# SHADOW on the WATER

Best Wishes!
Valerie J Rogers

# SHADOW on the WATER

**VALERIE ROOSA**

To order additional copies of this book, contact:
Xlibris Corporation
1-888-795-4274
www.Xlibris.com
Orders@Xlibris.com
48177

# CONTENTS

Dedicated to my husband, Frank with love.

Helping me steer my course as we sail through this life together, 'heaving to' in heavy weather, but always living under our true colors, until we reach our heavenly Safe Harbor.

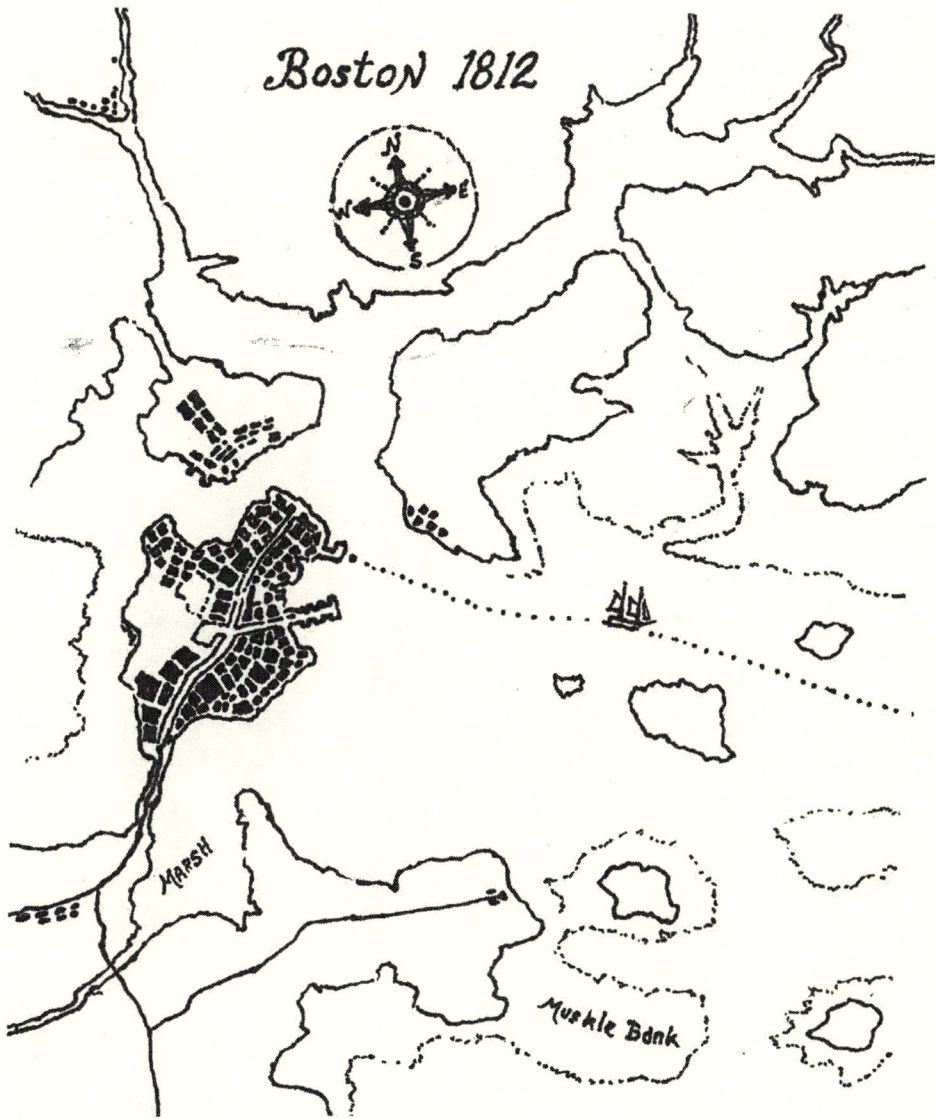

Boston 1812

The Course of the Lady Eleanor

The Lady Eleanor—Schooner

# CHAPTER ONE

## SECRET IDENTITY

Jonathon Strand sat at his breakfast table staring out to sea through the thick glass of his cottage window. His wife's voice seemed to be droning on and on in the background while his mind was contemplating the events of two nights ago when he had been a lonely witness of the vicious battle that had been fought at sea outside Boston Harbor. The same battle that had lit up the night sky with dramatic red fiery fingers of cannon shot and was accompanied by a flaming inferno as one of America's ships burnt to a cinder.

So this was war! The first sea battle of Mr. Madison's war, only two months old, but which would change his way of life forever. Lobsters would be hard to come by now that his quiet backwater had been invaded by warships.

Jonathon was a lobster fisherman. He lived two miles east of Boston in his tiny cottage made of wattle and daub, and situated on a small stretch of land amongst the mud flats and salt marshes of that area. He was a hardworking man, but struggled for a mere existence of a living by catching lobsters. He complained often to his wife that the growing expansion of the Boston town limits were encroaching upon him, and was the sole reason for the diminishing supply of lobsters.

His wife, Emily was not quite so concerned, for the lack of lobsters made her life easier, by stealing from her the task of taking the catch into town twice a week. It was a long and arduous trek, and the two miles seemed more like ten now that she was fifty three years of age. Lately she was only taking the journey once, so she was happy with the new arrangement. But mostly she was glad that this meant that they could go into town every Wednesday evening to the Methodist fellowship meeting, along with many other pious folk in the area. The meeting was always held in the beautiful home of Mr. and Mrs. Fitzroy, who lived in a large three story brick mansion overlooking Boston Bay, and where the couple hosted the local Methodists in their drawing room once or twice a week. The fellowship consisted of about eighty people, who came not only to be spiritually enlightened, but to taste of Mrs. Fitzroy's culinary delicacies which were laid out in abundance.

The little band of Methodists, who although gave no exhibition of bad behavior, were somewhat outcasts in the town. Indeed seventy five years earlier just after the great awakening of 1737 and 1738, they were persecuted to the point of violence. Now it was limited to the occasional slur or insult when one of them happened to be in a store, or the market place. But, nevertheless it resulted in them feeling somewhat like second-class citizens, despite the War of Independence which should have ratified their equal rights amongst all those that lived on American soil, and having settled all disputes to the contrary, should have been basking in the sun of religious freedom.

Still, these simple folk felt comfort abiding under the influence of the rich, while clinging inwardly, and somewhat emotionally, to the outdated English system of class distinction, with its royalty, piers of the realm, and noblemen in general. Yet publicly they spurned the attitude of lord versus peasant. Not that they were hypocrites, just that they enjoyed leaning on the laurels of the influential and pragmatic of Boston's society. It made them feel safe . . . comfortable. The Fitzroys took a certain pleasure in residing within their own little kingdom, especially Eleanor Fitzroy, who surrounded herself with every possible luxury; boasting of her excellent taste in furniture, porcelain, and fine silverware from the establishment of the renowned Paul Revere himself, master silversmith. This great wealth, which substance was amassed from her husband's fortune in shipping, only increased her appetite for the exquisite. She was indulged by her husband, Richard, who showered her constantly with expensive jewelry despite the sharp disapproval by the elders of their group.

Although their lifestyle was condemned by most of their Methodist friends, they secretly admired their possessions, and counted it a privilege to be able to enjoy them for at least one evening a week.

Jonathon Strand also tolerated the Fitzroys, but always left their house feeling somewhat contaminated, and was always glad to be back in his cottage surrounded by the familiar and simpler things of life.

Now at breakfast, with Emily still commenting on Mrs. Fitzroy's new gown, "The color of which was so becoming," she expressed, and which, in the eyes of the women, was, "Much more important than that nasty battle that happened the day before yesterday in the Bay of Boston."

The men had spent most of the evening discussing not only the battle and the apparent loss of one of their schooners to the British, and also the one they had purposely set on fire, but the rights and wrongs of President Madison declaring war on Great Britain. With all this political analysis the evening was gradually whittled away until they were all dismissed with nothing but a short prayer to show for it.

"I must be off, my dear," Jonathon said at last, unable to bear any more of the idle conversation. "I have to finish those repairs to the boat if I am to go out this evening and collect the lobster pots."

He kissed his wife on the cheek, and hurried out before she could answer him. He grabbed his old fishing coat and pulled on his boots, and made his way to a small outbuilding which was battered and scarred by the Atlantic winds. A place where Jonathon felt very much at peace despite the lack of adequate protection from the weather.

He took down his old, but well cared for tools, and turned his attention to his upturned lobster boat. The boat was his pride and joy, and he lovingly scraped at the place in the hull where it had worn through and needed to be patched. He pulled out some timbers from a corner which was piled high with wood of every size and description, such a pile that Emily often commented that he could build a new one from all the scraps that he had collected. He scrutinized each piece of wood carefully, and seemingly satisfied, set about to repair the boat.

By four o'clock in the afternoon the repair was finished, the hull sanded and freshly varnished, and although it was still a little tacky Jonathon turned it right side up, and slowly dragged the boat down to the water's edge.

There was just time for him to collect his pots and return home in time for supper he thought. He threw in a pair of oars, and shoved off. The shallow salty water lapped around the bow of the boat as he used one oar to push himself along in a punting fashion, until he reached deeper water. He pushed with his full weight against the oar for he was a large and burly man, and slowly the boat edged its way forward. There were lots of cattails growing along the edge of the mud flats, waving green and fresh in the wind.

Jonathon took a second look at what appeared to be an upturned canoe, not unlike a native American dugout. It was nestled amongst the cattails rising and falling quite gently. Jonathon changed direction. He was always interested in any piece of flotsam or timber that would enhance his collection, and as he rowed closer he saw that it was not a canoe as he had at first thought, but a large round timber about four or five feet long. It was black and tarred, and he soon realized by the jagged end that it was a piece of a ship, a mast most likely. He noticed a flutter of white on the far side of the timber, and realized with a start that a body lay alongside it. A man by the looks of things, lying on his back with his body in the water and his head sticking up above the surface. His face was framed by the wavering reeds and seemed to stare up to the sky, while embracing the piece of the mast. Jonathon noticed that his skin was white and lifeless looking, and encrusted with salt.

He threw his mud weight over the side, and jumped out of the boat. The water was up to his waist, and felt cold against his warm skin. Some poor devil washed ashore after the battle at sea he thought, as he waded towards the corpse. It wouldn't be the first body that he had dragged home in his little boat. The coast of Massachusetts was cruel and unforgiving, and the cemetery was littered with the unmarked graves of the shipwrecked. Now it seemed that fate had delivered another one onto his doorstep.

Jonathon studied the man that he had hauled up with a great deal of difficulty into his boat. He was not yet stiff, so Jonathon doubted if he had been dead very long. He had black hair, and looked to be in his mid-thirties. An officer perhaps? The man was wearing breeches and a ruffled shirt, which after its encounter with the sea, was covered with mud and salt, and encrusted with dried blood. The only injury that was apparent was a nasty cut on his forehead, which had plenty of bruising around the wound, and scarring on other parts of the body as well. Was he American, or an Englishman? Jonathon wondered. He sat on one of the thwarts with sea water dripping down his soaked body into the bottom of the boat. He stared intently at the man for a moment, there was something different about him. The victim had a certain look, quite unlike the other unfortunates that he had hauled back to shore on their last earthly journey. Jonathon leant forward and felt around the man's throat and chest. His body was not as cold as he would have expected. Then it occurred to him . . . perhaps the man was not dead after all; just unconscious. He felt like a fool. Was he too late? He sat there momentarily stunned, unable to collect his thoughts together. Then the years of experience took over as he propped the man up in a sitting position in the bottom of the boat. Jonathon draped his old coat over the stranger, grabbed one of the oars, and began punting the boat back through the shallow water to his little beach. He jumped out dragging the boat well up onto the sand before he gathered the man up in his arms, (who seemed immediately heavier than he looked) and staggered up the beach towards the cottage.

He kicked open the door with his foot, and stumbled into the kitchen carrying the limp body in his arms. He deposited the man into an old rocking chair next to the fireplace, and slumped himself down on a wooden settle. He was absolutely exhausted as he sat there extruding seawater and slime all over the floor.

His wife Emily came into the room. "For mercy's sake, Jonathon, what has happened? Who is that man?" she shrilled in a high pitched and slightly hysterical voice.

"I thought he had drowned," panted the fatigued lobster fisherman. "I think there may be a chance to save him if we hurry. Oh my Lord I am getting too old for this!" he panted.

"Well don't just stand there woman! Get some towels! we will have to get those wet clothes off of him at once." He knelt down beside the chair and began to peel off the sodden shirt, which gave little resistance for it was nothing more than a salt soaked rag. "Do we need the bellows for his nostrils?"

"I don't know yet," Jonathon replied. "We may!"

Emily left the room hurriedly and returned with an armful of towels, and Jonathon started to rub the man vigorously all over his upper body with a towel. The muscles were still taught and elastic to his touch, which seemed to authenticate life.

"We will have to cut off his breeches!" he turned to his wife. "Get some scissors my dear will you?"

Jonathon continued drying the man's body when he thought he saw a flutter of an eyelid. Just a hint of movement. He took the scissors from his wife and began cutting up one of the legs of his breeches. The scissors seemed blunt, and it was hard going.

Emily turned her head away in modesty as Jonathon reached the waist.

"Hurry, Jonathon, you are too slow! Do you want me to cut?"

"I can manage, woman, do you think you are the only one who can use a pair of scissors?" he growled. He decided to pull the other leg off, rather than continue to wield the blunt scissors. He put his big hands under the man's armpits and tried to lift him up a bit. With the manipulation into a new position, the man gave a slight cough, and his eyes opened suddenly, staring Jonathon straight in the face. The mouth opened as if to speak, but before any words could be uttered, he vomited a torrent of seawater down the front of his chest.

"You're all right now, son, we thought you were dead!" Jonathon said kindly. "Don't try to speak, save your energy. Come, Emily my dear, help me get him into a bed at once."

The elderly couple struggled to get the stranger into their own bed. Clad in a clean nightshirt the man lay there on the pillow with his eyes shut. They both stood looking down on him noticing with relief that, although he still looked a little pale, a slight color was now appearing on his cheeks. His chest rose and fell gently, and his breathing appeared almost normal.

"He needs a good sleep, that he does!" Emily said at last. "Poor thing! I wonder who he is?"

"I expect we shall soon find out," said her husband.

Early the following morning Henry slowly opened his eyes. He lay there staring around him trying to ascertain his whereabouts. Red checked curtains fluttered at the windows in the warm breezes of summer. He could still smell the sea air, and wondered if by some chance he was in Captain Street's Great Stern Cabin. Then it came back to him in a flash. His outburst of anger when he had picked up the Captain's sword. His flamboyant actions wielding a sword at anyone who dared to climb up onto the *Restitution*'s deck; threatening the American seaman with a pistol; pointing it at his head, he had been like a crazy man . . . incensed. He was astonished and shocked at his own behavior.

It was most unlike him, he was not a man to promote violence. Yet, when his own ship and his comrades had been threatened, and indeed some of them killed and wounded, he had become another person. He had acted like a lioness protecting her cubs. A seemingly supernatural strength had risen up in him until it overcame all reason, an uncontrollable and violent passion beating within his heart. Now it disturbed him greatly, and he felt mortified with shame.

But where was he now? A sharp pain pierced through his head as he tried to lift it from the pillow and stare around the little room. This was definitely not Captain Street's quarters. "I must be on shore!" he said out loud, at the realization that the room was not moving up and down with the motion of a ship at sea, something he had learned to live with for the past four months. Lying down he felt strange and awkward, and he thought of the sea . . . what an enemy it had been to him.

As Henry eased himself painfully back onto the pillow he remembered hitting the surface of the sea. The initial panic as the waves broke over his head . . . the frantic thrashing about with his arms and seeing pieces of driftwood strewn around him, but unable to grab hold of a single piece of it. Then gradually sinking downwards . . . the green florescent glow above his head as the pale light of the moon shone down through the waves. He remembered the myriads of tiny bubbles streaming upwards in perfect precision as they made their way to the surface, the light gradually fading . . . his lungs bursting. Thoughts of his beloved Elizabeth, that this was the end. But surely not this way? The darkness had gradually enveloped his helpless body as he began slowly sinking, until he had felt something hard and round against his shoulder. The merest bump, hardly noticeable, but his arms had reached out for something alien to that cold and watery environment, and what he had reached out for, he clutched with a grasp so tight that nothing in this world could have torn his hands from it.

The rest was hazy, and his head hurt trying to remember. But somewhere in his unconscious mind he could recollect surging upwards, it getting lighter. Then darkness again, cold and painfulness pressing upon him like a millstone. Henry shuddered. He struggled up in bed once again, this time on one elbow, and saw a glass with a pitcher of water beside the bed. He vaguely remembered drinking some, in the not so distant past. Probably during the night. Where was his wife . . . where was Elizabeth? Surely she would come soon. He took the glass up again, and held it shakily to his lips. He drank it gratefully, and the sweetness of it quenched his thirst considerably.

Henry closed his eyes once more as the sunlight in the room made all his senses throb. He tried to collect his thoughts into some semblance of fact, as he turned the past months over and over in his tired brain.

He heard voices in his mind, shouting orders. "Fire as your guns bear . . . That's tantamount to mutiny, Stapleton . . . the Royal Navy does not change its course for anyone!" He could hear Captain Weatherby's voice just as if he were standing in the room.

He sank deep into delirium again. He was in a thick fog now, chilled to the bone. He heard his own cry, "Ship, fine on the starboard bow!" The drums were beating to quarters, pounding in rhythm with his own pulse and the pain within his head. Then blackness . . . smoke . . . shouting. A vivid mental image of him handing a French flag to a young boy. Who was the boy? His son, Benjamin? No, the boy was in uniform. The pain was unbearable: perspiration ran down his face as he tried to force himself into consciousness. He mustn't give up. Then with a jolt he was wide awake.

The sudden noise of voices just outside the room startled him for a moment as he realized with shock that he must now be on American soil. The door opened gingerly, and an elderly couple entered the room. The man was tall and heavily built with a ruddy complexion. The woman, who Henry presumed to be the man's wife, was pale and slight. She was carrying a tray, with a bowl of something steaming hot inside. She set it down next to the pitcher of water beside his bed.

"How are you son?" questioned the man kindly, as he bent over Henry.

"Stronger," Henry managed to speak through cracked lips which were covered in salt sores from his long submersion on the salt marshes.

"I'm Jonathon Strand," the man said addressing Henry most politely. "And this," he said turning to his wife, "is my wife, Emily."

Emily bobbed a curtsey. "Pleased to meet you, I am sure."

They both stared at Henry for quite some time, when he suddenly realized they were waiting for an introduction.

"I am Henry Stapleton," he managed to utter.

"American or English?" questioned Emily somewhat harshly.

"Emily! Hush yourself, the man was at death's door," Jonathon scolded his wife. "It matters not what nationality he is."

Emily suddenly felt embarrassed by her haste to discern the stranger's identity, and turned away scurrying out into the kitchen on the pretense of something boiling over on the hearth.

Jonathon turned back to Henry. "Excuse my wife, son. It's the war, she's not normally that blunt. Do you feel strong enough to talk, or would you like to eat first?"

"I would really like some of that hot soup first, sir," replied Henry. "I think I haven't eaten for days."

"Certainly, can you manage it alone, or would you like me to spoon you some?"

"I'll try by myself, if you please." Henry took the bowl from Jonathon, and slowly lifted the spoon to his lips, took a few mouthfuls, and rested back on the pillow. Then Henry sipped some more as he let the warm soup soothe his parched throat.

Meanwhile Jonathon made himself comfortable on a chair at the foot of the bed, and started to relay to Henry the events of the last few days.

He informed him about the attack on the British squadron by the two schooners, local men of course, brave and loyal citizens of Boston. The loss of one ship, and the capture of the other.

The possible loss of fifty or more lives. Most of which had stated emphatically that they would, "Fight to the death," rather than be captured. The sadness at seeing their ship strike its colors. Jonathon had seen it all from his little shed near the beach.

Henry eased himself up on one elbow as he listened. Little did Jonathon realize (or did he?) that he had been part of that squadron. That it was his ship, the *Restitution* that was responsible for the heavy casualties that the Americans had suffered.

As Jonathon continued to relate the story, he was watching Henry's reaction to his news. Although he was not intentionally playing the role of interrogator, he, like many others in Boston, were angry with Britain. What was it going to take for them to realize that although America welcomed them as trading partners, their self rule and independency could not be infringed upon? America's rights (especially on the high seas) were flagrantly violated. In terms of religion, he supposed he leaned towards being a Federalist, for he was against violence and war. But, as far as politics were concerned (although he didn't claim to be that well informed) he concluded that he was definitely a Republican, a citizen that was prepared to resist evil in an aggressive way.

Bearing all this in mind, it was only natural that quite a large proportion of Bostonians happened to resent giving up some of the freedoms their fathers had laid down their lives for. They were also disappointed at the apathy of the local militia, volunteers as such, who had not joined ranks with the local seaman and fishing boys; thereby adding weight of manpower in his countrymen's attempt to burn the two British frigates.

And what part did this man play in the whole affair? Jonathon thought to himself as he looked at Henry, who was slowly refreshing himself with the food that Emily had brought in. Was he a British officer giving out orders for death and destruction? He forced himself to continue.

"Then I found you on the salt marshes, thought you were a gonna," Jonathon smiled. "I carried you back to the cottage . . . the rest you know."

"I am deeply grateful, you saved my life."

"Think nothing of it, I would have done the same for anyone. It's what we are put here on this earth for isn't it? To help people I mean. Whether they be American or English," he added.

"In answer to your wife's question, Jonathon. I am indeed, English."

"Thought as much!" Jonathon said smugly. "I know most of the young fellows around here, and you didn't look like a local."

"What will you do now?" Henry said candidly. "After all, I am an Englishman, and a sailor. And, of course, our two countries are at war. I expect you will be handing me over to the authorities." Henry quizzed him carefully.

"I won't be doing anything until you are completely well, don't you fret yourself on that issue. Even then, I am not sure *what* I will do. It is not something that can be decided upon that easily. It would be a hard decision for me, a peace loving Methodist at heart, to hand over a young fellow like you, whose destination would likely be a prison hulk. And few people come out of those stinking barges alive . . . we will have to see."

Jonathon got up, and walked over to the side of the bed looking down at Henry most sympathetically.

Henry grabbed Jonathon by the sleeve. "A Methodist did you say?" He stared disbelievingly into Jonathon's open and honest face. Then fell back onto the pillow and started to laugh. Henry laughed long and heartily until a pain in his stomach forced him to stop.

"What's so funny?" Jonathon asked warily.

"I am not your enemy," Henry smiled. "Far from it! I am a Methodist minister who was pressed into the British Navy four months ago, as I was paying a visit to friends in the port of Great Yarmouth, England. Here against my will I might add! In fact the British Navy is more my enemy than you, if I was to put it that way, I suppose." Henry paused, his face clouding over suddenly. "According to naval tradition, I will now be considered a deserter, especially if they think that I swam to shore. But you, on the other hand my friend, are a blessed and most honorable brother indeed!"

This time it was Jonathon's turn to laugh. "What a carry on indeed! Wait until I tell the wife. An Englishman . . . a sailor . . . a Methodist, and a minister to boot. Oh, what a carry on indeed!" Jonathon laughed until tears ran down his round face.

The sudden commotion brought Emily back into the room, and although she was not party to the gaiety, she couldn't help smiling at the bedridden Henry, and her husband who were rocking wildly backwards and forwards with mirth.

Finally, they were able to explain Henry's identity to Emily, who could only utter, "Upon my word!"

"Well," said Jonathon at last. "I have to get back to my lobster pots," he chuckled. "If there is anything you need don't be afraid to ask, and Emily will be pleased to get it for you, won't you, my dear?"

"Oh, indeed I will! No trouble at all."

"I will see you this evening then. Meanwhile get some rest," Jonathon said.

Henry held out his hand, "Thank you, Jonathon. Thank you indeed!" They shook hands firmly, and Jonathon and Emily left the room together chattering like a couple of magpies.

Alone once more, Henry fell into a more somber mood. His initial euphoria at finding Christian brethren here in this remote part of the world gave way to concern. He was faced with some very important decisions. Of course his only objective was eventually to get back to Elizabeth, and his family. But technically, and legally, he was a British sailor, and as such was expected to try to return to his ship, whether Captain Street thought he was dead or not. Maybe Street himself was dead? After all the Captain was struck down and wounded in that last battle when the Americans swarmed over the bulwarks of the stricken *Restitution*. His loyalty and duty should be to the British, yet he found no pleasure in the thought. This realization stunned him immensely. He would have to pray long and hard about the matter. His mind was still in turmoil, it was too early to think straight, and he was constantly reminded of this fact by pains he still felt in his body. He would have to get better first he concluded, he was no good to the Navy like this anyway.

Jonathon had not mentioned the British squadron, but his lack of conversation on the matter would seem that the *Restitution* and the *Providence* were way out to sea by now. Probably making repairs. They couldn't do that while still in Massachusetts Bay. The Americans could try another fire ship raid. They were almost successful. Captain Childers had been neglectful . . . complacent. It could go down as one of the most daring attacks on two British frigates in American history. What would Captain Weatherby think when he finally returned with the flagship, *Dragonfly*.

Henry sat up and looked out of the window. His room must not be facing the sea, for although he could smell it, all he could see were rows and rows of green beans climbing boldly up their poles with quirky looking white flowers budding out all over them as they gently swayed in the breeze. The pastoral scene before him, neatly framed by the bright curtains that hung at the windows, could have easily made him forget about the war completely. He let the beautiful smells of the garden soothe him. Jonathon was right, he thought, it was 'a carry on' indeed.

Henry sat at the breakfast table with Jonathon and Emily the following morning. He had talked endlessly with Jonathon the previous evening, well into the night in fact, and it had been decided by Jonathon, that Henry would stay put until he could speak with Brother Fitzroy . . . to ask his advice. Richard Fitzroy being such a prominent and influential citizen, and with a proper education. And like all men of his kind, Jonathon was under the misconception that education was the answer to every problem that arose in life. As if he, himself, had not been adorned with the same ability to exercise his rationale as the next man.

"I respect your decision absolutely, Jonathon," Henry stated emphatically. He had come to like and respect his host in the short time he had known him, and he would not presume to disagree with his advice. And so it was arranged for Jonathon to go that evening to visit the Fitzroy mansion in Boston.

After eating the delicious breakfast Henry felt much of his strength returning, so he decided to take a short walk on the beach. The sun was shining, and it was a good time to stretch his legs before the heat became too overbearing. It took only a few steps before he was wandering along the mud flats, watching seagulls lazily flying through the azure colored sky . . . it was a perfect summer's day. One that was so free of responsibility that Henry almost felt guilty. He certainly could not remember another day like it since he left England.

As Henry surveyed his surroundings he realized that this part of Massachusetts was not unlike the beaches and fenlands of Norfolk. His charming hosts had supplied him with a set of clothes, which although were too large for him, were at least clean and fresh. Jonathon had given him an old straw hat to wear, the first Henry had ever owned.

Despite his beautiful surroundings Henry felt a little ill at ease. For the first time in several months he was in charge of his own destiny. He could finally make his own decisions. On board a man-of-war, decisions were made for you, and life was so routinely exact that you were hardly expected to think from the time you awoke, until the time you laid down to sleep in your hammock for four precious hours of rest.

He wondered what was happening to the squadron, because looking out now on this day, with the sun glimmering on the ocean, you would never know that a bloody and savage battle had been fought, just a little way out there. There were no scars left behind in the sea, all the evidence had been washed away, unlike a land battle where it might have taken weeks to clean up the aftermath. Henry vividly remembered the fire ship, the smoke . . . the guns roaring, and his shipmates that had been killed. Savagely hacked down with a sword or an axe. It was now all part of history, and only the wives and families of those men that were killed would think about it, try to picture it the way it was in their thoughts. They would feel angry about it, and the heartache would be etched in their minds forever. An oracle to be passed down from generation to generation. Remembered by the few, pitied by many. It was also strange that only thirty six years earlier, the same year he had been born in fact, those who dwelt here had risen up in hatred against the English in their campaign for independence.

As a farmer who had grown up and lived in a remote part of England, it was hard to understand this hatred and resentment. His father, when he was still alive, relayed the general consensus of the time, (although he emphasized that it was not his own opinion) that surely the Americans had greatly prospered as colonies under the British Crown? What was a little taxation with all the profits they made? Still, he couldn't forget the other stories he had heard. The brutalities of the British redcoats in Boston, the apparent unfairness of the Stamp Act which was slowly squeezing out those coveted profits. He had to confess to himself that he had always felt a sympathy for the Americans, as did his father before him. He wished that his father had lived longer so they could have discussed the different views of politics more often. It all seemed such a long time ago. What would his father think of this present war? Now, once again, similar grievances had arisen, and brought the past hurtling into the present. A present that he was now unwillingly a part of.

He looked towards Boston. There were only a few number of vessels both large and small, sailing in and out of the harbor. Somehow they must be slipping through the British blockade, with only the two frigates on the station at the moment, but he had no way of knowing.

A haze was hovering over the town as the heat and humidity of the day wore on. Henry pondered on the proposed meeting of Jonathon and the Fitzroys. What were these people like? He felt a little nervous, his destiny would once again be in the hands of other people. He didn't want that.

He could see Jonathon from where he stood. He was about a mile off-shore, his shape bending over the side of his little boat, which bobbed about like a cockle shell. Henry admired Jonathon, he seemed an honest and hardworking man; the salt of the earth. He felt instinctively that the man was trustworthy, and without guile. It did not take a second look to ascertain his character, a person only had to gaze at his open expression to know what kind of personality lay within. He seemed to Henry more like a lifelong friend, than an acquaintance of a mere couple of days.

The sun seemed to relentlessly beat down upon Henry's head as he stood there, and he soon realized that he had put too much strain on his body by venturing out so soon. He must return to the cottage immediately. For although he felt quite strong, his lungs were still not what they should be after their contact with so much sea water, and his head had begun to throb again. He was still amazed that he had survived the whole ordeal, the mercy of God truly was abundant in his life.

Henry felt immediate relief from the sun as he stepped inside the cottage where Emily was busy in the kitchen. It took a few moments for his eyes to grow accustomed to the different light after stepping inside the cottage where he was shielded from the brilliant sunshine. He wiped the perspiration off his forehead.

"Well, Mr. Stapleton, how are we feeling today?" Emily questioned him as soon as he removed his hat and hung it on a hall stand next to the door.

"The sea air is very invigorating, Mrs. Strand. I am feeling better by the hour!"

"Would you like a cup of tea? I have hot water by the hearth," she continued.

"That sounds very good, it will be my first cup of tea since I left England," he sighed.

"Are you married, Mr. Stapleton?" Emily asked inquisitively.

"Yes, ma'am. My wife's name is Elizabeth."

"Children, I presume?"

"A son, Benjamin, aged twelve; a fine boy, and two daughters, Isabella and Flora."

"How delightful!" she smiled. "The poor mites must miss their father very much, and your wife too. Upon my soul she must be distraught to say the least."

"I wrote to her when my ship was in the middle of the Atlantic ocean. The letter was sent back to England on a Post Office packet ship. I am sure she must have received it by now. At least I hope so. I wrote again just before we arrived in Massachusetts

Bay. It was left under my pillow in my cabin on the *Dragonfly*, that was my ship Ma'am, before I was transferred temporarily to the *Restitution*. I only hope that it was found and sent back to Halifax, where I imagine it would be forwarded on."

"Oh, I am sure it will have been delivered by now, don't you fret none!"

Henry felt the overwhelming blackness of despair again, as he again thought of his family trying to go through life without him, not just the physical, but the emotional pain. His mind was full of unanswered questions, doubts about the future, his status quo, his very safety in this strange country. He seated himself down, and quietly drank the tea that Emily handed him, then with his eyes closed tried to shut out all the problems that weighted him down like a blacksmith's anvil. But despite the luxury of the hot tea gliding down his throat, the fears were still lingering in his mind like dark shadows across the moon, until sleep overwhelmed him, and he slumped down in the chair where he sat. Emily had long ago rescued the cup that tottered dangerously on the edge of the saucer as Henry had fallen asleep with the tea still in his hand.

The next thing that Henry was aware of, was the door bursting open to receive Jonathon. Home for his evening meal, and grinning like a Cheshire cat.

"Its all arranged!" cried Jonathon with a smug look on his face, as Henry leapt back into the realm of wakefulness.

"What is?" asked Emily before Henry could open his mouth to ask the same question.

"I've arranged for brother Henry to meet with the Fitzroys tomorrow night. They are quite looking forward to it, he will be the very first English Methodist preacher they have ever met."

"You went all the way into town?" Emily asked incredulously.

"Yep!" Jonathon said with a smile.

"Jonathon, as much as I appreciate all your efforts, pardon me for saying so, but how safe is it for me to go into Boston?" Henry asked cautiously. "I am sure that Bostonians will feel very revengeful towards any Englishman at this time, especially one that was on board one of the ships that battered and captured one of their schooners, and killed most of her crew."

Henry saw Jonathon's brow furrow into thoughtfulness. His initial excitement somewhat thwarted by Henry's remark.

"Well, I think that we must not dwell on too many of those facts. Of course I outlined the circumstances when I spoke to Mr. Fitzroy, and of how you came to be staying with us. But he and his wife seemed so overcome with the opportunity of meeting you, they paid no heed at all. So, like I said, it is all arranged for nine o'clock tomorrow evening. I suggested that time because I thought there would be less people out and about by then, and it will be getting dark. Not that there is any danger," he added hastily. "I will come with you naturally. Anyhow most of them city folks are just wealthy Federalists," Jonathon grinned broadly. "They won't care if you're British," he said with a twinkle in his eye.

"I hope not," Henry replied.

The following evening, Henry and Jonathon were shown into the large hallway of Edinburgh House. The large brick federal mansion was a sight to behold. Although the whitewashed walls of the interior were somewhat simple, the sumptuous red Persian carpet that covered most of the floor, more than made up for the simplicity. The hall was graciously furnished with a grandfather clock, and a long hall table upon which stood a beautiful Delft blue and white porcelain vase. A perfect companion to the red and white roses which were displayed in it. The scent of the roses was overwhelmingly strong, and the whole environment made Henry and Jonathon feel quite shabby in their everyday working clothes.

A starched and rigid butler bid them to wait for a few moments while he informed the Fitzroys of their arrival.

He returned almost instantly with the instructions that they were to enter the drawing room, where their hosts would join them soon.

"Mr. & Mrs. Fitzroy will receive you in about five minutes" the butler announced crisply.

The interim five minutes gave Henry the opportunity to absorb the luxurious surroundings in which he sat, also to ascertain what kind of people he was about to meet. The room was somewhat darkened, with tall French styled windows opening up to a view of Boston harbor. In front of the windows stood a large grand piano topped with a silver candelabra, which was flickering with candlelight. On the opposite wall was a white marble fireplace, with a handsome gilt-edged mirror hanging over it, and reflecting the last of the evening light upon the two men.

At the far end of the room stood an exquisite rosewood writing bureau with large claw feet. On top of the bureau was a Bible so large that it was akin to one Henry had seen in the British Museum. The rest of the room was scattered with large and comfortable armchairs, richly adorned in pink brocade with a gold leaf motif, and matching gold tassels. The room had a very definite feminine touch about it.

After absorbing all this affluence, Henry deduced that the owners of Edinburgh House, would be equally elaborate.

The two men sat patiently awaiting the entrance of their hosts. Jonathon tugged at his collar (which he was quite unaccustomed to wearing, but Emily had insisted that he wore,) as beads of perspiration trickled down his neck. Henry felt equally uneasy too, although he was used to these kind of surroundings which, although very impressive, were still not equal to the furnishings of Walpole Hall in the county of Norfolk, the stately residence of Lord and Lady Walpole. When in England, he and Elizabeth had visited the Walpole mansion occasionally. It was ridiculous really, he thought to himself, that he should be nervous of meeting these Americans. He supposed it was because he was used to the English aristocracy, and was somewhat comfortable among them while being able to converse with them freely. Of course at those times he was not under the threat of being considered a spy, or having his life in jeopardy because he was a foreigner. Not so in this time and place.

Would he find it more difficult to understand these rich people who were well known to imitate English social behavior, yet lampoon the monarchy openly and without shame? Still they had won their freedom bravely and honestly, and Henry had to admire them for that.

Henry's thoughts were finally interrupted as the twin oak doors opened to admit the butler once more.

"Mr. & Mrs. Fitzroy," he announced stiffly.

The couple that entered the room looked to be in their mid to late forties. Both were impeccably elegant. Mr. Fitzroy sported a mass of red hair, a throw back from his Scottish ancestry no doubt, though he was fairly short and broad shouldered. His wife, on the other hand, was tall and slim with black hair which was a sharp contrast to her pale features. She was dressed in a long silk gown the color of deep emeralds, with a hint of lace at her throat. The sleeves of the dress came down to her elbows where flounces of lace hung like waterfalls down her arms. She was a very handsome woman, and they made a striking couple, Henry thought.

"Good evening, gentlemen," Mr. Fitzroy said in a most welcoming manner. He shook hands with both of them in turn, and then turning to his wife said, "I would like to introduce you to my wife, Eleanor. Of course Jonathon we know you well, and you must be Mr. Stapleton," he said addressing Henry.

"I am pleased to meet you, sir, and delighted to meet you, ma'am!" Henry proffered a stiff bow to Eleanor Fitzroy, who in turn held out her hand to him.

"Please be seated both of you," said Richard.

Henry and Jonathon took their seats, while Fitzroy chose a seat beside the fireplace, to which position he looked most familiar with, and his wife seated herself on the piano bench with a flourish.

"Well, Mr. Stapleton, Jonathon has told me of the extraordinary circumstances which led to your arrival here in Boston. An extreme quirk of fate I must say. We could see it all from that window," he gestured past his wife and out to the bay, which sparkled with lights from the town in the growing dusk. "The fire ship, the battle; my goodness the noise was thunderous, positively deafening. Of course it was a great disappointment to us Bostonians to see our ships come to such grief! I have to confess, it nigh broke our hearts; the loss of men and valuable ships. Shipping you know, Mr. Stapleton, is our heart and soul, our lifeline you might say. Now, with a war on our hands there will be no more shipbuilding, or transportation of goods either, you can count on that!" he said bitterly.

Henry quickly observed that this meeting was going to proceed somewhat on the lines of an interview, although he could not understand why. Neither could he understand his own feelings of irritation. Fitzroy continued rambling on about the events and consequences of the battle for quite a few more minutes, and Henry felt very awkward. He didn't feel personally responsible. After all he had not fired a shot himself, and he had no desire to have been there in the first place. Finally, Richard Fitzroy made a pause and shifted himself in his chair.

"I hear you almost drowned, Mr. Stapleton?" He made a desperate attempt to change the subject. "What a dreadful experience! God be praised that you fell into our Jonathon's hands eh?"

"I am eternally grateful to him," Henry replied. "And to his wife, Emily as well. A wonderful brother and sister indeed."

"Quite so, quite so. Jonathon informs me that you are a Methodist minister in England. County of Norfolk I believe he said?"

"Yes, sir."

The conversation continued in trivial niceties for a while as Fitzroy continued to tell Henry about the fellowship meetings they held regularly at Edinburgh House. He reiterated on the early persecution of Methodists in New England, and how Methodism had grown almost to equal the numbers attending the Congregational churches of Massachusetts.

"That is well and good, Mr. Fitzroy, and how is the American Bible Society doing currently? I hear that they have now translated the Bible into the Mohawk language!" Henry asked the question, not that he particularly wanted to know every detail for he knew it to be the gospel of Saint John only, and not the complete Bible, but he desperately wanted to break the ice with this somewhat stiff couple. He longed to feel some warmth of Christian brotherhood between them, instead of being made to feel guilty about the fortunes of war.

"I am afraid I do not know, Mr. Stapleton. News travels slow, but I am sure you are right. What about some tea, my dear?" Fitzroy said turning to his wife. He seemed to be relieved to change the subject once more.

"Certainly!" Eleanor Fitzroy walked across the room and pulled a bell cord to summon a servant. "Please forgive me for my lack of hospitality, gentlemen," she apologized. "How could I have been so thoughtless after your long walk here. You must be in dire need of refreshment."

The atmosphere warmed considerably as Eleanor Fitzroy poured tea for her guests, and handed the cups to Henry and Jonathon. The china was delicate and fragile, and Jonathon held his nervously, unaccustomed to balancing a tiny cup on a saucer. The tea was of the highest quality Henry noted, no doubt imported from India with its fine black flavor. Eleanor handed round a selection of "petite fours." All three men politely took two cakes apiece, and while Henry carefully ate his, Jonathon had downed both in two bites, with the tell-tale crumbs strewn down the front of his shirt being the only evidence left behind.

"Tell me, Mr. Stapleton," said Eleanor Fitzroy addressing Henry. "Is it true that the most honorable composer, Mr. Mozart, is dead? Forgive me for asking, but I had heard a rumor several years ago of his death. You must appreciate, Mr. Stapleton, that news travels very slowly to this part of the world. Especially correspondence from Europe. I had heard this news from a somewhat reliable source, but since that time I have heard nothing to confirm it. There are only a few people in Boston that really appreciate fine music. I for one have a fondness for the art, and devote as much time as I can to playing. I have a deep regard for Mr. Mozart's twenty first piano concerto, it is one of my favorites!"

"Mine too," replied Henry. "But Mrs. Fitzroy, you surely must realize that the great maestro died about twenty years ago now."

"Oh, my dear Mr. Stapleton!" she uttered clutching her throat, obviously most distressed. "Is it that long ago? What a waste, and one so young too. A fever I suppose took him," she speculated. "I shall greatly miss his music. I suppose I will just have to content myself with those treasured pieces that he has already composed."

"Not a fever, ma'am!" Henry hesitated. "It has been rumored in these last few years that Mr. Mozart was poisoned, I am afraid to say. Buried in a pauper's grave too. They say it was jealousy, and the culprit likely to be another less talented composer of little or no renown. I am sorry if it brings you much distress."

"Oh! I can hardly believe it," Eleanor Fitzroy dabbed at her face which was flushed with grief. "That poor boy, it is a sad loss to the world indeed," she uttered hoarsely and continued shaking her head in disbelief.

Richard Fitzroy seemed a little annoyed that his visitor had disturbed his wife's emotions in such a way, and quickly changed the subject yet again. Not a particular lover of music himself, but he deeply respected his wife's love for it.

"Well, gentlemen!" he said forcibly. "Lets get back to the present. I feel, Mr. Stapleton, that there are several issues that we must contend with at this time. Although I am a firm believer in God, I am also a strong believer in my country too. I am just as much one of the "Sons of Liberty" as the next man, and I would in no way whatsoever wish to appear as a traitor to that freedom. But, notwithstanding, I have to confess, and I would add that many people here in Boston think along the same lines as myself, that I am not entirely in favor of this war that has been declared.

Mr. Madison has taken it upon himself to act hastily I believe. Without consultation . . . especially with the New England States. I know he inherited a lot of problems when he took office, and I am the first one to acknowledge that President Jefferson made his blunders. His Embargo Act, being one of the worst!" Fitzroy emphasized. He then paused thoughtfully and continued by saying, "Additional restrictions Jefferson made also impaired our overland trading with British possessions in Canada, along with Spanish possessions in Florida. So these last five years have been disastrous for people like me, Mr. Stapleton. A ship owner with ships standing idle. It has almost been our ruin, has it not my dear?" Fitzroy stated as he turned to his wife for support.

"Indeed it has, Richard."

"Federalist!" muttered Jonathon under his breath.

Fitzroy cast Jonathon a withering look. "Fortunately two years ago, after Mr. Madison took office, Congress instituted the Macon Bill, which reopened our commerce with all nations. However, I am ashamed to say many of the merchants here traded illegally at that time during the Jefferson period. I was personally opposed to it, and would not engage in the practice for conscience sake." He looked keenly at Henry. "Consequently we were only too pleased to resume trading with England, for she is by far and above our most beneficial trading partner. Unfortunately, and I am not proud to admit this, the merchants of Boston would far rather overlook the seizure of a cargo laden ship and a few impressed sailors than be at war with their benefactors.

Our views were in complete contrast to the "War Hawks" in Congress who want war despite the sacrifices of their New England brothers. The most notable of these representatives is Henry Clay, of Kentucky. He has fought tooth and nail to set up a pro-war faction in the government. They also claim that British officers in Canada are encouraging the Indians to rebel against the government. It is the same story in the South. The British are offering the slaves freedom if they rise up against their owners and fight on their side. It seems we are outvoted on every side. So, Mr. Stapleton, the meat of it is, that we are economically strapped and militarily impoverished. Why, America cannot boast of a single ship-of-the-line! Of course I am not giving out any naval secrets by that statement, although I do not hesitate to add that our seaman are some of the finest. Most of them cut their teeth with the Barbary pirate wars. Fine boys, everyone of them! Don't get me wrong either, we have some fine ships, the best of which is our very own *Constitution*, the forty four gun frigate built right here in Boston, by our own shipbuilders. The honorable yard of Mr. Hartt, a very good friend of mine," Fitzroy added.

"The reason I am telling you all this, Mr. Stapleton, and I do thank you for your patience, sir, is that although technically New England is at war with the British, I am sure there are many sympathizers to be found here in Boston. I think you will have to be careful if you plan to stay for any length of time, but I do not think you have to fear immediate arrest by the authorities either. Although I would suggest that you keep a sharp look out, any stranger might come under suspicion, naturally."

"I beg your pardon, Mr. Fitzroy, but I must interrupt you at this conjecture," Henry exclaimed. "I appreciate your concern for my welfare, but I think it only fair to inform you, sir, that my main objective is, and always has been, to return to England and my family. Although you are probably not an expert on British law, my claim has always been that I was impressed into the British Navy against English law. Unfortunately, up until this time, I have had no man who would agree with me or be willing even to discuss the matter. Something that has been the utmost frustration to me, as I am sure you can imagine."

"Absolutely, dear sir. Suffice to say that I would be in total agreement with your cause, and help you willingly in any endeavors you may undergo to bring this matter to a satisfactory conclusion on your behalf.

Look, sir, may I say at this point in our conversation, that you are more than welcome to stay at Edinburgh House for as long as you wish. I am sure that our dear Jonathon, and his wife Emily must be finding it quite difficult to accommodate you in their small dwelling."

"He is most welcome to stay with us!" protested Jonathon defensively. "Emily and I have been blessed indeed to have Mr. Stapleton reside under our roof, he is an absolute gentleman, that he is!"

"Of course, of course, Jonathon! No offence meant! But we have plenty of room here, just the two of us now, and the servants. A little bit of Scottish hospitality eh? Mr. Stapleton!" Fitzroy chuckled.

Henry looked apprehensively at Jonathon, aware of his hurt feelings, yet conscious of the added expense it would impose on his friends.

"Go ahead, Mr. Stapleton!" said Jonathon kindly. "I am sure it will be for the best in the long run I reckon. But you'll come and see us won't you, sir?"

"Of course, my dear friend, I will visit regularly. That is if you can put up with me. I have a habit of extruding seawater on decent people's kitchen floors!"

Jonathon smiled, and nodded his agreement.

"Well, I think that is quite enough for one night," Richard Fitzroy said. "We have plenty of time ahead of us to talk again. I will send for the chaise to drive you both home."

Henry was finally able to relax as Fitzroy rang for the carriage to be brought round to the front door of the mansion.

The two horses pulled them swiftly through the cobblestone streets of Boston, and out onto the Neck, that long strip of land that joined the peninsula of Boston town to the mainland. It was rougher going on the narrow Neck, and the carriage swayed alarmingly from side to side as it traversed the deep rutted track, and Henry and Jonathon had to hang on to the leather padded seats to steady themselves.

"Why is he driving so fast?" Henry questioned Jonathon as they continued this perilous motion, like two blackbirds hunched together on the branch of a tree.

"This is not the best of roads at night! We have to be careful, the Neck is full of all kinds of ruffians who would not hesitate to stand up a fine carriage like this. Little do they know that the occupants don't have a copper coin between them. Not to mention that neither of us have a weapon to defend ourselves," Jonathon laughed.

"It's the same the world over, my friend! A lonely salt marsh, a quiet street, it makes no difference."

The carriage streamed through the warm summer night, finally arriving at the top of the sandy lane that led to Jonathon's cottage, the silhouette of its thatched roof looked a lot like a spiky hedgehog in the darkness as Henry strained his eyes to scan the unfamiliar landscape.

"What did Fitzroy say to you as we were leaving?" asked Henry curiously as they walked the last half mile to the cottage.

"He said to be sure to bring you to the Sunday meeting," smiled Jonathon in the darkness. "And to bring your things with you."

"That won't be hard will it?" Henry replied. He stopped dead in his tracks for a moment and turning to Jonathon said, "These Bostonians are strange people; for the life of me I cannot understand them, Jonathon. The Fitzroys seemed very calm, considering their country is at war."

"I don't think they pay much mind to it! Bury their heads in the sand, and no mistake. I suppose it is hard for you to believe, but they just won't accept the war, brother Henry. Mr. Madison's war they call it. The people of Massachusetts will not allow their militia to be called upon, only for their own State's defense, if *they* in particular are attacked. That's the Federalist way!"

"If you don't mind me saying, Jonathon, isn't that a little selfish of them? After all you are supposed to be the United States."

"That's true, and I am dead against it personally, but I suppose it's a bit like the churches. I don't know what they are like in England, but here they can't agree on anything. In fact some of them don't even talk to each other, passing on the other side of the street, if you please."

"I am afraid it is the same in England with regards to the church, but the Navy, that's a different kettle of fish. I saw fierce loyalty on board the *Dragonfly*, and the *Restitution*. Not so much to the monarchy, but loyalty to the Captain, and especially to each other. A proper brotherhood they had, something that would put any church to shame, and no mistake!"

The moon shone down on the Bay of Boston, reflecting its silvery light on the gentle waves, and bathing the sea and shoreline with its misty illumination.

Long tufts of dune grass plucked at their legs, and grasshoppers and crickets leapt like jumping beans in all directions as the two men's feet disturbed them as they walked the final leg of the journey in silence.

The marshlands were far from quiet, Henry thought. The insect voices cried out incessantly into the warm and humid night, in wave after wave of croaking harmony. But he felt at peace, and he was at least thankful for that.

# CHAPTER TWO

## A SIGN OF THE TIMES

One by one the grand carriages began to arrive at the steps of Edinburgh House, as the aristocracy of Boston faithfully came to worship. Followed by those who were not quite as wealthy, and the downright poor who had walked many miles on foot.

The windows of the mansion had been opened wide, and fresh flowers adorned every room on the ground floor. Outside bowers made of festive colored red and white canvas with silk tassels adorning them, were scattered across the well manicured lawns, looking like a thirteenth century battle in array.

The shelters were set up to keep the hot sun from its occupants, and although the Sunday service was always held inside the great mansion, Eleanor Fitzroy preferred that her guests ate their food outside. This kept the children out of the house, and the crumbs off the floor.

Henry, together with Jonathon and Emily at his elbow, arrived amongst the throng of others that were being greeted on the huge columned portico by Richard and Eleanor Fitzroy. Eventually they were all seated in a vast library, with walnut shelves fitted from floor to ceiling, and furnished with rows and rows of chairs that had been specifically set up for the occasion.

After the prelude, which was given by a bewhiskered old man in a long black coat and white neck cloth, small thin paper backed hymn books were passed around, and the whole congregation sang a boisterous rendition of two of Charles Wesley's songs.

The room swelled with the sound of singing, and buzzed with the swishing of large fans on long six foot poles, that were being operated by two servants who stood one on each side of the library. Their faces showed benign indifference to the pleasantries enjoyed by the people that sat there, as they continued their monotonous task of keeping everyone cool.

Finally, Richard took his place before a small oak pulpit, with an arm like shelf attached at the side of it, upon which sat a heavy silver plate. Henry assumed this plate was for the collection of free-will offerings. Fitzroy smiled magnanimously at the people, and composing himself he announced in a well groomed and polished voice, "Ladies and gentlemen, brothers and sisters, I have great pleasure in introducing to you today a dear friend of mine, who is actually a Methodist minister by profession. Or perhaps I should say *calling*. He has also traveled a great deal while in England quite recently."

Richard had failed to tell them that the minister was actually born and bred there, thought Henry, as men and women cast admiring and smiling faces in his direction.

"Mr. Stapleton!" Richard gestured for Henry to stand alongside him. Henry moved towards the front, feeling somewhat embarrassed as he did so.

"Mr. Stapleton, would you honor us with a few words today?"

Henry stared at the people. He felt slightly nervous after the magnificent introduction. He was used to addressing large crowds back home . . . but here? He cleared his throat to begin. "Thank you, Mr. Fitzroy!" Henry told them briefly about the rise of Methodism in England, and how it was prospering in all aspects. He gave a lot more detail when he spoke of his own county of Norfolk, hoping that nobody would wonder why he had such excellent knowledge of that particular area, and yet was so vague about other places in England. But he needn't have been concerned, as the sea of faces looked back at him with much attention and admiration. He wondered also if they would pay any regard to the fact that this, '*well traveled minister,*' was dressed in long beige trousers and a checked shirt, instead of knee breeches and a neck tie, customary for a religious speaker. Would they notice how tanned he was compared to others of his kind? And had they failed to observe the fact that his hands were hard and calloused, which they would soon find out when they shook hands with him later, Henry mused.

After his brief message, there was more singing and prayers. Then suddenly it was all over, and everyone spilled outside into the sunlight. Men and women were bustling about, and children were darting between the bushes. Most folks were heading for the table which held several large glass punch bowls full of sparkling lemonade, anxious to cool themselves down.

"Please come and sit by us, Mr. Stapleton," said Eleanor Fitzroy touching his arm gently. "We would be most honored!"

"The honor is all mine, Ma'am," replied Henry as he took a seat beside them.

A butler held out a tray, and Eleanor took a glass and sipped it carefully. Henry took his, and stood it next to him on a small table. Another tray appeared out of nowhere with small dishes of crab fondue edged with tiny biscuits.

Henry could see Emily and Jonathon who were with the crowds around the big table. How he wished he could join his friends.

Emily's shrill voice carried over to him on the summer breeze, "Look Jonathon, Williamsburg cake!" Emily tugged at her husband's arm. "It takes six eggs to make one cake!" she stated knowingly. "Now you be sure to get a slice, you won't want to miss that."

"Yes, dear," replied Jonathon with a sigh.

The rest of the hot afternoon continued in idle trivialities, until even the most enthusiastic of the guests were beginning to look wilted. One by one, they started to leave, accompanied by the sounds of whimpering, tired children, and the impatient stamping of horse's hooves on the cobblestones, as the carriages waited in line to return their owners to their homes.

Henry said, "Goodbye" to Jonathon and Emily, and was at long last shown to his room by Richard, who escorted him up the elegant stairway.

The bedroom was bright and gracefully furnished like the rest of the house. There was a large Mahogany four poster bed which faced the window, with an excellent view of Boston Bay. Henry was grateful to be able to see the ocean, it made him feel closer to Elizabeth, and seemed to connect him in a strange way with England.

As soon as Richard had left the room, Henry threw back the heavy curtains around the bed which he knew would stifle him, and stop the circulation of what little fresh air there was in the room. It was hotter up here than downstairs, Henry noticed.

The Fitzroys had informed Henry that supper was at eight that evening, so he kicked off his boots and lay on top of the quilt to rest.

He must have fallen asleep, for he was jolted back to his senses when he heard a bell ringing somewhere downstairs. Supper he thought, while dragging himself into an upright position. His hair clung to his face with perspiration, and the palms of his hands felt sweaty. He quickly splashed his face with cold water that he had poured into a wash bowl from a pitcher left on the night stand for him to use. He dabbed himself dry with a towel, and smoothed back his hair. He hurriedly left the room and ran down the large staircase. He should not keep his hosts waiting, and in any case he was hungry, he decided.

Just the three of them sat around the long table, where they dined on the carefully prepared supper. After pushing back their plates following the meal, Richard suddenly excused himself and hurried from the room. He returned momentarily with a brown velvet bag tied with a cord at the neck. He dropped it (with its heavy contents) triumphantly on the table in front of Henry. He had a curious smile upon his face.

Henry stared down at it blankly. "What is it?" he asked his host.

"It's for you, my friend!" Richard said as he seated himself down on his chair, and leant back with an air of satisfaction. "Some of the men today gave me some remuneration for you. It's yours with their blessing," he continued.

"But, sir!" Henry protested. "They should not have done so, I never expected . . ." his voice faded suddenly as he realized that to refuse this gift would probably offend his new acquaintances, and even probably Fitzroy himself, who Henry was sure would have had some major part in such generosity.

"It's our normal custom, Henry."

"Thank you indeed then, sir, I am eternally grateful to you . . . to you all, of course."

"Only too pleased to help, my dear fellow . . . think nothing of it. Nothing indeed!"

The Fitzroys retired for the night, they looked tired and drained Henry observed as they left the room. Henry climbed the long winding staircase to his own room, and once inside he threw the bag onto the bed, and sat down and stared at it intently. He was almost afraid to open it, as if its contents held some venomous beast that might strike as soon as he loosed the cord. Of course he knew it contained money, he could hear the clink of coins as he had carried it upstairs. He spilled it out onto the bed. It was a stunning sight, he was almost spellbound as he looked down on the profusion of paper money, as well as coins of all sorts. Gold dollar pieces, and plenty of silver dollars. American money that he had never laid eyes on before in his life. His ship's pay had been in English currency, and that had gone long ago. But this! He had no idea of the value of it, though he knew it must be a very large amount indeed.

He ran his hands through it, fingering the coins and turning them over to read the inscriptions and dates. He smiled to himself; he felt like a pirate drooling over his ill gotten gains. What could he do with all this money? He would have to buy clothes he assumed. He must buy a gift for Jonathon and Emily, for their immense kindness to him, after all he owed them so much.

Finally he scooped it all back into the bag and put it into the top drawer of the bureau. He would deal with it in the morning. Perhaps he would take a walk through the town, it would give him time to think.

After conversing with some of the guests during the afternoon, he was particularly interested in visiting the Long Wharf, which, he was told, was the biggest in Boston, and jutted way out into the harbor on the east side. Some said it was a thousand feet in length, and normally was host to hundreds of ships from around the world. The China trade, the West Indies; Jamaica, all the world it seemed sought after the merchants of Boston. It was indeed the nation's seat of commerce, he had been told, with warehouses and dockside businesses lining each side of the wharf with an enormous density.

Henry lay sleeplessly on his bed for a long time, a lonely man now living in a mansion in Boston. No longer upon the high seas, with the constant ship's motion beneath him. No more hum-drum ship's routine, with bells clanging out the time every half hour; twenty four hours of the day. No sound of bos'un's pipes shrilling out orders of, "all hands," or "toe the line," when some sea officer was being piped aboard.

No anxiety of squinting through his telescope watching every sail on the horizon, trying to discover its identity, whether it was a friend or an enemy? When most of the time the ship's biggest enemy was usually the weather battering them constantly, as if it were trying to beat them all into submission.

That was all part of his past now, and Henry realized with a great shock, that he missed it all. The noise . . . the orderliness . . . the authority. Most of all he missed his friends. He wondered where the squadron was at this minute. He thought of the midshipmen, Christian Clark, and Freddie Baines, with their fresh faced enthusiasm of youth. Very much like his own son Benjamin. He was almost afraid to think of how much he missed his family, for it pressed on him with a heaviness that seemed to sap the very life out of him. He forced himself to ponder on the cantankerous Captain Weatherby, of the frigate *Dragonfly*, with all the responsibilities he had to the Admiralty, concern for his ship, and his men. His mind loitered too on Captain Street, brave and honorable, even if he often became a little flustered.

Henry was a bit unnerved by his unsettled feelings, it made him feel somewhat guilty about his current *easy* way of life.

For here he was in a stranger's house, eating their food, and for the first time in months, with money in his pocket. All these revelations resulted in a sleepless night of tossing about in the oppressive heat.

Henry left the Fitzroy mansion early the next morning. He had taken a hundred dollars from the money, and the rest he had put back in the drawer. There was almost five hundred dollars in miscellaneous coinage. He had been overwhelmed by the generosity of Bostonian Christians.

He walked down Congress Street away from the harbor, and turned right onto the cobble-stoned Milk Street. This road too, was fringed on both sides with fine homes built in red brick, and surrounded by well groomed shrubbery with wrought iron railings around the perimeters. Henry was enjoying the walk. The cooler morning air was stimulating, and he could smell the different odors of the harbor filling his nostrils. Everywhere you went in Boston, one eventually came upon the water, as the city was almost completely surrounded by it, except for the long narrow Neck which connected it to the main coastline.

He turned again, and very soon passed The Customs House, where every merchant who entered the harbor had to present their goods to be inspected by the customs men, who were never in anything like a hurry, and strolled around the dock carrying a stick and a look of self-importance upon their faces. Every one of them seemed to smoke a constant chain of cigars. Henry wondered if perhaps they were received as bribes for them to turn a blind eye to some of the imports. Cigars from Havana would be highly prized. Even Henry knew that. In England every businessman and diplomat seemed to smoke them, and they were *very* expensive.

Henry realized that the reason the customs men were in no hurry, was because once these ships were unloaded, then reloaded with American commodities, they would be hard pushed to exit the harbor with all the British men-of-war that were prowling along the eastern seaboard. Their precious cargoes would most likely end up in British hands and help finance the war against them.

The closer Henry got to the Long Wharf, which was his final destination, the more crowded it became. Teams of draught horses pulling long wagons filled with casks, and smaller two wheeled carts drawn by a single horse, were just a sample of some of the traffic that pushed its way along the wharf. The long dark wooden bowsprits of the many ships that were docked there, both small and large, all pointed towards the sky in a silent salute. So obstructive were the bowsprits of these ships, that they almost completely blocked one side of the street. Consequently, the multitude of wagons and pedestrians alike were sorely hindered in keeping the line moving along at a suitable pace.

The different aromas that tingled Henry's nostrils were quite amazing. The smell of codfish and herring, all mixed with the dusty herbal smell that was coming from the large wooden tea chests that were stacked high on every side of the street. Obviously the warehouses could not contain them all, and spilled their contents out through the open doors in profusion. The pungent smell of the spices that accompanied the ships of the

China Trade, were the most overpowering of all. Henry noticed the seamen wore brightly colored turbans on their heads, and had their broad chests bared with striped pantaloons on the lower half of their bodies. They loitered around these spice ships with a sharp eye on the crowds. Knowing how expensive were these precious spices, it was no wonder that each wore a double edged sword on their belts. Vicious looking weapons indeed, and enough to deter even the most brazen of thieves.

Several of the men looked suspiciously at Henry as he walked past. They gave him the impression that they would act first and ask questions later.

He moved away trying to show disinterest before they misunderstood his curiosity to be something more sinister. Henry knew that there would be one nation that was not represented here. His own! Of all the British ships that must have entered this harbor over the past two hundred years, on this date, August 1st 1812, there were none! No British seaman, no Union Jacks flying from the mast tops. But most of all, as far as Bostonians were concerned, no British goods that they loved and coveted, and would have gladly paid a king's ransom for.

As the morning wore on the wharf was becoming more crowded with people, and as the heat of the day increased, frayed tempers and lack of patience were starting to be displayed. Henry remembered noticing a Coffee House near to the entrance of Long Wharf, and began to retrace his steps with the hope of finding some refreshment.

The Ottis Coffee House was already beginning to fill up as Henry opened the door with its jangle of bells that announced every customer. The air was filled with smoke, and the smell of coffee laced with rum prevailed throughout the shop. Henry slid onto a long high backed wooden bench at the only empty table in the whole place. He looked around the room and noticed that most of its occupants were quite well dressed men, and deeply involved in conversation. There was not one woman to be seen in the place. In fact apparently they were not allowed inside under any circumstances.

This must be like the infamous Lloyds Insurance, of London, Henry thought. Which was technically nothing more than a glorified Coffee House, but was home to the insurance underwriters, and although he had never actually visited there personally, he had often heard the stories of fortunes to be won or lost in the place. And whenever a shipping merchant at Lloyds discovered the loss of his vessel, he could be found frantically searching out his own insurance broker, who would no doubt be sipping his coffee in the House somewhere amongst the close knit group of ship owners.

Here in the Ottis House a dark haired man embracing a white apron around his middle, came up to Henry to ask him what he would like to drink.

"I'll have a pot of coffee, and a pork pie!" said Henry.

"No pork pies, sir," answered the heavy set waiter, looking at Henry in amazement, and with a certain element of curiosity about his request for *English* food.

"What do you have to eat then?" Henry enquired.

"Beef and carrots, oyster soup, steak, codfish, and we have an uncommonly good cherry pie," replied the waiter breaking out into a big smile. "The best on the Wharf and no mistake!"

"The oyster soup, and cherry pie will suit me fine."

"You still want the coffee?"

"Of course!"

Henry settled back while he waited for his food to arrive, his eyes scanned the room with interest as he immersing himself in the atmosphere of this American establishment. It was just as noisy and unruly as any ale house in England he observed.

Presently a tall and thin elderly gentleman paused at his table. "Excuse me, Monsieur," the stranger spoke softly, "May I please share your table?"

Henry nodded, and gestured to the bench on the other side of the table. He was not seeking to engage himself in any conversation, especially with a stranger. He had to be cautious.

"You are indeed very kind, sir," replied the man, removing his hat and placing it carefully on the seat beside him. The stranger took out his pocket watch and looked at the time. Henry noticed it was an expensive gold fob watch with fine engraving on the front of the case. The man snapped it shut, and looked sharply across the table at Henry.

"And what is your trade, sir? If I may be so bold as to ask."

Henry hesitated, surprised at the open enquiry of the man. My, the Americans, or should he say the French, were extremely outspoken and frank, he thought to himself. Things were beginning to get very awkward and he was annoyed at being forced to speak.

"At the moment, I have none," replied Henry with a stony face.

"Come, come, my dear sir, a gentleman like yourself can hardly be without employment."

"With respect, sir, I am not in the habit of divulging my personal business to a complete stranger!"

"I see . . . you do not have to explain yourself to me, Monsieur, I must beg your forgiveness, I have been ungracious, sir. Why you do not even know my name. Let me introduce myself. I am Count Pierre Thibidaux, at your service my young friend." The elderly gentleman stood up, and held out his hand across the table and shook Henry's warmly.

Henry said, "My name is Henry Stapleton, and I am pleased to make your acquaintance."

"You are from Boston, Mon Ami?"

"No, I am from the country," replied Henry uncomfortably, welcoming the arrival of his food as a distraction from his predicament.

"And which *country* is that?" questioned the Count, peering deep into Henry's eyes.

Henry felt a sudden panic, fear momentarily gripped at his heart like a vice. Who was this man who had guessed his secret within minutes of their meeting, like a fox sniffing out his quarry, and perhaps waiting his opportunity to seize its prey. Beads of perspiration started to collect on Henry's forehead, and he fumbled in his pocket for his handkerchief.

The Count whispered, "Do not be alarmed, my friend!" he said kindly. "I have visited England often, before the Revolution . . . the French Revolution, that is. I have many friends there still. I am familiar with your speech. It is not unlike the Bostonian dialect, and would go undetected by most people here I am sure."

Count Thibidaux leaned forward and laid his hand gently on Henry's arm. "Your secret is safe with me, have no fear." He sat back easily and not waiting for Henry to reply said, "In many ways we are alike, you and I. Far away from our own countries and our kinfolk. The stories are different, but the heartbreak the same eh? We are twisted together by fate, like a loaf of braided French bread." The Count smiled, and continued.

"I will tell you my story if you like, then, if you feel free, you may in return tell me yours, my friend. Unless of course you can converse in French? That would make it more . . . convenient for you."

"My French is mediocre at best, I think I prefer to continue our conversation in English," said Henry.

"My name, as I have already told you, is Count Pierre Thibidaux. I was once the owner of extensive lands and a beautiful chateaux about thirty miles on the west side of Paris. I lived there with my wife. We had no children!" he stated sadly. "But alas she died of a bloody flux seventeen years ago." He lowered his eyes, which seemed to swim with tears at the mention of his loved one, and for a moment his face was frozen with fear and emotion. The Count then continued more carefully. "When the revolution broke out in 1789, we of the aristocracy were not surprised. There had been rumblings for years. The King's officials were insulted and abused, and the common people began to arm themselves and meet secretly, plotting to overthrow the Monarchy. Maybe it would never have come to revolution, but the previous year had been a disaster, one of the worst summers in living history. There was a terrible draught in the early spring, everything withered and died. Then when the rains came, it was too late, and continued too long. The countryside was flooded and the precious good earth was washed away in rivers of mud. There were no crops, and no crops meant no bread. Consequently a poor man was never separated from his aching stomach. The region around Paris was hit the worst, and wheat had to be shipped in from other parts of the country, making bread, the common mainstay of a poor man's diet, too expensive!

He paused while the burly waiter returned and took his order. When he was out of earshot, he continued. "After that the whole atmosphere became explosive . . . a powder keg. We had to live life very cautiously, almost lay low if you know what I mean. We did not leave our estates for many weeks at a time for fear of our lives. But we hung on, hoping for the best.

During this short period I became a member of the Emigres, a faction of high Nobles that were planning to flee the country, and live in exile while trying to conspire with foreign dignities to somehow rout the rebellion. England would have been a natural place of refuge for me. Quite naturally they were terrified of the political influence an out of control revolutionary government would have had on their own country."

"Britain's commerce would be in ruin within months if revolution had spread to England," Henry replied enigmatically. "Hungry people do not often have sound judgment . . . there must always be someone in command of the ship, as it were."

"You are most wise, Monsieur. So, I wrote to the British Admiralty who were trying to send small boats for us. It was a race against time! The other members escaped successfully, but we were hindered. My wife was sick at the time and unable to travel by sea. So when news came of their escape, I took what fortunes we could carry on our persons, and we took our carriage and traveled to western France. To Bordeaux, where I had some distant relatives living.

We stayed in that area for four long years, during which time I became very involved in my cousin's shipping business, and invested most of our money in that trade.

In 1791 we heard that our King and Queen, together with the royal family, had fled for their lives, leaving a manifesto behind denouncing the revolution and all it stood for. They were expected by the people to head up the new Assembly of Government, the King being a figurehead only. Of course they would not, and could not, condone this appointment. Then when the Queen was murdered along with thousands of others without even a trial . . . we knew it was time to leave France, knowing that no one was safe from the guillotine.

Even Bordeaux was not safe from the 'Reign of Terror.'"

"How so?" asked Henry between mouthfuls of food."

"There were terrible reprisals inflicted upon the Gironondins in our area, which followed the Revolutionary government's ratification of the 'Convention' to mobilize all citizens to serve as soldiers. It was absolute anarchy. The State also approved the use of violence to crush any resistance. Nobody could be trusted . . . everyone was in fear of being denounced as a traitor to the Revolution." The Count's face sagged heavily and he slumped down in his seat, as if the very thought of it all was like a knife wound.

The two men let their conversation lapse as the waiter deposited a bowl of oyster soup before the Count, who sat staring at it for a second until finally lifting the spoon to his mouth. Henry noticed the old man's hand shaking a little as he ate.

"My dear Count, you have my deepest sympathy and condolences. I cannot imagine what terror you have lived through. It makes my own miseries seem like chaff in the wind in comparison to your own," Henry said.

The Count let a watery smile appear on his face for just a second, then he continued somberly.

"It was after these atrocities that we made our plans to come to America. But alas my wife, Marie, passed away two weeks before we were due to sail, so I was forced to come alone. I have lived here in Boston alone and in exile ever since, but for an old and trusted servant who would never leave me, and is indeed my only source of comfort and a reminder of my past."

"You did not return after the peace came?"

"Without my Marie . . . I saw no value in it. Too many memories!" he said sadly. "But all the while I go on about my own troubles, you will excuse an old man like myself, Monsieur."

"No excuses necessary, none indeed! I hesitate, my dear Count Thibideaux, to relate my own circumstances, they seem so insignificant in comparison . . . so minute."

"Every man bears his own burden, Monsieur, whether it is large or small. In the eyes of the beholder it is tres grande, very overpowering. I would be pleased to hear your story, my friend," he uttered kindly.

"It's a long one," sighed Henry. "But I thank you for your indulgence. Meanwhile, I am compelled to ask, sir. Can I rely on your integrity as a gentlemen not to reveal what I am about to tell you? My life could be in grave danger if I were to be discovered."

Count Thibideaux raised one eyebrow a trifle, and softly replied, "You have my word . . . as a Nobleman."

"It seems like a lifetime ago now," Henry murmured. "These past few months have seemed endless, more like years than months. I am from the county of Norfolk, in England. I am a farmer, but primarily I am a Methodist preacher."

"Ah! Somehow I detected the angelic look in your face," interrupted the Count.

"I do not wish to bore you with all the details, but suffice to say that I was on an errand of mercy in the port of Great Yarmouth, in England, when suddenly, and without mercy, I was captured by a gang of sailors from His Britannic Majesty's Navy, and rowed out immediately to one of the King's ships anchored in the harbor." Henry seemed obligated to withhold the name of the frigate, *Dragonfly*. He did not know why.

"The ship set sail almost immediately, and I did not have knowledge of its destination. I was very ill treated at first, and was not allowed to speak to the captain until three days had elapsed. I finally gained an audience with him, but he was most unsympathetic, and very immune to my protests of unlawful internment, my being a minister of the gospel and exempt from such service . . . or so I thought," Henry said wryly.

"You have a wife, a family that you left behind perhaps?" asked the Count.

"Both! My wife's name is Elizabeth, and we have three children. I miss them terribly."

"They too must be as distraught as you," said the Count, with great sympathy.

"It does not bear thinking about! I try very hard not to in fact, but how can I push them out of my thoughts," Henry said unconsciously touching the scar on his forehead, which was just beginning to heal.

"Then what happened? Did you see any action while on board? After all, our native countries are at war are they not?"

"Sadly, sir! But in answer to your question. With the French a minor engagement, but with the Americans, several! And culminating with a very intense battle just over a week ago out there in the bay," Henry nodded towards the window of the Coffee House.

"Yes, it was the talk of all the coffee houses, a sad loss for America I am sure. I am afraid that my loyalties are confused these days, but for better or for worse, I live in America and confess my allegiance towards her now."

"Naturally, Count Thibideaux, as it should be. However, it was during that last battle that I fell overboard I am afraid!"

The Count raised his eyebrows in amazement, but remained silent.

"Unfortunately," continued Henry, "I cannot swim. I was washed up on the shore unconscious, as one that was already dead. But fate had other ideas . . . I was discovered by a lobster fisherman who carried me to his cottage, where I had the good fortune to be revived."

"Upon my word, what a remarkable story, you must be deeply indebted to this fisherman."

"Indeed I am, and to his dear wife also. They nurtured me as one of their own."

"Did they know you were . . . ?" The Count leant forward so that he would not be overheard.

"Eventually . . . yes," said Henry outguessing what the Count's next question would be.

"They did not care?"

"Apparently not! For they confessed to be Methodists, like myself."

"Mercy for mercy's sake!" said the Count with astonishment and admiration on his face.

"Now I am staying with a man who is in a similar business as yourself," continued Henry.

"Oh, and who is the man? Perhaps I know him?" replied the Count.

"A Richard Fitzroy, he has his residence on Congress Street. He, and his wife have also been most gracious to me."

"You are staying with him incognito?"

"No, he is fully aware of who, and what, I am. I would not eat a man's bread and live in deception." Henry felt a little angry at the question.

"Of course not, my dear friend. I can see that you are a man of *true colors*."

"Without a doubt that is an accurate statement, sir," Henry replied. "But I hasten to say, that with all the uncertainties I am experiencing right now, I feel more like a shadow on the water. My life is fluid . . . with no tangible reason for my being in Boston. Indeed a shadow!"

"I can understand your feelings exactly. They are not unlike my own over these past years. But, I do believe I know your kind patron. In my business it seems inevitably so."

"So I can count on your discretion, sir? Henry asked anxiously."

"Absolutely!"

"Well, Count, it seems that we have both finished our meal, and our coffee has grown cold, so if you do not mind I think I should be on my way. I still have some errands to attend to before I return to Edinburgh House. One of which is to buy myself some new clothes!" Henry said looking down at himself, and feeling rather embarrassed at his state of dress. For he could not help noticing how elegantly the Frenchman was dressed with his pale green velvet coat, and a plum colored neck cloth.

The Count stood up. "Forgive me for taking up so much of your valuable time, Monsieur. Perhaps we can meet again, soon?"

"I would like that. How will I contact you?"

"I live on State Street, a small house next door to the old State House. You may call upon me at any time," he said with a stiff bow. "And remember, your secret is safe with me."

Henry watched as he walked away, his thin frame held high as he proudly carried himself with dignity, like the true aristocrat he was. He waited a few discreet moments before leaving the coffee house himself.

As he walked back towards the main part of the town, he soon noticed a store with an exclusive looking sign that read "Drapers—Men's & Women's Apparel."

He walked inside the shop, and a small shrewish man scurried out from behind the counter, and Henry knew immediately that he was at the man's mercy. Very soon he would be parted from some of his silver coins.

# CHAPTER THREE

## FREEDOM IN SIGHT

Jonathon and Emily were sitting near their kitchen window, when through the thick mullion windows of the cottage they saw a figure struggling down the lane with several boxes and packages in his arms.

"I wonder who it can be?" cried Emily, peering through the glass with a puzzled expression upon her face. Jonathon stooped over her shoulder to get a better view.

"Why it is brother Henry, my dear, don't you recognize him?" he replied with a smile on his face that spread from ear to ear. Jonathon flung open the door, and Henry staggered through with his purchases.

"Oh, it is so good to see you again, Mr. Stapleton!" said Emily all red faced with excitement. "We have missed you, that we have!"

"Aye, my boy, but we hardly recognized you in all your finery!" Jonathon said looking Henry up and down; noticing his new white breeches and dark green coat. "Silver buckles on his shoes too! See, Emily my love, a fine gentlemen indeed he looks now!"

"Thank you, dear friends. Let me tell you of my great indebtedness to you Bostonians." Henry was breathless, and not just from the journey down the sandy lane. "It was an absolute God send . . . the money I mean."

"Money?" Jonathon asked curiously.

"Yes, you remember last Sunday at the Ftizroy mansion? Well apparently the good townspeople enjoyed my extemporary description of Methodism in England so much, that they decided to show me their appreciation in the form of a financial gift. A great deal of money I can tell you, my friends, and quite unexpected of course!"

"God be praised!" said Emily. "If ever a person deserved some good fortune after all you've suffered, Mr. Stapleton, it is you."

"And . . ." said Henry with a curious twinkle in his eyes. "I have brought some presents to the people who are the dearest to me on this side of the Atlantic," he proclaimed with a flourish.

"Upon my word, Mr. Stapleton!" gasped Emily sitting down in a chair next to the fireplace, as she wiped her hands on her apron. Her eyes were sparkling with excitement.

"Sit down too if you please, Jonathon," said Henry.

Jonathon sat obediently on a bench, while Henry rummaged through the packages and boxes that he had strewn on the floor of the kitchen.

"This one is for you, dear Emily!" Henry held out a square box neatly wrapped and sealed with wax. Henry watched with pleasure as she carefully broke the seal and undid the string. She lifted the lid almost as if she were scared to look inside, and pushed aside the soft white paper to reveal a strikingly handsome dress of gray and black silk.

"It is the very latest fashion the Draper informed me," Henry said.

Emily gasped in wonder as she jumped to her feet clutching the dress to her neck. "Why, it has a high waistline, and a straight skirt that falls in such elegant folds," she uttered, her face suddenly wreathed in a smile, and then just as quickly she looked as though she would burst into tears.

"Oh my!" Emily said at last. "It's the most beautiful thing I have ever seen, Mr. Stapleton." She smoothed her hands carefully over the silk. "Look, Jonathon!" she cried, holding the dress up to her shoulders. "It is the new Empire line that you see in shop windows. Not an old hoop-skirted crinoline . . . I can throw away my old hoop now," she laughed with joy. "Thank you, Mr. Stapleton! Thank you from the bottom of my heart!"

"You are most welcome, Ma'am."

Emily was still hugging the dress tightly to her as Henry handed the other two boxes to Jonathon.

Jonathon was much more reserved. "Henry, you shouldn't have . . . you didn't need to . . ."

"If a man can't share his good fortune with friends, it would be a sad day indeed," replied Henry with conviction as he watched Jonathon timidly opening his gifts.

The first box revealed a fine pair of black leather boots, the kind that came right up to the knee. Jonathon looked down on them in shocked silence. Henry thought for one moment that his friend did not like his present, but as he observed him more closely he saw that he was overcome with emotion, and unable to speak.

"The Draper said that if they did not fit he would gladly exchange them," Henry said.

"Oh, do try them on, Jonathon!" said his wife full of excitement.

"I will Emily, presently. I would like to open the other box first," he said with a very serious look on his face.

The second box was made of wood. It was long and flat, and the lid was lightly nailed down. Jonathon slowly reached out to a cupboard close by, and pulled out a long piece of metal to pry open the lid. He peeled it back, and inside lay a small woodworking axe made of finely forged steel, and with a beautifully carved oak handle. There was also a leather belt laying alongside the axe, with a special holder for the blade of the axe to be hooked through when attached to the belt.

Henry could tell that his friend was very affected by his gifts. He was a man that had acquired everything in life by sheer hard work. And items of such expense would be considered as a frivolous purchase. Something Jonathon could never have afforded to buy in the normal way of things.

Emily could sense it too, she knew what a proud, but soft hearted man he was, and it pleased her that he had received the gifts, for the axe would be an excellent tool for him to work on his old boat.

"Let's all have a cup of tea!" Emily said at last. "This definitely calls for a celebration I would say, wouldn't you?" She looked lovingly over to her husband, who nodded in agreement.

The two men shook hands heartily, and Henry noticed his friend's eyes were swimming with tears as they did so. Jonathon quickly looked away to hide his embarrassment.

"I can never repay you, my dear boy," said Jonathon as they drank their tea.

"You have already paid me a thousand times over, in more ways than I can ever describe."

After a happy hour or so of conversation, Henry stood to leave. "Well, I must be on my way," he said at last. "Thank you so much for your hospitality . . . and the tea!"

"We hope you will come back soon," said Jonathon, with Emily clutching tightly on his arm.

Henry left the little cottage, and started the long walk back to Boston. So much had happened in the last two weeks he thought, as he paced wearily along the coast road towards the Neck. He automatically glanced out to sea, his eyes squinting as the late morning sunshine reflected on the blue waters of Boston Bay. It was almost as if he was expecting to see the squadron again. He knew they were out there somewhere, he could almost feel it. The frigates, *Dragonfly*, *Providence*, *Viceroy*, and the two schooners. Then there was the frigate, *Restitution*, commanded by Captain Street, the last ship he had been on board and which may very well have become his tomb.

What now? he thought. He could not drift along with these people indefinitely, no matter how kind they were to him. "I must get back to England," he sighed. His heart ached as he thought of his wife, Elizabeth, and anger for the British Navy welled up in him once more. This war that had been propitious in separating him from his family, when would it end? Up until this time there was not much news of how the war was progressing. Apart from the presence of the British squadron continuously blockading out there somewhere in Massachusetts Bay, and probably along the whole of the eastern seaboard too, (which was general knowledge,) compounded the fact that commerce was at a standstill, while daily life was continuing as normal.

He wondered if the average citizen even cared much about the conflict with Britain. They certainly did not seem overly anxious to participate. Individuals had obviously made a stand for their beliefs, hence the fire ship attack. Mostly young men of course. But the Militia were languishing; resting on their laurels.

The President was unpopular it seemed, yet why would the people with enough independent spirit, spurn their hard won freedom in such a way by showing so much disloyalty to their own elected government? All this in order to maintain their commercial enterprises Henry presumed. What did they fight and die for in 1776, he wondered. At least the Loyalists had had the courage in to flee the country rather than be hypocrites. They had made their decision, even if it was a poor one.

What progress had been made here in thirty six years? Perhaps most of the heroes of the 'Declaration of Independence' were too old to hold up the battle flag and gather the country to unity once more. Or perhaps they had died in the subsequent years? News arrived in England back in 1799 that George Washington had passed away. But what of the others?

He chastised himself inwardly. Why should he even care about these people. Yet strangely he *did* care. For people like Jonathon and Emily, the Fitzroys; the Count. He was shocked by his own feelings. He was unable to think of these people as 'the enemy' anymore, and in no way could he harm a hair on their heads, not for anything. If America was invaded by English soldiers, and the war leapt from the sea to the land, where would his loyalties lie? Where was his heart? With the British Navy, or America?

He had heard that the Quakers were refusing to fight. 'Objectors,' was the new name they were given. Unable to fight for conscience sake they had been flung into prison as traitors. Left to rot under cruel jailors, with a public that despised them, and all they stood for.

Henry had a certain amount of sympathy for them, they were almost like the martyrs of old, caring not for their own lives, clinging only to their Faith. To a certain degree he shared the same persuasion, he was guilty of the same feelings. *But*, he told himself, if people did not fight to rid themselves of tyranny, oppression and injustice, they would be consumed by it; overrun by the enemy, and ultimately deprived of their hard won freedoms. Be it commerce or politics, and in his own particular case, faith in the Creator God, all culminated surely in the 'pursuit of happiness' these people conversed about often. He realized with a shock that some of his own beliefs were being challenged. He was not entirely the pacifist that he thought he was. The same old questions were whirling around in his head. At what point does a man stand up and fight? How bad does it have to get? What are you prepared to fight and die for? A person had to be resolute. The old pain in his head returned.

By the time Henry had reached the narrow Neck of Boston, the sun had long ago been smitten by storm clouds. The first drops of rain began to fall that proceeded the sultry storm that was making its presence felt in the southern sky. The heavens became dark and lowering, and before long thunder was booming loudly and lightning crackled all around him, on a landscape where he was the highest point.

A sudden thunder clap deafened him, and he instinctively dropped down into a crouching position, it seemed a natural reaction considering the horrific engagements at sea he had already endured, and for a few moments he was back on the

*Restitution*, and imagined that cannon balls were whistling over his head.

Those battles were still too real in his mind. The sound of the big guns; the acrid smelling smoke; the screams of the dying and wounded. A bolt of lightning struck a single dead tree just ahead, a lonely sentinel in the middle of the mud flats. The flames licked down the trunk of the tree as it split in two pieces, sending splinters in all directions. It seemed at every turn there was a reminder of those intense battles at sea, and this war that you could almost smell in the air.

By the time Henry got to the outskirts of Boston, the storm was in full force, sending heavy rain driving into his face with a wind so strong that he had to lean against it to make any progress at all. The sand from the rough track was being whipped up around him, and stung his hands and face. He slipped and stumbled in the ruts as the road became more and more flooded in the torrential downpour. He was soaked to the skin, and his new white breeches (now splattered with mud) seemed to mock at him. All is vanity he thought looking down at himself, and all is very temporary.

Finally climbing the portico steps of Edinburgh House, Henry fell breathlessly into one of the chairs that were placed there for a more tranquil occasion. He rested for a few minutes while rain dripped off him and left immense puddles all around his feet. His coat, neck cloth, and even his shirt were sticking to him like limpets. Kicking off his filthy shoes (minus one silver buckle) he sat watching the trees in the beautiful gardens, bending over at an alarming angle as the wind tore at the branches. It was as if they were paying homage to an unknown entity.

He dared not enter the house, and leave pools of water on their impeccable carpets, he thought. A gentleman would never do such a thing. A gentleman! The word seem to ring in his head. At present he was living a life of frivolity in comparison to his life in the British Navy.

At last Henry entered the door of the mansion, the butler looked at him disapprovingly, and sniffed as he hurried towards the kitchen muttering under his breath as he went. "I'll send a servant to help you with your wet clothes, sir," the butler said begrudgingly.

"No, matter!" Henry replied, and slowly climbed the stairs to his room with a firm resolve to talk to Richard Fitzroy later about the possibility of him finding some gainful employment. If he had to live in Boston against his will for a while, he might as well earn his living. He had been at leisure too long. He was strong enough to work, and he fully intended to do so.

"I will certainly give it some thought," said Richard, rubbing his chin as they sat at supper that evening. The heavy curtains were pulled over the windows even though it was still light. Eleanor Fitzroy hated storms, and the air was still sultry with occasional thunder rumbling menacingly in the distance.

Henry actually felt more at ease now that the matter of his employment had finally been broached. Richard had made light of the matter, almost as if he would rather have Henry there as a guest, perhaps speaking at the Sunday meetings like a personal resident bishop. But Henry finally convinced Richard that he was not accustomed to boredom, and in any case people would start to talk, causing gossip to fly like blossom on the wind. Then perhaps people would start to wonder who he really was!

"You are absolutely right, my dear sir," Richard said. "I suppose it can't go on indefinitely. Of course we have to consider your safety too. There are some in this town if they knew your true identity, would like to see you hang!"

"Republicans?" Henry smiled.

Richard coughed with embarrassment. He rubbed his chin again and said, "I will make some enquiries first thing in the morning."

"Thank you, Richard."

A week later it had been arranged for Henry to go down to the Customs House near Long Wharf, to meet with a Mr. Benjamin Harrison. Mr. Harrison was well known to Richard Fitzroy, for he had dealings with him on matters with regard to the many vessels that Richard owned. There happened to be a vacancy in the clerical department, and Mr. Harrison needed someone with good writing abilities. It seemed like a fair assessment of his expertise thought Henry, although it was his handwriting abilities that had been the cause of his being transferred from the frigate *Dragonfly* to the *Restitution*.

Henry walked once again in the direction of Long Wharf. Seeing the ships in such profusion seemed to tantalize Henry with all their opportunities for his freedom. Notwithstanding, Henry was grateful to Richard, and hoped this appointment would lead to his employment at the Customs House. It would give him the opportunity to stay abreast of current affairs, the more people he met outside the precincts of Edinburgh House the better. And wherever there were sailors hanging about, there was always a lot of *talk* going on.

Mr. Harrison was a large robust man in his late fifties with long dark whiskers. He was smartly dressed in black coat and trousers, unlike the uniformed Customs Officers who strutted about the wharf with a stick in hand, and their noses in the air, as if they could sniff out smuggled goods wherever they were hidden.

Harrison welcomed Henry warmly, and certainly had no airs or graces about him. He offered Henry a chair, and after brief civilities asked him to copy a few sentences from a bill of laden, to test his penmanship.

"That will be fine, young man!" He expressed his pleasure at Henry's neat and flowing handwriting. "Yes, that will do very well. When will you be able to start your position?"

"As soon as you wish, sir."

"Tomorrow will be excellent then. You will be here at seven in the morning!"

When Henry arrived at the Custom House early the next day, he was greeted by the sight of a dozen or so men hanging around the door of the Customs Office. Some looked angry, while others were waving their arms in animation.

"Damned coward! that's what I say," said a red haired man with a hint of an Irish accent.

"Don't tell me you would have done any differently, Sean," said another man poking him in the chest playfully.

"Like hell I would!" yelled back the man named Sean. "And don't push me neither, or I'll be plastering your face."

The rest of the men chuckled, and nudged one another sarcastically as they seemed to goad the Irishman more and more. This was just the kind of start they liked to the morning, with enough wrangling to last them the rest of the day. The men's raucous voices were carrying through the morning air like crows in the tree tops.

"What is it?" Henry asked a man on the edge of the crowd, which by now was beginning to swell.

"I've just given them the news that the commander of Fort Mackinac surrendered to the British, three weeks ago."

"Fort Mackinac! Where is that?"

"It's an island north of the Michigan Territories, we had an outpost and fort there," he replied. "Until the Limey's took it, that is! You must not be from around here, mate, if you don't know that," the man said looking at Henry somewhat strangely.

"Oh, I have been abroad," replied Henry nervously. The man was still occupied with his news, and the turmoil it had caused, to concentrate much on Henry's answer. Henry was relieved, but he pushed the man for more information.

"How do you know this?"

"I was there, mister! Me, crewing on the *Friends Good Will*, fine little square topsail sloop she was. We left Detroit loaded with tobacco, whiskey, casks of nails, and other dry goods, north bound for Mackinac Island. The Master, Mr. Lee, was uneasy during the whole passage up Huron, even though we carried the ship's owner along too.

All the rumors of war with the British, that was all we had on our minds, every man jack of us. We've had enough of 'em hi-jacking our seaman. Trade is important you know, mister, that's what Mr. Williams always says! That's why he built the sloop in the first place, a right industrious man he be. Why, he was born near here, in Roxbury. The first man from Massachusetts to open a dry goods store in Detroit! There's money to be made in the North West Territories, he staked his life on it. Lot of good it'll do any of us now," he shook his head sorrowfully.

"What happened to you?"

"Well, we didn't know it at the time, but the day after we sailed, war was declared! So we couldn't warn them at the fort. Then we offloaded all our supplies in the normal way. Those soldier boys gave us a hand too, real hospitable to us they was. Little did they know what was round the corner for 'em. The next morning the Master, Mr. Lee, told us to put our backs into loading military supplies, and that we were chartered to carry cargo for the army. Soldiers too! That was a bit insufferable, mister. Soldiers, they 'aint like sailors you know. Can't stand on their feet for five minutes. Then they're all down below throwing up their guts, whilst we had to handle the ship in all weathers on our south bound passage to Fort Dearborn. Lake Michigan can conjure up some wicked weather you know. Those north-west winds can rattle the teeth in yer head!"

"I can imagine," Henry smiled. If only the man knew who he really was.

"I for one was glad to get rid of the human cargo," continued the man. "And with a fair wind we sailed back north. Fort Mackinac we counted as our half way point to 'back home.' We was all looking forward to a 'friendly tot' upon arrival at the island. We luffed up, saw our flag flying from one of the block houses on the fort, and looked forward to some sleep. Then we lowered our tender, and pulled for the shore. You could have knocked me down with a feather when we were all arrested by those red-coated bullocks. We was marched off at gunpoint, then informed that, 'We were now on British soil!' Flying false colors they were.

They took the *Friends Good Will* as a prize, the poor soul. She was almost new, nigh broke Mr. Williams' heart it did. We wanted to fight for 'er, but it was useless. They released us prisoners eventually, and gave us our parole. Didn't want to feed us most likely. But they kept our brave ship! I hate 'em for that, mister!"

"Understandably so, but remember the winds of war often blow in the opposite direction."

The crewman of the *Friends Good Will* stared at Henry for a split second, as if trying to read his thoughts, then turned away and merged back amongst the seething group of men.

A large crowd had now formed, and was becoming more and more unmanageable by the minute, as one man shouted loudly to the Irishman who seemed to be at the axis of the mob. "There was women and children in the fort, Sean, and civilians in the village. The commander couldn't risk their lives, not with those blood thirsty redcoats." He spat a wad of tobacco from his mouth viciously.

"Hog wash!" Sean O'Boyle replied viciously. "Them's Army women, they knew what to expect! Any rate, they could have picked up a musket and stood by their men! Same as our women did in the war for independence." His eyes were blazing now, and Henry could see that he was a man motivated more by his fists than by his mouth.

"Naw! Cowards, that's what I say! They were probably all blind drunk more like it. How could they let the British creep up behind them unawares. After all they were in a fort, for all love. You couldn't get much better protection than that!" O'Boyle sneered.

"Pity the poor bugger that was sleeping on watch!" mumbled someone in the front of the crowd. The mob roared with laughter

"You'll all laugh on the other side of yer faces if the British try to land here in Boston, or get control of the Great Lakes," growled O'Boyle as he grew more and more angry with every passing moment.

Although Henry didn't much approve of mob violence, or the lack of self-control the man O'Boyle displayed, he could not help admire his loyalty and love for his country, which, he was presumably at least willing to fight for.

"Lay off it, Sean, you're no different to anyone else," yelled another member of the crowd. "Except you're Irish!"

The crowd roared out again in uncontrollable laughter. O'Boyle lunged at them, throwing himself bodily amongst the men with his arms thrashing about in all directions and punching everyone in his path.

Henry watched with a certain amount of amusement as the crowd surged first one way, and then another. They were like a swarming rabble that looked a lot like bees protecting their hive, and with the red-headed O"Boyle in the thick of it.

Far away a whistle blew, which seemed to have a sobering effect on the rioting crowd, and gradually, one by one, they fell away not wanting to spend the night in jail.

Just at that moment Mr. Harrison arrived with the keys to the Customs office. "Come in, Mr. Stapleton," he said, and all but pushed Henry through the door. "Never mind them," he nodded to the crowd as it dispersed. "It's just high spirits! Sean O"Boyle . . . he takes it all too seriously. It's not the first occasion! Sometimes it's worse! There's actual damage done to merchandise and property. I'm glad it broke up when it did."

Henry smiled and said, "It did not offend me in the least, Mr. Harrison."

"Good!" was the short reply.

"Well, how was your first day of labor?" asked Richard as they sat at supper in the large dining hall of Edinburgh House. The butler fussed and fumed as he directed the servants carrying huge dishes laden with food to the table.

"Just fine, sir. Mr. & Mrs. Fitzroy . . . Richard and Eleanor, if I may be so bold," Henry said hesitantly. "I heard news of the surrender of Mackinac Island in the Michigan Territories, whilst I was on the wharf today.

Richard and Eleanor exchanged glances, but did not reply.

"I spoke to a crewman of a sloop called, *Friends Good Will*, which had been lured into the fort under false colors."

"Yes, the news is everywhere, together with the usual speculations I am afraid." replied Richard with a big sigh.

"I'm sorry to hear it, sir," said Henry with genuine feeling. "The crewman of the sloop said it would have a big impact on America's trade. Richard and Eleanor stared at him for a few moments with shocked expressions upon their faces. There was a hint of fear in their eyes.

"Thank you, Henry," said Richard at last. "We appreciate your commiseration."

"At least there was no loss of life!" offered Henry as an afterthought.

A silence fell on the little gathering, and they ate their meal in silence. Each one of them captured by their own thoughts and concerns.

Just as coffee was being poured, there was a loud explosion, just as earth shattering as any broadside fired by the *Dragonfly*. It reverberated around the harbor causing sea birds to take instant flight, and Edinburgh House shook to its very foundations. The candles on the table seemed to flicker in a momentary suspension, and the coffee cup that Eleanor was holding to her lips, fell to the floor with a clatter.

She leapt to her feet in terror, clutching her throat with her hand in a gesture of absolute fear. "Oh my Lord!" she whimpered. "We are being attacked! Is it Bunker Hill all over again, Richard?"

"It's all right, my dear," soothed her husband, as he ran to her side and put his arm around here shoulders. "It is all my fault, I should have told you my sweet. Don't be alarmed . . . Henry, my deepest apologies to you too, sir."

Henry shrugged in unconcern. "I am no stranger to the sounds of war," he admitted to them, and quickly resumed his place at the table.

Richard began explaining to his wife. "I read in the newspaper this morning, that the Governor of Massachusetts has decided to restore our defenses. Fort Warren, (that's the old fort situated at the mouth of the harbor,) has been equipped with some formidable guns, and manned by a few dozen militia men. They chose to start practicing their gunnery this evening. The militia needs the experience, and it will give the blockading British squadrons something to think about," he added. "I had forgotten all about it until they just fired the guns. I am so sorry, my dear!"

"Apologize to my ears, Mr. Fitzroy," snapped Eleanor in an uncommon show of bad temperedness. "War! War! War! That's all we talk about these days," she bemoaned.

"Well, I am sorry to weary your ears, Eleanor, but the fact of the matter is, we *are* at war, whether we like it or not! And as such, we will have to suffer all the inconveniences and deprivations that might go along with it."

Eleanor stared back at her husband in silent defiance. Her hands trembled in the light of the candles, as she kept her mouth in a firm thin line. Finally, composing herself she said, "How many cups and saucers will be broken before this practice stops Richard? Tell me that! Now call for the servant at once to clean up this mess . . . I am all together too upset to speak with anyone for the rest of the evening."

The servant appeared after Fitzroy rang for him, and removed the broken pieces of china from the carpet, and dabbed up the coffee stain. Eleanor sat stiffly until he had left the room, made her apologies, and walked out with a flourish.

Several more shots were fired from the fort during the rest of the evening, as the two men sat facing each other across the table. "I wonder what the British will do next?" exclaimed Richard, almost thinking out loud. "Henry, I don't suppose you have any . . . . ?" Richard stopped before he embarrassed himself, realizing that to continue in this line of conversation would be in extremely bad taste.

"Henry, if we were to read between the lines," Richard said in a somewhat cynical tone.

Henry stopped him in his tracks before Richard could go any further. "You forget, sir, I was a common seaman for much of the voyage across the Atlantic, and as such I knew nothing. None of us did! Even Captain Weatherby didn't know his assignment until he opened his sealed orders in mid-Atlantic. And the men," he paused with a loud sigh, "Why, we didn't know our orders until the enemy was in sight! We were barely given the courtesy to think for ourselves. If you'll forgive me for saying so, I think you fail to understand the protocol and ways of the British Navy, Richard. Even an Admiral is not always privy to the whims of the Diplomatic Service."

"I am sure you are absolutely right," replied Fitzroy humbly. "Let us speculate no further with that line of conversation."

Henry left the table and walked over to the window. He drew back the curtains and inhaled some fresh air, even though it was tinged with the smell of gunpowder as the smoke from the harbor was hanging languidly in the sultry atmosphere of the evening.

"It also said in the newspaper," Richard spoke once more, "that they are going to install a boom across the harbor. Of course there is only one area that is deep enough for large ships of war to enter, the rest is too shallow, and some places even dry on the ebb tide. Still, they will have to make sure that there are no gaps in the booms nevertheless, and there will be sentries posted too, no doubt."

Henry returned to take his seat back at the table, but he couldn't help wonder what Captain Weatherby would think about that information, perhaps there were British spies even here in Boston.

Maybe people would suspect that he himself was guilty of spying. God forbid! He recognized though that he certainly had a unique alibi if he *were* a spy, that is if one could possibly feign the appearance of almost drowning, and inflict a scar on his own head that nearly killed him, and was only just healing. Not to mention the stabbing pain that affected him often and unexpectedly. He chuckled inwardly to himself. As if his life wasn't in enough danger here, than to consider undergoing intelligence work

Richard broke into his thoughts. "I am afraid that the war is accelerating, Henry, no matter what we think or feel. There is no turning back the clock now for any of us. It's all or nothing! Sink or swim!"

Henry was aware of Richard's voice droning on and on. He was not purposely being rude, and was still able to maintain eye contact with his host, but his mind was elsewhere. as once more he lapsed into daydreaming about his escape back to England. And with the current news as just related by Fitzroy, those dreams were fast fading into oblivion. What with booms across the harbor, and the presence of a manned fort armed to the teeth with ponderous weaponry, Boston would soon be sealed up like a tomb. But escape he must whatever the cost, for his very life and happiness depended upon it.

One thing was certain, he was going to need a ship . . . a ship bound for England. His chances were slim to non-existent at present as he remembered all the shipping pressed in at Long Wharf. No ships were either coming in or leaving Boston. He imagined it would be the same elsewhere. Almost like a siege, he thought. No wonder Richard looked perturbed.

Henry looked over to where Richard sat (who had long since retired to an armchair,) and was now leaning back comfortably and silently staring at the ceiling. No doubt he was worrying about this war, and what it would mean to him personally. His business would suffer, perhaps even be annihilated. The fortunes of war can often determine a persons success or failure, Henry realized. The debtor's prison in England were full of such people, and were impartial to its guests' integrity.

Henry dragged himself from his silence, and asked Richard, "What will become of your ships now that the blockade is here in earnest?"

Richard looked up with a certain surprise at Henry's question. "To be absolutely honest, I am faced with great uncertainty. A ship that is sunk in a storm has its monetary reimbursement, via the insurance companies. But a ship that is unable to get either in or out of her home port . . . that is money poured down the scuppers indeed. There is no insurance against that!" He shook his head in dismay. "Many of the ship owners that I have talked to lately are considering applying for a Letter of Marque."

"What exactly is a Letter of Marque?" asked Henry curiously. He had heard vague talk about it in his short experience in the British Navy.

"It's an application to the Government to transfer a ship's papers, from merchantman, to privateer."

Henry knew what a privateer was, he had heard the wild stories. A pirate's dream was to become a privateer . . . a plunderer on the high seas, with a legal document in his pocket to sanction his attacks on shipping of any nation that physically resisted them, whether they were at war with that particular nation or not, and also absolve him from all reprisals. Henry could imagine what life would be like at sea with such ships roaming the oceans like a pack of sea wolves.

"There will be definitely some unscrupulous rogues that will put to sea with, or without, a Letter of Marque," Henry stated emphatically. "You can be sure of that. You yourself have given the matter serious consideration then?" Henry asked Richard with care.

"I have! I cannot sit idly by and watch my hard earned money slowly dwindle to nothing. I suppose Eleanor would not be in favor of it, but it cannot be helped. Women don't always understand these things do they?" He looked up with a smile.

"I suppose not," Henry said.

"They are incapable sometimes of seeing the whole picture, they tend to focus on the one issue, and not take account of the overall view. Of course I love her dearly, but I cannot be influenced by her in any way. This is serious business Henry! If I emphasize the possibilities of the subsequent losses that could be incurred by doing nothing, I am certain she will see reason."

Henry was surprised that Richard rambled on about his wife so, for he had always found that once Elizabeth was completely aware of the facts of any serious situation, she seemed to readily accept any possibility that might lead to the solution. He was fortunate, he thought to himself.

"What about a crew?" Henry was amazed how easily naval questions were streaming from him, almost like it had become second nature to him.

"That's another story," said Fitzroy. "There's plenty who would want to go . . . who have the courage, and a strong conviction of patriotism, but most of them have families at home to feed. Months away at sea, with no guarantees of success . . . with only a glimmer of prize money and riches, not to mention the danger, and a real possibility of never returning! It bears thinking carefully about before a decision like that can be made by any man, don't you think?"

"Except for those who have nothing to lose!"

Richard Fitzroy looked at him keenly, as if Henry's statement had struck him between the eyes like an axe. A man like yourself, he thought to himself. Was Henry offering his own services? Or merely making a statement? It was not a question you easily asked a man, to put your life on the line with no guarantees of success. Richard thought that such a commitment would have to be given from the heart of a man's own conscience, even though obviously Henry had nothing to lose on this side of the ocean. He had already taken extensive risks. But he was the right age; strong, and with naval experience, and being English . . . he may think like an English sailor, and have knowledge of the ways of the Admiralty. Richard didn't want to admit the honesty of Henry's previous statement, that 'ordinary seaman in the British Navy didn't know what was happening until the enemy was in sight.' He had convinced himself in his own mind that this was *not* the case, and Henry would be a convenient ally, which would definitely be to Richard's advantage.

"You are right, Henry," Richard replied at last. "Not a man such as myself, however. I am too old, and my dear Eleanor would not hear of it, and that's a fact! Maybe others . . . younger men perhaps?"

"It would take you a couple of months at least to gather a crew, the right armament; provisions for at least six months," Henry added.

"I must say, Henry, you have become quite the commander, you sound as if you had been at sea for years instead of only a few months." Richard looked at him with a certain admiration.

"What suitable ships do you have Richard?"

"The largest is a brig . . . older, fifteen years or more. Only two six pounders!" He looked embarrassed. "Not a man-of-war, especially in her condition that's for certain! Her *below decks* could be altered . . . right now she is set up as a merchantman."

"A brig is not really fast enough to make an attack and retreat with the spoils," Henry said knowingly, "as I am sure you are aware. Do you have any schooners?"

"Only one, on the slightly smaller side," Richard uttered apologetically.

"How small?"

"One hundred and twenty five feet sparred length. Ninety five feet on deck, fore and aft rig. The *Lady Eleanor* is what we call her. We use her more for pleasure than anything else. Eleanor hates to travel by carriage on long distances, she loves the sea, born and raised in Gloucester . . . her family still live there. We used to spend a month up there during the summer, but this year . . ." he shook his head. "Well things are different now," he said regretfully.

"The way you describe this *Lady Eleanor*, she sounds like a useful and appropriate vessel."

"She's lively alright, and her main cabin is very commodious. Eleanor had it furnished with the finest of furniture. She won't give up her comfort, even for a month," he laughed.

Henry could imagine it. He could also see in his mind's eye, the beautiful furnishings spattered with blood, or smashed to smitherines. A canon ball had no respect for elegance, and chain shot was worse, especially if it were fired by a frigate or a sloop of war. And there must be plenty of them just over the horizon in Massachusetts Bay. Henry felt carried away with excitement . . . the possibilities running through his head like lightning. He pulled himself down to earth, checking himself as if his mind were the sheet of a mainsail that was controlling the wind of restraint in his heart. Maybe things were moving too fast?

"How long would such a document take to obtain?" Henry found himself reverting to logic again, thinking clearly for he must be patient, and bide his time.

"I don't know, except that anything that involves the Government is bound to take a long while. If I apply immediately, who knows? We might all be surprised!"

"Has anyone else obtained this documentation yet?" Henry asked.

"Not as far as I am aware, and I must say I would like to be the first one to leave from Boston anyway. I have a strange feeling, Henry, that the window of opportunity may be short lived. The British Navy is spread thinly right now . . . you of all people must know that. But if ever the war with France is over, and with the ensuing peace, we could be locked up in our harbors for ever. Time is of the essence . . . I feel it in my bones." He punched one fist into the palm of his other hand with grim determination.

"For the time being though, I would like you to come down to the harbor and take a look at the *Lady Eleanor*, see what you think of her. Would you come?"

"Certainly, I would be most interested in seeing her."

Over the next few weeks, Henry visited the *Lady Eleanor* several times. She was all that Richard had described. In good condition! Well maintained, and with a jaunty rake to her two masts that seemed to whisper, "Take me out to sea, and I'll show you how to fly." Henry had no doubts about her whatsoever, and was certain that she would be a speedy, and very seaworthy craft. Just the kind of vessel to outrun any frigate or ship-of-the-line that she may encounter, yet large enough to carry the weight of metal needed to board and capture the average merchantman. She was currently berthed at India Wharf, which was quite near the Long Wharf. Her cargo had long since been unloaded, which made her empty and sad looking, but surprisingly free of vermin. The reason was, no doubt, the round faced, green eyed, and much overweight gray cat who was sunning herself on the top of one of the hatches.

The last few weeks had also brought a surprising number of seaman, both young and old alike, knocking at the door of Edinburgh House, much to the disconcertion of the lady of the mansion, although the preliminary interviews were usually quite brief depending on the age of the applicant. Henry was amazed at how fast the news of the impending voyage of financial opportunity had spread throughout Boston, despite the fact that Richard had insisted on the highest degree of secrecy.

It seemed that the lust for prize money had got completely out of hand, and was spreading like a fire through a hay barn. Every tavern and coffee house in the community was a hot bed of speculation, and every mother's son had sworn to make his fortune while serving his country at the same time.

It was during this time that some of the most important news of the war so far, arrived in Boston. The USS *Constitution*, captained by Isaac Hull, had apparently come upon HMS *Guerriere* off of the coast of Halifax, Nova Scotia. The *Constitution* was south bound heading towards Bermuda, when they were hailed by an American privateer, who informed Isaac Hull that an English man-of-war was seen traveling south on the previous day. That was on August 18th. Captain Hull was overjoyed, and clapped on all sail. Two hours later, the masthead lookout on the *Constitution* spotted the *Guerriere*, and with the wind out of the north-west at a lively eighteen knots, the American frigate soon ran down to close with her enemy.

Captain Dacres, of the *Guerriere*, was also anxious to fight, and 'hove-to' until the *Constitution* closed. Both ships then sought the best position for forty five minutes.

The *Guerriere* fired first from a long way off, but Hull had only presented the *Constitution's* stern as a narrow target. He was calculating that the British frigate would be out of range. His own guns were at the ready, and double shotted with grape. Finally veering off, Hull opened fire hitting *Guerriere* with a full broadside that shook her from stem to stern. The British retaliated, but within thirty minutes of the battle the *Guerriere* was a floating dismasted wreck, rolling in the heavy seas. It was the first victory at sea for the American Navy.

After the return of the *Constitution* to Boston Harbor at the end of August with the *Guerriere*'s prisoners, including Captain Dacres, the whole of Boston was jubilant.

On September 5th there were great celebrations held all around the city, including one at Fanheuil Hall, where a great banquet was laid out in honor of Captain Hull, and his crew. These current events had suddenly put the American Navy into the role of victor instead of the vanquished.

They were tired of the British creeping into their harbors at night all along the Massachusetts coast, with their undersized raiding parties destroying a numerous amount of small shipping. Some folks even said that the British set their watches by the town clock in Gloucester.

There would be no more of the British making sport of them by firing their muskets at cattle grazing along the edge of the mud flats, just for target practice. Bostonians could at last hold their heads up high, unlike the citizens of Nantucket who were openly supplying the enemy with meat, fish, and other supplies.

Naturally the Fitzroys had been invited to the great victory celebration, and Richard had persuaded Henry to come along too. He sat with the Richard and Eleanor at one of the densely populated tables in the middle of The Hall, the three of them giving their full concentration on the rhetoric of the evening's events.

Suddenly the whole assembly erupted with, "Huzzah for Captain Hull!" and one of the officials announced loudly, "May we ask you one last question, Captain Hull before this evening is over?"

Captain Hull stood slowly to his feet. "Certainly, my dear fellow! Ask away!" Hull smiled broadly, much to the appreciation of his vast audience.

"Is it true, sir, that during the battle against Captain Dacres, you became so excited that you actually split your breeches?"

The whole assembly of people held their breath in anticipation of Hull's answer. Not a sound was uttered, nor a plate rattled.

Hull's face turned very serious. "It is true, sir, but . . ." he held up his hand to stave off the crowd's response . . . "my dignity was restored when I refused the honorable captain's sword, which he endeavored to hand over to me when he came on board the

*Constitution.* Instead I challenged him with, "Your sword you can keep, sir, but I'll trouble you for that hat!"

The laughter rang out to the rafters of the building. This was a day to be recorded in American history; glasses were raised to the honorable Captain Hull, his officers, and the gallant crew of the frigate *Constitution.* Fists banged loudly on the banquet tables as the guests showed their approval.

"Ladies and gentlemen!" said the Master of Ceremonies, standing to his feet after the last of the tributes had been given. "A toast to Captain Hull, and the remarkable ship the USS *Constitution.* May she never be defeated!" A loud cheer swept over the occupants of Faneuil Hall, and the crowd went wild once again; shouting with relish, and throwing their hats in the air in a most unceremonious display of patriotism and emotion.

If Richard Fitzroy had any doubts at all about his privateering endeavors, they were washed away like a footprint in the sand, after hearing the account of the stunning exploits of the American frigate

And so, on September 6th 1812, Richard sat down at his desk and wrote with enthusiasm.

> *Dear sirs,*
>
> *Referring to the Act of Congress concerning letters of marque, subsequent prizes and prize goods. I have to request of you, as the person employed by the Secretary of State, a commission for the schooner called, The Lady Eleanor. Burthern ninety six tons, and mounting nine guns. Owned by Richard and Eleanor Fitzroy of Boston, in the county of Essex.*
>
> *The crew to consist of fifty five persons to reconoiterre on the high seas.*
>
> *Your most humble and obedient servant,*
>
> *Richard J. Fitzroy*

Richard addressed the request to Charles Winthrop, Collector for the port of Boston. He carefully blotted the wet ink on the document. It was a brief letter, but to the point, he thought.

No need for any flounces and curves, not with Governmental affairs. He laid it to one side on his desk, he would show it to Eleanor later. He was sure that she would be kindled with enough patriotism to be in full agreement. Especially after their attendance at the banquet last night, held for the foremost citizens of Boston. Eleanor had clapped her hands in approval with the hundreds of others, as a challenge was put forward to all the citizens of Boston to drive the enemy once and for all from their shores.

He would also show it to Henry, and try to find the courage to openly ask him to take part in his plans.

Richard broached the subject at supper that evening as the three of them sat quietly eating their roast pork.

"Must we talk of war over supper," complained Eleanor. "I am sure Mr. Stapleton would like to enjoy his meal." She looked at her husband with a great deal of disapproval on her face.

"Sorry, my dear. Perhaps later then? In the drawing room?" He looked across at Henry who said nothing, but nodded his head in answer to the question.

Later that evening as the sun was dipping over the trees in the west, the two men sat facing one another on each side of the fireplace. There was no fire in the grate, as this was September, but the brass andirons that protruded into the hearth shone like stars as they reflected the soft candlelight of the room.

They sat for some while in complete silence. Henry had already read the letter of request to the Port Authority, which lay on his lap as he relaxed in the chair. The humid atmosphere of the evening was causing both men to perspire heavily . . . or was it anticipation of the change that would effect all of their lives, Henry wondered as he loosened his neck cloth and tugged at his shirt, which stuck to his chest like a wet rag. Would he ever get used to the American climate? Perhaps he would not be here to experience another summer? He sincerely hoped not.

"Well!" said Fitzroy at last. "What do you think?"

"It is an opportunity for you, Richard, and if you are fortunate enough to be successful it will compensate for your losses in the shipping business. Who knows . . . perhaps the war will not last too long, and then life can return to normal," Henry said hopefully.

"What about you Henry, what is to become of you?"

"Richard, are you asking me to participate in this venture? If so . . . for goodness sake say so, and stop beating around the bush for Heaven's sake. You may not realize it, but you have done nothing but indirectly allude to the possibility of my participation in your enterprise. I have turned it over and over in my mind since you shared with me your intentions. In fact, I have laid awake at night going over the consequences of such a voyage. I do not seek the prosperity of course, and naturally I would have no desire to ever return to Boston . . . forgive me for saying so. But if there were any way in which I could manage to get to a foreign port (preferably one that was sympathetic to Britain) it would mean the possibility of me getting back to Elizabeth and my family."

"I cannot give you any guarantees, my friend, you do understand?" said Richard.

"Of course! I would have to take my chances on that count. Under normal circumstances in peace time, I would not hesitate to agree to become a member of your crew. I'd willingly offer you my services after all the kindness you and Eleanor have shown me since my arrival. But, there are some other issues that would have to be overcome in order for me to throw my lot in with you this time."

"Pray continue," said Richard sitting very calmly, but portraying a smile on his face as he began to see the outline of his plans beginning to take fruition.

Henry thought Richard looked very much like a small boy on Christmas morning. His plump cheeks were all red with excitement, as he mopped his forehead with a large white silk handkerchief. The very air in the room seemed to crackle with anticipation.

"First of all," said Henry quite seriously, "there is the matter of taking up arms against my fellow human beings. There is no way that I could be persuaded to take a life in cold blood. Only in self defense . . . and even then I would have to be hard pushed to willingly retaliate."

"My dear fellow, we are of the same persuasion in these matters! Have no fear."

"Richard, let me be frank. Although I am a virtual prisoner in this country, I cannot be a prisoner of my own conscience. I must be true to my convictions. In recent months, I have had to face the reality that war is often inevitable, no matter how hard we try to avoid it. Every generation has to face these age old decisions, in some part of the world or other, regardless of our nationality.

I have also come to the conclusion that war is not murder, and those that are called to the service of their country do not violate any Biblical commandment if they fight with honor, and kill only as a last resort. This is, of course, my personal opinion you understand (though I never thought I would ever confess such,) but the circumstances that fate has now bestowed upon me has forced me to question my own pacifism, whether I like it or not. These were questions that I had to wrestle with from the time I was impressed into the British Navy. I was literally dragged from a life of pacifism to a life of war and killing. But I tell you the truth when I say, that thus far in my life I have never killed a living soul, and still hope to God I never have to."

"Although I would not take a man's life deliberately," Richard answered hesitantly, shifting about his chair. "I *also* would defend myself if I were attacked, and my life was threatened," he added nervously. "Yet I have to also consider my shipping business . . . its state of affairs . . . its success. Privateersmen sometimes have to kill, it is unavoidable, we would only be stealing from the enemy. Isn't that fair? Wouldn't that be justifiable?"

"Richard, we could all hope that enemy merchant shipping will haul down their colors quickly, as soon as they get a warning shot across the bow, and before there is any loss of life. But in reality it's not always like that. Some may prefer to fight to protect their possessions. Richard, Jonathon calls you a Federalist. Is that the Federal viewpoint in general? It seems that you are against the war with England because it deprives you of your wealth through loss of trading with your enemies (despite the fact that your freedom is once again in jeopardy and your country's rights are being violated,) yet you are willing to kill to protect your enterprises and way of life. Forgive me, but it seems to contradict all that Americans honor, and hold dear in life. I have lived here long enough to comprehend that ideology."

"This is the very thing that I wrestle with, Henry. In many ways I envy you your decision. Your mind is so clear cut. It is something that thus far I have been unable to convince myself of. I know of many here in America that defend your position absolutely. Neither do I condemn them. Not at all, but in all of my years of business I have never yet been in the position to put my convictions to the test. Until . . ." he paused, looking Henry straight in the eyes, "Until this war broke out, and then I met you . . . all the discussions we have had together . . . I am afraid I am a little ashamed."

"Richard, the last few moments on board the *Restitution*, when the boarders were coming over the bulwarks yelling and screaming damnation to everyone, and wielding their cutlasses and boarding axes, I saw one of them strike Captain Street to the ground. He was wounded severely in the shoulder, and before I knew it I felt overwhelmed by a great surge of anger, and picked up the sword from the deck where the captain had dropped it.

I raged along the taffrail thrashing the sword in all directions, wielding it backwards and forwards, not caring if it found a mark or not. Nobody was going to stand in my way! My ship, my captain; my country. I was blinded by my emotions. Nothing else seemed to matter. All that I believed in seemed to go by the board, I acted like a mad man, it was as though I had lost all sense of reason. I had a loaded pistol in my belt and I pulled it out without hesitation, and aimed it at one of the boarders who was intending to shoot me in the face.

But, before he could pull the trigger, Captain Childers, with the frigate *Providence*, who was standing off from the *Restitution*, fired at the American schooner with a broadside which slammed her against the *Restitution's* side. It was then that I lost my balance and fell into the sea. I still can't say whether or not I would have fired my gun to save my own life. The rest of the story you know."

Henry put his head in his hands as if to blot out the memory, but it was still so very real to him, just as if it had happened yesterday.

"To tell you the truth Richard," he said looking up at last, "I am still not one hundred percent sure of my position. It haunts me like a specter from the past. I have seen killing bring out the brute beast in men, savagery at its worst. Yet these same seamen sit sobbing over a dead sailor as they stitch him up in a hammock . . . kissing his head before the last stitch encases them in the canvas shroud, and the memory of their shipmates' faces are gone forever. They are for a short time as tender as any woman.

Then as the drummer raps out 'beat to quarters' again, and the cry of 'all hands' echoes round the timbers of the ship, their tenderness is heaved over the side as effortlessly as the dead body hitting the water. I think that maybe they cannot allow themselves the luxury of grief. Perhaps they would lose the motivation to fight. Fight to win, I mean! I don't know."

"Henry, nobody would hold it to your account, you know, if you *had* pulled the trigger."

"I know that."

"Well, the way I have to justify any actions of self defense, is that I put it immediately into the realm of hypothesis. What if I were walking down the street, and some ruffian attacked me, with robbery or murder in his heart? Would I stand there with my sword still in its scabbard? I think not! Why it's the very reason I wear it in the first place. I am sorry, Henry if I am rambling somewhat, in any case these situations may never arise. You may very well sail out of Boston Harbor with God's blessing, and never have the misfortune to run into any British men-of-war," Richard said unconvincingly. "Then you may never be put to the test."

Henry wasn't convinced, he knew the British Navy too well, but he realized he didn't have many options and he was desperate enough to try anything.

"So what do you think, brother, can I count on you? It would serve both of our purposes you know!"

Henry stood to his feet, and walked over to the window to look out over the harbor. The sun had long ago set, and a pale moon was reflecting it's twin on the ocean. The sounds of the night began to penetrate his ears, and the gentle late summer wind ruffled the curtains and blew softly in his face. He stood there staring out to sea, as if he were in another time, another place. Henry felt the pain in his head again for a moment, and it began to throb. Another reminder of all his trials.

Henry turned sharply to Richard.

"I'll go!" he said simply.

"Henry, my dear fellow! You won't have any regrets, I'd stake my life on it." Richard shook Henry warmly by the hand. "You'll see England again, mark my words!"

"It would be my greatest desire, my friend!"

Richard scurried out of the room leaving Henry alone with his thoughts. Would he really be able to escape Henry wondered? Leave this country . . . these people . . . see his beloved Elizabeth again? Would he ever run his hands through his own soil that was probably left untilled at this moment, in the far away county of Norfolk, one of the remotest coastal areas of England. So much work to do there!

The sights and sounds of his farmland wormed its way gradually into his mind. This time of the year the fenlands would have wildfowl nesting in the reeds. The windmills must be turning steadily in the wind, grinding the precious grains of wheat. The harvest would be in full swing now, he thought. The bright golden stooks of wheat, standing like sentries in the fields, waiting to dry out in the sun before being loaded on the wagons. The larks and swallows flying lazily through the sky. Men working . . . almost as hard as any crew on a man-of-war. They could count the fruits of their labor without holding a sword in one hand, and a pistol in the other. No deeply ingrained self-admonition of 'one hand for yourself, and one for the ship?' Or else possible disaster.

He dragged himself away from his thoughts and allowed the present to filter back unhindered through his mind.

He had much to do, Henry told himself. He wanted to see Count Thibideaux before he left Boston. He had visited the old man several times since their first meeting, and Henry liked him immensely. The Count appeared to be much of the same character as Henry's old French fencing master, and just as mysterious. Henry would like to say goodbye to him before he sailed, he felt obligated, although he couldn't totally understand why. A whim perhaps? And of course there was Jonathon and Emily . . . that would be even harder.

Richard had reckoned on about eight weeks to provision and prepare the *Lady Eleanor* for sea. He was being optimistic, Henry thought, considering that the weather would be changing all too soon.

The sea . . . that broad and natural barrier that lay between countries, separating them one from another. And the only method of traversing these great oceans was by ships that plied backwards and forwards, that neither tempest or inclement weather could stop. Every ship's voyage was filled with danger, and never guaranteed that a mariner would be propelled onto his own home shore, despite his hopes and dreams. The sea was only for the brave of heart.

Henry tried not to think of all the uncertainties that lay ahead as he made many journeys to, and from, India Wharf, in order to help with the preparations for the first voyage of the schooner under her new commission. After many weeks passed by, he knew every step of the way by heart, and even people he passed seemed to be familiar to him as he nodded politely to those he met in the streets.

Richard had more than enough names on his crew list now, and he was painstakingly narrowing it down to the allotted amount.

He had shown the tentative list to Henry one day while they stood in the Great Cabin of the *Lady Eleanor*. Henry noticed Sean O'Boyle's name was on the roster, and he hoped the man would not be a trouble maker once on board. He trusted the man's loyalty was a lot stronger than his temperament.

"The one thing now that I have to contend with, Henry," said Richard, "are the guns. There are to be nine of them. I am not sure what caliber to get. Do you have any suggestions? Would eighteen pounders be *too* heavy do you think?"

Henry laughed out loud. "I am not the expert on these matters that you seem to think I am. But in my short experience at sea I would say eighteen pounders would be totally unsuitable. She's not a frigate you know," Henry smiled. "I would hate the *Lady Eleanor* to sink at her berth with the weight of too many guns. Did she carry any when you used her for pleasure?"

"Just a swivel gun on the bow . . . just in case. There were years of peace after the Revolution, consequently not much need for weaponry, certainly not to sail the short distances around Massachusetts Bay. I have a feeling that this is going to be much more complicated than I imagined," Richard said with a sigh.

"Perhaps you could transfer some of the guns from your other vessels," suggested Henry. "The other ship owners would most likely be glad to unload some of their excess armament as well. They surely won't be using them while they are bottled up here in the harbor."

"An excellent suggestion, I will look into it as soon as I am able. Can't think why it did not enter my own mind," he added ruefully. "No sense in spending vast amounts of money unnecessarily is there?"

"Richard you will need at least one high caliber gun on the foredeck, it's the most crucial one of all. The first one to be fired, given your intentions. I would suggest a nine pounder. They are heavy so you will have to strengthen the bow of the ship, brace up the foredeck if necessary. Get some carpenters on the job as soon as you can would be my advice."

"Excellent idea, Henry! I will scour the whole city of Boston if necessary," Richard remarked. "And now I must leave you for the time being, I have an appointment with a Captain Winters. He is fairly young, but an excellent seaman, so I am told. Apparently he knows these waters like the back of his hand, and with a captain secured at last, I will have my full complement of men," Richard said with real satisfaction. "Then all we have to do is wait for the commission. Let us trust it will not be too long in coming, Henry, eh?"

# Chapter Four

## THE COLD VOYAGE

Two months passed by, and the rakish ninety five foot schooner, *Lady Eleanor*, lay quietly at her moorings at India Wharf. She was at last ready for sea. Her freshly painted exterior was a beautiful blue reflecting against the stark November sky. She was fully equipped with her total of nine guns, four six pounders on each side of her flush deck, and specially installed with heavy trucks, blocks and tackles.

Fitzroy's pride and joy was the one nine pounder mounted in the bow. The gun was large and took up extra space which would be a little tricky when loading and firing, but the extra weight on the bow was tolerable, and Richard had taken Henry's advice about the extra strength built into the foredeck.

Richard had bought the gun from Count Pierre Thibidaeux, the Frenchman, who was only too willing to part with it at a modest sum. When Henry had introduced Richard to the Count, it was evident from their conversation that the two men had met several years ago at one of the local assembly balls, which Richard and Eleanor had attended.

Apparently, Richard had informed Henry, the elderly Count never took to the floor, but sat and watched the dancers in silent reminiscence. Henry could imagine the old man sitting alone, thinking of the wife of his youth, his Marie, the one and only true love of his life. What a gracious existence they had together back in France, during those peaceful days before the uprising.

Henry went often to the *Lady Eleanor* to check on her progress, and noticed that now she was also fully rigged with white number one canvas on her two masts. The sails were neatly and expertly furled on their booms, and her standing rigging was freshly tarred. She was provisioned to the hilt with the best that Boston could supply in the way of food considering the blockade, and she had a water supply for many months at sea.

All was now ready, and everyone involved with this venture had to be content with just waiting . . . and waiting for the commission from the Government.

The Fall came and went, and Boston was knee deep in wet and rotting leaves that blew around the town, and lay in great heaps in the streets and alley ways. Smoke curled up lazily from the chimney tops, as the nights became more and more chilly and the days were beginning to grow shorter, as was Richard Fitzroy's temper, which Henry couldn't help notice.

The coveted Letter of Marque still had not arrived. Richard was furious with the Government, feeling his opportunity was being blown away like the fallen leaves.

The lack of response from the State Department was also taking its toll on Henry, who was becoming more and more anxious as each day passed. Although he kept busy with his employment at the Customs House, and all his evenings were spent helping with the *Lady Eleanor*, as darkness shrouded Boston each night Henry noticed people were growing increasingly more suspicious of his comings and goings as time went by. It seemed to get worse as the peoples' personal deprivations ensued. There were more shortages of food than before, and Richard had had to set a guard at night so that the schooner was not raided of her provisions.

Henry could not move around quite as freely as he once did, and there was much talk and gossip in the taverns. Of loyalty, patriotism, and spies. Any quite innocent event or meeting, or even a social function, was immediately dubbed as, *'devious'* or *'underhanded,'* by the daily newspapers.

Henry had had plenty of time over these months to recapitulate some of his own personal plans. Would he really be able to set foot in a foreign territory other than America, and rendezvous with a ship bound for England? And in the meantime, while he waited here in Boston, would *he* be considered a spy? His real identity was still only known to a handful of people. Was his life in great danger? His world was full of shadows.

Henry knew deep down in his heart that he would never go back on his word to Richard. He would embark on this voyage, it was his only chance. But his hopes and dreams seemed to dwindle as the year was fast coming to an end.

The weather was becoming noticeably colder now, with bitter winds sweeping the town. The merchant ships lashed to the wharf with their cargo holds empty were bouncing around on their moorings, while masts and spars groaned and creaked, and blocks rattled and banged as the ships were tossed from side to side.

Boston was a picture of dreariness as old men wandered along the waterfront in thick winter coats, puffing on their pipes and dreaming of the town's former glory as they spent hours staring at the rain soaked ships until the icy cold finally drove them back to their homes.

Henry wondered what winter would be like at sea on the North Atlantic. He had heard the chilling stories whilst on board the *Dragonfly*. Of sails and ropes frozen stiff and unmanageable, with bone chilling cold that could not be overcome by any human being. Cases of frostbite, with the surgeon having to remove blackened fingers or toes. Or worse still, a seaman slipping on some icy spar, and falling into the merciless and cruel sea, his cry unheard in some vicious snow storm that could envelop a ship in minutes and turn it into a frozen fortress. Every life on board was endangered by the enormous extra weight of ice on the rigging that made any ship perilously top heavy, forcing her to gradually sink as each subsequent wave made the situation worse. Finally she would no longer have the strength to rise to meet another.

It was December 15th when the Letter of Marque arrived, and with it brought great joy and excitement at Edinburgh House. Secretly though, Henry was concerned that it might be too late in the season to sail. Richard had never crossed the Atlantic, even in the summer time. He had no real knowledge of life at sea. Yet somehow he knew Richard would not change his plans at this stage, and being unwilling to discourage his friend in any way, Henry did his best to be a partaker of the good humor that was displayed, and offered his heartiest congratulations to his benefactor.

The date that had been set for the *Lady Eleanor* to start her voyage was December 22nd, which only left them a week to take care of the last minute details. During that time Henry found himself loosing his appetite somewhat. Whether it was anxiety or not, he was unable to tell. He had put on a few extra pounds since living on shore, unaccustomed as he was to life mostly sitting at a desk, so he wondered if he would regain his leanness once he was at sea again. Outside the concept of war and foul weather, life at sea was usually pretty healthy, with all the fresh air and plenty of opportunity to keep busy with the work about the ship. A vessel at sea was also immune from any land borne diseases until it resumed contact again with terra firma. Other maladies that normally afflicted seamen on a King's ship, were those contracted by deprivation of certain foods. This would not necessarily be encountered by privateersmen, who usually made frequent re-provisioning stops whenever possible, especially if they were fortunate enough to bring in a prize through the blockade. This was probably the most dangerous effort of their careers, for failure would mean re-capture of their prize and a permanent berth aboard a British naval ship of war as an impressed sailor. Henry was all too familiar with that!

After a night of fitful sleep, Henry got out of bed on the morning of December 20th. He stretched his arms above his head and slowly walked across to the big window, and threw back the heavy bedroom curtains. He looked out across the bay where the sky was the color of lead. The cold air on the slightly warmer water of the sea, was producing spasmodic puffs of fog on the surface, like a boiling cauldron on the hearth. It had become his usual routine lately to stand for a few moments looking out across the Bay of Boston. It had become such a familiar view to him after all these months at Edinburgh House, that the only changes he ever noticed were the weather. The impending winter season with all its hardships was sneaking up rapidly, and had become all too important to him.

Henry started to turn away when he realized with a shock that this morning's view was different. He hastily took up his position again in front of the window and kept a steady gaze on the sea. Every few seconds their appeared to be several ships drifting along in the fog. Then, as suddenly as they had appeared, they were enveloped again with the white vapor. This strange phenomenon gave them the appearance of ghost ships, with their blackened masts and spars in sharp contrast to the bleak wintry sky. They appeared to be there one minute, and gone the next.

Henry stared once more in disbelief. Could it be . . . ? He frantically pulled on his breeches with remarkable speed, and hurtled down the winding staircase to where he knew Richard's solid brass telescope lay in its usual place on top of the bookcase by the drawing room window. He quickly removed it from its case, and clapped it to his right eye. He thanked God for his excellent eyesight, for if he had not been endowed with the ability to see beyond the range of the average man, he would probably have dismissed what he had seen from the upstairs window as a trick of the imagination. Henry strained his eyes intently for several minutes as he adjusted the telescope to the correct range. He carefully wiped the lens with his pocket handkerchief occasionally, and studied the ships as they drifted in and out of his vision amidst the dense fog. But there could be no doubt in his mind . . . the squadron was back!

Henry could count all six ships in turn as they sailed in a neat line of formation, the four frigates, *Dragonfly*, *Providence*, *Restitution* and *Viceroy*, and the two schooners, *Vixen* and *Starlight*. He had spent so many hours on watch all those months ago as a lookout on the frigate *Dragonfly*, it was as though their outlines was etched into his brain.

Suddenly all the memories came flooding back in a lifelike manner. He saw the faces of the crew so clearly in his mind, just as if he had just gone below deck for a few moments and then returned.

Henry sat down heavily on the piano stool with the telescope in his lap. It was unbelievable! After all this time when the British squadron had presumably been patrolling at least twenty miles off shore, they were back in force! He had to get another look. He took up his position at the window once more and watched as the frigates seemed to be standing off now, while the two schooners plied backwards and forwards in the shallower waters closer to the land. They would be acting as the eyes and ears of the flagship. Henry's heart was pounding hard as his hopes of escape dropped like a stone sinking to the bottom of a pond. He had to warn Richard! Were he and Eleanor awake yet? Probably not!

Henry could hear the sounds of the butler, and the other household servants clattering around in the kitchen with breakfast in preparation. He'd wake Richard up immediately and give him the bad news. Henry was half way up the stairs when he stopped abruptly in his tracks. There was no point in telling them now, he decided. Another hour would make no difference.

"Perhaps you should delay the enterprise until the spring," said Henry carefully to Richard at breakfast, after he had informed the whole household of the shocking news. Eleanor nodded her head in agreement. Henry could see that Richard was bitterly disappointed, but a certain stubbornness was etched on his countenance as he shook his head persistently.

"No, Henry! It's now or never, we cannot afford to wait another six months. Who knows what might happen in the meantime. We have all grown complacent in Boston, with the *Constitution*, and other ships coming in and out of the harbor at their leisure, while the British squadron was out of sight, but not out of mind, I might tell you! No, I am willing to take the risks, and I think I can speak for all the crew . . . they are as anxious as I am. Delay will only bring more deprivation and misery to the families. The *Lady Eleanor* sails on December 22nd, come hell or high water! Or the British come to that!"

"Very well, Richard, Henry agreed. "You are right! We cannot wait!"

So the stage was set. There could be no change of plans, no regrets. Only God could be the judge whether it was the right decision or not, Henry thought. But now that the action was about to begin, Henry felt a strange excitement within the pit of his stomach, and he realized that he was actually looking forward to whatever fate had in store for him. He still had nothing to lose he reminded himself.

On the ebb tide of December 22nd very early in the morning, and long before daylight, a fore and aft schooner slipped out of India Wharf unnoticed by most of the citizens of Boston. In the center of the harbor the *Lady Eleanor* sailed past the little wooden lighthouse structure erected on one of the numerous islands there, with its lamp of whale oil diligently glowing with a faint light as snow flurries were starting to drift down from the leaden clouds that hung overhead. It was bitterly cold. Every man that didn't need to be on deck was down below.

There was a complement of fifty-five sailors on board, including Captain Winters and Henry, who had officially signed on as general crew.

The wind was out of the north-east, and was blowing a strong twenty knots. The *Lady Eleanor* carried all her sails, and was heeling sharply over with the waves creaming along her sides only inches from the gunnel. The spray licked up her sides and ice cold seawater smashed into her bow. Her nine guns were securely lashed on her flush deck, and she was ready for whatever fate had to offer her.

Henry stood at the taffrail, his eyes watering with the salt spray. He was back at sea again, but the movement of the ship under his feet did not feel unfamiliar to him and he braced himself easily as the schooner heeled over suddenly, then quickly righted herself. He was finally saying *goodbye* to this land, he thought.

Henry had bidden farewell to the Count, who had shaken his hand warmly with genuine affection and informed Henry that he would be happy to receive him if he ever returned to Boston again. The old man had given him a worn woolen boat cloak, which Henry suspected had accompanied the Count when he had fled from France. He was grateful for its warmth now.

He had paid one last visit to the little cottage on the salt marshes that morning while it was still dark, in order to pay his respects to Jonathon and Emily. Jonathon had given him a hearty embrace, obviously overcome with emotion, and unable to utter any words at all. None were needed of course, his face said it all.

Emily was much more demonstrative, openly crying as she kissed him squarely on the cheek. "God Bless you, Mr. Stapleton," she said with quivering lips. "I hopes you get back to your wife safely. Our prayers are with you . . . for your safety on that cold ocean!"

Henry had left the cottage quickly, he hated *goodbyes* that seemed so final. He gripped the little bag that Emily had given him containing some fruit cake. "For you only," she had instructed him, "Not to share with anyone else. It has two pounds of dried fruit in it. Should last you a month," she had informed him with a smile.

Henry had walked back up the lane, and stepped into the open carriage where Richard had been waiting for him. The driver flicked his whip between the horses ears, and they had continued their journey to India Wharf.

Henry felt strangely contented as he felt the heave of the schooner beneath his feet, it was as though the *Lady Eleanor* was a living thing, and as anxious as he was to leave her moorings. He stared back at the harbor until it had disappeared from sight.

The plan for evading the British squadron was simple, Richard had carefully informed him the night before. The *Lady Eleanor* was to stay on the east side of the bay, if the wind complied, then sail between Governors Island and Apple Island. There it would be shallow, and with the wind in its current direction there would be no risk of ending up on a lee shore. With the wind squarely on the schooner's beam, it would try to push them over towards Middle Ground, the island that was dry on the three quarter ebb. They would have to take great care, and take continuous soundings. Then they would creep slowly into the shoals, for the *Lady Eleanor* drew only nine feet. After that they would drop anchor and wait. Hopefully that would put them out of range of the British guns, even if they were spotted by one of their lookouts; which was quite likely. The *Starlight* and *Vixen* would not be able to come in that close to the shore, for they were more deep drafted then the *Lady Eleanor.*

It was fortunate for Captain Winters that Henry was familiar with the specifications of the enemy ships. Henry was sure that the British would not try a small boat assault either, for the schooner could blast them out of the water before they got anywhere near, and they would have no supporting fire power from the squadron whose guns were out of range.

The Americans had a solid plan and they would wait for the darkness of night in order to make their escape. With no moon to light their hideaway, it was hoped that they would not be detected. At this time of the year Captain Winters reckoned they should have about thirteen hours of darkness in which to outrun the British.

Once free of the coast, the *Lady Eleanor* could out sail anything the British had to offer. She was fast and lively, and every man on board was proud to sail in her. It wasn't a perfect plan, and there were plenty of risks of things going wrong, but it was all they had, and there was no room for improvement.

The *Lady Eleanor* was kicking her heels as they left Apple Island far behind to their stern, and set their course for north-east by east.

By three in the afternoon the wind had shifted slightly, much to the delight of Captain Winters. He had no desire to engage the British; not that he wouldn't like to, but he was no match for four frigates and two schooners. He would have to run like a rabbit! Even one of their schooners would be more than a match. No, it had to be Yankee skill and seamanship to the fullest if they were to achieve their purpose. If they had to make a fight out of it, they were ready, but to become successful privateers they must escape the blockade. Every man aboard had a cutlass, two pistols apiece, and a stack of boarding pikes, and axes that lay near the foremast; enough to fell a forest. They were armed to the teeth.

Captain Winters gave orders for a hot meal to be served before it got dark. That way the crew would be fully fed, and free to give their utmost attention to the feat of outrunning the British blockade.

As far as Henry knew, they were the first ship in Boston to obtain a Letter of Marque, and the first privateer to be leaving this harbor since the American Revolution.

The cold was eating away at Henry as he came on deck to get some air, even though he was not officially on watch. Below decks it was not only stuffy, but it was beginning to wreak with the smell of tobacco and liquor. He could see the concern upon the Captain's face at the thought of having most of his men too drunk to be able to concentrate, or stand on their two feet when they were needed. To counteract his concern, Captain Winters gave the order for at least twenty men to come on deck and start to chip the ice from the rigging which had already began to form. He did not want to have their hiding place discovered by the shrill chinking of hammers and chisels once they were at anchor, and cloaked in darkness.

In response the men set themselves vigorously to the work, and for the next two hours slivers of ice in all shapes and sizes came crashing to the deck like frozen bolts of lightning. Anybody not actually engaged in hacking off the ice had been ordered to stay below, or risk being thrust through with a spear of ice. Only the helmsman and a few men left to tend the sails remained huddled by the binnacle in front of the wheel, where they had rigged some strong canvas overhead to shelter them from the falling ice. Winters threatened a flogging to any man that split a sail during this de-icing procedure. Henry decided to join those at the helm.

As the schooner's anchor finally plunged into twelve feet of icy water, they made ready to play the waiting game. Less than an hour to total darkness now, and the frosty air bit deep into everyone. Most of the men shuffled below to get out of the cold, but Henry and some others that were ordered to stay on watch, stayed huddled behind the bulwarks and took advantage of all the shelter from the wind they could get.

Their ship was currently positioned thirty five miles east of Boston Bay. But for every mile they had traveled, the British schooner, *Vixen*, vigilantly sailed eastwards in hot pursuit. She kept her distance to about three miles away, and finally hove to. Neither ships could fire their guns for they were well out of range of each other, and both of them knew it.

The persistence of the *Vixen* was very aggravating to the crew of the *Lady Eleanor*. Every time they looked towards the horizon, there she was! Imposing; threatening, and ready to strike like a snake. Her dark silhouette against the bleak December evening was a constant threat to their safety. There was no concealing themselves now. They had nowhere to hide.

"Captain Winters, don't you think it rather foolish to try to make it through shoal water at night?" Henry suggested to the Captain. "We can't shine a light for fear of the British seeing us as soon as we make our move, and even with a man on the bow with a lead line, there is every possibility of hitting a rock."

Winters scowled at Henry. "So you think I'm foolish do you?"

"No, sir! Not you personally, but it would not be the most prudent thing to do would it?"

Before Winters could answer, Mr. Crook, the Sailing Master, suggested lowering a small boat, and towing the *Lady Eleanor*.

Henry quickly interrupted them both again and said, "But that means we would have to keep rotating the men at the oars, and in this wicked cold wind . . ."

"Let me look after my men, Stapleton," Winters growled. "Tomorrow we'll try to outrun the British on the slack tide, just before the ebb. Then we can use the receding tide to help us stay off the shoals. And I have decided to take this action *not* because you recommended it neither! I'm the captain on this ship, and I give the orders! Do you hear?"

"Yes, sir!" Henry replied, but he noted their was an antagonism building between them already. Every man on board was subject to this captain's decisions, and Henry felt strangely uneasy with this fact.

At first light on December 23rd, the wind had changed from the north-east to the south-east, and was blowing a gale. Orders were given to put out extra anchors to prevent them being blown on shore to certain destruction.

The privateers' cause was being tested at the very onset of their journey.

The *Vixen* had clawed her way back out to sea for the same reason the Americans had set extra anchors. She was still visible though, even hull down. If Winters had made an attempt to make a run for it, the *Vixen* with the wind behind her would be able to run down on them in minutes. It was a waiting game with this unexpected wind change, and no mistake about it, Henry concluded.

All that day the wind blew with a vengeance from the south-east, while the shallow water produced a booming surf that was comparative to a Pacific island.

Farther off shore the waves marched towards them like an army in regular formation against them, constantly bombarding the *Lady Eleanor* who lurched violently up and down to her anchors like a duck tied by its neck.

The *Vixen* was still in sight, and Henry observed that she was on a beam reach sailing backwards and forwards; biding her time. He was sure that the rest of Captain Weatherby's squadron would have beaten their way back into deeper waters by now. They were not in sight, even through a telescope.

All day long the wind howled out of the same quarter, causing the *Lady Eleanor*'s spars to groan and shudder with the strain. It was about four in the afternoon, with all hope gone of their escaping that day, that a snow storm came up out of the north west. Visibility was down to only a few feet as their whole world was surrounded by the stark whiteness of the falling snow. Captain Winters decided that setting lookouts was a complete waste of time, much to the thankfulness of the crew who thought it most inhumane to send a sailor out on such a night.

The following morning was Christmas Eve, and the hatches were opened to reveal two feet of snow on the decks. The blizzard had passed, but as Henry looked around him the guns were so shrouded with snow that they looked like large white dogs standing guard on deck, and they were so frozen that any contact with them would cause a man's skin to stick to the metal, tearing flesh from bone.

It did not take the crew long to shovel the snow from off the decks of the ship, and it fell into the water creating a white slush that floated around the hull.

Henry looked out across the salt marshes and mud flats, where the reeds now brown and stubbly were sticking up through the water making a sharp contrast to the icy wilderness that lay around them. There was no sign of life for miles around, and what little wildlife there was, went scurrying for shelter at the sight and sounds of human beings.

Everyone knew, especially the Captain, the urgency for a change in the wind soon. If they didn't break free they would face the danger of becoming ice bound, and would have to return to Boston to wait until the Spring.

Although it was Christmas Eve nobody was in high spirits. The usual festivity that would be humming on shore, was almost non-existent on the *Lady Eleanor*. Fears about the failure of the voyage were being openly discussed by the hands, and tempers were starting to fray. It was not good for sailors to be cooped up for too long with little work to do, it made them inevitably turn to drink. Then from drink to the possibility of them taking over the ship. This would be mutiny in any situation, and it could become a very ugly situation.

Mr. Samuels, the ship's cook, tried desperately to swing the mood by rustling up some pre-Christmas fare for the men, even though most of them must be contemplating it could be their last meal before they tangled with the British schooner, and fought for their lives. In the meantime they ate the boiled turkey, turnips and bread. When they had finished eating, the cook had prepared a special treat. He carried in the finest and largest plum pudding that Henry had ever seen. It must have been prepared many weeks ago, probably by Samuels' wife. He set it down in the middle of the long table in the main cabin, where every seaman was crowded in.

"Nobody touches it yet, do ya hear!" Samuels snarled. He poured brandy expertly over the top of the pudding, took flint and steel, and set fire to it. The flames licked upwards engulfing the pudding completely.

In the darkness of the cabin the men sat in silence staring at it, their faces illuminated for a moment by its glow while their shadows danced around the cabin walls. Then as the flames died, Mr. Crook, the master, lit the lanterns. Captain Winters was sullen and withdrawn from the men as he watched all these proceedings with a cold stare.

"Right, hold out your plates lads!" said Mr. Samuels. "The Captain first!" He cut out a large wedge of the pudding and slapped it down on the Captain's plate with a flourish.

Henry held out his plate with the rest of the men. What a difference to protocol on board the *Dragonfly*, or any King's ship, Henry thought. The Captain would most certainly be dining alone in his private dining room. The officers would eat in the ward room; the common sailor on the lower gun deck, eating between the big guns, with their tables hung on ropes from the deck beams overhead, and lazily swinging with the motion of the ship. On a King's ship, Henry reflected, it all seemed so long ago, and he ate in relative silence amongst these men, most of them drunk and probably not in a fit state to fight if they had to. What would happen tomorrow? Would they be forced to go back to Boston, or would they have to fight the British. Once again his life was in danger.

Before the crew of the *Lady Eleanor* turned in for the night, the wind had subsided considerably, and moved two points to the south. Captain Winters was elated, and despite the fact that a pale moon had arisen over the sea, and Mr. Crook's nervousness about navigation, he was determined to make a run for it straight away. Never mind caution, it was time the mouse sprung the trap laid by the cat. The element of surprise was gone anyway; the British schooner had been tracking them from the start, and knew their exact location. She would be watching, waiting, and ready to pounce. One long tack should do it, thought Captain Winters, and they should be able to sail directly parallel with the coast as close as they dare. It would be dangerous, one false move and they would be aground. They could not 'go about' on the other tack, for that would bring them within range of the *Vixen's* guns.

A leadsman was put in the fore chains to make sure of their depth, his skill would be more important than that of the Captain at this juncture.

"Not the fourteen pound lead," snapped Crook, as the leadsman reached out to tie it onto the lead line. "The five pound one will be adequate in this shoal water," Crook muttered as the leadsman raised his eyebrows.

"Aye, aye, sir."

"And don't bother to arm it neither, we all know it's sand and broken shell. Hell we can practically see the bottom!"

"Yes, sir."

"All hands to make sail," Winters yelled, and a dozen men ran to each mast.

"Heave away, boys!

Prepare to weigh anchor! Hands to the capstan, look lively there!"

Mr. Jones, the *Lady Eleanor*'s first mate, reported, "Anchors straight up and down, sir."

"Well, Jones, what are you waiting for? Get it hauled up and catted away as soon as possible!"

Mr. Crook, the Sailing Master, stood at the wheel awaiting his instructions from the Captain. He had his heavy coat pulled tightly around him with the collar turned up to the top of his ears to keep out the wind, and he pulled on his thick woolen gloves as he gripped the spokes of the wheel tightly in anticipation of orders. Soon the *Lady Eleanor* would become alive in his hands as she felt the pressure of the wind in her sails. Although it was no longer snowing the wind felt raw, and seemed to cut through the Master's clothing like a knife.

"Anchor's aweigh," came the cry from the bo'sun.

Henry turned his attention to the men hoisting the mainsail and mizzen on large wooden hoops that slid slowly up the mast, which lifted the giant sails almost to the peak. The gaff topsails had not yet been set. These were relatively small triangular sails with a small boom running along the peak of the sail, which, when sheeted home were fastened tightly by the halyard making the small boom almost perpendicular with the mast. He had seen many such schooners in the Great Yarmouth roadstead in time of peace.

The *Lady Eleanor*'s headsails, and her two big sails shivered in the wind as she hovered there uncertainly.

"Steer a course east, by north-east, Mr. Crook, yelled Winters."

"East, by north-east, sir, full and bye," the Master repeated turning the bow of the schooner onto her course. Her main and mizzen sails filled with the strong wind and bellied out like the two graceful wings of a swan. The *Lady Eleanor* groaned and creaked as she came to life, while she cut through the reeds at a spanking pace. Mr. Crook stood stalwartly at the wheel, carefully gauging the ship between the shallows and just enough water to keep her afloat.

The leadsman's mournful cry could be heard constantly, "By the deep, four fathoms! He had already felt the white calico marker that indicated the five fathom mark slip through his fingers, although he could not see it in the darkness. Everything had to be done 'by touch.' By the mark three!" The seaman was sweating with nerves now as he fingered the three leather strips tied in the line that had just marked the three fathoms.

Crook winced when he heard three fathoms. Only about ten feet under the keel.

"A spoke to starboard, Crook! What's the matter with you, man!" Winters snapped.

Henry caught the Master's eye, and he understood that the man had to wait until he got the order from Winters, or else suffer the consequences. He sensed the man would have automatically moved the schooner over if he hadn't had to *wait* for orders.

The crew swarmed around in droves, every man to his allotted task. Henry stood by the taffrail, he had not been given a specific job yet, and he had the feeling Winters was purposely avoiding giving him one. Henry walked towards Captain Winters with determination. He was not going to be intimidated by a tyrant.

"Have you got a moment, Captain?"

"What can I do for you, Stapleton?" Winters replied, not bothering to stop what he was doing, but gazed out to sea with his telescope clapped to one eye.

"I was thinking that I might be of more use to you, I can hardly stand around watching the men at hard labor. Shoveling snow and lending a hand generally I have been doing willingly, but I have a lot more to offer than that."

"What can *you* do?" questioned Winters arrogantly, with his Boston drawl.

"Well, I learned to reef and hand sails as a topman once, and . . . ."

"Unfortunately we do not have any yards with sails attached to them on this vessel," Winters replied sarcastically, "and steering is too dangerous for you through these shallows, it would take a man of *real* experience. I would not want to tear out the bottom of my ship, Mr. Stapleton," he said coldly.

"I am quite aware of what kind of rigging the *Lady Eleanor* has," Henry said belligerently. If only Winters knew, Henry reflected, that I have steered a 38 gun frigate in the heat of battle, with guns blazing and men dying all around the deck, but he kept quiet. He knew his words would be wasted.

All of a sudden Captain Winters swung round on Henry, and staring him straight in the face threw back his head and laughed out loud. "So it seems you are out of a job at this moment, sir," he said with a smug look on his face. "But if we ever get out of this thin water, then you can be sure I will find a watch for you at the helm, just to keep you out of mischief," Winters' exclaimed, snapping his telescope shut. He handed it to Henry unexpectedly. "Perhaps you would like to take a look at the *enemy*?" Winters had a strange look in his eyes as he uttered that remark.

Henry took the telescope from the Captain, and studied the horizon carefully. There was the *Vixen* alright. Still in her same stalking position as before the snowstorm had hit them. What did Captain Winters think about him? Henry wondered as he looked out across the cold ocean at the British schooner. It was clear that he disliked Henry. Of course his true identity had been revealed to the Captain, but no one else was privy to the information. Henry knew that Winters only tolerated him because he was in the pay of Richard Fitzroy, and for no other reason. Had Henry still been on board the *Dragonfly*, and met up with the *Lady Eleanor* at sea, things would be very much different. Captain Winters would most likely be at Henry's throat with a cutlass, and the man would not hesitate to cut him down as the *enemy*.

It was ironic that the squadron had chosen this point in time to return to Boston. Henry remembered last summer. The summer of 1812, when war had been declared, and when Captain Weatherby had decided to split the British squadron to work between the ports of Boston, and Newport, Rhode Island, and while alternating between the two thus endeavored to blockade them both. What made it harder, was that each time Weatherby set out for the *other* harbor, he had to weather Cape Cod, that great hook shaped peninsula that stuck out in the Atlantic Ocean like the blade of a sickle. Thus costing him extra miles, and constant vigilance. For the distance between each port was more than a hundred and twenty miles.

It seemed so long ago as Henry's memory took him back to the ward room on *Dragonfly*, with the kindly Mr. Plumb, the ship's Sailing Master, as they had intently poured over the charts together. Just the captain's clerk then, but because of his ministerial experience and a college education, it rendered him the only possible choice for the position after Weatherby's clerk had been killed. It had given Henry certain privileges, but it also put him at closer quarters with first Lieutenant Fox who hated him with deep hatred, and would have found any excuse to see Henry flogged or hanged from the *Dragonfly*'s yardarm. It made no difference to Fox.

Henry tried to push these thoughts out of his mind as he studied the *Vixen* through his glass. He did not personally know anyone on board, and had only caught a glimpse of her captain when Weatherby had ordered all the captains on board for a meeting. *Vixen* was a hefty topsail schooner, and in a single ship to ship action at sea, the *Lady Eleanor* would not stand much of a chance against her. *Vixen*'s gun crews were well trained, every man familiar with the peculiarity of his own weapon, and knew how the rest of his mates would react under fire, their calm discipline would hold them in good stead. The British were sticklers for gunnery practice.

The *Lady Eleanor*'s only hope was her superior speed. The schooner was very fast, Henry had already observed her performance in stays, and Mr. Crook was making an excellent job of steering the ship through the shallows. A slight turn of the wheel to starboard then to larboard as he steered the ship through large slabs of ice, his sharp eyes taking in every inch of the water up ahead while his eyes bulged as he squinted into the pale moonlight. The closer they stayed to the coastline the safer they would be from the British. Then, when they had left their pursuer far enough behind, they would turn east, and head for the open sea. After that? Henry could only take a guess. It was left to Captain Winters to decide what waters he wanted to hunt down enemy shipping in.

Winters and Fitzroy originally had planned for the *Lady Eleanor* to head north after leaving Boston, perhaps sail to Nova Scotia? The Cape Sable area on the southern tip of the province seemed an excellent choice for them to put Henry ashore, row him in to a remote part of the coastline on a dark night, and at the same time look for some unsuspecting British merchantman that may be sighted. But with this wicked weather maybe Winters would change his mind, and head for the warmer waters of the West Indies, and prey on enemy shipping there instead. Bulging merchantmen loaded with expensive goods were beginning their voyages across the Atlantic Ocean to the hungry European markets. That's where the teeming multitudes lived in comparison with the sparsely populated Americas.

All through that harrowing night they sailed on, every crew member had his eye fixed on the shallow water on their larboard side, and also cast their heads over their shoulders constantly, to judge their distance from the schooner, *Vixen*, who was not letting up her chase for a moment. She was always there . . . hour after hour.

Much to the everyone's disappointment, when daylight came they still had not put many miles between them, and the enemy. Mr. Crook said it was because of sailing so close to land with all its eddies and tidal variances, while the British had the ocean beneath their keel.

Things would get better when they were in deeper water Henry rationalized. They must escape at all costs.

On board the schooner, *Vixen*, every hand had been roused up and was standing at the ready. They had 'beat to quarters' long ago. In fact the moment they had seen the *Lady Eleanor* hoist her sails. Every larboard gun was run out, the decks were sanded, and cartridges lay ready to be used the moment the order was given. Every man knew that sooner or later the American schooner would have to break free from the shallows, and when she did, they were confident of a victory. The schooner would make a fine addition to the squadron. They had nothing to fear. They were an experienced crew and their gunnery well practiced. They mistakenly assumed that the American vessel had drummed up a crew at the last minute. And although it was recognized that Boston was the largest seaport in America at this time, and her sailors well seasoned, they relied on the fact that seeing the British squadron in their national waters, would have the affect of '*intimidation by a superior force.*'

Fortunately, what the Americans lacked in numbers her volunteer sailors made up for it in enthusiasm and spirit. The few hands that were experienced, were also confident that they could quickly shape up the landlubbers over a period of a week or two. Relying heavily on the philosophy that a man learns fast when his life is at stake, and the smell of prize money is in his nostrils.

It was now Christmas Day, Henry realized, and apart from an extra tot of rum issued to the men that morning as they stood ready by the guns, there was nothing said or done to recognize the day as anything special. Henry felt gloomy, and along with the sadness came thoughts of home *again.*

He could picture the large brick house in Ludham, with its thatched roof and Dutch gables, designed in the same style as the houses of the Flemish weavers. It had been built in 1603, the very year when the first King James, the ill fated son of Mary Queen of Scots, had begun to reign. Hawk Common House, where generations of Stapletons had lived ever since. Like himself all had been farmers and landowners, their portraits still hung in the large hallway, and up the curved staircase, where they looked down on their ancestors with mute expressions. What would they think of the present Henry Stapleton standing here on the deck of the *Lady Eleanor*? Preparing to fight against his own countrymen, cold and shivering like the others on board the schooner.

Henry's thoughts were again of Elizabeth, who with their children would be preparing to gather at the big table in the dining room for the festive meal, where he would normally be seated at the head, looking down at his wife at the other end, and with the children seated on each side. This year would be different! There would be an empty place at the head of the table. Had old Mr. Baldwin managed to bag a brace of pheasants? Henry wondered. Elizabeth would do her finest with the roast potatoes that would positively glow by the light of the big fire. Had Benjamin got enough wood in? His mind skipped about, contemplating all the details of the life he was missing in his anxiety about the family. The Christmas pudding would follow the dinner, in which Elizabeth would have hidden some small coins. A few farthing perhaps? Or maybe she was penniless? No, he mustn't think that.

Elizabeth's face would be radiant in the light of the candles, and her bright blue eyes would be lovingly studying the expression on the children's faces as they carefully ate their pudding, being ever-so-careful not to crunch their teeth on a coin. The shrieks of joy and laughter as they discovered something hard amongst the black and moist pudding in their mouth. After supper they would all sit around the large stone fireplace. It would be quiet and peaceful. Henry closed his eyes for an instant, the cold wind seemed to freeze his eyeballs in their sockets, and his eyelashes froze to his cheek bones. Was it snowing in Norfolk he wondered? as he imagined the dining room decorated with holly boughs that the children would have cut with their own hands from the woods. For a moment he could smell smoke as it drifted from the smoldering logs on the hearth, and wound its way up the big chimney. He could visualize Elizabeth, small in stature with golden hair like a cornfield, sitting quietly in a chair . . . her mind far away. Was she thinking about him? Did she miss him as much as he longed for her? Had she given up hope? Surely she must be devastated with worry, wondering if he was still alive or not.

The children would be playing with their gifts by now, not noisily though, for respect for their mother, and her suppressed grief. They would all be thinking of their father and of happier times. His mind was still there in Norfolk as he opened his eyes and stared hard at the British man-of-war.

As Henry watched, a sudden puff of smoke came from the *Vixen*, and was instantly whisked away in the strong wind. It brought him back sharply to the present as a plume of seawater arose about a hundred yards away on the starboard side of the *Lady Eleanor*. The *Vixen* had missed her target, but the English ship was obviously testing her range, and for Captain Winters it was 'a mite too close,' as he informed Mr. Crook to hold to their present course.

Well into the forenoon watch the wintry sun was shining, and the ferocious wind was curling stiff white caps over the surface of the sea. The ice cold spray was lashing their faces and causing them to appear red and spotted.

Captain Winters had ordered the guns run out, but didn't see the chance of ever using them. The one gun that may have been brought to bear, Fitzroy's pride and joy, was the long nine pounder on the bow, which was useless at this point unless Winters went to the trouble of hauling the big gun aft. No! he would save it for when they turned east, and made the final run into deeper water, and the *Vixen* would then be on the *Lady Eleanor*'s starboard bow. Then he could make the British wince.

The *Lady Eleanor* was handling beautifully now, her sails taut and drawing well, and every rope tightly secured and singing in the wind like a finely tuned violin. As she gradually worked clear of the shallows she began to pick up speed, her bows dipping and rising with a regular motion dividing the sea with precision as she tore through the ocean like a fox terrier.

Henry looked around at the men, most of them looked fairly relaxed as they leant against the rails. Sean O'Boyle was grinning from ear to ear and Henry wondered if he had had one tot of rum too many. Was he three sheets to the wind? The rest of the mostly young faces were eager and alert. They ducked in unity as another of *Vixen*'s six pounders danced across the waves and fell short, but sent a swathe of green water over the gun crews on the starboard side, and soaked them with icy cold seawater.

"Close!" said Crook to Winters, who grinned and shrugged his shoulders in reply. Henry thought that maybe Winters did not want to alarm the rest of the men by his nonchalant attitude. Or was it cold-heartedness? This captain seemed to be a strange kettle of fish, Henry concluded.

"Beggin' your pardon, sir," said Crook to Winters. "We're quite close to Cape Ann!"

"I am fully aware of that, Mr. Crook, and I know your concern for the rocky shore in that area. I hope to wear ship before long."

"Good!" said Crook, the tone of his voice showing relief, but uttering *"about time"* under his breath. He was angry with the Captain. Winters was not demonstrating enough caution considering he held the lives of every man on board in his hands. Crook was a shrewd old man, wizened by sun and wind, but an artist at ship handling, and his experience was as old as Noah's ark itself.

# CHAPTER FIVE

## THE DUEL

The *Lady Eleanor* was wearing every stitch of sail that she possessed, and wearing it well. With the wind strengthening she was heeling over at an alarming rate. A prudent captain under normal circumstances would have reduced sail long ago. Henry was very much aware that the more she heeled, the more of her vulnerable hull the *Lady Eleanor* was exposing to the British guns. A shot taken below the waterline would take men away from the guns and send them to the pumps. Of course this would reduce her speed dramatically. This was the most critical moment the ship had ever endured, she was certainly not so sorely pressed under the regimen of the Fitzroy outings on Massachusetts Bay.

The men on her decks were leaning at a thirty degree angle to her deck planking to keep themselves upright, which made movement on board very difficult. Doubly so, because along with the heeling of the ship, there was also a bucking motion as she

107

rose and dipped violently, sending seawater crashing over her bow, and rushing aft along the deck. The force of it almost swept the men off their feet before it escaped through the scuppers and ran down the sides of the ship. Each time the schooner's bow plunged headlong into the waves, Henry held his breath as he waited for her to rise, while the ice continued to coat the ship with every submersion. Could she endure this punishment? How long before she lost all buoyancy to rise again? The nine pounder on the bow was making it worse, it was so heavy for a schooner of this size. Nobody had realized that they would have so much ice to contend with.

The two masts shook and shuddered with a great resolution as the schooner's hull tried to shake the water off of her, like a wet dog. Henry breathed out a sigh of relief.

Work below decks had come to a standstill. No food could be prepared, and everything was lashed down to prevent a flying missile injuring the men, who had wedged themselves into a position where they were able to grip onto anything stable. The *Lady Eleanor* continued to lurch along in this fashion, a complete captive of the wind and waves, hour after hour.

The rocks of Cape Ann were now visible to Henry even without the use of a telescope as he steadied himself on the muzzle of a gun. His eyebrows had long ago turned white with frost and his very breath was freezing against his face. He could just visualize the cape looking slate gray and ominous. The rocks stood well above the magnificent spray of seawater that was freezing as fast as it touched the stone cold granite. They were heaped up like a giant's causeway leading to a frozen fortress. It was a breathtaking sight, one that Henry had never experienced before, with such bone chilling cold that was so foreign to all that English weather could ever produce.

He noticed that Mr. Crook now had an assistant to help him wrestle with the schooner's big wheel. It took everything they had to hold her on course. Out in the open sea they could have lashed the wheel in position. But here, so close to the shoreline they were afraid to let go for a moment. If they lost their footing for an instant the wheel could spin out of control, and send the *Lady Eleanor* foundering onto rocks that would grind her hull timbers to pieces within minutes. Any survivors would freeze to death before they could swim for the shore. Beyond the craggy rocks lay the stone quarries of the area. Rich in granite needed for buildings, along with ballast for ships, enabling them to weather such turbulent waters as these.

As the *Lady Eleanor* started her gradual turn eastwards, she was sailing even closer to the wind. One more compass point and her sails would be flapping, and she would be in irons. She was still trying to weather the Cape, which protruded some nine miles out into the Atlantic Ocean. Captain Winters was relying on the fact that the British man-of-war would find it even harder, being a topsail schooner and not able to sail as close to the wind as he could. He knew that every mile ahead would be the most dangerous of their voyage so far.

The *Vixen*'s captain would be doing everything in his power to cut them off, and soon the *Lady Eleanor* would be in range of the *Vixen*'s guns.

Winters was tensely gripping the bulwarks as he watched the Cape. Once free of its grip, the open ocean and the Gulf of Maine would be before him, and his superior speed would leave the British ship far astern. The *Lady Eleanor* was still racing along at twelve knots.

Captain Weatherby and the rest of the squadron were still a dozen miles from Boston. His schooner, *Vixen*, had been out of sight for two days now, and he was getting anxious about her whereabouts. Felkes, Weatherby's steward, brought in some hot tea and set the pot down on the table in the Great Cabin.

"Mind it don't slide off the table, this weather is no picnic is it, sir?" Weatherby sipped it gratefully.

Much to Weatherby's annoyance things were not ticking along like clockwork. The squadron was scattered somewhat, and as soon as the *Vixen* returned, with or without her prize, Weatherby was ready to return to Newport. He would face another grueling trek around Cape Cod. Perhaps this time he would stop at Nantucket Island. The Islanders were friendly enough, and he was getting short of supplies. He also needed some whale oil for his lamps. There was no other place in the world where it was more in abundance than Nantucket. Her great whaling ships plied the waters of the Pacific Ocean for three or more years at a time, eager to supply the world's hunger for the oily, putrid liquid. Nantucket Island's mariners were some of the world's most famous, though fiercely clannish in their outlook. Their Quaker heritage was prominent in their lifestyle, and business ethics, except when it came to selling their wares to outsiders, Weatherby chuckled to himself. But who was he, after all, to complain about his benefactors?

On the *Lady Eleanor*, Henry heard Winters ordering, "All hands on deck," they were ready to put the schooner about. The moment had come and destiny's door lay before them. Whatever the outcome there was no other course left open, for to continue would put the ship on the rocks of Cape Ann. On the new tack Henry realized that Winters was putting the *Lady Eleanor* on a converging course with the *Vixen*. The British man-of-war was still on their starboard quarter, about two miles away now, with her guns visible in a row of murderous black metal. Ready to take aim and strike.

"Hands to mainsail and mizzen sheets!" Winters yelled through his speaking trumpet, the sound of his voice was whisked away immediately in the cold ferocious wind.

"Put your helm up, Mr. Crook," said Winters stiffly.

Immediately Crook and his assistant swung the wheel hard over to starboard with all the strength they could muster. "Helm's a lee!" replied Crook, his voice cracked with the dryness in his throat. The *Lady Eleanor* came up into the wind obediently, and paused momentarily as if unsure of what was expected of her. Every sail was flapping thunderously, her jibs cracked like whips as the wind sought desperately to tear them off the bowsprit and blow them away like a Monday morning wash. Henry and every available man were bracing themselves and straining with every muscle they had to haul in the sheets, hand over hand they worked quickly to put the ship on her new tack. "Two-six-two-six," the bo'sun shouted to the men. These seconds seemed like minutes as they waited for the outcome.

"Put you backs into it men!" yelled Winters. "Don't let her get stuck in irons, or we're all as good as dead!"

Slowly the *Lady Eleanor*'s bow came through the eye of the wind, her whole motion felt like a horse plunging up and down. The rocks beneath the surface seemed to reach up with their arms as she pitched and rolled over their ugly gray heads. Her sails shivered as they lay powerless, then with a great lurch the schooner slowly moved forward as the wind took hold of her sails, then they bulged out in perfect harmony as the *Lady Eleanor* surged off on her new course. The men cheered loudly and Henry marveled at the strength of the wind, and how much they were at its mercy. There was no arguing with it once it was harnessed, and he realized they were set for a wild ride. The chase was now in earnest.

The men looked exhausted, and blood oozed from the frozen raw flesh on their palms, with droplets of bright red dropping onto the deck, and taking on the appearance of red berries from a Hawthorn bush that had fallen in the snow.

Henry felt frozen stiff, but very thankful that with the sails trimmed, the schooner was steering true on her new tack. The wind was now coming over the larboard bow with such destruction that the impact made the *Lady Eleanor* hesitate each time a wave struck her hull. Her bowsprit was pointing towards the British schooner *Vixen*, like a great finger pointing the way to the battle.

The two miles between the two ships soon began to lessen, and Henry could just make out a smudge of navy blue, which he knew would be the uniforms of the English officers that were on board. He reasoned that the *Vixen* would fire first, using her bow chasers. He wondered if they too had a nine pounder on board?

"Stand by the nine pounder!" cried Winters to the men on the foredeck, as if he had read Henry's thoughts. "Steady there! Hold your fire men!"

Henry kept a keen eye on the *Vixen* and saw a red flash, and then a puff of smoke that climbed up the foremast of the *Vixen* like a huge thunder cloud. Seconds later the ball from the *Vixen* fell a little to the larboard side of the *Lady Eleanor*, sending a torrent of water in his face and taking his breath away for a moment. A repeated cloud of smoke . . . and another ball fell with a whoosh into the sea on the starboard side. "Six pounders," he called to the men who grinned back at him, and at each other, but it did not cover the anxiety they all felt. Any moment the British could alter their course slightly and fire a true broadside which could sweep them off the foredeck like rag dolls.

"Put your helm up two points closer to the wind, Mr. Crook," growled Winters. "Keep the headsails drawing . . . don't loose us an inch or we'll be in big trouble."

"Aye, aye, sir."

Another ball tore over their heads, this time missing the mizzenmast by inches, but ironically tearing their flag from its lashings. The fifteen stars and fifteen stripes, the symbol of their nation, was torn in two and drifting out of sight rapidly in the *Lady Eleanor*'s wake. The men let out a groan, as if their own personal hopes and dreams had been swept away too. It seemed like a bad sign to them, for most sailors were extremely superstitious. They also saw it as an insult, as if the English had slashed it in half with a sword, or compelled them to strike their colors, something they would never do. It made their blood boil, and they cursed out loud.

"Keep your mind on what's going on," roared out Winters. "It will be your heads next time if you don't concentrate. Stapleton!" Winters sneered. "I want you behind that gun too," he shoved Henry roughly in the shoulder.

"Don't push me, Winters. I'll obey orders, but you'll not lay a hand on me!"

Winters cursed him out loud. The men didn't seem to understand what was going on between Stapleton and their captain.

Henry stepped behind the gun, and steeled himself for what lay ahead.

"Hold fast!" screamed Winters above the noise of the wind, then stumbled back to the helm after instructing the gun crew on the foredeck. The six pounders had been run out at intervals along the deck, and were manned and ready if they should be needed. Winters pulled out his sword and lifted it high above his head. He stood near the helm with his legs slightly apart, balancing himself with the motion of the ship.

"Fire!" yelled Winters, bringing his sword down in a great swipe towards the deck. The first ball went awry, and he scowled at his men menacingly as if to forbid them to make another mistake.

The *Lady Eleanor*'s nine pounder was loaded and firing in rapid succession. Henry grabbed the big sponge on a long rod, and sponged out after each shot. He had seen it done many times, it came naturally now. Surely this was self defense? This was not in cold blood! What else could he do? He had an immediate mental image of Christian and Freddie . . . boys at war. He forced the thought of his own son Benjamin away out of his mind too. This was not the time or the place for sentiment.

The big gun recoiled across the foredeck again and again, making the ship shudder from stem to stern. It rumbled back on its truck and was brought to a stop by the tackles that held it. Henry saw the *Lady Eleanor*'s shot rip through the rails of the *Vixen*, sweeping two English sailors aside like toy soldiers. He swallowed hard, shaking his head with remorse.

The direct hit on the British was infectious, and the gun crew danced around in an euphoric state with wild eyes and grinning faces. The rest of the crew broke out in a cheer. Henry helped two sailors use hand spikes to get the gun into position to fire again, while another blew gently on the slow match. The rammer stepped back and afterwards Henry sprang into action again the moment after the gun had fired, so that more shot could be loaded.

The *Lady Eleanor* sailed on unscathed, the two schooners were now less than a half mile apart, and drawing closer together like great magnets, with each vessel starkly contrasted against the wintry sky. Again a huge jet of orange fire roared out from the *Vixen*, like a flaming inferno, and a ball wheezed through the air with a hideous whine. Henry threw himself down on the deck as wooden splinters showered over his head. He turned to look behind him and saw the *Lady Eleanor*'s mizzen mast and spanker sail had gone by the board and was dangling over the side, amidst a maze of blocks and rigging.

The *Lady Eleanor* soon slowed down dramatically as the broken spar trailed in the water like a great sea anchor. Mr. Crook managed to keep her on course while a dozen men rushed to the side with axes and hacked away at the cordage that was holding the mast prisoner. They worked like mad men to free it.

Henry saw two sailors lying near the scuppers. One had a giant splinter in his stomach which protruded out through his back, soaking his clothes in a sodden mass of blood. The man sat in a slumped position with his lifeless eyes still staring down at himself, with a look of shock and disbelief on his face. The other lay screaming nearby, his right leg pinned under a section of the mast. Henry raced aft, grabbing a metal hand spike that lay near one of the six pounders. He frantically used the spike like a great lever to lift the mast enough for the man to roll free then pass out in agonizing pain. Without waiting for orders from Winters, Henry lifted him carefully and staggered below with the man in his arms. As he looked over his shoulder Winters looked stunned and confused.

The smaller guns were still firing, deafening Henry's senses. It was slightly warmer down here he noticed as he descended into the relative quiet of below decks. The man's warm blood soaked into his clothes with a sickly smell. The seaman was swiftly taken from him, and laid out on the big table, where the day before they had eaten their plum pudding. He could tell by the look on the surgeon's face, and the grim looking bone saw in his hand that the leg would have to come off. Mercifully the man may stay unconscious through the nightmare operation, and when he awoke . . . it would be all over. Or just beginning Henry thought. He scrambled up the companionway just as the surgeon was tightening the metal tourniquet and giving orders for the loblolly boy to be ready with the Laudanum to help kill the pain, then catch the amputated limb in a bucket.

When Henry came on deck again it was to the serenade of the *Lady Eleanor*'s starboard guns blazing. The entire spar deck was thick with smoke, so that it was hard to see what was happening. The mizzenmast had at last been hacked away, and was disappearing in their icy foaming wake.

Because of this serious setback, the two ships were almost level with each other now. The British man-of-war had a few marines in the tops hailing musketry down on them, and at the same time the first of her larboard guns were brought to bear.

Henry saw the *Vixen* take a shot into her hull. She seemed to wince like a puppy, but continued her onslaught with all the pent up fury of her British commander.

The battle went on with vicious intensity as each ship launched its weight of metal against the other. Wave after wave of bombardment exchanged between them, and when the smoke had cleared, Henry was met with a sight that he had not expected to see. The British schooner's bowsprit had fallen victim to one of the *Lady Eleanor*'s well aimed broadsides. It was completely shot away, leaving nothing but a stump behind with a snub nosed *Vixen* looking absurdly foolish with her ornate figurehead now in perfect view. The fox's head, with it's teeth bared in a goulish smile was left totally intact, except for a few chunks out of the gold paint.

With the loss of her headsails, it was all over for the British. The *Vixen* swung up into the wind with her yards and sails flapping furiously. The Americans held their breath as they watched her foremast topple gracefully over her side, taking dozens of English sailors with it. Henry heard their cries as they fell into the sea. In the cold ocean they would last but a minute or two. Their heads bobbed momentarily in the waves before the ice and cold took them down to their watery grave.

The *Lady Eleanor* seemed to kick her heels as she drove heavily on through the pounding waves, despite the loss of her mizzen. She was still under fire from the *Vixen*'s starboard battery as she clawed herself free. A few last musket shots rang out, and slammed into her. Then, they were free of their attackers at last with the open ocean before them, and with not another sail in sight. Every man jack on board was a picture of sweet jubilation. A whole swarm of them ran to the stern and waved their fists at the receding British ship.

"Merry Christmas!" they roared. "That's one present you didn't expect to receive!" They shrieked and howled wildly, leaping in the air and slapping one another on the back as they did so.

Henry couldn't help smile at their simplicity, almost like children who had scared away the school bully. Another two men had minor wounds, the rest were unscathed except for frostbite and a few bad bruises.

"One dead, three wounded," commented Captain Winters to the sailing master.

"You were lucky, that's a fact," said Mr. Crook smugly.

"Yeah," drawled Winters. "They'll lick their wounds for a while, but they'll be back, mark my words. Wherever there is an ocean, there is a British ship somewhere on it," he said angrily.

"Head east, Mr. Crook, we have repairs to make and a destiny to keep."

"East it is, sir. Full and bye."

Despite the stumpy remains of the mizzen, the *Lady Eleanor* made excellent progress punching her way out into the deep water of the Atlantic Ocean. The heavy swell now crashed over her bow as she forged on like the Trojan she was, reveling in her new found freedom. This was her natural environment, and Henry thought that if ships had any character, the *Lady Eleanor* seemed to bristle with the excitement she felt.

A jury rigged mizzen was in place by the time the evening meal was served, and although the schooner would not be able to ride to a full gale, Captain Winters was satisfied with the work.

They would sail east, and then turn south to seek a harbor further down the coast, in order to get a complete refit and be ready for sea again. He would avoid New York, and the Chesapeake He had had enough of the British blockading squadrons who were concentrating on the larger ports. Maybe Port Royal, in South Carolina? That was a fine and dandy place he thought, and large enough to have shipyards to take care of the schooner's repairs. As far as the Englishman, Stapleton, and the promise he had made to Richard Fitzroy to put him safely ashore somewhere, they could both go to hell as far as he was concerned. Despite the money he would be paid for completing the job when he eventually returned to Boston, Winters decided that it was not a priority. Prize money was what he was after, not some high minded act of human kindness, and what Fitzroy could pay would be *nothing* in comparison to the lucrative business of privateering.

The cook did a splendid job for the Christmas supper. Every man on board thought that they had a lot to celebrate. The birth of the Christ child, and their narrow escape from the British. They ate their food with relish and good cheer, pausing only long enough to show respect for the dead by lifting their glasses to their fallen shipmate, whose body had been stitched up in sailcloth, weighted with shot, and already gone over the side.

Henry was not so jubilant, although he tried not to show it. He had overheard Winters talking to the master about Port Royal, which was in the opposite direction he had hoped the ship would be sailing. Gone were his hopes of being put ashore at Cape Sable. He had enough common sense to know it could not be helped, what with damage to the ship they could hardly head north, where British ships were in abundance in the area, and with no place to get satisfactory repairs done. Soon they would be bound for the South, away from New England, and more importantly, as far as he was concerned, Old England!

This new change of plan had really daunted Henry's hopes. He had felt certain that he would soon be on his way home. He could not understand why God had allowed this to happen to him.

117

Surely he was entitled to some small favor from the Almighty? Anger rose up in him, born out of disappointment without doubt, but nevertheless what a blow it seemed. He was needed back in England, he reasoned. There was a purpose. Elizabeth needed a husband to take care of her, not to mention his family and friends who ardently supported his vision for the area, where perhaps another great awakening could yet be born. Every turn of events in his life seemed to be thwarting his own hopes and desires. How could it be so? How many more years would it take?

Henry stood up from the table, and left the warmth of the cabin with its band of happy sailors. His departure was unnoticed as he climbed the companionway steps with a heavy heart. Up on deck there was only a handful of men attending to the working of the ship. With a quick look around him Henry could observe that the horizon was clear. He looked up high above him to the top of the mainmast, where a man sat huddled there, a cold and lonely figure muffled in a heavy coat with his hat pulled down over his ears, faithfully keeping watch as he scanned the horizon for any strange sail that might appear.

Henry slowly climbed the ratlines despite the bitter cold wind clutching at his clothing. Higher and higher he dragged himself upwards, his fear of heights overcome long ago. Henry seemed to get satisfaction in torturing his body with cold, in order to forget his anger and frustration.

The man was startled when Henry's head appeared suddenly over the edge of the small platform. The roaring wind had muffled all sounds below.

"I'll take over for a while," Henry offered.

"Are you sure?"

"Certainly, I expect you could do with some hot food, it is Christmas Day."

"Sure can, matey! Most grateful to you."

The surprised seaman hurried down the ratlines, eager to find shelter from the brutal weather. Henry squatted on the small platform. It was quite tiny in comparison to the fighting tops of a frigate. It was not usually a part of a fore and aft schooner's rigging, but quite adequate to get a bird's eye view of the ocean. Henry looked down where the head of the staysail was fastened about six inches below him. He could easily reach out and touch it from this roughly made platform, which was little more than a wooden basket.

The motion of the ship was sickening up here, more like riding a horse. Worse! There was a rope harness strapped to the mast with two loops that a man could slip his arms into. Henry sat there with his back to the rough timber of the mast, his stomach churning over as he tried to keep his eyes trained on the horizon rather than look down to the deck far below. From this height the *Lady Eleanor* looked ridiculously small and disconnected to life up here.

Henry sat in this rigid position for over an hour. He soon realized that depriving himself of comfort did not obliterate his mind, or his feelings. It changed nothing . . . except his body temperature.

"Get down here this instant," barked a voice from far below.

It was Winters, and his face betrayed his temper. He was yelling before Henry's feet touched the deck.

"I'll trouble you to ask permission in future before you act on one of your own whims, Stapleton. You cannot take matters into your own hands here, you know. This is my ship and my command, no exceptions, no excuses! You follow my orders, and mine alone. In other ships and circumstances you would have been flogged." Winters looked meaningfully into Henry's face. "I trust this will be the last time my authority is flaunted!"

Henry bit deep into his lip, he did not answer. This kind of man was past reasoning with. Instead he stared coldly back at Winters, defiantly. He knew his eyes said a lot although he had to clench his hands so tightly that his finger nails dug deep into his palms.

"Well? How about, aye, aye, sir! Isn't that what they say on English ships?"

Henry still couldn't bring himself to answer, and Winters turned away abruptly on his heels and stormed over to talk to

Mr. Crook at the wheel. Crook was impervious to the Captain's vicious tongue. He hadn't understood the remark to Stapleton, but he was too old to be flustered by such a caitiff individual as Winters.

Henry knew that he had to get a grip on himself, and on his feelings of anger towards Captain Winters. It was obvious the man despised him, and he had to admit that the feeling was mutual. There was something about Winters . . . something sinister, almost evil. Nothing that he could put his finger on . . . as yet, just a gut instinct way down inside the pit of his belly. But it was going to be a long voyage he thought, and they were all locked in together between these wooden walls. Like being in the belly of a whale. Henry hoped that he was not to be compared to the angry prophet, Jonah.

To recapitulate; Henry was, at least, still alive, which was quite an achievement considering all the battles he had endured, and in three different ships. The frigate, HMS *Dragonfly* and the encounter in the English channel last year with the French ship-of-the line, the *Rose*. Then on the *Restitution* with Captain Street in command, and now he was on board the *Lady Eleanor*, and had survived yet another battle. Quite a feather in his cap he mused, for a humble minister from the village of Ludham.

During the following few weeks as they ran down their southing under easy sail, they only sighted one solitary sail on the horizon, hull down, and heading north. The crew had to be held in check as they wanted to give chase. A rebuke from Winters vividly describing the serious repairs still to be carried out, soon cooled their enthusiasm. Henry wondered if any of the crew were beginning to regret their decision to sign on as privateersmen. Financial gain at the moment was non-existent, and likely to remain so for some while to come. Most of the men must have families at home that depended on them to be their providers, and with a country at war, they could all look forward to hard times ahead. It would be a long wait for them, Henry conjectured sadly. Many children would be going to bed hungry at nights, waiting for news of the exploits of the *Lady Eleanor*. Why was it always the children? All over the world and whatever the culture, war affected them the most.

Winters and Mr. Crook spent many hours pouring over charts in the cabin below, plotting and planning. The smell of tobacco and spirits wafted up continuously from the overhead hatch. Henry wondered if they kept their minds clear enough to command sound judgment, if the need arose. If a British man-of-war was to appear out of nowhere they could be caught unawares, and they would end up as a lawful prize of the British Navy.

Although Henry had let the Captain's outburst of temper ride over him, he could not forget it. He mistrusted the man intensely. Winters seemed moody, dangerous ... sudden outbursts of temper. His hatred for the English was very evident, and presumably, judging by his attitude, this included Henry also. But what were his motives in this war? Money? Power? Presumably both. These were the two main ingredients that often made nations take up arms against one other, and what England was currently fighting tooth and nail against in Europe in order to oust the dictator, Napoleon Bonaparte. Countries were even now falling under his tri-colored flag like a pack of cards. Politics were driven by commerce in any nation.

Henry wondered if the *Lady Eleanor* would ever get back to Boston. The town had gained quite a reputation for blockade running in the months prior to the *Lady Eleanor*'s departure, allowing a few merchantmen to slip out under the wing of one or other of the naval vessels, thereby outwitting the British. And now, here he was aboard the first privateersman to exit Boston, roving the eastern seaboard to hunt down enemy shipping and take them as a prize. Fortunes could be made if the cargo was sold in the right port, and could actually yield more financial gain than the ship itself. But it was a risky business. An American ship had to run the blockade to get out, and they would have to penetrate those same blockades to get back in with a prize. Winters would probably burn the prizes anyway, once he had unloaded what merchandise he could squeeze on board the *Lady*

*Eleanor*, and cast the survivors into the sea and let the them drown. Henry didn't care much for *financial* gain. Money meant nothing to him.

Henry remembered the long discussions with Richard back at Edinburgh House, on the defeat of HMS *Guerriere* last summer by Captain Isaac Hull's *Constitution*, which had first heightened public awareness to the war. Then just as the fire of victory was beginning to smolder and die away, the *Constitution* defeated another enemy ship, the *Java*, off the coast of Brazil in mid December 1812. The *Constitution* was then under the new command of Captain William Bainbridge, who sighted the British ship. She was a new French built frigate, captured only a year previously by the British, and brought into their service immediately. After a wicked engagement, which cost the *Constitution* her steering wheel, and the *Java* her three masts, it was all over for the British frigate. *Java*'s Captain Lambert was mortally wounded by a musket ball. The first lieutenant immediately took command and tried to re-hoist the flag of the smitten ship. *Constitution* bore down again and took up a raking position. The red ensign on the British man-of-war was immediately torn down with great haste as a signal of their surrender to the Americans. The badly holed *Java* was burned by Bainbridge's crew, and apart from the prisoners, the only souvenir of the battle was the *Java*'s wheel which Bainbridge installed on *Constitution* as a replacement for his own shattered one. The new wheel would be a badge of courage to all who steered with it, and a constant reminder of their defeat of the enemy.

Henry's thoughts again wandered back to the *Dragonfly*, and her crew. He had seen the *Guerierre* at anchor in Halifax, when the squadron had arrived early last year. She was one of Vice-Admiral Sawyer's ships, and he could imagine what effect it would have had on the British public, and on Sawyer himself. After all, it was the Vice-Admiral who had once said, ". . . what, that handful of fir built American frigates, with their bits of striped bunting at their mastheads, and manned by illegitimates and outlaws . . ." Statements like that could not be kept hidden from the masses.

Not while there were curious seamen lurking near the hatches of the great cabins of their admirals and captains. There was not much that could be kept secret for very long on board a King's ship, nor could it be hid from the press. The Times of London would make mincemeat of the defeat, and the Admiralty would be venting their outrage on the unfortunate captains who happened to be in Portsmouth at the time.

How easy it was for Henry to now anticipate peoples' reactions based on his short experience in the Royal Navy, with its close tie to politics and public opinion.

Henry chuckled to himself as he thought of Felkes, the grumpy old steward. His friends, Christian Clark and Freddie Baines, lively youngsters like his own son Benjamin. Full of life and youth. He could picture in his mind's eye, Benjamin dressed in a King's uniform. How proud English boys were to wear it, and how soon it could be saturated with the blood of mere children. Henry shivered. He knew if he ever got back to England he would have a new dimension of thought when it came to war at sea. He would never be the same again . . . never!

"Daydreaming, Stapleton?" said Winters suddenly appearing from nowhere. Henry tensed his whole body. He had not seen him approach. It unnerved him, and he reminded himself to be more cautious of this habit he had acquired of disappearing into a world of his own, and being rendered oblivious to his surroundings. It could prove to be very dangerous.

"Ah, Captain Winters!" Henry declared. They stared at each other for a moment. Winters had eyes of steel, cold and hard. A face that you could not trust, a person that you did not want to turn your back on. Yet it did not make any sense! This was the man that was supposed to help him to get ashore. In fact he was being paid by Richard to do so, and yet?

"Just thinking of home," he replied honestly. Winters looked at him in a calculative and aloof manner. "So, have you decided on a destination yet?" Henry continued, trying to turn the focus away from himself and pull some information from this man with a mask of iron.

"I suppose you are anxious to make your *escape*, Stapleton. Well, I can tell you this, it will not be for quite a long while yet. I must get to Port Royal, or Charleston to undergo repairs. I cannot let you go ashore when we arrive," he replied sourly. "The whole political feeling in the South is a far cry from the passive attitude of Boston. The War Hawks in Congress live up to their reputation, and have a strong following for their cause amongst Southern gentlemen. Their hatred towards the British is very acute, and should your identity be discovered . . ." he paused, his lips curling slightly at the corners as if to suppress a smile. "Well, suffice it to say that a minister would not look very comely kicking on the end of a gibbet."

"A gibbet does not paint a pretty picture, whatever the nationality," retorted Henry defensively, with more than a note of sarcasm in his voice. "It is enough that men are hung for a crime committed, but to be hung for being a citizen of one country or another, is unthinkable!"

"Damn your eyes! Don't play games with me, Stapleton. You clergymen are all the same! Cowards the lot of you if you ask me. You will not fight for your country, and all the while you try to talk your way out of tight corners. What will you fight for, eh?" Winters poked Henry roughly in the chest, his face contorting with anger. He sprung forward and thrust himself within inches of Henry's face. He was torn between his hatred for the British, and his financial compensation for the safe passage of this particular Englishman, as Richard Fitzroy was not willing to reimburse him in full until Stapleton was safely clear of American jurisdiction. Winters was compromised by his future payment.

"I'll fight for what I believe to be right, that's my privilege. But no man calls me a coward, sir!" cried Henry, trying desperately to control his rising anger. It was at times like this that Henry almost regretted his commitment to peacefulness. "Captain Winters, you'll not persuade me to take the first action if that is your intention!" Henry knew that the Captain was assuming that he would 'turn the other cheek.' Winters was an example of humanity at its worst, taking advantage of a man's integrity.

"Huh! Do ya think you have control of me then, Stapleton? I'm captain on this ship, and don't you ever forget it! You can live or die it makes no difference to me," his words spat out like venom, and echoed in Henry's ears like thunder.

"I'll defend my rights if I have to," Henry replied hotly. "Your kind will goad a man into making the first move, then use your *so-called* authority to cut him asunder, and stand un-condemned for it. But I can assure you, without a shadow of a doubt, that if you strike the first blow, I will fight you!"

"Are you challenging me, Stapleton? You are beginning to sound more and more like a mutineer, and that brings us back to the subject of hanging again, doesn't it?"

Henry felt like a fox cornered by a pack of hounds. He was breathing with short bursts of air as he struggled once more to keep his anger under control, while still maintaining eye contact with Winters at all times. Henry noticed that Winters' right hand was resting on the butt of the pistol stuck in his belt, with his fingers twitching nervously.

"Oh, I will *challenge* you, Mr. Winters!" Henry said coolly. "To a duel . . . but not to the death. A test of skill in that fine old art of swordsmanship, within the context of honor. Whoever draws first blood to be the victor! Do you agree to my terms?"

Winters raised his eyebrows, a look of shock slowly spread over his countenance like a cloud passing over the sun. His angry face receded into a sardonic smile.

"Very well, Stapleton! Tomorrow morning at nine! I will be happy to oblige you. I'll assemble the whole crew to be a witness to this *duel*. Then we will see what kind of swordsman you are! It will be great entertainment for us all!" Winters spun round sharply and walked away, leaving Henry staring after him.

Henry was shocked by this latest turn of events. Apart from his few moments in defense of Captain Street, on board the Restitution before he fell overboard, it had been many years since he had handled a sword. He had taken lessons as a young man from a little known Frenchman, an aristocrat, who had taken up residency in Ludham to live quietly in seclusion. The villagers said he was a refugee, who like many of his kind had fled from the Revolution that was sweeping across France at the time.

As young boys he and his friends called him simply, Frenchie. They had scrumped apples flagrantly from his orchard whenever they felt like it. And when some of the boys were caught in the act, they received a sound boxing of their ears from the French Master, but it did not deter them for a moment. The minute Frenchie's back was turned, they would scale the wall surrounding his orchard, like a hoard of miniature soldiers assaulting a castle wall. Victory was won only when the ripened apples were theirs. Nevertheless, Frenchie was an excellent swordsman, a master of the art. Later he had taught Henry everything he knew, and now at this moment in his life Henry was most grateful for that tuition. He hoped that the passage of time would not be his enemy, and cheat him out of his victory over Captain Winters.

Henry stayed on deck until the evening, for the weather had modified slightly as they had continued their passage south. Not exactly warm, but not the cold bite of winter that they had experienced in the Bay of Massachusetts. Its wintry clutches receded with every day of southing they made. The *Lady Eleanor*'s progress was slow, and she had to forge way out into the Atlantic and sail almost directly south to be away from the British merchant convoys which were always escorted by British-men-of-war, as they sailed along the regular trade routes. This meant that the schooner was forced out far enough to be sailing against the warmer waters of the Gulf Stream which ran at about eight knots at this time of the year, accompanied by its turbulent seas, which no captain in their right mind would try, unless he was trying to hide from a superior force. And Henry knew that they still had to weather Cape Hatteras, and sail west of Bermuda (one of the major British naval stations, where the concentration of warships would be amplified even further.) It was going to be a long voyage, and as provisions and water diminished things could get only worse amongst the men.

The crew were standing aloof from Henry now that they had obviously been informed of the imminent contest that would take place the following morning. Their cold glances and muttering oaths were bandied about quite openly. The news of his challenge had quite naturally swept through the ship. It was evident by their behavior that they were whole-heartedly behind their Captain, with a fierce loyalty that would have been admirable on any ship. Perhaps they didn't know the *real* captain.

When Henry finally climbed down the companionway hatch he could hear voices raised in excitement.

"I'll wager a silver dollar on the Captain!" said Sean O'Boyle confidently.

"Of course you will, Sean. Trust an Irishman to make a safe bet."

"I should think the odds are slightly tilted in your favor," laughed another.

Henry marveled at how soon the men had conceived the idea of a wager. The rest of them laid their bets one by one. Captain Winters' name was chorused continually as the crew pushed forward with their money in their fists, amidst the smell of whiskey and tobacco. The hands fell silent as Henry reached the bottom of the steps, and one by one they started to leave the big table with angry looks flung in his direction.

"Just a minute shipmates!" A large man stepped forward out of the darkness of the cabin. The only black man on the ship. 'Black Jacks' they were labeled by sailors around the world. Henry had heard him called, Weller by name. The black man was well known for not speaking very often, and although he was free born he kept himself to himself as if a natural barrier were between him and the rest of the crew. Weller came forward and sat down at the table. He wiped one hand down the front of his red shirt, then laid both his hands palms down on the table. Massive hands, Henry thought, like those of Goliath. You only had to look at the man to see that he had experienced a lifetime of toil, and yet he couldn't have been more than forty five years old. He had a stained handkerchief tied around his head, and beads of perspiration were on his brow.

Weller finally moved one hand to reveal five silver dollars under his right palm. The coins shone brightly in the dim light of the cabin. "Well," the black man said slowly and deliberately, "if you want my opinion, and probably most of you don't value it, my money is on Mr. Stapleton. Yes, sir, a finer gentleman as ever walked the deck is he. It's written all over him. He'll be true to his colors, you'll see if I am not mistaken. You fools can do what you like with your money, easy comes easy goes is what I says. Yes, sir, indeed!"

"You're crazy, you damn Sambo!" cried Fryers the master's mate. "But we'll take yer money just the same." He snatched it up and thrust it deep into his pocket where it jangled along with the rest of the crews' wagers. "Any more bets on the preacher?" Fryers grinned. "It's a sure thing mates that he'll lose. What does a preacher know about fighting eh?" And before anyone could stop him Fryers drew out his dirk and stabbed it deep into the table with such force that the handle quivered momentarily. "We'll see tomorrow morning who's the best man, Captain Winters or your scraggy preacher here, and that's for sure!"

The rest of the men roared with laughter, most of them were too drunk to realize what they were doing. They slapped Fryers on the back heartily as they staggered to where the keg of whiskey was stored, and helped themselves to more.

Henry wondered if any of them would be in a fit state tomorrow morning to even comprehend what was going on.

Henry was alone as he stood by the table with the black man. He sat down and held out his hand to Weller, who shook it with a powerful grip. Henry thought it felt like a leather mitten the man's hand was so calloused, but Weller had an honest face with deep penetrating eyes.

"Thank you for your vote of confidence. It seems as if you are my only ally, Mr. Weller."

"I could hardly bet against a preacher could I? My mammy and pappy would turn over in their graves. Besides, what do those fellers know? Stealing whiskey whenever they can, and three sheets to the wind most of the time, they don't really give a hoot about prize money. Just so as they can git out of their responsibilities. Most of 'em anyway," Weller muttered. "I likes yer Mr. Stapleton. I think you've got a good 'eart. I can tell that by looking at yer. God's will be done tomorrow."

"Thank you, Mr. Weller, I hope I won't let you down. That was a lot of money you laid down, and I think you will be one of very few that have put their hopes in me."

"Call me Joshua, Mr. Stapleton, that's my given Christian name."

"Very well, Joshua it will be from now on."

"Well, I best be getting on with my work now." Joshua stood up slowly and resolutely, stretching his powerful frame as he did so.

There was a strange nobility about the man Henry thought, as he watched him walk away. Much more so than many English aristocrats he had met. Joshua Weller was humble for humility's sake, Henry concluded. A rare quality in this world. He couldn't help feel an alliance with the man, despite their diversity of birth and circumstances, there was a compatibility of character between them both.

Off watch once more, Henry lay in his hammock with the sounds and smells of the sea all around him. The *Lady Eleanor* leapt vigorously beneath him as she plunged onwards keeping true to her course. Sleep eluded Henry as he turned things over and over in his mind. He thought about the following day. He doubted his swordsmanship. It had been a long time since he had drawn a sword from its scabbard. And then never in anger, only for sportsmanship and a little friendly rivalry amongst the other students, and later with his friends. Always watched carefully by, and under the expert eye of, Monsieur LaSalle. At the slightest hint of foul play he would haul the young men aside and lecture them on gallantry and protocol. Deep down though, they were all a great joy to the Frenchman's heart. He took pride in his young prodigy, and he never let them know that he was completely aware that they called him Frenchie behind his back.

These anxieties hung around Henry like a dark mist, as he swung with ease in his hammock with the motion of the ship until he finally slipped into a deep sleep. He opened his eyes after what seemed like just half an hour, and realized that he was being awakened to the sound of the men on deck, swabbing and holystoning the fine oak timbers of the Fitzroy's schooner. Holystoning, a thankless task that most seamen hated. Decks were wetted with seawater then sprinkled with sand, and scrubbed vigorously with a small stone the size of a prayer book by men who were down on their knees as they worked on each section of the ship's timbers, slowly working fore then aft with the lay of the grain until the job was finished. It seemed strange to Henry that Winters would adopt a British tradition like holystoning, considering how much he loathed the English and their ways. Perhaps he fancied himself having the same type of control over these volunteer privateersmen, as British commanders had over pressed men, who couldn't answer back even if they had a legitimate cause. In most cases any form of verbal retaliation would be a hanging matter. The British Navy flirted with mutiny on a daily basis. Captain Winters certainly didn't need a sentry at his cabin door to protect him from his crew as did a British naval commander. Was he a tyrannical man below the surface?

Henry noticed that the weather had already turned quite warm considering that this was mid-February, quite like a spring morning. He leapt out of his hammock, pulled on his breeches and buttoned on a clean shirt. He picked up the black leather belt with its sword clip attached to it that Joshua had brought to him late the previous evening, and carefully buckled it around his waist. He was ready! As ready as he would ever be, he thought to himself as he climbed the companionway steps. It was a quarter to nine, fifteen minutes remaining before the duel was to commence. Henry walked decisively to the bow of the schooner, and stood looking at the sea which was sparkling crisply below him with its uniform waves breaking evenly under the *Lady Eleanor*'s bow. A sudden burst of spray hurled seawater over him soaking his shirt and momentarily causing him to catch his breath. The water felt cold on his skin despite the warmth of the morning air.

The men were going about their everyday duties, it was just another day at sea for them. Nobody spoke to him, just cold stares as they passed him by.

At the appointed time Winters came up on deck. He looked fresh Henry thought, as though he had slept extremely well, and was completely unperturbed to all intents and purposes. The Captain was dressed in brown breeches, and black boots. He wore a shirt made of deer hide similar to those worn by the woodsmen that Henry had seen in Halifax. An excellent deterrent to the point of a sword, and in stark contrast to the thin cotton shirt that Henry wore himself. Winters had made a cunning choice indeed!

At nine the crew began to assemble themselves, each one extending their encouragement to Captain Winters as they crowded around him. There was an air of excitement amongst them together with wide grins at the prospect of making some money, as well as seeing their Captain exonerated. Winters confidently strutted over to where Henry stood, his face hard and taut as he approached.

"Mr. Stapleton," he said very formally. "Alas, you look a little tired. Anxiety perhaps? Or didn't you sleep well?" His voice bore a note of sarcasm and smugness.

"I had adequate sleep," responded Henry curtly.

"Mr. Ratby will be my second," continued the Captain. "And who is yours?"

Henry felt embarrassed and stupid. How could he have forgotten such a simple dueling etiquette as selecting a second?

"I will be his second!" a voice cried out, and Joshua came forward out of the crowd of men. He looked tall and intimidating as the crew stepped aside to let the big black man pass through their midst.

"Your servant, sir," Henry nodded to Joshua with a smile.

"So be it!" Winters said sharply, with a look of annoyance upon his face.

The two seconds conferred briefly in whispers, then stood aside. Mr. Ratby nodded to the Captain as a signal that everything was in order.

"First blood," Joshua reminded Ratby with a harsh look.

Winters sneered, but said nothing. "Well, Stapleton, here we have a selection of weapons," he drawled as he pointed to a dozen swords laid out in display on the schooner's cabin top. "They have all had an edge put on them," he continued. "So it's up to you to make your choice."

"I believe the choice is yours, Captain Winters. According to the rules, the one challenged has the right to choose his weapon first."

Winters muttered something under his breath then inspected the swords carefully. He picked them up one after another, and flicked his wrist several times to test their weight. He finally chose a heavy sword with a gold hilt, twisted to look like the strands of a rope. The blade was wider than most dueling weapons, more like a cutlass Henry observed.

Henry's keen eye had already spotted the weapon of his choice. It was a thin sword, about thirty six inches in length. On the silver hilt it had a pattern of the fleur-de-lis finely engraved on it. Probably made in France. Perfect, Henry thought. The guard at the base of the hilt was large, but looked adequate enough. The blade itself was engraved with miniature figures resembling angelic beings. Henry took it in his hand, and, as he suspected, it was as light as it looked.

The two opponents stood facing each other between the foremast and the mizzen. Henry noticed that the decks had been well sanded beneath their feet. The sun felt warm on his face, and for the first time Henry had the opportunity to take a good look at his adversary. Winters was not quite as tall as himself, but thick set, bordering on heavy. A formidable man indeed. His lips were thin, and his green eyes were narrow and set well apart. If he hadn't been a privateering captain, he might have made a prize fighter, Henry thought.

Winters paced around the deck in small circles, like a cat locked in a cage. He seemed somewhat nervous and uneasy.

Ratby called out, "Salute your opponent, then you may begin the contest."

Henry drew his sword and raised it vertically, the hilt level with his chin in the time honored way of duelists for the past four hundred years. Winters raised his reluctantly in acknowledgement. The two men took up their positions. Henry, with the manner of a professional in the 'on guard' position, and Winters with his sword held forcefully in his right hand while his left hand hung loosely by his side.

Henry took the initiative and made the first thrust. Winters was quick to parry. Then he made a sudden lunge, bringing his sword down in a hacking movement. Henry parried and stepped back quickly. The morning air was split with the sound of cold steel.

The hands were craning their necks and jostling forward to make sure they did not miss a strike, their voices swayed together in unison as they murmured their vocal endorsements.

Winters lunged again. Henry attempted to parry, but the two weapons clanged together with a ringing sound, and held for a moment in a crossed position. Henry quickly thrust his sword upwards, Winters did the same. Their swords were still locked together at the hilt. Henry felt the weight of the man and measured his strength. The Captain's eyes were inches away from his own, his warm breath panting in his face. Henry could smell the rum. The hatred was there in his eyes too, Henry could see it plainly. It flashed through his mind that Winters was not as confident as he had first appeared to be, and had hoped a tot would relax him a bit. It was also apparent that Winters was no swordsman, and would try to make short work of it. Henry summoned all his strength to push the man free.

Now they circled each other more warily. Another thrust and parry with swords clanging harmlessly. Henry watched the Captain's movements like a hawk. It was one thing dueling on solid ground, but quite another matter trying to fight on the rolling deck of a ship. With every lurching movement the *Lady Eleanor* made, both men had to keep their balance. Another hacking motion from Winters. This time Henry felt the wind as the blade of Winters' sword swiped past his ear. Henry had seen it coming and managed to jerk his head aside just enough for the thrust to miss. It had been close enough . . . too close. Henry made a sharp riposte, and they both lunged and parried, each man trying desperately to find his mark, and prove himself to be the victor in this contest. One of them had to nick his opponent, enough to draw blood so that the duel would be declared over, and 'honor satisfied.' If Henry were vindicated, would Winters concede to apologize? Henry doubted it.

The pace grew faster now, Winters was desperately trying to bring the whole thing to a rapid conclusion. Henry noticed the Captain was falling short of breath, that he was beginning to pant, his chest heaving in an out violently as he sucked in air through his teeth. There was a brief pause as Henry sought out Winters' weakness, a possible chink in his armor so to speak. Another half circle . . . steel was clashing against steel, and Henry felt the vibration of each blow running down his right arm. Now he was fighting with his back to the main mast as Winters slashed this way and that with wild erratic movements, then he lunged at Henry with all the force of his body behind him. Henry tried to side-step the thrust, but caught his foot in a ring bolt fastened to the deck. He lost his balance as the Captain's sword tore into his shirtsleeve. His right arm, his sword arm, was pinned fast to the mast like a dart, and Winters' sword was deeply embedded in the wood. Henry had felt no pain so he knew that he was not wounded.

He heard a roaring cheer, as Winters withdrew his sword from the mast and sprung back into position. Henry was amazed that so many were lusting for his own blood. The sea of faces laughing and jeering at him, like a crowd that accompanied a felon to the gallows, making sport of his misery.

Henry never took his eyes from Winters' face, he could not let his guard down for a second. The duel was not ended . . .

*yet*. Gripping his sword tightly, though his palms were sweating, Henry still felt strong . . . alert and thankful again for the sword's light weight, its finely engraved hilt glinting in the sunlight as he prepared to fight again. He caught sight of Joshua amongst the crowd of men, his only friend. Joshua's huge black arms were folded across his chest in a defiant posture. Their eyes met for a fleeting moment as Joshua grinned and nodded his approval. A gesture that greatly encouraged Henry. He was not alone. There was at least one ally on this ship.

Henry advanced more vigorously now, thrusting the point of his sword towards Winters' bulky frame. He no longer paid any attention to where he could make a strike, but lunged at any place he thought he could penetrate the Captain's defenses. Winters parried it aside once again, but by now he was cruelly out of breath. Standing there clutching his sword with both hands, the tip of his weapon pointing towards the deck, Henry thought he looked done in. He would let the Captain catch his breath, there could be no repercussions. If he was to win, it would be the honorable way.

Winters gathered himself together once more, and gasping for breath he let out a stream of curses from his mouth. Once again the Captain staggered forward with his sword still held in both hands. He lifted it high over his head, and with his face contorted with rage, he swung his sword in a great arc. It hissed through the air with a strength that only a mad man could produce.

In that split second Henry knew that if Winters' sword reached its mark it could have taken his head off. His right arm came up automatically to defend himself, though he realized with dismay that Winters was not dueling to draw blood alone. This was not just a contest of skill in the context of chivalry and honor, Winters was going to make it a fight to the death. He was out to kill him. In Winters sadistic mind the rules had undoubtedly changed.

Henry thrust the blow aside, but the sheer weight of it, and the full force of Winters' body that was behind it, sent Henry to his knees, completely off balance.

Winters took the opportunity of thrusting his boot into Henry's stomach with a vicious kick. Henry dropped his sword with a clatter as he doubled over in pain. He knelt on the deck, his eyes swimming. Had Winters broken his ribs? Henry tried to move but the pain was crushing.

"Now beg, Stapleton," leered Winters over him. "Or say your prayers!"

Henry heard the men shouting . . . cheering . . . others cursing out loud. Protests from the seconds were ringing out as the sea of faces swept past him in a blur. He was down for about five seconds, but it felt like five minutes.

"I won't beg to the likes of you," Henry gasped as he struggled to his feet sweeping his sword up from the deck in a lightning move with his left hand, and quickly tossed it over into his right.

Winters laughed coldly. "Not praying either then Stapleton? Seems to me you have run out of alternatives."

Henry was angry now. What kind of man was he dealing with? A coward? A bully? It was more than likely that Winters had killed many times. In cold blood perhaps? Henry could see that Winters was over confidently trusting in his own strength now that he had knocked the wind out of him. Henry had to take advantage of the moment and act quickly. He made a sudden lunge at Winters, this time with skilled accuracy. The Captain cried out, and clutched at his left thigh, staring down in disbelief as a red stain began to appear on his breeches, slowly spreading to the size of a silver dollar.

The crowd of seamen gasped, and a murmur rippled through the men. The air was sparked with tension.

Henry stood there glaring at his opponent. It was finally over, his honor was still intact. He held his blood stained sword up towards Winters in a silent salute. The sight of the wounded man gave him no pleasure. Slowly and deliberately, he took out a handkerchief from his pocket and wiped the blood from his sword. He turned away, and quickly sheathed it in the scabbard that still lay on the cabin top, and re-attached it to the clip on his belt.

He was just about to thank Joshua, and pay his respects to Mr. Ratby, when the crowd of men suddenly parted, and Henry saw an enraged Winters limping towards him with a blood thirsty howl that sounded like a tortured animal. His cry echoed around the ship with a bizarre sound that mingling with the sound of the waves crashing over the bulwarks of the *Lady Eleanor*. The Captain's shadow loomed up over Henry like an old grisly bear, his sword was raised ready to strike a death blow.

Before Henry could draw his sword from its scabbard again, he was aware of Joshua stepping between them, a pistol drawn from his belt. One quick move and he had Captain Winters by the throat with the pistol leveled at his temple.

"First blood has been spilled I believe. Your blood! The contest is over, Captain Winters, *sir*," Joshua said dryly. "Mr. Stapleton here is the winner, fair and square like."

"Take 'em both boys," shouted Winters over his shoulder.

"Yeah!" shouted Sean O'Boyle. "Get 'em! Who needs the likes of them. A preacher and a Sambo, they make a good crew. Pity there's only two of 'em eh?" The men lurched forward as one body.

"Stand fast!" yelled Henry, hurriedly drawing his weapon and holding them back at sword point. He looked over at Joshua who pulled himself up to his full height, the barrel of the pistol still pressed tightly against Winters' head.

"One more step, and I'll blow his brains out. Don't none of you have any pride? Mr. Stapleton was the winner by a long shot, and the Cap'n," he paused momentarily, "the Cap'n acted more like a coward if you asks me."

The men hesitated, mumbling amongst themselves. They were shocked and angry by the natural authority with which the black man had taken control of the situation. They stood down at last, cursing Weller and Stapleton alike. They seemed to sense that these two men meant what they said.

"You'll swing for this, Weller," said Winters through his teeth. "You're done for now! Both of you," he shouted.

"You men throw your weapons down, then line up where I can see you all," ordered Joshua. "You others get the cutter into the water, and look lively there if you have any regards for your Captain's safety. No tricks! And nobody moves! Is that understood?"

"How long do ya think you can hold us all at bay," growled O'Boyle.

"Long enough!" Henry said menacingly while carefully moving from side to side with the tip of his blade stretched out towards the men, until his was able to pick up one of the discarded pistols that lay on the deck, and thrust it into his belt. "And while you are at it O'Boyle, toss that powder horn and bag of pistol balls over here to me. Throw the other weapons over the side. Quickly now." While O'Boyle reluctantly and slowly tossed an assortment of weaponry over the side, several of the hands started to lower the boat into the sea cautiously, their eyes were flashing wildly looking for a way out of this situation.

Henry snapped out to them sharply, "Just a minute! We'll have one of the swivel guns mounted in the bow, the nine pounder goes overboard!"

Henry was aware that he didn't have time to spike all the other guns, it would be too long and complicated, and he couldn't afford to have too many of the men moving around on deck at one time, it was too dangerous. They couldn't control fifty men for much longer even if they did have Winters at the other end of Joshua's pistol.

Nobody moved.

"The nine pounder goes overboard!" Henry repeated as he put the point of his sword under O'Boyle's collar, he could feel the steel tip pressing against the man's throat. Henry chose four men to move the big gun with hand spikes. They shuffled forward, staring at Winters as if to ask his permission.

"Do it," Winters growled reluctantly.

Again the waiting . . . the tension, the sounds of the ship as she groaned and creaked with the sails flapping and blocks rattling until . . . the splash, as tons of metal hit the water as the big gun went over the side. Henry was relieved. The long nine was his biggest fear. He knew that at this point he was relying heavily on the crew's loyalty to their captain. Otherwise they could easily be killed if the tide of seamen turned on him.

Henry spoke abruptly to Mr. Crook, the Master. "I'm sorry," he said to the old man, "but I will have to borrow your services for a short while. We will go below!" Henry steered Crook at sword point down the hatchway.

"I won't resist you, son," said Crook once they were out of earshot of the rest of the crew. "I know where we're going," he said softly as they moved aft towards the stern of the ship. "The tiller ropes?"

"You are a shrewd man, Mr. Crook, and a good one I may add. The tiller ropes it is. I have a sharp edge on my sword, I believe it will do a fine job."

"I'll do it for you, Mr. Stapleton! You can trust me. He pulled out a knife that had been concealed on the inside of his boot. If I was in your position, I'd have done the same. Winters is a fool!"

Henry stared into the old man's eyes for just a second. "Get to work then."

While Henry and the Master were below, Joshua still had his iron grip on the Captain. "Now," said Joshua, nodding to the nearest seaman. "This is how it will be. I want a sail and some hemp and cordage thrown in the cutter, a cask of water, and some food." He cast his eyes around at the men who growled menacingly at him, and made haste to fetch the food and water. With the cutter bobbing up and down alongside the schooner, Joshua started to back himself slowly towards the entry port, the protesting Winters struggling to free himself.

"For pity's sake, Weller. Would you have me bleed to death?" he moaned.

"You'll live," replied Joshua coldly, the pistol held unrelentingly against his temple.

As the last strand of the tiller ropes, (which were twice the size of a man's wrist) parted in two, Henry raced back on deck. The crippled schooner could not pursue them for some time. One last thing to do, he thought, as he rejoined Joshua.

Henry cried out, "Lower the second cutter over the side!"

The *Lady Eleanor* had only two small boats that she carried on deck. He had to make sure the crew didn't take possession of the remaining one. The second boat splashed down into the sea and Henry swiftly cut the rope that held her. She drifted slowly to leeward with her painter trailing alongside. She bobbed quietly across the waves getting smaller and smaller as each white crest broke over her transom and tossed her this way and that.

"Would you leave us without a boat too?" shouted O'Boyle. "We'll see you both to Davey Jones, do yer hear me! You won't get far, and when your food runs out you'll be shark bait. Ha, ha!"

Henry stood with his back to the entry port as Joshua and Winters climbed over the side. He followed quickly after them, and all but fell into the cutter as it heaved up and down on the swell. Joshua shoved Winters down hard in the bottom of the boat.

Henry cast off hurriedly, and called up to the men who were peering over the gunnel in sheer disbelief, as they watched the abduction of their Captain.

"When we are out of range," he yelled up to the men, "You'll get your Captain back, he can swim for it!" Henry grabbed the tiller, and sat down in the stern sheets. Joshua handed him his pistol and he kept it aimed at Winters.

The black man took up the oars and effortlessly began to row away from the *Lady Eleanor*.

"We'll get 'em, lads," Winters shouted back to his crew in a more subdued voice, his face red with anger and embarrassment. "We'll do for them alright, mark my words. I'll see 'em both hanged, if it takes me a lifetime!"

"Shut your mouth, Winters, your not captain on this vessel," growled Joshua between gasps of breath.

The *Lady Eleanor* gradually slipped away to leeward as Joshua rowed hard into the wind. Winters sat low in the boat, smelling of sweat and seawater, and cursing in mumbled tones.

As the gap widened between the ship and the cutter, Winters turned to Henry and snarled out, "Damn your eyes Stapleton! To hell with promises, and a pox on Fitzroy and any man that would try to help an English scum like you."

Joshua paused from rowing for just a split second as he heard these words. His back seemed to stiffen slightly, and Henry realized that this was probably the first time the black man was aware of his true identity. If he had any opinions on the matter he did not show it, and continued rowing like a man in complete control of his feelings.

When the cutter was over a mile away from the schooner and out of the range of the six pounders left on board, Henry ordered Winters to take to the sea. He slipped over the side cursing as he went, and began to strike out for the *Lady Eleanor.*

Henry reasoned that the schooner would hoist all sail as soon as they had repaired their steering, in order to close the gap between her and their captain.

"Joshua, they won't attempt to fire the canons for fear of hitting Winters," Henry stated. "In the time they take to pick him up and get him back on board, we should be able to set some sail on the cutter, and set a course. There is just enough breeze to make our escape. We can sail much closer to the wind than the schooner. We left one good man on board though," said Henry wryly.

"Who's that?"

"Master Crook," Henry replied with a smirk. "He gave me this!" He dug deep in the pocket of his breeches and held up a small pocket compass in a wooden box.

"Well I'll be . . ." said Joshua. "Don't that beat all."

"So, friend Joshua, we have only one direction to sail in, and one possible landfall. And that's the east coast of America, God help us. Let's hope it's commodious in more ways than one!"

# CHAPTER SIX

## THE LONELY OCEAN

That night the sun set on a small boat in the midst of a quiet ocean. The occupants, Henry and Joshua, had long since hauled down their tiny sail in the dying breeze. Both men were exhausted.

Henry now had time to reflect on the dramatic turn of events that surrounded him. Here he was, an English minister impressed into the British Navy at the beginning of last year, and spending most of that time living out perilous times on board the frigate *Dragonfly*. Then his transferal to the *Restitution*, the fire ship incident, the battle that almost killed him, and followed by the long lonely months spent in Boston nurtured under the secretive wing of Richard Fitzroy, a rich Federalist. And now here he was in the early spring of 1813, finally fleeing the decks of a privateer after a dual with its captain who had tried to murder him after the official end of the dual.

At the present, Henry was drifting along with a most unlikely companion, who treated him more like a brother. A tried and true friend indeed! Joshua was a man of giant stature and strength, but deep down the black man harbored a gentle nature. He had signed on with the *Lady Eleanor* to make some prize money. He had never been to sea before. It was hard for a black man to get a job in a predominately white society, especially now that America was at war. The jobs were metered out carefully to preferred individuals only.

Captain Winters had been bent on taking Henry's life from the beginning of the Lady Eleanor's departure from Boston. It was just a matter of time and the right circumstances, and he would have succeeded, had Joshua not stepped in and protected him. This single noble act had cost Joshua his freedom and he was now an outcast, and possibly considered to be a traitor.

Henry couldn't help feel responsible for his well being now that they had in their possession only a few days of food and water, along with the small compass, and with no other means of navigation. A sextant, certainly tide tables or charts would have been invaluable to Henry. But that was just wishful thinking. And Joshua was not a seaman, strong and willing as he was.

Henry knew that they must head west, to the perhaps hostile and unknown American coastline. Their only surety was that it would be somewhere south of Cape Fear, which they had weathered two days ago in the *Lady Eleanor*, before the duel was fought. Henry had kept a constant vigil on their position since they had left Boston, and Mr. Crook had always been happy to share their progress with him since that time, very willing to pass on his years of knowledge to anyone with a keen interest in navigation. The old master had described Cape Fear in great detail. Situated on a large promontory jutting far out into the Atlantic Ocean. The last sea boundary of the southern most border of North Carolina, on the tip of Smith Island near the mouth of the Cape Fear River. According to Mr. Crook it was surrounded by treacherous waters and currents. By Henry's calculations, they must be now literally on the same latitude as Bermuda, owned by Britain and teeming with British men-of-war.

Henry looked across the waves and squinted, as the sun reflected harshly off the surface of the sea as its crimson light was being slowly strangled by oncoming darkness with the last rays fading gracefully into the western sky. Twilight was here.

The evening was uncommonly warm, and the humidity which was heavy in the air soaked through everything onboard the little boat. Their hair stuck to their foreheads giving them both the appearance of wax figures. They leaned back on the gunnel in a propped up position. Henry had his knee resting against the tiller, steering the boat as he occasionally checked his compass bearing. He must stay awake and alert. There was not much comfort for either of them as they stretched their limbs out on the damp timbers of the cutter. They were too tired to row with their sore and aching muscles, so were content to drift idly with the current until morning light.

Few words passed between them, and soon Joshua fell into periods of fitful sleep, and Henry fought back the temptation to shut his own eyes. Every now and again a few waves slopped over the side of the boat, bringing him back to reality, and the cutter was soon completely swallowed up in darkness with not even the light of a moon to illuminate their surroundings. Their only world was this little boat. It was their only hope. The only thing that stood out in the inky blackness, much to Henry's amusement, was Joshua's extraordinarily white teeth, which seemed to jiggle and gleam in the dark like a specter with no body. Henry smiled to himself and closed his aching eyes, it was just the two of them now.

Between bouts of fitful sleep, Henry pondered on what lay before them. Captain Winters' words seemed to ring in his mind, as he had warned of the inhospitable attitude of the southern states towards the English. He wondered too, how Joshua would fare. A black man at large in a slave-holding state. What would become of him? Both were in mortal danger of a different kind. The one could find recompense at a whipping post, and then off to a plantation somewhere. With himself, a more permanent fate. The end of a rope . . . on a lonely gibbet, as an enemy of the United States. He mustn't think of his wife, Elizabeth, and whether he would ever see her again. He was beginning to think that their reunion would not be in this world. He must not dwell on these fears, it would cloud his judgment. He must concentrate on survival. It was his only hope.

The following morning broke with slightly cooler temperatures, but a savage ocean. The wind had slowly strengthened during the early hours, and now it blew so hard that the salt spray was stinging their faces without mercy.

Atlantic rollers were careening down upon the little boat in savage rows, like gray bearded soldiers marching in formation upon a helpless enemy. Stone faced looking waves set with destructive determination as if they felt mirth at having the privilege of overpowering such a small boat. The white spindrift foam was blowing off the top of each wave, and making a good imitation of Old Father Time with his sickle raised on the verge of reaping his watery harvest.

It was impossible now for either Joshua or Henry to row against such a monstrous sea, or to hoist the tiny sail. It would be madness in this weather, and the wind would likely tear the canvas from the small spar in seconds.

They shared a cup of water between them, and ate a few dry ships biscuits each. Their little cache of food was now in great danger of being spoiled by seawater. Joshua tied what was left in a bundle and lashed it under one of the thwarts, the driest place he could think of. Henry secured the only cask of water to the side of the boat, for fear of it breaking loose and being washed overboard. Both men were fully aware that the fresh water was more valuable to them than food, and they must protect it at all costs.

"Looks like a squall coming," Henry said breaking the long silence between them.

"Aye, it does, Mr. Henry," replied Joshua. "We will have to keep our wits about us if we are to survive it."

"In perils of our own countrymen, in perils of the sea," Henry verbalized St. Paul's words out loud, as he stared out at the approaching squall line. "And you don't have to keep calling me, Mr. Henry," he said with a grin.

"You's Mr. Henry to me! And that's alright," Joshua said. "*Mr. Henry,*" he repeated good-humoredly.

Within minutes the squall line hit the little boat with such force that it lifted the vessel up and tossed it on its side, like a discarded toy. As the boat righted itself it was half full of seawater and wallowing badly. The heavy rain lashed down on them without mercy and soaked them through to the skin.

"Help me dismantle the swivel gun, Joshua, it'll sink us like a stone. We have to throw it overboard!"

They stared at each other. In those split seconds they both knew that they would be throwing away their only defense against a sizeable enemy vessel. It took but a minute, and they hardly noticed the splash with the ferociousness of the sea that was pounding them.

"We must bail," yelled Henry.

"What with?" screamed Joshua, his strong voice carried away with the sound of wind and rain, as he desperately fumbled about in the bottom of the boat on his hands and knees. He held up a tin cup with a look of triumph on his face. Then he laughed hysterically, as the rain blinded him and ran down his cheeks.

"I think we need something a little larger than that," Henry yelled, as he too, started to pull at the variety of spars and canvas laying in the bottom of the boat. At last he grabbed a piece of canvas about the size of a hammock. "This'll do," Henry gasped and gave one end to Joshua. They both held two corners each as they allowed it to fill with seawater, and bailed it overboard like a child is tossed in a blanket. Time after time they hauled and bailed, until they could hardly distinguish the sides of the boat as they wrestled against the incoming waves.

"I don't think we can keep this up much longer," gasped Henry as they emptied another twenty gallons over the side.

Joshua looked stunned, as though he saw no reason to continue any longer.

The green seawater continued to swamp the boat, wave after wave, until the two of them were so overcome with exertion that they sprawled out lifelessly. They were up to their waists in water, and their little craft was awash as they clung onto it until their fingers became numb. Whoever had built this boat, Henry thought, must have been a craftsman, for most would have opened up at the seams by now.

The pain they both felt in their muscles was almost unbearable as they drifted in and out of logic. Fatigue overtook them. They hardly cared anymore. Henry knew that they must stay awake, they must continue bailing, it was their only hope.

Another giant wave drowned them with such intensity, that the canvas they were holding was ripped from their clenched fingers as they desperately tried to hang on as it began to disappear over the side of the boat. As stunned as they were, Henry threw himself over the canvas pinning it down bodily before it washed away completely. He was completely underwater while he hung over the side of the boat desperately hoping to retrieve their miserable bailer. He couldn't breathe. His lungs were full of seawater, and he was choking as he yanked the sodden canvas back on board the cutter. He spat out seawater as he fought to get his breath back. Henry was breathing so hard that the veins stood out on his neck and forearms as his strength seemed to ebb away. He stared angrily down at his numb and reddened fingers holding only a small portion of the canvas that remained, for the treacherous sea had torn it in pieces, and left them with no physical means of fighting back.

Henry looked quickly at Joshua who lay there inert staring up at the sky with unseeing eyes. Henry could see that he was still breathing as his chest heaved in and out against his wet shirt.

"Joshua, are you alright? Henry asked. Joshua did not reply, and Henry knew that he no longer cared whether they lived or died. Henry made a weak effort to keep the boat afloat as best he could, but there was no spirit left in him. Maybe the sea would win in the end anyway. Maybe it *was* hopeless?

At about four o'clock that afternoon the storm stopped as suddenly as it had started. The lightning no longer stabbed at them with fiery fingers, and the thunder was an occasional interlude as the sea turned a strange turquoise color, and a watery sun could just be seen behind the scudding clouds.

"Rest, Joshua, I'll bail out the last of the seawater," Henry gasped.

At last with minimal seawater swilling about their feet, the two of them lay resting until the boat bubbled along easily on the ocean's surface. They watched with fascination as slowly the waves returned to normal size, and their horrific battle with the sea began to fade like a forgotten nightmare—only to be replaced with fears of survival.

Thankfully their cask of water was still intact, but their small supply of ship's biscuits was thoroughly soaked, and looked like a pathetic gruel mixture.

"We'd better eat it immediately, it'll spoil soon anyway," Henry said.

Miraculously the tin cup had survived the storm and Henry scooped up the mixture by the cupful, and handed some to his companion.

It was eagerly consumed by Joshua because of the nourishment that it brought, but the seawater taste made it bitter to the palate. "I knew it would come in handy," he cracked a smile as he tapped the side of the cup with his blistered fingers.

"Make the most of it, Joshua. It could be your boots tomorrow!"

Joshua pulled a wry face.

Henry was aware of how weak they both were, for the two of them had already been in the boat for thirty six hours, and their legs were stiff and painful.

Henry carefully scrutinized the horizon his reddened eyes squinting as he did so. There was nothing to see but the lonely gray expanse of ocean. Maybe he should be grateful he thought. There must be plenty of British men-of-war scouring the eastern seaboard. He also noticed that there was not a solitary sea bird to be seen. A sure sign that land was still a long way off.

"At least we can hoist the sail again now, Mr. Henry," said Joshua cheerfully. He stepped the small mast and hoisted the little lug sail. The wind was steady now from the south-east, and the cutter pushed its nose bravely into the swell with the wind on her larboard quarter.

With nothing more to occupy them, Henry lashed the tiller so that the boat would stay on her westerly course

"How far do you think we are from the land," ventured Joshua at last.

Henry shook his head, "No way of telling really," he answered as he rubbed his chin which had a stubbly fresh growth of beard. "We could have drifted for miles in the storm. Land could be a hundred and fifty miles away . . . even more."

The reality of their predicament pressed them both into silence. No food left now whatsoever, and no chance of getting any either, unless they happened upon a fish or two. As they had nothing to fish with it was most unlikely.

Finally Henry spoke, "With a small cutter like this we'll be lucky to make three knots with this soft south-east wind blowing steady like it is, and that doesn't take into consideration our drift to leeward. At this speed . . . it could take days, even weeks to sight land."

"Are you really an Englishman?" asked Joshua, breaking into Henry's conversation suddenly.

"Yes I am! Does it make a difference?"

"Not really! Not anymore! In some ways I am just as much an outcast as you are."

"I am sorry I ruined your chances of prize money, Joshua, by falling unwittingly into league with me, you did yourself no favors."

"What's done is done. I'd do it again most likely," replied Joshua ruefully.

"Do you have a family?" Henry enquired, genuinely feeling sorrow for the man whom fate had laid in his pathway, and who had helped him so much.

"Naw! Just me now. My father died when I was a boy, and my mammy died of typhoid two years ago." He shook his head sorrowfully as the memory of her was obviously so very painful to him.

"I'm sorry. Christian folk I imagine?"

"Yes, sir! Yes indeed," Joshua replied in a very defensive tone.

"I did not mean to bring back painful memories for you. They are at peace now, Joshua, you know."

"I knows that, but I just miss them—that's all. Especially my mammy . . . Winnie was her name." He looked down at his hands, rough with years of toil. "She worked hard for me, Mr. Henry. I only wish I could do the same for her now.

Things were bad for blacks then, even in the North. Most of us were treated like slaves, even though we were not! But even those who were born free like me did not have much work, and no respect from white folks. She always told me there was dignity in hard work, that it was a God given privilege for a man to earn his living. As for the respect . . . well we still gets none of that do we?"

There was just a note of sarcasm in his voice, but Henry did not blame him. In fact he had a great admiration for the man. He doubted if he would still be alive if it had not been for Joshua's intervention after the duel ended with Captain Winters, or in the storm last evening. Alone he would have drowned. "Well if you will excuse the pun, we are both in the same boat now," smiled Henry. He paused leaving Joshua alone with his thoughts for a few moments.

"My family are all in England," he struck up the conversation again. "My wife, Elizabeth, and our three children, Benjamin, Isabella and Flora. I miss them too. Sometimes so much it makes my heart ache, and I pray to God that I will one day be back with them on my farm. Where there is no war. No war on the land anyway. Yet, here I am in an open boat in the Atlantic Ocean going who knows where . . . with you. Rather ironic don't you think?"

"We are all in God's hands, Mr. Henry, regardless of our circumstances. I truly believe that."

"Yes, I can see that you do Joshua. I give you joy of your complete trust, my dear fellow. If I could choose any companion in this plight of ours, I could not have picked a better man than you."

Joshua suddenly clutched Henry's forearm, and pointed over his shoulder. The sudden fear in his eyes made Henry turn his head rapidly.

"A ship!" Henry gasped out loud. He stared in disbelief at the threatening shape of a man-of-war, hull up on the horizon. He chided himself that he was not keeping a better look out.

"What shall we do, Mr. Henry?"

For a short while Henry was overcome with a mixture of real fear and confusion. If the ship was English he would be counted as a deserter, and he'd not see another day on this earth! If she was French; it would probably mean impressment for both of them. Henry's mind reeled in horror at the thought of being in the exact same situation he was in a year ago. After all he had gone through . . . all he had endured. Only this time on an enemy ship. It was too much to bear.

"Let us pray that it is Dutch," he murmured.

Joshua did not answer, his face was an open book of dismay.

"Let's try to outrun it, Joshua," Henry said impulsively. "We can trim the sail! The wind is favorable."

"Whatever you say Mr. Henry. But there ain't much hope is there?"

"We *must* try," Henry's voice crackled in desperation. He felt like a sitting duck as he sat in the sternsheets gripping the tiller. To take no action went against the grain. Joshua hauled in the mainsheet to trim the sail, then stared at the man-of-war, not daring to take his eyes off her for the merest second.

They sailed close hauled for about half an hour as the ship just hung there on the horizon like a vulture, dark and forbidding. They could not see her colors. Most ships were inclined to fly false ones when they thought it prudent. So it was still anyone's guess as to her identity.

"We're sailing hard on the wind, but our course is now south, we're just running parallel with the coastline—going nowhere," Henry said bitterly.

After another hour of this frantic effort to widen the gap, and beating hard to windward all the time, a small white sail appeared in the distance like a seagull unfolding its wings. It seemed to surge towards them at a fast rate. As the vessel got closer it looked larger than their own small cutter.

This is going to be a cat and mouse game, thought Henry, as evening approached rapidly. The ominous looking man-of-war still seemed to lurk on the horizon, a dark onlooker behind a curtain of salt spray. He and Joshua scrutinized the unknown ship's small boat as they carefully watched its progress. It drew nearer and nearer, and got larger by the hour. Soon they could just make out a flag streaming out from the masthead.

The two men held their breath as they watched this drama unfolding before them. Henry felt a strange uneasiness . . . a bizarre feeling inside his gut. His life seemed to be one disappointment after another. Was destiny playing a taunting game with him? He had somehow thought, no *expected* things to improve, as if he was molding his own life and steering his own course. Instead the play was already written, and he but a mere player.

Henry looked at Joshua, despite the fairly cool weather after the storm, beads of perspiration appeared on the black man's forehead, though his jaw was set firm. At this moment the future was very uncertain, and they both knew it.

He glanced down in the bottom of the boat, where the French sword still lay there glinting in the dying rays of the sun.

Henry said at last, "Whatever happens Joshua we must keep our freedom."

Joshua nodded, but said nothing.

"I never thought I would live to say this, but in all my days at sea I never believed I would be grateful for the onset of darkness," exclaimed Henry as the twilight enveloped them like a damp coverlet. "Too bad we weren't able to see what flag they were flying, I'll keep to this southerly course though, regardless."

Another day was ending, and their watery existence in this small boat without food for two days, was beginning to sap every ounce of energy from them. They tried to get relief by drinking several cups of water each, despite the fact that it should have been rationed if it were to last. This unconscious foolhardy act caused them to hope that the water would somehow draw their attention away from the aching feeling of hunger within the pit of their stomachs.

Henry could no longer see their pursuers in the small boat, nor the lumbering man-of-war. Had they lost them?

The wind dropped as darkness fell, which was quite common in that part of the ocean. Lulled into a false sense of security they tried to snatch a little sleep. Their strength was failing, and Henry knew that tomorrow would only make matters worse. Even if they could escape their pursuers, without hope of any food soon they would literally watch their lives ebb away like the tide. It was the responsible decision for him to try to find this strange ship they had spotted. Maybe it was Dutch, or even Portuguese? Perhaps they were trying to run away from their only means of salvation?

As dawn broke they peered steadily out over the sea looking for any signs of the mysterious boat, for the slightest smudge of white that would betray the presence of a sail. For a moment there was nothing but a lumpy sea all around them.

Then through the morning mist, like a phantom lingering in first light, was the shape of a massive warship. It was ship rigged with three masts, and her spars were blackened with tar. She was carrying a cloud of canvas opulently pale and yellow, which pushed her through the waves with intrepid beauty. With her small boat retrieved, the ship was little more than a mile away.

"Quickly, hoist the sail!" shouted Henry, all thoughts of surrender gone from his mind. Their own sail looked like a mere handkerchief in comparison to the man-of-war. With pale faces Henry and Joshua saw the colors streaming from the mizzenmast.

Their worst fears were confirmed. It was the blue, white, and red stripes of the French flag. Even from that distance they could hear French voices chattering excitedly, and Henry could easily see a little cluster of officers on the quarterdeck. Immediately his mind jumped back to a year ago, when the *Dragonfly* had come upon the *Rose of England* in the English Channel. The voices . . . the battle . . . pulling down the French flag with his own hands.

"Oh my Lord, she's a seventy four!" he cried almost falling off the thwart. His quick eye had seen the two rows of gun ports, and what that represented in fire power.

Joshua looked at him somewhat dazed. "What's that?"

"A seventy four!" repeated Henry, impatiently. "Joshua, that's a ship-of-the-line out there."

Joshua stared at him, somehow the meaning of Henry's statement seemed to elude him. In his world, a schooner was the biggest ship he ever saw. The significance was sadly wasted.

That means there are likely to be more than one of them," continued Henry in a matter-of-fact seamanlike fashion. "A ship-of-the-line usually fights in a fleet action. They are the largest rated ship that any nation possesses. Some are even bigger, with 120 guns and three rows of ports."

"Is it a lost cause, Mr. Henry?"

Henry shook his head in disbelief, he couldn't in all honesty look Joshua in the eyes without betraying his own feelings. Before any ideas of trying to escape again engulfed them, they saw a puff of smoke spit out from the ship's bow. Within seconds a large waterspout erupted a few yards in front of them.

"Bow chaser! A shot across the bow is the universal signal to 'heave-to' and surrender . . . or answer to the consequences," Henry said mournfully.

Joshua dropped the tiny sail without any hesitation, and the *Lady Eleanor*'s cutter rolled lifelessly from side to side. The two men sat perfectly still, their shoulders drooped. There was no more fight left in them. Henry's deeply tanned face was pale from hunger and exposure as he stared down at the bottom of the boat. The French sword still lay there, amazingly it had survived the storm, and its very presence taunted their hopes of freedom even more.

Joshua still had the pistol stuck in his belt. He fingered it lightly as if contemplating a last desperate effort, then he let his hand slip down by his side submissively as he realized that his powder was more than wet.

"Ohe du vantardise!" came a cry from the ship.

"What did they say?" asked Joshua.

"They are hailing our boat," replied Henry.

Joshua looked shocked that Henry understood what they were shouting. "Do you speak French then?"

"A little!

*La Dame Eleanoir*, canot," Henry shouted back to the voice from the ship.

They both watched almost unemotionally, as a small boat splashed down over the side of the seventy four. With a haughty faced French midshipman sitting in the stern sheets, the strong arms of the boat's crew rowed silently across the waves to the two waiting men.

# CHAPTER SEVEN

## PRISONERS OF WAR

The dark and smelly orlop deck of the seventy four, was a sharp contrast to the open ocean. Henry and Joshua sat despondently on two upturned casks. Their only comfort was that they had eaten a small quantity of bread given to them by their captors, together with a bucket of water, if you could call it such, for it smelled foul and had a green slime floating on the surface.

"It makes me nervous, Mr. Henry," admitted Joshua. "Hearing them all chattering a lot of nonsense. All I have heard them say is allez! this, and allez! that. Surprised me when you spoke French, Mr. Henry. An educated man you are then?"

"It's a long story. But the French language . . . I have a little," explained Henry as he remembered the French merchants he had often sold many of his sheep to back in Great Yarmouth, England, especially after the drought.

"Enough to keep me out of the Bastille," he smiled faintly. "Have no fear Joshua, I have no doubt that you will be freed to work on board this ship. After all, you are an American citizen. With me, I am afraid it will be different."

"But you are a man of God, don't that count for anything, even in France?"

"Can you trust a nation that back in the late nineties was torturing and killing Roman Catholic priests; destroying Christian artifacts. Every Christian was persecuted. Why they even changed the calendar in their furor to rid the country of anything that was esteemed holy."

Joshua was aghast. "What kind of maniac would do a thing like that?"

"A lawyer if you please! A certain Maximilien Robespierre, the leader of the radical Jacobins."

"Did everyone feel that way?"

"No, thankfully they were in the minority, but the philosophy was catching. The result of people living in fear, no doubt. If you were a Christian with an allegiance to God, or a Royalist, even though they had already guillotined the King and Queen, you were automatically considered an enemy of the Revolution. Therefore guilty of treason."

"Well, bless my soul, it weren't like that here in America!"

"You were fortunate, Joshua, though freedom always comes at a high price, it does not mean that we should lose respect for human life. War is one thing, crazed mob violence and killing, is another. There are ethics, even in warfare. We should fight under our own colors, and wear our own uniforms. In order to tell the world who, and what, we stand for! Strangely enough this is not the first time I have had this kind of conversation." Memories of Edinburgh House and his long conversations with Richard leapt into his conscience. Henry sighed, "As to my own personal fate . . . we shall soon see."

"It will pain me if they splits us up, Mr. Henry. We have been through a lot together. Couldn't you say a few words for me? Tell 'em I am a bad seaman or something. If they keep me on board this ship, I swear I will take the first chance I can to escape, even if it means jumping overboard."

"No, my friend, you will do no such thing! You wouldn't last five minutes, and fifty French marines would shoot you down without mercy. I will do my best Joshua, but it seems in this world our rights seem to matter little to anyone lately. Least of all on board a ship of war."

"Allez! Allez!" cried a French marine as he approached them out of the darkness. His musket was being waved from side to side as he poked and prodded them in the back, herding them towards the companionway steps. "Allez! allez!"

"Here we go again," mumbled Joshua shuffling to his feet and glaring at the guard fiercely. "Ignorant pig! No good French scum!" he sneered at the marine. The Frenchman obviously did not understand a word, but the expression on Joshua's face was easy to read in any language. The marine jabbed his musket at Joshua with a string of curses. Joshua clenched his fists.

"Easy," whispered Henry, sensing the big black man's anger. "There will be time enough for that later."

They groped their way up the steps from the orlop deck where over a thousand feet of anchor cable lay coiled. The smell from it was so strong with all of its encrustations from the sea stuck to it, that it almost made them vomit. They were glad to get up to the berth deck above, where hundreds of sailors slung their hammocks. The smell was not much better up here either. A combination of human perspiration and unwashed clothing hung strongly in the air, together with that waft of garlic, hated by all Englishmen. Up still further they climbed, and all the while the Frenchman was jabbing them in the back and goading them constantly. One set of companionway steps led to another until they finally emerged on the upper gun deck, where with the open gun ports made the air feel almost fresh.

After being so long in the dark, their eyes hurt as they stared at the squares of daylight through the gun ports, where a brilliant sun was shafting pleasantly through each opening. A sharp contrast to when there was a heavy sea running, and these same square ports would be closed tight, forcing men to stumble around with lanterns.

They walked on past the huge cannons lined up, and fastened to their tackles, like fierce black bears kept on a leash. Henry soon realized that their destination was the Captain's cabin, as they were marched unceremoniously under the quarter deck to an ornately decorated door of the commander-in-chief. A French marine stood stiffly at attention outside the cabin, wearing white cross belts over his chest, not unlike his English counterpart, and shouldering his musket with deference.

The two men were mustered brusquely into the Great Cabin, where a carefully groomed man in his mid forties sat behind a desk.

"What is your name?" the Captain addressed Henry curtly.

"What is *your* name, sir?" replied Henry in a very retaliatory voice. He had no intention of being pushed around by an officer in the French Navy, any more than he had initially been dealt with by the British. He had not been pressed into the French service, merely plucked by them from the sea.

The man stiffened at the obvious incivility. "I am Captain Dupont, and this is His Imperial Emperor's ship-of the-line *Phoebe*. I repeat, sir, you will give me your name and a brief account of why you were drifting about in the Atlantic in an open boat. You will notice that I speak in English to protect my motives and maintain secrecy, so again I ask, what is your name, and please verify which ship you are from ?"

"We are from the *Lady Eleanor*, privateer, out of Boston," interrupted Joshua in a matter-of-fact voice. "America is not at war with France, and that's all you need to know. We thanks you for rescuing us."

The French captain jumped out of his chair, walked hastily from behind his desk, pushing past his first lieutenant who was standing with his hands behind his back as he did so, and stood and faced Joshua. Dupont, although small and stocky, struck Joshua viciously in the mouth with the back of his hand. His many jewel studded rings caught Joshua's bottom lip, and brought blood quickly to the surface.

"Who gave you permission to speak, you black ox? You are nothing more than a worthless piece of flotsam. Don't you know that the likes of you speak only when you are spoken to? Or when you are addressed by your betters! They should have drowned you at birth. Is this man your slave?" asked Dupont indignantly, turning to Henry.

"He is a free man! As free as you, or I," said Henry angrily. "You have no right to strike him so. He speaks the truth."

"I can see that you are quite a pair! Birds of a feather no doubt?" said the Captain striding back to his side of the desk. "But you *will* divulge your identities, and your intentions to me immediately, or you will curse the day you were born! Both of you!" Dupont pulled out a lace handkerchief from his pocket and lightly fanned himself with it. "Now," he said composing himself, "shall we begin *again*?" He stared at Henry with his narrow eyes blazing with fury.

Henry was not willing for Joshua to suffer any more abuse, especially on his account. So he accurately gave an account of himself from the time they had sailed from Boston, carefully omitting his true identity as an Englishman. He feared the worst. Something told him that this Frenchman would not be easily deceived, and Henry's particular Norfolk dialect, although not unlike the Bostonian speech, would probably betray him eventually.

"I see," said the Frenchman. "Of course you are English, that much is obvious, and from your sunburned features your story is quite likely true. Now, sir, your name?"

"Henry Stapleton, Monsieur. And this is my good friend Joshua Weller."

"The black man's name is of no consequence to me," snapped Dupont. I'll deal with him later.

"So, you claim to be Monsieur Stapleton, an English privateersman on an American ship. Now, what of this sword?"

the Captain asked, taking Henry's dueling sword down from the bulkhead where it hung, and drew it carefully from its scabbard. Dupont turned the weapon over and over in his hands.

Henry realized that the Captain was totally absorbed by the sword that he had acquired while on board the *Lady Eleanor.*

Dupont laid it carefully down on his desk. The fleur-de-lis engraved on the silver hilt seemed to dance in the sunlight that streamed through the enormous windows that spread across the entire stern of his great ship-of-the-line.

"I am sure, Monsieur, you as an Englishman have enough knowledge to know the sword is French."

Henry nodded in agreement. "A fine sword indeed, it served me well!"

Dupont stiffened at Henry's words. His face was full of suspicion. "You had the very good fortune to come by it, sir, it is quite rare. A superior weapon! One of a kind! In fact I am very familiar with its owner. You see the sword belonged to my late brother, the Marquis of Carrillion." The Captain picked up the weapon and turned it lovingly over in his hands, smoothing the blade with the tips of his fingers as he did so. He was obviously lost in in his own thoughts, and Henry detected a flickering sadness in the Captain's eyes.

"Pray tell me how you came by it, Monsieur Stapleton.?"

"Certainly! It was my weapon of choice when I fought a duel with Captain Winters on board the *Lady Eleanor.* I have no knowledge of the sword's origin."

"I see," said the Captain slowly. "And you make a habit of fighting duels with American captains?

"No, sir! It was an unavoidable situation . . . a matter of honor."

"Ah! Honor, it makes a cruel mistress."

"Indeed, sir. But pardon me for saying, you seem extremely affected by the presence of my sword," said Henry somewhat sympathetically.

"My brother was murdered, Monsieur! In Boston, over a year ago now. He was, how do you say, an Ambassadeur for the

Secretaire d'Etat for our country. He was a very young man, almost *too* young for such an appointment of State. He was cut down in the prime of life. He too was challenged to a duel! He also was a victim of honor. The young are impetuous are they not? Jacques was an excellent swordsman though, trained in the court of France itself. But alas . . . there was foul play." Dupont hesitated, "I need give no further details, only to say that I have pledged my soul to avenge the death of my brother, no matter what steps I may have to take."

"You have my deepest sympathy, sir," Henry said, and although he disliked the man for being his captor, he could not help feel a certain amount of sympathy for him.

Captain Dupont took a deep breath, as if physically taking charge of his emotions. "A fine sword indeed," he said at last. "Of course you will have no further use for it, so I will in due course return it to my family in France. Fate has granted me an unexpected respite, a sweet revenge in a way.

Now, to get back to the matter in hand. You, as an Englishman," he waved his hand lightly in Henry's direction, "are my prisoner. Your black man will join my crew. If he wishes to stay at your side he must profess to be your slave! It's that simple," said Dupont as the former hardness returned in his voice.

"I must protest!" said Henry, his tanned and weathered face flashing with indignation again. "Slavery is abolished in both of our nations."

"Do not be naïve, Monsieur, the trafficking in slaves is illegal indeed, but it is still not against the law to be a slave owner, even in *your* country."

Henry bit his lip, he could not refute the man's words, and he hated to be pushed into a corner, but he said, "At least England did not revoke the emancipated slaves like Napoleon did in Saint Domingue eleven years ago."

"A mere slave rebellion in Haiti does not constitute freedom for all blacks!" Dupont spat back. "Perhaps Napoleon was . . . a little foolish . . . possibly. But that emancipation was instituted by the Revolutionary government. I am a Marquis, an aristocrat, we need blacks to labor in the fields. Are we supposed to do the donkey work ourselves Monsieur? Sheer nonsense! So, I repeat my question. Does this man profess to be your slave?"

Joshua stepped forward, looming over the desk his head brushing the deck beams above as he did so. "I *am* his slave," confessed Joshua defiantly. "He bought me in Boston for . . . for a fair price. I accompanied him as his personal servant on the *Lady Eleanor.* That's right, isn't it, Mr. Henry?" Joshua turned pleadingly towards Henry who could tell by the look in his eyes that this strange friend of his, for some reason known only to himself, wanted to stick by him no matter what the personal cost.

Henry's own silence was enough answer for Dupont, who smiled cynically with satisfaction.

"That is correct," said Henry gravely, deeply touched by Joshua's loyalty. And may God forgive me for this deception, he said under his breath. It was the only way out of a bad situation.

"So, you will both be held captive until such time as we return to France," continued Dupont. "Or, if the opportunity arises, you may be exchanged for some of our own prisoners. I can, of course, also offer you the high privilege of serving our country in His Imperial Emperor's navy. Many of your countrymen have done so you know," he said smugly.

"That is one privilege that I have no intentions of making myself available for," Henry replied, his self-control beginning to slip. The thought of being enslaved in yet another navy overwhelmed him like the angry waves of the ocean.

Without bothering to answer, Dupont had the two men unceremoniously ushered from his cabin, and Henry and Joshua slowly retraced their steps under the watchful eye of the guard. Back down to the orlop deck they found themselves once again sitting on upturned casks.

Both men knew that their time on board the *Phoebe* would not be of a sanguine nature. Living deep in the bowels of a ship-of-the-line was not to be compared with the deck life of any ordinary vessel, where sea breezes blew away the cobwebs of the mind. It was dark, smelly, and damp down here. Rats ran unchecked around them day and night, and living in this limpid dark atmosphere beleaguered them completely. It was a place of depression and impending disease.

The only clue to any sense of normality was the faint sounds from the crowded decks overhead. The dull striking of the ship's bell at the changing of the watch, and hundreds of bare feet running continuously about their duties. They could hear the endless mournful sound of the sea as it bubbled along outside the massive wooden hull, with all the creaks and groans of the ship's timbers as she dutifully threw herself against the weight of the sea.

Every now and again they heard the sound of indiscernible voices, some loud, some faint, but all in a language that was mostly foreign to them. Henry's French was fairly limited, and he and Joshua felt like strangers in another land.

Their life on board the *Phoebe* was becoming monotonous, to say the least. The only diversion was a few handfuls of ships biscuit, riddled with weevils that was brought to them daily, along with a pitcher of stagnant and slimy green drinking water.

Consequently, the two men had many hours in which to talk about their future, but most often the conversation was quite mundane and hopeless. Henry's talks with Joshua were about anything and everything, just to while away the time. But at night, (and Henry only knew it was night because of less activity on the deck above,) his thoughts were engaged in plotting and planning.

During these restless hours, Henry tried to estimate how many knots the ship was making. What kind of weather was being endured? He could tell the latter by the way the ship was shouldering the sea, her steadiness beneath their feet, and in combination with the angle of her heel. Perhaps he could estimate their position? His keen mind was constantly reasoning . . . fathoming as he lay on the hard deck planking. His body ached, but he had to stay alert mentally. He had to be ready when the window of opportunity finally arose. If it arose? He prayed to God it would.

Henry arose and paced about in the darkness, it was hard for him to accept the events that were happening in his life again, seemingly to fulfill no good purpose whatsoever. Yet, he had to stay resolute in his hopes for better circumstances. Henry had no control of his destiny, and he was constantly assessing the possibility of how he and Joshua might escape. For to be on a French ship as an enemy prisoner, was no different than being in France itself. This ship *was* France, and the yard arm was just as close as any guillotine.

Henry regretted his own decision a thousand times over, when on that fateful day in early Spring of last year, he had walked into the Stars and Grapes Inn. The day when a simple act of kindness had turned turtle on him, and resulted in his being pressed into the British Navy. The day that changed his life! So much had happened since then . . . so great a hardship, with death and destruction his constant companion. Now, it seemed more like twenty years ago.

Henry wondered at the progress of the war with America. Most people in England would, no doubt, be looking forward to a swift conclusion. It was a well documented fact that the American Navy was very small, which surely the British could destroy in a matter of weeks with her hundreds of ships at sea, despite their entanglement with the French. He wished he could have the opportunity to question Captain Dupont about such matters, somehow drag out naval intelligence. Henry had a strong feeling that Dupont would also like to speak with him, to probe him about his acquisition of that beautiful French sword, and how it came to be on board the *Lady Eleanor* in the first place? Was the Captain telling the truth? Perhaps the previous owner *was* the murderer of his younger brother.

Could Captain Winters be so vile as to engage in foul play? Henry knew in his heart that the answer was, *yes*. It was more than a distinct possibility. After all Winters had tried to kill him when the duel between them was officially over. If it had not been for Joshua's courageous and timely intervention, he would be a dead man by now. Captain Winters was clearly a man of few scruples. An angry and dangerous man, Henry concluded. One that could not to be trusted under any circumstances. The ethics concerning a duel to determine a person's honor had been in effect for hundreds of years, and strictly adhered to. To the best of Henry's knowledge, even the rules of war were still honored by *gentlemen* of any nationality. Most of the time quarter was expected, and mostly given. The previous owner (if indeed it was Captain Winters, and Henry felt sure it had to be), the man had violated the rules and made the sword an intrigue not only to Dupont, but to Henry at this time. He was involved. How deeply?

Henry thought about Joshua. The big black man would be outlawed in Boston, when, and if, the news of his coming to the aid of an Englishman ever leaked out. It did not bear thinking about. He was most likely doomed to be a fugitive for the rest of his life.

Exhausted Henry threw himself on a pile of straw that was littered with rat droppings. Not even the comfort of a hammock was offered them. He wondered how many other prisoners had slept on this same crude bedding? How many crushed dreams of freedom and their homeland were snuffed out on this refuse heap? Some would be waiting for the cat o' nine tails, others for the halter at the end of a yard arm, run up by their own mess mates. For Henry Stapleton and Joshua Weller, Providence had not yet played her final card. Eventually Henry drifted into a deep sleep.

"Mr. Henry, Mr. Henry," Joshua shook him awake from a dream in which Henry was on his farm in Norfolk walking peacefully through the hayfields with his dog, the big black border collie who was fondly known as George. The dog always followed him everywhere he went. The dream was so lifelike that Henry could still smell the fresh mown hay, pungent and aromatic in his nostrils. As awareness returned, the fresh smell of hay was replaced by the foul odors of the *Phoebe*'s orlop deck. Joshua was leaning over him, his kindly face shining with sweat as he gestured with his thumb towards the guard standing over them both.

"Wake up, we've got company," Joshua whispered.

Henry sat up with a start, struggling to bring his mind back to the present. The guard nudged him to his feet with his musket.

"You are wanted topsides!" the French marine jeered as he shuffled them along.

Stumbling with each step to the pitch and roll of the ship, their limbs felt stiff and painful as they slowly climbed up the steps. Both men smelt foul from their confinement, and their clothes were filthy rags.

This time Dupont received them in his shirtsleeves, and he wrinkled his nose as they entered the cabin. He loosened the white stock that seemed to be too tight for his fat neck, and his plump hands hung limply from the expensive lace cuffs. No more epaulets and gold lace displaying his rank for the moment. It was a much more informal Dupont who sat across the desk from them this time.

Henry felt very aware of his own unkemptness, and especially his unshaven face which was now sporting about an inch of beard. He knew how the French loved to use perfume and toiletries, he was sure Dupont must despise their stale and fetid smell. It had been five weeks since they had been picked up by the *Phoebe*, and the heat and humidity of summer was very evident even behind these wooden walls.

Dupont motioned Henry to be seated. "*You*," he said turning to Joshua. "Stand!" Henry winced inwardly, but Joshua seemed to play his part well, and showed no outward signs of annoyance.

As soon as he was seated, Henry took the bull by the horns and asked how the British were doing in the war. He had to find out, and this may be the only opportunity for him to get any pertinent information from Dupont. The Captain seemed irritated by his outspokenness, but recovered his composure quickly.

"For your information, Monsieur Stapleton, I fear the British have lost face many times since the beginning of this war. Of course I am sure you are quite aware of the loss of their *Guerriere*. The British *Java* too, went by the board. Alas she was French originally, the British had her for only a year before the USS *Constitution* took her. That must have made Whitehall bite their tongues."

"Yes, I had heard of that while I was still in Boston," Henry replied stiffly.

Dupont continued, "Then the ultimate insult thus far that the British Navy has had to endure, is that little American sloop-of-war, the *Wasp* I believe she is called. Fought and destroyed the infamous HMS *Frolic*, a much larger vessel than herself. It occurred last October did it not?" Henry nodded.

"Oh, and we mustn't forget in the same month, the illustrious Stephen Decatur who with the *United States* captured the British *Macedonian*. What a feather in America's cap," Dupont chuckled openly. He was obviously enjoying every moment of his discourse.

"Then a crowning glory for the Americans, their Mr. Madison announced a Navy ball to be held just before Christmas. Of course they were all there. The Congressmen and their wives, all the rich and influential in Washington. Then the introduction of their most noble heroes, 'La grand cinq.' America's five most loyal captains. The honorable Isaac Hull, John Rodgers, the very young, but upcoming, Oliver Hazard Perry, David Porter . . . and of course the popular and handsome, Stephen Decatur, who has come a long way since his fight with the Moors in North Africa."

"All Edward Preble's progeny," Henry interrupted, "and Stephen Decatur was one of his own. Decatur is indeed a legend in New England after he crept into Tripoli and re-took and burned the *Philadelphia* in his little *Intrepid*."

Dupont glared at Henry with distaste at being stopped in the middle of his list of British defeats. He took a pinch of snuff from a small snuff box on the desk, then slowly and precisely sniffed it up both nostrils with a great effort of self-control, and continued by saying, "I understand the banquet was illustrious. The finest of foods . . . despite the blockade," Dupont smiled knowingly.

"Then after the food, and the wine . . . the grandest moment of all. The captured British flag, hauled down from the mast of the *Macedonian*, was ceremoniously carried through the crowd and presented at the feet of Mr. Madison's wife. Dolley, he calls her. They say she clutched it to her heart, then laid it on her lap for the rest of the evening. A somewhat course woman, or so I am told. All frills and ostrich feathers! She wears them apparently to mask her lack of great beauty. Brazen too, they say."

"On the contrary, Captain Dupont," Henry could no longer bear his prating. "I have it on good authority that Dolley Madison is a very modest woman, with impeccable manners. A Quaker, so I am told. Diligent too. They say she is the first one awake at the President's mansion, and goes about in a plain gray dress with a dust cap upon her head, just like one of the servants. A deeply religious woman too, despite her lavish parties and elegant clothing. And I do believe she has her gowns sent from France!"

"Touche," replied Dupont. "Then I suppose we must forgive her," he said smiling. "We must put it down to her unique way of hosting. I believe she had much practice in the President Jefferson era, who was, I am also told, a total bore at his own receptions. Mrs. Madison no doubt has a lively wit to match her blue eyes. So perhaps I am too hasty in my opinions. In any case, enough of this petulant talk," said Captain Dupont abruptly, displaying a great deal of irritation.

"Indulge me with one further question, Captain Dupont," Henry asked carefully. "Have you any news of the British blockade outside of Boston?"

"Come now, I can hardly give away secrets to America's enemies, even if you are in my custody."

"I am not an enemy of America, sir. I have the greatest admiration for her citizens, and what is more I owe my life to many of them. Including Joshua here."

"Yes, yes, your eh . . . servant," Dupont sneered.

Joshua caught Henry's eye and smiled. He stood bracing himself as the ship pitched and rolled under his feet. He was impervious to the Captain's remarks, and true to his promise he remained silent. Joshua was reconciled to the fact that Henry would somehow find a way out of this mess. This Englishman was different, he had sensed it from their first meeting on the *Lady Eleanor*.

"More to the point of this conversation, and the reason I had you brought to this cabin in the first place," Dupont continued with much annoyance. "There is, you might say, a great gulf between us. One which puts me in very difficult straits. You see I have been absent from France for almost a year, in the far east, you understand. Most of the news I acquire is from passing ships. I stopped at Haiti upon my return, in order to replenish my stores, and obtain fresh water. It was there that I was greeted with the disturbing news that France no longer has a strangle hold on Cadiz. Our naval force had besieged that city for over two years. Our ships covered the Bay of Cadiz like bees round a honey pot. But alas, apparently last August that all changed, and it was with a sad countenance that I set sail from Haiti. I had set my course for home, hampered as the *Phoebe* is with marine growth on her hull, when I came across you and your man drifting about in the ocean."

Joshua shifted about on his feet, and Henry heard him breathe deeply. He must be as impatient as he was for Dupont to stop going on and on in his boring voice.

"Yesterday we sighted a vessel outbound from France, it carried the most devastating news of all. Our most honorable Napoleon Bonaparte has suffered a great defeat at the battle of Borodino, just outside of Moscow during the month of September last year. He lost almost 32,000 of his men. He then entered Moscow, but most of the occupants had fled the city trying to burn it as they left. He waited and waited to try to make a treaty of peace with the Russians, before returning to France. All through September, they were short of food, and winter was coming. Then he could wait no longer, he marched his men from Moscow in a retreat pattern. But it was too late. The snow came, and men and guns were left behind buried in the snow and littering the countryside as they marched back to France. Those who he left behind, were tortured and killed by marauding Cossacks.

Alas, news travels so slowly it seems, for here we are only just receiving the bad tidings."

Henry stiffened, his heart beating with suppressed excitement. This was indeed incredible news. A triumph in the long run for England if Bonaparte was defeated. It would bring an end to the war with France. He smiled openly but knew that Dupont had sensed his elation, and was extremely annoyed by it. Angry almost.

"Everything went wrong," continued the Captain glaringly. "Bogged down with snow on their return; lack of food for his troops; stricken with disease. The soldiers dropped like flies. A leader that started with an army of thousands, left with only a few hundred." He shook his head sadly.

"This is a great loss for France. I have to be honest with you Monsieur Stapleton, I hate to speculate . . ." He paused as if he were unwilling to admit to his own thoughts. "I will come to the point, do any of us know how long this war may last? Indeed are we still at war at all?" Dupont leaned back in his chair with a deep sigh, his air of arrogance knocked out of him for a few minutes. He sat there stiff lipped and taut faced.

Henry took advantage and asked, "If England is not at war with France," he said trying desperately to respect the man's feelings, "we should no longer be your prisoners."

"You are my prisoners until we reach France," snapped the Captain testily. "Nothing has changed."

Joshua was a lot less diplomatic than Henry, and stood there with a broad smile upon his face. He was enjoying himself for the first time in weeks.

"This tragic event will, of course, affect England's war with America," Dupont said directing an ice cold look at Joshua. "The full force of the British Navy could now be leveled at America. England will have ships to release from the channel fleet; those who have been on blockade duty for years, and I suspect that many of the English sailors will be sent directly to America without so much as setting foot on their native soil first. From one blockading duty to another," he smiled cynically. "I doubt very much if your *Lady Eleanor* will ever return to her home port of Boston."

Dupont's comment was directed more towards Joshua than Henry.

"But that is all mere speculation on your behalf, Captain Dupont."

"The noose will be tightened, Monsieur Stapleton, will it not? America will pay the price I am afraid, she will most probably be starved into surrender."

For the first time in his entire life, Henry was lost for words. He sat motionless staring stupidly at Dupont. Full of suppressed emotion, and shocked by his own feelings. He realized that he felt sorrow for America, the fledgling nation struggling against the mighty British Empire. He had to admire their courage, their cockiness . . . even their awkwardness. Like the stripling David standing before the mighty giant, with all the odds against him, yet victorious. Yet Henry was an Englishman, and should therefore show loyalty to his King and country. His country he loved, but respect for King George III, well that was a different matter. How could he respect a man like him. It was common knowledge that he was insane. The country had been guided almost totally by his son, George the IV, who had been the Prince Regent for many years, and although sane, was an insatiable gambler and the ruination of his father. Posing as 'a very polished gentleman,' the Prince Regent was also an accomplished blackguard. He was far too tolerant of the Tories, turning a blind eye to the many reforms that England was crying out for. Morally and socially he was as incompetent as his father was insane. They were both the subject of many cruel jokes in the ale houses of England.

There were uprisings against parliament, and it was rumored that the Prince Regent was so unpopular, (this was when Henry was still in England), that the public hurled stones at his carriage when he was attending important matters of State.

How totally unlike America's tenure for politics. Democracy in England was like a wandering spirit, a Will O' The Wisp. The British outwardly pursued it with diligence, but in reality, just like the spars of a ship, it frequently went by the board.

"Stapleton!" Dupont's voice sounded strangely lucid and distant, like a drowning man hearing voices on the surface. "Monsieur Stapleton, I fear your mind has escaped you."

"I beg your pardon, sir," Henry was jolted back to the present by the Captain's tone.

"Now to get back to the prevailing reason I have given you the privilege to return to my cabin," continued Dupont, "you must give me more details about your acquisition of my brother's sword."

"I've already told you, Captain, I have no knowledge of its origin. It was on board the schooner . . . one of many swords. I can tell you no more than that. You cannot get blood out of a stone!"

"Then ask your servant what he knows? I will not speak to the likes of him directly."

"Joshua speaks for himself, Captain!"

Dupont sneered at Joshua, took another pinch of snuff, and focused his gaze on Henry as if Joshua didn't exist in the cabin.

"Mr. Henry has told you the truth, I only know that it was one of the weapons owned by Captain Winters. It was on the ship when I came on board!"

"Your *slave*'s information may, or may not, be accurate," Dupont replied. Perhaps you are the pretender, Monsieur Stapleton? But, nevertheless you and your slave will be detained until we reach France. You are dismissed."

Henry burst out, "Is that all you have to say, Captain? '*We are dismissed*' when you have insulted my integrity and accused me of being a liar!" A fierce battle raged within him as he tried to control his anger.

Henry took a step towards Dupont, but he saw the Captain's hand reach towards the drawer of his desk, where, no doubt, he had a loaded pistol waiting for such a moment as this.

"That's all," rapped out Dupont.

Henry caught sight of Joshua tensing his muscles, he knew the big Black man would stand with him if they were to resist. But this was not the time or the place. The marine sentry guarding the Captain's cabin would shoot them down without a second thought. 'Nothing more than prisoners trying to escape,' would be entered into the Captain's log if they embarked on any foolish notions at this present time.

The usual tide of early summer storms were lashing the east coast of America as the great ship-of-the-line, *Phoebe*, plowed her way through the crashing waves. She was heading east-north-east, back out into the deep Atlantic, and forging into that warm current of water that would slowly carry her across the ocean, and back to France. She was in reasonably good repair because Dupont had riches enough to endow her with the many extras to keep her in good stead. Her hull above the waterline was brightly painted and her rigging freshly tarred. Her gun ports were tightly closed and her guns were neatly secured behind them. She had a perfect compliment of thirty-two pounders on her lower deck, and the normal total of thirty guns on her upper deck. These were tough twenty-four pounders, ready and very able to do maximum damage. She carried twelve pounders on her quarter deck and forecastle. A formidable battleship.

The *Phoebe* was a very seaworthy ship, although a little ostentatious, and Dupont loved and pampered her like a woman. If any of the ship's company spoke evil of her, or cursed her, they would suffer the wrath of his tongue, and more if necessary.

For all her immense size and splendor, the *Phoebe* was struggling in this wicked weather. Gale after gale came slamming through, and lifted up the ship's stern as one gigantic wave after another passed under her counter. She was reefed right down to storm sails. Captain Dupont was very irritated, he had barely made a hundred miles in ten days as the wind drove the *Phoebe* off course.

Deep below in the orlop, Henry and Joshua stumbled about like drunken men, as it became almost impossible to stand upright. It was naturally far worse for the seamen on the weather deck. "All hands aloft," was cried almost continuously as the sailors constantly changed the sails on the two decker, or hurried to repair the blocks and running rigging that were being ripped from their moorings. Everyone was soaked like drowned rats, and their temperaments became just as vicious. What would normally take only thirty minutes, now took hours as they beat the wet and heavy canvas sails into submission with their bare hands. The yards became slippery and dangerous as the men fought to hold on for their lives on the wildly plunging ship.

The evidence of the bad weather, not that they needed any, was the fact that Henry and Joshua were now experiencing the company of numerous sailors. Their groans and moans penetrated the comparative silence normally experienced by those on the orlop deck. Their surgeon, a funny little Frenchman with a droopy mustache, was busy day and night, attending to their cuts and bruises together with a huge quota of broken bones. The patients seemed to be in high spirits though, despite their pain. It did not surprise Henry one scrap. Far better to be down here in the dry, even with a broken limb, than to be dueling with death up there a hundred and twenty feet in the air like mountain goats, with the sea boiling beneath them like a cauldron, and the wind clutching at their clothing to try to tear it from their limbs. These poor souls who had nothing but rags on their backs, old clothing that had been snatched eagerly from the ship's supply of slops, considered themselves fortunate indeed to be down in the wooden bowels of the ship.

Eager to dispel the boredom of life down here below the waterline, Henry and Joshua offered their assistance to the surgeon. Henry's small knowledge of French, along with various gestures was enough for him to understand the instructions given by the little surgeon. The man was grateful enough, and bumbled around like a large bee nodding his head as he went, saying, "Merci, Monsieur, merci!"

Joshua was considered a very likeable fellow indeed by the French sailors, and he spent his time in encouraging the injured sailors, using Henry as an interpreter. The men laughed at his efforts to make himself understood, as he ambled around pointing to things and repeating the words in French as Henry explained them carefully to him. The whole spectacle was made more hilarious to the men, by the sight of the big black man stumbling about as he bent over double to avoid hitting his head on a deck beam above. Mirth was contagious no matter what the language spoken, Henry thought to himself. He admired Joshua for his willingness to make a fool of himself in order to bring good cheer to those in pain. Given different circumstances they might be at each others throats.

As the days wore on, the ship resumed a more regular motion, and the casualties became less frequent. The little Frenchman was happy that he was down to his last three patients, all of which had broken arms. In order to celebrate the dispersion of the violent weather, the surgeon offered them a tot of rum. Henry made his excuse, but thanked the man nevertheless. He preferred to keep a clear head, and he had not tasted rum since he had tried it as a prank when he was a boy. Now as a minister he hated it for all the poverty and deprivation it brought upon the families of drinking men, especially in his area of Norfolk.

Even sailors were destroyed by it. Although fate sometimes allowed them to finally return to their families after serving in the Navy, the habitual tot of daily rum (even though it was watered down) and the six pints of beer per man they drank while on board ship, gave way to a bell striking subconsciously when it came to the time of day when the rum had been issued. The memory of it lay just beneath the surface long after they had left the service, and spent idle times wandering on the beaches while watching the King's ships as they stood in to land, and anchoring with their pendants streaming from the mastheads. Or when they dragged themselves from tavern to tavern in search of a generous officer who may remember that they had served together, and drop a few coins into grateful hands.

Henry could understand sailors needing 'Dutch Courage,' as it was called, just before they had to fight the enemy and look into the teeth of their guns. And definitely it helped kill the pain before, and after the surgeon's knife. Still, the little French surgeon had made the offer out of kindness, for that Henry was thankful.

As the ship returned to her normal routine, and life became meaningless for Henry and Joshua again, the two men tried to determine their current position by the time elapsed since they were taken prisoners, and the fact that the ship was trying to return to France against the strong head winds which would have driven her well off of her original course. The *Phoebe*, a mere pinprick in the Atlantic, must be somewhere between New York and Boston, they finally concluded after much discussion and piecing together of a crude map they had made by laying pieces of straw out on the deck boards. Certainly no further.

One morning a guard was sent to bring them up on deck for a period of fresh air. Henry marveled at Dupont allowing them such a luxury as they walked along the starboard gangway on the main deck, that narrow part of the ship's deck plan that ran along both sides of every battleship, stretching from the quarterdeck to the forecastle. The center part of the ship was open with wooden deck beams that stretched horizontally across to the larboard gangway. The Captain's gig, the jolly boat, and their own small cutter that they had escaped from the *Lady Eleanor* in, were all lashed down on these beams. Snug with canvas covers over them, they were always ready for any order from the Captain.

Henry gazed longingly at their boat as they walked past it. Escape had seemed so close when they had been drifting towards the American shore. He remembered with regret how they had thrown the swivel gun overboard during the storm to lighten their vessel. The gun now lay on the sea bed worthless to anyone, and now their cutter was the property of the French Navy. A tiny prize of war waiting for such a time that it could be swayed up by the bosun's mates with block and tackle, and all at a moments notice at any whim of Captain Dupont. Yet despite their new taste of freedom on this crowded ship-of-the-line, he and Joshua were always only three feet or less from the marine guard that walked behind them, his musket (with bayonet affixed) always at the ready.

Today, Henry noticed it was pleasant weather, and the sun penetrated his thin ragged shirt as he felt its warmth on his back. The wind was fresh, and white wave tops were to be seen everywhere surrounding the ship. Joined in perfect formation they stretched out to a seemingly endless horizon. The wind ruffled his hair and Henry felt almost human for the first time in weeks.

The great ship-of-the-line was flying all possible canvas, even studdingsails, aloft and alow, making her look strangely top heavy. The men on board took little notice of the two prisoners, for like sailors in any navy there was little time for anything but work. To pause long enough to notice them would probably earn them a crack from the starter, which was a short rope with a large knot tied in one end, and wielded by a bosun's mate across the unfortunate sailor's back for neglecting or not concentrating on their work.

Henry saw the Captain standing on the quarterdeck. He was immaculately dressed, with his legs apart and his hands clasped behind his back. His fat little neck and head turning this way and that, like a child's puppet. He caught Henry's eye for a moment, but quickly turned away with a proud look and a lofty jerk of his head, as he strutted off like a peacock the sun glinting on his gold epaulettes, while his beautiful sword hung on his hip as he hastily returned to his cabin. There was no need to wear the sword of course, the ship was not 'at quarters' but Dupont liked to parade himself, he obviously enjoyed his position and all the pomp and ceremony that went with it.

Their guard was just about to usher the two men down the forward hatch when a shrill cry came from the lookout on the foremast cross trees.

"Ohe sur pont, voile!"

"Where away?" cried the bo'sun.

"Two points on the larboard bow," came the reply.

The guard paused for a moment as the curiosity of the whole ship was electrified by the news, and every head was turned to strain their eyes to windward. The lookout was able to see a vessel on the horizon long before the men at deck level could. The guard lingered to wait for the news, this was probably the only highlight of his boring day. But he positioned himself carefully so that his two prisoners were still secured.

Five minutes later, with the Captain dutifully informed, every officer on board was training their telescopes on the approaching ship. Henry and Joshua were equally excited, maybe their destiny was about to change?

"Goulette," yelled the lookout.

"Schooner," Henry said to Joshua translating from the French.

"Americain goulette," informed the lookout.

Henry and Joshua glanced at each other.

The French officers looked somewhat relieved, they were on their way home and did not welcome another battle to endanger their chances of returning safely to their homes and loved ones.

The American schooner was flying along with every stitch of canvas bulging to the wind. "She's got the wind in her teeth," said Henry. "She's positively driving along!"

"She has her tail between her legs if you asks me, Mr. Henry, and more likely that's the reason," replied Joshua pointing.

"She's being pursued by two ships! No three!" Henry corrected himself. He squinted into the sun. "There's the third," he gasped pointing excitedly to three ships, which although hull down were quite distinguishable now to all on board. All five hundred and sixty men on the *Phoebe* watched the chase evolving before them.

"Beat to quarters!" roared the Captain, who had now appeared again on deck after being informed by his lieutenant of the sighting. Dupont pulled at his neck cloth and his face reddened as he stood clutching his sword in an agitated state as he paced up and down.

The pursuers must be British, Henry thought to himself, or why else would the schooner flee so? "They must be putting all their hopes in a French ally for protection," Henry whispered to

Joshua. "Yet they don't know for sure at this distance that the *Phoebe* is French."

"You're right," Joshua replied. "They don't know!"

"They do now!" Henry announced as the tri-colored flag burst thunderously from its lashings as French sailors finished hoisting their colors.

Henry's keen eyesight carefully observed the two vessels at the head of the chase, he needed no telescope. The ships were schooners also, and the rakish cut of their masts were strangely familiar to him. The third was definitely a frigate. Its neat rows of black and white gun ports made her identifiable. Even as he watched, a puff of smoke appeared from the frigate only to be blown away instantly in the brisk wind.

This time Joshua had no need of interpretation. The sharp rapping beat of the drums all around them was understandable even to him.

Suddenly the gap between the hunter and the hunted seemed to widen. All three of the pursuing ships had luffed up into the wind, and Henry could see signals being hoisted from the frigate. The American schooner drove on wildly towards the French ship-of-the-line, she was running for her life. Now that she was closer they could see several shot holes in her mainsail.

"Strike the studding sails Mr. Wigoire," ordered Captain Dupont to his first lieutenant who instantly relayed the order to the bo'sun, and men swarmed up to the fighting tops in response to the twittering calls. The studding sails were quickly heaved down and neatly folded in large squares, secured like great white cushions perched on the platforms of the fighting tops.

The sentry escorting Henry and Joshua, was brought back to earth with the ominous drum beats. He pushed Henry in the back with a painful jab and a surly look. Henry clenched his fists, but submissively he and Joshua allowed themselves to be ushered down once again to the grim orlop deck. This time it was not the quiet place of refuge it once was. The rumbling on the decks above as the big guns were rolled out, sounded like a thousand thunderclaps. The excited voices of the French sailors rang out everywhere as they picked their way around all the unnecessary trappings of the Captain's cabin, which had been hastily brought below by his steward to be stored out of harms way. The Great Cabin, even in a ship of-the-line, was just another gun platform during battle.

The American schooner came smartly up in the lee of the *Phoebe* with all her sails flapping wildly as she spilled her wind. The top of her masts were barely as high as the mainsail yard so tiny was she in comparison with the great ship. A sea of faces lined the bulwarks as Captain Dupont called down with his speaking trumpet.

"Ohe du bateau?"

The man that appeared to be her captain looked slightly confused. He presumably did not understand French. After conferring momentarily with the master he guessed that the *Phoebe* was asking for identification.

"The *Lady Eleanor*, privateer, out of Boston, Massachusetts," came the nervous reply after some hesitation.

"Send your captain on board immediately," snapped Dupont, and waited impatiently as a line was tossed over the side.

"I am the captain!" replied a heavy set man dressed in brown breeches and a deerskin shirt as he clambered up the side It was with great difficulty that the Captain ascended upwards, clumsily falling over the large rounded tumblehome of the *Phoebe*. Strong arms hauled him up the last few feet. The master of the *Lady Eleanor* scrambled up quickly behind him.

Lieutenant Wigoire welcomed them aboard in perfect English, "You will come to the Captain's cabin immediately," he said stiffly. By this time Captain Dupont had hastily retreated to his *place of authority*, and comfort. The captain and the master of the schooner dutifully followed Lieutenant Wigoire into the shadow of the quarterdeck, where the most sanctified place on the ship was located. The Great Cabin.

"Captain Dupont, of His most Imperial Emperor's ship, *Phoebe*," announced Dupont stiffly. "Please be seated."

"At your service, sir! Captain Winters of the *Lady Eleanor*, privateer, and carrying a legitimate letter of marque from the

United States Government," Winters declared in a decisively monotone voice.

Dupont stiffened at the name, his hands suddenly clenching tightly. He sat in momentary silence, just staring at them. Winters and the master exchanged looks, they had noticed the sudden change in Dupont's demeanor.

"This 'ere is Crook, sailing master of my ship."

The Captain stared deeply into the face of Winters, his eyes narrowing with sudden hatred. "It seems as if I have heard of you, Monsieur."

The two men shifted uneasily in their seats.

"I don't think so, Captain," Winters replied nervously, beads of perspiration showing lightly on his forehead.

"You will both await my return," snapped the Captain. "My lieutenant will remain to keep you company," Dupont snapped, as he retreated into his sleeping quarters through a small door on the starboard side of the ship.

"He's a strange fellow," said Crook to Winters in a low growl.

Winters said nothing. The name of this French captain was vaguely familiar to him, he felt visibly shaken.

In the few moments that the Captain was out of their sight, Winters and Crook quickly observed the luxury and extravagance that surrounded them, and even with most of Dupont's fine furniture and trappings already stowed below, the fine carvings in the woodwork of the *Phoebe* was starkly visible, and made the Americans extremely nervous and uncomfortable. They had never witnessed the interior of such a ship before in their whole lives. The great stern benches were upholstered in a striped silk brocade, which ran the whole width of the ship. This was broken by the two elaborately carved doors which led through to the stern gallery, which was like a balcony with a roof, where the Captain could walk out and survey the sea from the rear of the ship in complete privacy. Free from the rain and the elements, where nobody on deck could witness his comings or going. This must be a privilege that was highly pleasing to Dupont.

It reminded Winters of some of the elaborate French houses he had seen in New Orleans. So many Frenchman . . . Frenchman . . . his mind worked furiously as he strove to remember the name, Dupont.

"Do you know this 'ere captain?" Mr. Crook asked suddenly, breaking into Winters' thought pattern.

"Are you questioning my word, Crook? If I say's I don't know 'im . . . then I don't know 'im!"

Crook didn't bother to answer, he knew the Captain to be a liar, and he didn't trust him. He was a dangerous man! God knows what he will get me into this time, he thought as they sat their nervously. He had also noticed that Lieutenant Wigoire was watching them both closely, his face terse and pompous with one hand resting easily on the pistol stuck that was stuck in his belt.

Captain Dupont returned to the cabin carrying a beautiful sword, and carefully laid it on the desk in front of him.

Winters stared at it in sheer disbelief. It was Stapleton's sword. Anger welled up inside of him as he thought of the man. He should have killed Stapleton long before he had challenged *him*. Stapleton, with his fancy swordplay. 'First blood' should have been 'last blood.' He would never forget how Stapleton had humiliated him in front of the men. Dueling . . . his mind continued to race. Dupont . . . that name. It all suddenly flooded back with horror. The events of a year ago on the wharf that night in Boston. Another duel, and the hatred he felt for the young Frenchman with the dark brown eyes. His cries for mercy. The feel of his sword as he felt it slip into the young man's body, the blood soaking through the exquisite clothes. The look in his eyes as he died without a sound from his lips. The valuable sword he had picked up when he thought nobody was looking, when everyone was crowding around the youth. The cries of, "Foul Play," coming from the mob as he hurried into the darkness.

This Captain must be a relative of the boy, Winters conceived. Not the father though, this man was too young. A brother perhaps?

Winters was beginning to sweat more profusely now. His fingers ran around his collar as he tried to loosen it. His eyes darted this way and that like a caged animal looking for a way of escape. He must know who I am Winters thought. The look in Captain Dupont's eyes, his comment about my name. The appearance of hatred burning into him right now like a red hot iron as Dupont stared at him across the desk. Winters wished he had surrendered to the British. Although he despised them too, they were more likely to have a sense of justice than this Frenchman. Now it was too late.

Mr. Crook, the Master sensed Winter's fear, but was looking naively confused at the tension building in the cabin.

"I believe you knew my brother," Dupont said coolly, wringing a lace handkerchief in his hands as if to suppress his emotion."

"I . . ." Winters shut his mouth tightly, unable to speak. Not wishing to incriminate himself by anything he might, or might not, say.

"I am waiting, Monsieur," said the Captain coldly, his steely eyes seemed to look right through Winters, who was desperately trying to keep his hands from trembling as he shifted about uneasily in his chair.

"It was a fair fight Captain, I swear it," Winters blurted out fearfully.

"That is not what I heard," continued the Captain. "Murder is what I heard, Mr. Winters. Cold blooded murder, by a cold blooded killer! Jacques was hardly more than a boy, and you were supposed to be a man of honor. Do the Americans lack honor Mr. Winters? Or are you the fly in the ointment? Answer me man! Do you deny it? Do you deny you killed my brother Jacques, or will you add lies to your crimes?"

Dupont waited tensely for Winters to answer. He could barely contain his emotion. His mind was telling him to snatch up the sword that lay before him and run Winters through with it, but he kept his self control. This man's punishment was to be reserved for the coward that he was. Mr. Winters would have his day, and very soon.

"Do you have anything further to say, Monsieur?" the Captain said collectedly.

"Like I told you before, it was a fair fight! We had Seconds, ask *them*. We followed all the rules. I gave the lad every opportunity . . . he knew the risks. By God he was the one that challenged me. He was arrogant, stiffed necked, always coming it the Toff. You Frenchies all think you are high and mighty. I've told you once, and I'll tell you again. It was a fair fight!" Winters was beginning to show signs of retaliation despite the situation he was in. He was losing his self-control.

Dupont leapt to his feet, grabbed the sword and lunged forward across his desk holding the tip of the blade to Winters' throat. The Captain didn't utter a word, he just stared at Winters with his eyes blazing.

All this time, as if unaware of his own personal danger, Crook, the Master of the *Lady Eleanor* was staring at Winters in utter disbelief. He could hardly believe his ears or eyes. His loyalty was now stretched to the limits. He wanted no part in murder whether his Captain was guilty or innocent. He could see by the expression on this French captain's face that he was bent on revenge of some kind.

Dupont slid round the desk, still with the point of the sword touching Winter's adam's apple. Winters leapt from his chair, and automatically took a step backwards until he felt the cabin wall pressing against his back.

Dupont slowly lowered his weapon and said, "Mr. Winters, you personally, will be held in my custody until I decide what to do with you. As for your schooner, you have two choices! She can make a run for it, minus her captain, although I doubt if the two British schooners would take very long to catch up with her. Then it would be certain death for most of the crew. Or, she can stand and fight alongside us. She would be a handy vessel for me to have in battle, considering the lack of agility of my ship-of-the-line."

Winters rubbed his throat considering the possibilities. "And if you win this battle against the British?" he retorted.

"France is not at war with America, Mr. Winters, so I cannot consider your ship a prize. If we win, you shall have one of their schooners as *your* prize. I daresay your navy would appreciate another vessel to fight the British. They should pay you handsomely for her." Dupont hated to discuss business with Winters in any shape or form, he only wanted to seek revenge for this murderer of his brother, and to hell with the protocol and politics of war.

"Which is it to be then, Mr. Winters? Don't take all day, time is running out for you."

"It's not much of a choice really is it?" answered Winters begrudgingly. "I'll stand by you against the English, Captain. But only if you forgets this business with your brother. I want no retaliation against me after the battle is won. Bygones is bygones so to speak, and I'll sail off with me prize without having to look over my shoulder, if you get my meaning," he added slyly.

Dupont's face contorted with emotion, as he clenched his fists. His heart was engaged in a deadly conflict with his mind. What good was revenge if he lost the encounter with the British? The *Lady Eleanor* would tip the balance of fire power in his favor. Not to mention her speed, which would have the effect of a dog baiting a bear. One British frigate of 38 guns plus two very nimble schooners against one ship-of-the-line. The situation would be risky. Perhaps he could avenge Jacques death some other time . . . a duel perhaps? He moistened his lips with his tongue as he realized what possible promotion would be in store for him if he were successful in bringing a powerful British frigate under his lee as a prize, plus one of her schooners. For the honor of France, and perhaps his brother too.

A tap on the door interrupted his thoughts. A very thin midshipman entered with his hat under his arm. "Quartermaster's compliments, sir, and to tell you the British frigate is three miles off now, and the two schooners have stood off north and south of us. Sir, if you please, the Bo'sun thinks he recognizes the frigate. It is *La Libellule*, sir."

"Ah! the *Dragonfly*, yes I know of her . . . and her Captain. Tell the master I will be on deck momentarily."

"Yes, sir."

Turning to Winters Dupont said, "I agree to your proposition with much reluctance, if I may say so."

"I has your word on it then?" Winters said in an almost pleading voice.

"You have my word, Mr. Winters," Dupont said bitterly. "Your sailing master will return to your schooner, but you will be detained! Now, if you will excuse me," he uttered with a note of sarcasm. "I have a battle to fight, and honor to defend!"

Wigoire escorted Winters from the cabin, and Crook making a hurried bow, fled this French fortress. He never gave Winters a second glance.

# CHAPTER EIGHT

## BROADSIDE FOR BROADSIDE

Franklyn Weatherby, Captain of His Majesty's frigate, *Dragonfly*, was leaning on the quarterdeck taffrail watching the French ship-of-the-line. He could see her plainly enough now without the use of his telescope. Henry Stapleton would have identified her long ago. He had amazing eyesight. Strange how Weatherby thought of Stapleton at this moment. He shook himself mentally. Too many of his crew had lost their lives since last summer. Stapleton was just one more victim of the press gang. Thousands of them had gone over the side since Napoleon had set his sights on invading England. There was no sentiment in war. That was the way of the service. No remorse for shipmates killed in action. A captain had to stay detached. That was the loneliness of command.

Weatherby observed the French ship once again, she had rigged with fighting sails, topsails and topgallants flying nicely in the quartering breeze. Weatherby could not believe his good fortune. The ship was a third rate, which meant she had less than eighty guns on her two gun decks. The ships were very well matched, and after a year of tedious blockade duty he was now on the threshold of justifying his existence in these waters. A smile spread slowly over his broad Yorkshire face. The trivial pursuit of the American schooner had yielded a much larger quarry.

He had sent *Starlight* and *Vixen* to get as close to the big French ship as possible, but not to fire until he gave the order. Which meant that midshipman Baines was frantically laying out the colorful signal flags around his feet.

Weatherby felt very self-confident. He had not let gunnery practice lapse since leaving Halifax last spring. Was it really over a year ago? he asked himself. Most British officers were surprised that the war with America had lasted this long. They thought that the American navy would quickly be laid to rest. They had been wrong. Still his own men were ready for anything. He smiled as he looked down on them from the quarterdeck rail.

Lieutenants Fox and Bradley were talking on the leeward side of the quarterdeck, giving him the courtesy of his side of the ship undisturbed. The fresh breeze on his cheek, the familiar wake chuckling under the transom leaving a pathway in the sea, and with the prospects of battle in his heart, Weatherby felt exhilarated. It was time to make decisions.

"We shall beat to quarters!" he cried with a loud voice.

The sharp beat of the drum echoed through the timbers as the whole ship became alive with movement. She would soon be in her natural element, the purpose that she had been built for. War at sea! This would not be mere target practice, oh, no! Weatherby conjectured. The *Dragonfly*'s guns would soon be hot with constant use. The Black Dogs, as the crew affectionately called them, would soon be hurling out their mighty weight of metal against the enemy. Weatherby let his thoughts drift back to other engagements from the past, as he listened to the sound of the drum. How many battles had it introduced in his career? How many of the brave had fallen? He decided not to let this melancholy thought intrude upon his good humor, and assured himself of victory. He prayed the losses would not be too great . . . this time. Something that a frigate captain always prayed for. He had the windward position, and this was to his advantage.

The American schooner was beating towards the *Vixen* at a flat out rate, trying to intercept her before she could close on the ship-of-the-line. It looked like she would be the first of his ships to engage the enemy. Weatherby hoped her twelve six pounders would be up to the job. He remembered how this American schooner had got the upper hand of the *Vixen* last time, (though he had not witnessed the battle himself). There would not be another defeat.

"They are equally matched sir," said Bradley at his elbow, as if reading his thoughts.

"The *Vixen* is heavier, though the American is faster," Weatherby said. "But why has the Yankee decided to throw in her lot with the Frenchman? I had well expected her to make a run for it."

"I don't know, sir! It's rather strange to be sure."

Weatherby said, "They're leaving the ship-of-the-line somewhat unguarded. They will be divided now. A bad move."

"Gives us a better chance though, sir," Bradley said enthusiastically.

"Aye, Mr. Bradley, a chance is all we need."

As the *Dragonfly* drew closer, tension grew throughout the ship. The men on the gun decks were stripped to the waist in readiness for the hot work ahead of them. They had all tied handkerchiefs around their heads to keep the sweat from running down into their eyes, and spoiling their aim. It was also a flimsy attempt to deaden the noise when the guns eventually fired.

"They look like a crew of pirates instead of sailors in the British Navy," commented Mr. Plumb, the Sailing Master. "Still this will be harder than pirate's work, hotter too, mark my words."

"They'll soon be climbing up over the Frenchman's bulwarks brandishing their cutlasses, while yelling and screaming like demented beings," replied Weatherby. "Or else standing on the deck of the *Dragonfly* repelling French boarders. I hope it's the former, Mr. Plumb."

"Yes indeed, sir."

A hush grew over the ship, it would be a another mile before they were within range of the *Phoebe*, yet as the men watched through the gun ports, every nerve was tensed as the big ship-of-the-line formidable as she was became more distinguishable across the waves with every passing second.

Lieutenants Fox and Bradley were standing by the gun crews, their swords drawn in readiness as a signal for the men to start firing. No verbal command would be heard once the big guns started to fire. Midshipmen Christian Clark and Freddie Baines, were also assigned to a gun each. Their young fresh pimply faces drawn and pinched with worry lines as they waited for the command to fire!

Christian was trying to rally and encourage the men as they stood poised for action. Weatherby could hear him speaking softly to the gun captain and his crew. Clark was only a boy, but old enough to know that the crew were thinking of their wives and loved ones at home. This quiet moment may very well be the last thoughts they have on this earth.

The men liked Christian. He was a good honest lad, always optimistic in the face of danger, considering midshipmen were just as easily struck down by a flying splinter or the prime target of a French marksman who had them in his sights. More so since they wore the uniform of an officer. But Clark never showed any fear in front of them, and they respected him for it.

Suddenly the quietness of wind and water was shattered by a full broadside from the ship-of-the-line. Hot orange tongues of fire flashed out from the ship's side in astonishing unison, belching out mayhem and destruction. The *Dragonfly* was now in range of her guns. Every thirty two pounder, twenty fours, and twelve pound shot fired as one. Even two miles away the billowing smoke was awesome as it was swept along the wave tops like a living emetic substance completely obliterating the shape and size of the *Phoebe*. The thirty two pound balls fell short, but sent up a virtual waterfall cascading over the larboard bow of the *Dragonfly* as the spent balls from the *Phoebe's* starboard battery plunged into the ocean. Two of the twenty fours found their way into the hull of the *Dragonfly*, somewhere between wind and water leaving deep pock marks as the only visual evidence of the impact. Weatherby knew it would be a different story below decks.

"Engage the enemy!" commanded Captain Weatherby. The signal flags broke loose from the masthead of the *Dragonfly*, relaying the command to the schooner, *Vixen*, who was on a broad reach, and closing with the *Lady Eleanor*. Upon seeing Weatherby's signals, *Vixen* turned her helm to larboard and began to run with the wind on the same course as the American schooner, laying parallel with her.

At the same time Weatherby sent a signal to the schooner, *Starlight*, to sail across the *Phoebe's* wake. If Captain Brooks could rake the big ship's vulnerable stern with his handy little six pounders, *Starlight* could do considerable damage to the ship-of-the-line.

Mr. Crook, the Master on the American schooner was a little nervous. The *Phoebe's* second lieutenant, obeying orders from Captain Dupont, had come on board to take command of the ship, and Crook was very uncomfortable knowing that his schooner, for all intents and purposes, was under the command of the French navy, and not his own country's flag. The men were scowling, and the Master knew that they did not have their heart in the matter, especially as their Captain was a prisoner of the French somewhere on board the ship-of-the-line. They deeply resented the fact, for many of them had been in favor of making a run for it. It was all Crook could do to persuade them against mutiny, regardless of the promise of Winter's eventual release, and the possibility of prize money from the sale of an English schooner.

Yankee pride was very important to most of them. It went against the grain to look up and see the French flag flying at their masthead instead of their own handsome stars and stripes. It weren't natural.

Noise and smoke thundered across from the *Vixen*, who had fired her guns at almost the same moment the *Lady Eleanor* had fired hers. There seemed to Captain Weatherby little damage on either side, but the small six pounders were easy and quick to reload, and within a minute both ships were loading and firing at each other like deadly scorpions.

Weatherby turned his attention now to firing his first broadside. He was purposely sailing on a broad reach, with the wind fresh and steady on his larboard quarter. He estimated that at this angle the *Dragonfly* would present less of a target than if he sailed directly down wind. And he could still bring his guns to bear.

"Prepare to fire! Fire!" shouted Weatherby at the top of his lungs.

Lieutenant Fox on the larboard battery brought down his sword with a vengeance, and the *Dragonfly* reeled under the broadside as her fourteen guns on the larboard side recoiled across the deck. As the thick acrid smelling smoke started to clear and rolled away down wind, Mr. Plumb shouted in Weatherby's ear, "The *Vixen*'s been badly hit, sir."

"So Soon?" Weatherby saw to his dismay that the *Vixen* seemed to be in deep trouble. Her headsails had been shot away. A victim of that deadly first broadside from the American ship. Her jibs and stays were drooped over the bow of the ship in a mass of tangled ropes and canvas, together with most of her foremast, and all of it floating on the surface of the sea. Now she had lost all headway and was dead in the water.

"*Vixen*'s a sitting duck!" Weatherby groaned out loud to the sailing master.

"I'm afraid you're right, sir. She's unable to answer to her helm. Look, the wind and waves are beginning to turn her slowly and persuasively up into the wind. Her mainsail's flapping and cracking like a whip!"

"See that! The American has gone about, Mr. Plumb, her crew has tacked back to position themselves to fire their portside guns. The *Vixen* will have to fight for her life! God save us if they board her. I'm afraid she has failed to live up to her namesake this time, she's no longer the sly fox sneaking in for the kill," Weatherby sighed deeply. "She's more like a terrified chicken in a hen house waiting for her fate, poor blighters!"

Even the crew of the *Dragonfly* could see that the American schooner would be upon *one of their own* in minutes, the *Vixen's* Captain needed every man on board at the starboard guns to continue firing, and ready, if needs be, to repel American boarders.

Unlike the *Dragonfly*, all the *Vixen's* guns were mounted on the spar deck where the wind whisked the smoke away immediately after the guns were fired. This helped the gunners to be kept cooler by the sea breezes. On the negative side there were no gun ports to crouch behind and seek protection. On the gun deck of a frigate, the walls were painted red to disguise the blood that would ultimately be splattered about as men died, either by the enemy's weight of metal, or from a splinter of wood from their own ship scything through their soft flesh. Even the guns that they served . . . their own guns, could turn and bite them viciously if they broke loose from their breechings. It was a horrible end to a man's life, yet there was always another to take his place to feed the never ending hunger of the canon.

While the battle was raging, Winters was detained in a small cabin leading off from the wardroom. He felt angry and frustrated. Dupont had tricked him out of his ship, and he felt a great repulsion for the man. What if the French lost? He'd not only lose his ship, but he would end up a prisoner of the British. With all the gunfire going on would there be anything left of the *Lady Eleanor*? Now that he had more time to reflect on the events of the past few hours, Winters had come to the startling conclusion that Henry Stapleton and Joshua Weller, were almost certainly somewhere on board this ship. They were still alive. The sea had not got them after all. For there could be no doubt that Dupont had relieved Stapleton from ownership of the sword. He must have plucked them both from the ocean. They were probably being held as prisoners down below. Weller may have joined the French and was up on deck fighting, but he doubted it. The way Weller protected Stapleton . . . Stapleton, the thought of him made him sick with hatred as he strode to the door of the small cabin and shook it furiously. It was well and truly locked, secured with a bar of wood that had been inserted between two metal brackets on the outside, making it doubly protected. He smashed his fist against the solid oak cursing loudly, but the door was as strong as the very ship itself.

Eventually Winters sat down on the cot, and listened to all the sounds of a ship-of-the-line at battle stations. A whiff of powder began to curl under the crack of the door and stifled him. He heard the loud shouts of the French crew, and the rumbling of the big guns across the deck planking after they had been fired, as they were re-loaded and hauled back into position. It was all deafening to his ears. He felt like an animal in a trap, unable to move or escape. Outside this door a battle was raging with the cursed British. And there was one Englishman in particular that he would like to annihilate, to wipe off the face of the earth forever. Winters started to convulse with anger.

Captain Dupont had immediately recalled the *Lady Eleanor* as soon as he realized that the *Vixen* was in irons, and of very little threat to him. The *Lady Eleanor* dutifully tacked back towards the big two decker, and her instated French lieutenant was debating whether to sail between the *Phoebe* and the *Dragonfly*, (who were very close together now) or set a course to sail behind the ship-of-the-line on her larboard side. Thus putting the big ship between him and the *Dragonfly*. Safe for a short time under the *Phoebe*'s lee.

The French lieutenant quickly decided on the latter course of action. He would try to come around the *Phoebe*'s stern and engage the other British schooner.

The *Phoebe* was concentrating all her fire power on *La Libellule*, the hated *Dragonfly*. She wasted no shot on the schooners, they would be mincemeat once he had dealt with the frigate. Wave upon wave of iron hurtled across the waters in the direction of the British frigate, and just as viciously *La Libellule* returned broadside for broadside until the smoke from both ships was like volcanic dust hanging just above the surface of the water, making it difficult for the gunners to fire accurately.

Instinctively the Dragonflys just kept on firing back. They all knew that the enemy was out there in that thick bank of smoke. Men were coughing and choking as the bitterness entered their throats and lungs.

Wreckage on both ships lay scattered on their decks, while fallen spars lay in the water between the two ships like floating forests. The piercing screams of the wounded could be heard everywhere, and even more frantically the cries from those in the water who were clinging desperately to any piece of flotsam they could hold on to, for most seaman couldn't swim and they knew that their chances for survival or receiving medical attention now was almost impossible.

Those wounded on deck were only slightly more fortunate, they were being carried below where the surgeon's bone saw and assortment of knives awaited them. The unfortunate souls struggling in the sea would die more quickly.

"Prepare a boarding party," cried Wetherby to Lieutenant Fox. "The *Dragonfly* can't take much more of this," he said despairingly. "We must bring an end to this misery soon!"

"Yes, sir." Fox yelled at the Bosun, who was already anticipating the order and was ready to pipe the orders that would send the Bosun's mates amongst the men where they would browbeat the crew into obeying the Captain's orders.

The two ships were so close now that any minute their yards would touch, and they would be tangled in a deadly embrace. It would be the best thing, Weatherby reasoned. They had been firing the big guns at point blank range for the past fifteen minutes, now some of his Royal Marines would be able to crawl out on the yards from the fighting tops, and swing down easily onto the main deck of the ship-of-the-line. He watched with pride as midshipmen Clark and Baines were mustering their men around them, who had all seized boarding pikes, and stuffed pistols in their belts, two apiece. Each man a cutlass swinging on his hip.

"Steady as she goes, Mr. Plumb, I intend to ram the Frenchman," Weatherby said excitedly.

"Aye, aye, sir."

"Do your best to put our bowsprit under theirs, that should hold us together until we can board her."

"Yes, sir," said Plumb obediently.

"And Mr. Plumb . . ." their eyes met for a second. "If I should fall today don't surrender. Remember that!"

Plumb nodded. They had sailed together long enough for him to understand exactly what Wetherby meant. Amidst the seriousness of the moment, Plumb had to smile to himself. The Captain had said the very same words at least a dozen times before, in previous battles. The most amusing thing about the conversation was, that he as the sailing master, being always at the helm, made *himself* the 'prime target' of the day, in *any* battle, on *any* ocean. Smite the helmsman and perhaps the ship would be out of control for just a few minutes before another man could step behind the wheel and take his place. Whereas there was always another officer to take command of the ship should a marksman gun down any figure who bore a gold epaulette on his shoulder. Still these things had to be discussed in advance, and Plumb was more than accustomed to it by now.

"Pity the *Viceroy* had to go back to Halifax for repairs, sir. She would have tipped the balance."

"She certainly would, Mr. Plumb."

"The Restitution and the Providence, sir. Any chance they . . . ?"

"At least forty five miles east of us . . . not enough time . . . we'll have to make the best of it."

"Just us, and the *Starlight* left then, sir. We've been in worse straights!"

"Indeed we have, Mr. Plumb."

Young Captain Brooks commanding the British, *Starlight*, saw the American schooner plunging ahead with spray bursting over her foredeck as she slid down the larboard side of the *Phoebe*. With the smoke from the big ship's guns, she was now rendered invisible to his concentrated observation of her, obliterated by the immense silhouette of the ship-of-the-line. He guessed at once that the American schooner had hoped to surprise and intercept him as the *Starlight* attempted to sail across the stern of the *Phoebe*. He must get a broadside off in a desperate attempt to cripple the ship-of-the-line before he met up with the Yankee. How close was the *Lady Eleanor* sailing to the big ship? He rapidly tried to gauge her speed and distance. He knew he ran the risk of an almost head on collision with the American schooner because of this startling tactical move of theirs. It would be hard to make an accurate estimation of her speed and progress while the American was out of sight.

The wind was hard on *Starlight*'s larboard beam, but the *Lady Eleanor* must surely be heading almost into the wind, close hauled, Brooks concluded. And the only option open to the American would be to go about on a starboard tack. Anything else would be suicide. Logically she would sail as close to the *Phoebe* as she could for maximum protection, but by the time her bow was level with the *Phoebe*'s stern then she would have to strike off on her new tack. Brooks thought when this happened he would have a clean shot at her. But first he must give his full concentration on his attack on the *Phoebe*.

"What's our speed?" Brooks said turning to the master.

"We must be making nine knots, sir."

"Steady as she goes then," he snapped at the *Starlight*'s master.

"Aye, aye sir."

Captain Brooks realized that once he had opened fire on the *Phoebe*, he may just have time to reload and fire another broadside into the American, if she sailed right across his bow, as he hoped.

*Starlight*'s little six pounders were aimed high, as she heeled sharply over on a beam reach. The men at the guns were standing at the ready, with their handspikes poised to lever the guns round when the gun captains had estimated the range.

The *Starlight*'s senior gun captain was an old hand at the game. He stood there with a well worn quadrant in his hand. He had already estimated the range of his shots by roughly calculating the height of the enemy's masts and by observing the heel of their own ship, he could thus estimate the angle and range of his guns. He was a cool and collected character . . . he knew his job well.

Brooks was paying strict attention to Captain Weatherby's previous signals, every shot was to be aimed below the waterline. Indeed that was all he could expect anyway, with his small ship heeling hard over they could hardly be expected to make a sweep of the quarterdeck. In comparison to the ship-of-the-line they must look like a pond yacht. Brooks was hopeful nevertheless. The main challenge he had to deal with was the *Phoebe*'s stern chasers. The two upper deck chasers would not be able to fire because of the sharp angle down to the little schooner. Now the lower deck guns . . . that was a different story. If they could get their aim right? Even one of those twenty four pound balls could slice the *Starlight* in half at this close range, cut her through like a piece of French bread.

Musket fire from the quarterdeck would be another problem. The Frogs would be lining the taffrail with their muskets at their shoulders, ready to unleash their deadly barrage. His own marines would try to pick off as many of the enemy as they could. Every shot must count.

Captain Brooks looked keenly at his men, who showed no outward signs of fear, but tension was etched on their faces. He knew that once the French opened fire he could rely on them to stay focused on what they were doing, they were trained for such situations, as ready as they could be. Ready to die if necessary.

The Captain saw that the gun crews were trying hard to keep their powder dry, as huge crashing waves came sweeping over the bow and foamed wildly along the deck with a fierce hissing sound. The men's bare feet were wet as they stood there waiting for Brooks to give the command to fire. All the sand that had been spread previously on the decks by the ship's boys in order to stop them slipping, had long been washed away. They would have to trust in their own ability to keep a footing when the guns began to fire.

A great cry was suddenly heard from the hordes of Frenchmen lining the bulwarks of the *Phoebe*. They hung over the edge cheering wildly as the *Lady Eleanor* rushed past them on their intercepting course with the *Starlight*.

"Viva la Americaines," they yelled with great gusto as they raised their muskets high above their heads in a rag tag salute. In turn the Americans raised their hats, and gave a loud responding cheer, their faces were lit triumphantly as they raced past. They looked exhilarated, and confident of victory.

"Fire!" Captain Brooks shouted to the gun crews, and the *Starlight*'s little six pounders flashed out with a thunderous roar as she fired hard into the stern of the ship-of-the-line. It seemed as if the British schooner reeled on her beam ends as the guns lurched backwards, and the gun crews expertly stepped aside to let the guns recoil on their lashings. The spongers were back on the guns in seconds, shoving their long rods with wet rags bound to the tip of each one, quickly down the mouth of the cannon to put out any sparks from the previous cartridge, making them ready to reload with shot.

"Run out! Fire!" someone screamed from within the cloak of black enveloping smoke.

The powder boys below decks were nursing their wooden boxes like a child hugging a puppy. Each square box with its wooden lid held four cartridges which looked like miniature sacks of flour, instead of the deadly gunpowder bagged up in a very light sacking. They were just the right size to fit down the muzzle of a cannon. When the gunner's mate had issued out the cartridges, carefully handing them over for fear of any spark that may touch off the whole magazine, the boys came running up from down below yelling, "Make way for powder! Make way for powder!" as loud as their young lungs could utter. As soon as the boys had delivered their precious cargoes to the appropriate guns, they raced below to the ship's magazine to collect more; leaping over any obstacles lying on deck as only the young can do as nimbly, and then diving down the hatchway like apes from the Rock of Gibralter. No wonder they called these youngsters powder monkeys.

Most of these thin and scrawny youths were urchins whisked off the streets of some coastal town back in England, and were far more suitable for the job than a full grown man.

Sometimes when the ship was not in action, the sailors would chase the boys down the hatchways, just for the fun of it. They swore it kept the boys on their toes as well as putting the fear of God into them.

"Fire as you bear!" Brooks yelled again. Another full broadside was loosed on the *Phoebe.*

Brooks gripped a starboard ratline as he screwed up his eyes to see what damage they had inflicted. The salt spray splattered him in the face with every wave that passed. He seemed oblivious of the fact that the French marines could mark him down easily from their positions on the *Phoebe.* His navy blue jacket with its prestigious gold buttons, twelve in all, and grouped in twos to show that he had less than three years service, were gleaming down the front of his chest. His one gold epaulette on his shoulder made him stand out like a bright bantam cock amidst the rest of the crew who were dressed in their motley array of seaman's attire.

*Starlight's* guns fired once more, and Brooks looked almost surprised as pieces of the ornately carved stern gallery from the enemy ship flew past him in a shower of wood splinters. He was jolted back to reality as a seaman near him screamed as a splinter stabbed into his thigh like a knife, the blood spurting from him like a fountain.

"Get that man below at once," Brooks cried. "Stand by your guns . . . steady m'lads, don't let them ruffle your feathers! Easy now!"

The grimy faces of the gunners watched their Captain with an intensity that only extreme loyalty could produce. They were breathing hard, partly because of the hot work at the guns, but mostly out of excitement and the wild madness of battle. Their faces were aglow. They had scored a deadly hit on the Frenchman! Most of the stern gallery had been blasted away, but what was more important, they had made three nice round holes as neat and evenly placed as if they had been put there when the ship had been built.

"Reminds you of the Trinity don't it?" chuckled a seaman as he stared with amazement.

The hit was right at the waterline, and from now on every wave that crested up the transom of the mighty ship, would start to send gallons of water through the gaping holes. With most of the bulkheads removed during a battle it left a clear passageway for any shot to crash unrestricted down the whole length of the ship, making it more deadly, and creating more damage, to both ship and any human flesh that stood in its pathway. On the *Phoebe* the incoming seawater would prove just as devastating. With any luck the leak would not be readily noticed as most of the French carpenters would be busy filling other shot holes already inflicted by Captain Weatherby and the *Dragonfly*, the British flagship.

"Now my beauty," Captain Brooks whispered to himself as the American schooner was still hidden from his sight. "Any moment now you will have to come out from behind that ship like a young lion, but we'll be ready for you," he breathed.

As Captain Weatherby squinted through the smoke, he could see now that the *Vixen*'s Captain must have given orders to rig a jury fore-mast, because small figures like ants were swarming over the *Vixen*'s bow, wielding axes . . . cutting away the debris. All the clutter of stays and sails that were trailing over the side and bubbling in the water, were being hacked away with fervor. It looked like the *Vixen* was not about to be excluded from the battle after all, and her crew were doing their best to get the ship back into the action. They had a chance to strike a blow at two nations . . . France and America. Although why the American schooner was now under French colors, Weatherby could only speculate.

With his own guns still firing non-stop Weatherby was closer than ever to the *Phoebe*, it was just a matter of time, and it looked from where he stood at the con that the *Starlight* had managed to hit the Frenchman somewhere in her stern. A fine piece of seamanship and gunnery indeed. If they lived through this day, Captain Brooks would probably get the frigate he always wanted. He could visualize another glorious oratory in the Gazette with its list of England's brave captains. There would also be a list of the deceased, and in years to come many would remember this day. Would he himself survive to outlive the stories that would be told, both truthful and exaggerated, by those who supped their ale in the Taverns along the south coast of England. All those hopeful young officers on half-pay, tantalizing themselves with the possibilities of honor and glory as a frigate captain.

"Stand by to board!" Weatherby roared out at last.

# CHAPTER NINE

## NO WAY TO RUN

Henry was thrown across the table as he assisted the *Phoebe*'s surgeon, who was in the middle of removing a musket ball from a French sailor's stomach. The impact and blast of the three cannon balls that the *Starlight* had launched through the stern of the ship, had fallen dangerously close to where he and Joshua were working. The surgeon and his loblolly boys were operating beneath the swinging lantern in the dark and gloom of the orlop deck. They barely looked up after the explosion for they were so engrossed in their work.

Henry grabbed the edge of the makeshift surgical bench to stop himself from falling face down into the man's bloody entrails, which were carefully being sewn back into place.

Joshua had the gruesome job of placing the amputated limbs, and other gruesome body parts, into a bucket for disposal later.

"It's enough to make you sick," he choked out, while screwing up his face in disgust. His eyes strangely protruded with horror in the murky gloom of the lantern, where only a small circle of light illuminated the grisly work. The sweet sickly smell of blood was everywhere, permeating the very timbers of the ship. The surgeon, although competent, gave no heed to the blood that flowed unchecked onto the floor, where it became a hazard to those who were forced to walk through it, and finding it more and more slippery underfoot.

Through the terrible cries of the wounded, the unrelenting sound of the guns crashed out above them. Henry felt as though he was in the very depths of hell itself. As the non-serious cases were brought down, the injured were able to relay current events that were taking place up on deck.

"The English are real close . . . almost alongside," one man said shaking his head in disbelief. "And four of the big guns have been overturned by enemy fire, they weigh tons," he reported. "Gun crews all killed . . . No mercy . . . no mercy!" he shook his head again.

Henry and Joshua exchanged quick glances. The British were close then, things must be really heating up, thought Henry. He put his hand on the man's shoulder. "How many British ships?" Henry asked in his faltering French. The man looked puzzled, his eyes were glazed with pain.

"Trois," he murmured. "Frigate . . . and two schooners. But we put one of the schooners out of action," he replied with a note of satisfaction in his voice.

"What are the odds for the British?" asked Joshua grabbing Henry by the arm.

"One frigate and a schooner against a ship-of-the-line and a schooner . . . not good I am afraid," replied Henry. "But a frigate is faster than a ship-of-the-line, so your guess is as good as mine."

Joshua looked uncomfortable. Henry realized that the man must be having difficulty with his loyalties, should the *Phoebe* be captured. The schooner, an American, and a French ship-of-the-line. Neither were his enemy.

"Aw, what does it matter!" Joshua mumbled at last. "Any way you look at it we'll be prisoners with all, or one of 'em. Ain't no doubt about that!"

"More than likely," Henry sighed.

The seawater around their feet, mixing with blood and sand, felt cold and uncomfortable. The realization that the sea was surging through those shot holes began to put great fear amongst the wounded, especially those who could not walk.

"You!" said the surgeon to Henry. "You speak French, go up and find the carpenter's mate, and tell him to get someone down here to plug these holes. Else we will all be swimming around like rats! God knows what will happen if water gets into the magazine," he said jerking his thumb over his shoulder towards the ship's magazine where the gunpowder was stored. Without dry powder the big guns would soon fall silent.

Henry stumbled up the companionway steps, gulping fresh air as he went. He pushed his way through throngs of seaman going in every direction. Sweating profusely he made his way up to the spar deck. Musket fire, and the big guns belching out smoke and mayhem up here made it difficult to see, but his eyes quickly sought out anyone wearing a French officer's uniform. After all, he had no idea who the carpenter's mate was.

Henry looked around him quickly as he saw that he was in the fray and fury of the battle.

Musket balls whined past him as he made his way through the smoke towards the quarterdeck. He grabbed an arm bearing epaulettes rushing past him heading in the opposite direction.

The lieutenant looked at him with anger and disbelief as Henry asked him for the carpenter's mate.

"Charpentier, s'il vous plait," Henry yelled at him trying to make his voice heard over the deafening sound of the cannon fire.

"How the hell do I know," the lieutenant shrieked back. "Somewhere below no doubt." He pushed Henry briskly aside and disappeared into the smoke.

If Henry thought the noise from the guns was loud when he was below, they were magnified ten times over up here. Wave after wave of broadsides thundering through the afternoon; the ship reeled beneath his feet as if an earthquake had it in its grips. Powder boys scuttled around his feet like pigeons in Trafalgar Square, as he weaved his way back to the companionway steps through a debris of fallen spars and ropes. Another musket ball slammed into the bulwarks inches from his shoulder. He shouted once more for a carpenter, but nobody knew or even cared it seemed up here. Just voices screaming, "Re-load! Run out! Fire!"

Henry leapt down the forward hatch, and somehow, as he made his way through the maze of passages, he found himself in what seemed to be the *Phoebe*'s wardroom, where the officers ate their meals. It was lined with a row of small doors on each side which were the tiny cabins assigned as sleeping quarters for the officers. Naturally the wardroom was empty, each man being at battle stations. Just as he turned to leave and make his way back down to the orlop deck, he heard a loud banging and shouting coming from one of the cabins. There was a stout piece of wood barring one of them. Someone must be locked inside. Another prisoner perhaps? The shouting and cursing continued. Henry became rooted to the ground. The voice was calling out threats in English, cursing and blaspheming like nothing on earth. Not just an English voice but one with a strong Boston accent. That voice, it was familiar to him. Who was being held prisoner? The shouting stopped suddenly. Henry tried to rack his brain . . . to remember. He paused for a moment. Should he free the man? He took a step forward, hesitated, then turned abruptly. He had no tools in which to remove the wood from the door, anyway there was no time, he would need a carpenter's tool he thought ironically.

Henry had to return to the orlop deck as quickly as possible, he didn't like leaving Joshua by himself, and the wounded there may be in danger of drowning. He hurried down more steps, the smell of seawater mixed with all kinds of other materials seemed to smother him. He had no difficulty in knowing what direction to go, for a veritable stream of wounded men were being carried below in his wake. Their agonizing cries and groans pierced through his ear drums. The cost of war . . . paid out in human flesh.

"Did you find the carpenter?" said Joshua eagerly.

"No, it's like looking for a needle in a haystack up there. Nobody seems to care anyway," replied Henry.

"There's more wounded coming down by the minute," said Joshua ruefully.

"I know, it's pitiful, even if they are French."

"They are human beings! Someone cares about them, I guess," answered Joshua.

Henry said, "There's no doubt about our own plight, Joshua, the seawater in the hold is rising fast, I've noticed the difference since I went topsides. It's ankle deep now, and within an hour it's likely to be worse, we'll not be able to ignore it much longer. Some drastic measure has to be taken." He looked around hopelessly.

"We're still prisoners, Mr. Henry."

"I know!"

"Can we make a run for it?"

"No way to run, Joshua, my friend."

"*Vixen*'s got sail on her again, sir," reported the *Starlight*'s first lieutenant to Captain Brooks.

"Well done the *Vixen*," said Brooks. "There may be prize money after all then," his eyes shone with anticipation.

Brooks couldn't think too much about *Vixen* at this split second, he must concentrate on what he was doing. With *Starlight* aggressively plunging through the waves, the little schooner was still taking enemy fire, yet so far she had not endured any major damage. Brooks could hardly believe his good fortune. He removed his hat briefly, and wiped some spray from his face with the back of his hand, and as he looked up . . . the American schooner burst into sight from behind the ship-of-the-line, like a racehorse jumping a fence at the Newmarket races. Every sail on the American was taut and drawing hard. She was totally unscathed, the only vessel in this battle so far that had not yet been hit by enemy shot. Not a scratch, she looked almost as if she had just been launched down the ways on her maiden voyage. She looked magnificent, her dark blue hull shone in the pale sunlight as seawater cascaded over her, creating all shades of blue and green in her reflection. With all the smoke and filth of battle downwind of them, the American vessel looked pristine, a picture of beauty and splendid seamanship.

"My God she's fast," exclaimed Brooks with a great deal of admiration. "Well this is it . . ."

The American schooner was a little farther away than he would have liked, but eventually their paths would *have* to cross. *Starlight* was still on a beam reach, he must wait . . . just a little longer . . . he must hold his fire until just the exact moment, then he would bear up on the same tack as the American, close haul his wind so he could bring his starboard guns to bear, then loose his broadside. Brooks quickly gave orders for the larboard gun crews to join the starboard gunners. They could use the extra men, and it would increase his rate of fire.

"Stand by to larboard your helm, I'm going to bear up shortly," he rapped out to the Master.

"Aye, aye, sir."

Once in every captain's lifetime there came a moment of opportunity, and in the next thirty seconds Captain Brooks realized that this was his moment. No carefully laid plans, just a question of providence placing you in the exact position at the right time. He felt excitement clutch at his throat, and his blood started to course through his veins vigorously. He noticed that his heart was beating wildly against his uniform coat.

"Stand by your guns!" he cried.

It was as if the crew somehow had knowledge of this latest plan that was being etched in Brooks' mind, for they gave a rousing cheer. They too, had seen the *Vixen* bravely tacking back into the line of fire. That plucky little schooner was now hard on the heels of the *Lady Eleanor*. If they played their cards right, the American would be caught in their cross fire. It had to be perfect timing with no allowances for error. It would be mere seconds now before the *Lady Eleanor*'s Commander would realize his predicament, and have to take some kind of evasive action. But what?

Brooks let his mind race. If he stayed on this beam reach he would risk a collision, but could force the American schooner to change her course, head her off so to speak. He quickly turned to the helmsman.

"Stand by to luff a little!"

"Aye, sir. Standing by."

"Then lay her as close hauled to the wind as you can," Brooks shouted. "Steady as she goes . . . easy now. The American will have to fall off the wind, she's *got* to! They would be fools to risk their ship in a collision," he informed the Master, his eyes ablaze.

"Aye, sir, if indeed it *is* their ship? You never know what tricks a privateer may pull."

"It's possible the French have a hand in the matter too," replied Brooks. "Still, it changes little at this point of the engagement. In for a penny, in for a pound!"

Brooks stared hard at the enemy ship through his telescope, watching for the faintest ruffle of the headsails that would indicate she was changing course. If he could edge *Starlight* over a point to starboard, he could force the American to change course, and bring her even closer to the *Vixen*, who was closing the gap behind them. The American schooner would be well and truly sandwiched in the middle of the two British ships.

"One point to starboard."

"One point to starboard it is," replied *Starlight*'s helmsman.

Now she would have to make her move, Brooks concluded. He felt the strain on his eyes as he kept them glued on the enemy schooner. The French flag flying at her masthead was streaming out in the strong wind. Why the dickens was she flying those colors anyway?

He was overjoyed to suddenly see that the *Vixen*, as if anticipating his move, had hardened up and was sailing as close to the wind as she possibly could, considering her hasty repairs. It would just be a matter of time before the American would be caught in a pincer movement. She was committed now, there was no tacking off and escaping, she was just where the British wanted her to be.

To any casual observer the three schooners made a beautiful sight plunging through the sea each sending forth prestigious white bow waves before them. Every sail sheeted as tightly as could be with the sun gleaming upon each sail with a soft orange glow. Each one was as graceful as a bird. The picture was completely free of smoke, for the black murk created by the two larger ships still firing incessantly at each other was drifting away to starboard and rapidly dispersing as the big ships were left behind. The ocean was pristinely clear, and the battle had unwittingly divided itself in two parts. The *Dragonfly*, His Majesty's frigate, in combat with the *Phoebe*, His Imperial Emperor's ship-of-the-line, while the schooners, looking like terrier dogs in a street fight, were snapping and growling menacingly at each other, ready to tear out the throats of their opponents.

The net was closing, and the American's only chance was that of outrunning her two attackers. If she could keep up her extraordinary speed, it would be down to a question of superior seamanship. Yankee courage against British experience, who had hundreds of years of victory beneath their belts on every ocean in the world.

The *Lady Eleanor* was slightly smaller than her opposition, narrower in the beam and only ninety five feet on deck, but one hundred and twenty five feet including her bowsprit, as opposed to the two British ships measuring one hundred and ten feet on deck apiece. But small meant faster in any man's navy, and her crew had every confidence in her abilities.

"Shake out the cobwebs," called Crook the old Sailing Master, and the men threw themselves into the work.

On the *Phoebe*, Henry was dismayed to realize that he was now standing knee deep in filthy water, which swirled around him.

Everything that had been standing on the floor of the orlop deck was now bobbing about. Even the wooden buckets of bloody amputated limbs were floating around in a macabre dance. There was still no sign of the ship's carpenters.

"Are they going to let us drown?" Henry snapped to Joshua? Are the French so blind that they can't see their own ship is in trouble? I don't even hear the pumps going."

"Perhaps they are deliberately trying to commit suicide," Joshua said sheepishly.

As if reading Henry's thoughts, (for the Frenchman had no understanding of English,) the surgeon sent one of his loblolly boys to report the matter to Captain Dupont. Henry watched the concentration on the surgeon's face as he continued to operate, completely oblivious to his surroundings and circumstances. This was dedication and compassion to the core Henry had to admit. Foolish though the Frenchman may be.

"We'll move up to a higher deck when I have finished with this patient," the French surgeon announced abruptly. "You, and your friend, will help carry up the wounded, it's more dangerous up there from the gunfire, but we have no choice. The worst cases can be dealt with on the ward room table instead of down here. The rest . . . alas there are so many, they will have to lay on the lower gun deck despite the guns." He shook his head in despair, then turning to Henry said, "When they are all brought up, save yourselves! Do I have your word you will carry out my instructions first?"

"You have our word!" Henry replied.

Henry knew the odds against those being taken to one of the gun decks. Their survival would be almost impossible, not to mention they would be under the feet of the gun crews. It was like condemning them to certain death. The French surgeon had no other choice, it was a grim decision he had made.

"I don't like the looks of this," said Joshua. "We'll all be committing suicide!"

"We had better get on with it," Henry said, his mouth set in a thin line.

They both picked up a wounded Frenchman in their arms, and staggered towards the companionway hatch. The men they carried groaned with intense pain as they were moved, while blood oozed through the crude bandages and soaked Henry and Joshua's own clothes as they took on the appearance of one of the patients themselves. The rest of the less serious cases slowly dragged themselves in the two men's wake, forming a human column of horrific proportions.

As they reached half way up the companionway ladder, the ship gave a tremendous lurch to starboard, making a horrible groaning sound as she did, much like the dying sounds of a mortally wounded whale.

Henry slipped, and hit himself hard on the shoulder as he desperately tried not to drop the man he was carrying. "I'm afraid the ship is sinking faster than I thought. She'll come to a point when her buoyancy will give way to the weight of the incoming water. It's just a matter of time," Henry called over his shoulder to Joshua who was close behind him. Joshua looked terrified.

"If they don't get the pumps working soon it will be too late," Henry gasped.

"What about the wounded?" asked Joshua.

"There is very little hope for them," replied Henry looking down into the pale lifeless face of the man he carried in his arms. "This one's dead already, poor devil!" He laid him down carefully, and quickly closed the man's staring eyes with his fingers. We'll keep our promise though!"

"If the guns don't get 'em the sea will," said Joshua angrily.

By the time the worst cases were delivered to the ward room, the American prisoner that had been detained there must have been released. The room that had been the scene of damnable shouting and cursing was now empty. The door was open wide and swung backwards and forwards aimlessly with the motion of the ship.

Unknown to Henry, Winters had been released, under the promise that he would fight against the English. Captain Dupont had lost a lot of men and was now willing to release his prisoner to help fill the gap in the ranks of seamen. He knew Winters was a tolerable swordsman and Dupont was convinced that the British would attempt to board very soon.

The *Dragonfly*'s sails were pock marked with holes, as a grim faced Weatherby stood tirelessly near the helm. Like Dupont, some of his men had been killed, and many more lay below mortally wounded. *Dragonfly*'s mizzenmast had gone by the board with its maze of sails and rigging littered about the quarterdeck. The sailors' axes flashed in the sunlight as they fought like demons to get it cleared. Weatherby tried to maintain some sense of dignity as the men worked literally around his feet. The two stern guns were out of action now . . . gun crews dead, but for two men.

"This is hot work, Mr. Plumb!"

"Yes, sir. Not too hot to handle though, sir."

"Speak for yourself. I'd rather not have my breeches scorched by the French."

Weatherby removed his hat and wiped the perspiration from his brow, then promptly jammed it back on his head again as a powder stained Midshipman Baines rushed down the larboard gangway towards him, dodging this way and that as musket balls whined around him as he stumbled and tripped over the splintered pieces of the ship, and the bodies of the slain.

"A message from Lieutenant Fox, sir!" he said breathlessly. "He needs more men at the guns."

"Very well, Mr. Baines, take a message to Lieutenant Bradley to send over some of his men.

"Aye, aye, sir."

He scampered away in his oversized silver buckled shoes, which even after all this time at sea, he had not yet grown into. His feet tapped clumsily across the deck to deliver the Captain's orders.

Just at that moment, the deafening crash of a cannon ball from the *Phoebe* scudded across the deck. For a moment Captain Weatherby could see nothing but smoke and flying splinters.

When it cleared he could see fourteen year old Freddie lying on his left side among the shattered blocks and rigging. His right leg was completely shot away just below the knee, and blood was pumping unchecked from the stump that was left behind. Weatherby could see that the lad was losing consciousness fast as his screams and sobs slowly subsided. Even through the smoke Weatherby could see how white the boy's face appeared, as white as the tabs on his lapels, which was now splattered with his own blood.

Weatherby screamed to a nearby seaman, "Get a tourniquet on Baines' leg! Use your neck-tie man if you have to! Get him down below to the surgeon immediately!"

"Aye, aye, sir."

"And be careful with him! Hurry, man! Hurry!" Franklyn Weatherby felt hot tears of anger run from his eyes. All the midshipmen were as dear to him as if they were his own sons. These thirteen and fourteen year old boys were not only his personal pride and joy, but they were the future of the British Navy. "Oh, Freddie," he sighed. He muttered a quick prayer as he pulled his attention away from the limp body of Baines being carried below, and forced himself to keep his mind focused on the attack. The *Phoebe* was listing over badly to starboard, and was much lower in the water than she was an hour ago. She must be taking on water rapidly.

"She's sinking, sir," exclaimed Plumb excitedly.

"I can see that, Mr. Plumb. I am not blind! Her rate of fire has slowed considerably as well," he added.

"Looks like only two guns left in action, sir," Plumb shouted back breathlessly. "Has water got into her magazine do you think? Maybe her powder is wet, sir."

"More than likely," Weatherby replied. He turned to the old Master, and with a dogged determination said in a very calm voice, "Lay the *Dragonfly* alongside the enemy, Mr. Plumb. It's time we stopped dawdling and boarded this bugger!"

Plumb grinned. "Aye, aye, sir," he replied, and obediently spun the wheel hard over. "Hard to larboard it is, sir."

"Avast firing!" Weatherby yelled down to the larboard gun crews. "Stand by to board the enemy," he shouted to Lieutenant Bradley.

Dozens of sailors made their way towards the mainmast where boarding pikes, axes and cutlasses were stacked around it in readiness.

"Steady as she goes, Mr. Plumb. And try not to scrape too much paint off the hull," he said wryly.

Plumb chuckled to himself, Weatherby's humor had a steadying effect on him. They had served together and been good friends for many years . . . he prayed these would not be their last few minutes together.

# CHAPTER TEN

## A MATTER OF HONOR

The *Dragonfly*'s red-coated marines were firing with deadly accuracy at the French sailors, considering the denseness of the smoke. These were hardened disciplined soldiers that were attached to every naval vessel in the service, and made up about one fifth of the complement of men on board every British fighting frigate.

Now that the *Dragonfly* was alongside the ship-of-the-line, they could hear the screams of the wounded coming from the French ship amidst the incomprehensible sound of the cannons.

The crew of the *Dragonfly* were assembled now in groups along the larboard bulwarks with their boarding pikes and cutlasses gripped tightly. The officers had two pistols apiece stuck in their belts, with their swords in their right hands. They crouched down behind the bulwarks as French musket fire hailed down on them like rain, as they waited for the impact of the two great ships as they crashed together. Periodically they would peer over the edge to try to see their opponents, but the smoke was so thick that it made their eyes sting. Weatherby's men were wild-eyed and ready to fight: anxious to get among the enemy.

At least twenty of the Dragonflys stood poised on the gunnel, holding a grapnel iron attached to a long rope coiled efficiently in their hands. As soon as one of these men were shot dead by the enemy, another grabbed the line from his fallen brother and leapt up to take his place, standing ready to make another cast that would grip the bulwarks of the French ship with one of the grapnel's three pronged iron hooks, and then draw them closer and closer together until both ships would be locked in a deadly embrace. Once that was accomplished there would be no escape for either vessel unless the lines were hacked away. They would soon be at close quarters with the French.

Captain Dupont stood on his quarterdeck shouting orders. He could see the English captain appearing periodically between the clouds of smoke, and as it cleared, the defiant Weatherby stood on his quarterdeck glaring over at him, and out of the corner of Dupont's eye he saw the British colors streaming proudly in the wind. The *Dragonfly* was about to prove her reputation at his expense.

Dupont had previously heard of her naval prowess, and knew for a certainty the British were ready to board him. He swallowed hard, his mouth felt parched and dry. The odds were against him now that his ship was sinking, and he had lost a third of his men. Plus another hundred or more were wounded. Most of them lay helpless on the lower gun deck while the surgeon was in the wardroom sawing limbs off of seamen laying on the same table he had carved many a roast chicken dinner upon while dining in company with his officers.

At this moment Dupont would rather be at home in France, sitting with his wife at the elegant table of their dining room in their beautiful chateaux. He had served his country for long enough, and except for the lunatic Napoleon, who would not be content until he ruled the whole world (including invading

Britain itself,) things might be different. He clenched his fists behind his back. So this was a hero's death? At least he would be with his young brother again. Yet he still had not avenged his brother's death. To die himself was better than being taken a prisoner, but what of *his* prisoner Winters? Dupont still had not resolved *that* matter.

As the battle raged on before his eyes, seamen and officers dropped around him like flies, their screams of pain rang in his ears as he set his lips in an even line, determined as he was to eradicate as many Englishmen as he could before the end came.

Without orders from any officer, the French surgeon signaled to Henry to take one of the severely wounded men into Dupont's Great Cabin. The sentry that usually guarded it was busy guarding one of the companionways to stop any cowardly seaman from sneaking down to hide from the battle that was raging.

Henry hesitated for a moment, he knew it was a violation even in the French Navy, but what did he care now. Within seconds he and Joshua helped carry the man over to the Captain's cot. The work was exhausting, they were both saturated with sweat, and the blood of the wounded. As they laid the man down, Henry was very much aware they were alone in the Great Cabin. The stern chasers housed there were out of action and the men that served the guns had abandoned them to fight elsewhere.

Henry's eye caught sight of the sword, his own dueling weapon when he was on the *Lady Eleanor*, still hanging above Dupont's desk on the bulkhead. Momentarily the two men stared at the sword. It seemed untouched, almost serene. A silent witness of the macabre scene around them. Impulsively Henry grabbed the sword from off the bulkhead, its blade cold against his sweating hands. He held it for a moment, then looked around furtively as if someone could see him. The only eyes that were in the cabin other than Joshua's were too glazed over with pain to see or care.

"The surgeon is waiting for us," muttered Joshua, he'll send someone in a minute to get us."

Henry looked about quickly and whispered, "Wait a minute, Joshua! I must have time to think."

"What's the good?"

"We have nothing to lose?" Henry retorted. "We've given our parole, but maybe . . ." Joshua had already left the cabin.

Henry stood holding the sword. He clenched it hard in his right hand. He had to use it or find a hiding place for it . . . he knew he still couldn't use it to kill in cold blood, but somehow in his mind it was a symbol of their freedom. He staggered back towards the wardroom clipping the weapon onto his belt as he went. It seemed to fit naturally there. The ship listed badly beneath his feet suddenly and it was all he could do to keep his balance. He had been at sea long enough to know that the *Phoebe* must be sinking fast. It seemed so hopeless.

Rats were scuttling around Henry's feet freely, having been driven from their nests deep down in the ship. They too were trying to escape as the water rose higher and higher. Their squeals sent a shiver down Henry's back. Eventually he passed a small room adjacent to the wardroom where the door was propped open with a small wedge. He took the sword and put it behind the door with the hilt hanging over one of the hinges. It was hardly noticeable, he concluded. Not a place one would normally expect to find a sword hanging. It was a good hiding place he told himself. Time for them was running out.

In the ward room Joshua gave him a curious look, but said nothing. The smell in the place was overwhelming, the sickly odor of blood penetrated their nostrils. The wounded never seemed to stop coming, and their groans became like a dirge that permeated the very soul. There were so many crammed in the comparatively small room that even the surgeon could hardly move. The battle was more imminently noticeable up here, the never ending boom of the guns seemed to be all around them, and the stifling choking smell of smoke was unbearable. It was almost impossible to treat the wounded as the whole ship seemed to vibrate and lurch every second. And all the time blocks and wreckage fell on them without mercy.

"The firing has become more spasmodic now," Henry said to Joshua as the *Phoebe* shuddered. This was due more to the impact of the British guns firing at her rigging with chain shot, rather than from the recoil of the *Phoebe*'s own armament.

"She must be well and truly stricken," Joshua said.

"It is true, M'sieur," said the surgeon wiping his hands down his blood stained shirt. "The last report was only our mizzenmast still stands. The old lady, she groans and moans as if she is being tortured. She is too tired to respond to life."

On the frigate *Dragonfly*, midshipman Clark ran breathlessly towards Captain Weatherby.

"Sir," he gasped. "The American schooner has struck her colors, the red ensign is now flying," he said in a peremptory voice.

"Good lads," said Weatherby. "Stand by to signal *Starlight*."

"What signal, sir?"

"Set a prize crew, then board the ship-of-the-line, with all haste."

"Yes sir! And sir . . ." he paused momentarily. "What news of Baines?"

"I have heard nothing yet, Mr. Clark! He is in God's hands, now try not to worry."

At least Freddie did not have to endure the horror of the surgeon's saw, thought Christian as he ran back towards the boarding party standing at the ready. It was hard to imagine Freddie with a 'peg leg' he being so young. He smiled a little at the thought of it, then almost instantly regretted his warped sense of humor.

"Alright men, have you all got your arm bands tied on? Don't want any of you to kill your own shipmates," Christian shouted. Men's eyes instinctively glanced down at their left arms where a thin white strip of canvas was tied, the identifying mark of the Dragonflys.

The last broadside crashed out seconds before the *Dragonfly* and the *Phoebe* collided slowly and with all the dignity of a couple of stout ladies at a ball, thanks to the expertise of Mr. Plumb as he laid the *Dragonfly* alongside the Frenchman in a perfect display of seamanship. The grinding sound was horribly loud as every timber on both ships seemed to cry out in protest, and a mass of ropes and blocks rained down from the heavens and littered the decks below.

"Boarders away!" bellowed lieutenant Bradley, and with his sword gripped firmly in his hand he pointed it towards the enemy ship. "To me, Dragonflys! At 'em lads!

The men surged forwards, flinging themselves up the side of the *Phoebe*, her huge tumblehome making it easier for them to clamber up. Bradley led his party up and over the bow. Lieutenant Fox attacked the midships, and young Christian was assigned to board the quarterdeck.

"To me Dragonflys," Christian yelled as he led his boarding party across. The men screamed like tortured beings from hell as they swarmed up, and over the sides of the French ship-of-the-line. The clash of steel and pistol shots soon drowned out the noise of the men's screaming as they strove in mortal combat.

The crack of the muskets in the French fighting tops seemed to increase in a volley as the British seaman boarded the *Phoebe*. Several were hit mortally hard, and fell screaming through the small gap between the two ships, those that weren't crushed to death could be heard crying until they hit the water. Then the cries stopped.

The rest of the men that made up the boarders behind them surged forward in a great press; a living, seething mass of men; their faces set like a mask as they threw themselves onto the French.

"Repel boarders, repel boarders!" Captain Dupont cried out in desperation, and each man searched out an opponent in the crowd.

A good proportion of the British marines had also launched their attack, their bright red coats with white cross belts standing out as sentinels amongst the mass of fighting seamen. They looked like red beetles busily carving a way through the crowd.

They fired a volley, and then deftly reloaded their muskets with incredible speed. Then fired once more.

The battle on the main deck spread out in small groups, as British and French seaman alike engaged their respective attackers. The only guns being fired now, apart from the muskets, were the occasional ring of a pistol shot followed by a scream from its victim as they fell with blood oozing from the small neat round holes created by a deadly accurate pistol ball. How could death be so tidy?

The carronades on both ships had now fallen silent as every gunner was now engaged in hand to hand combat with the enemy. The swords and boarding pikes were now in full play as the clash of steel rang out everywhere.

Another horrific crash of timbers grinding together, as the British schooner *Starlight* came smashing along the larboard side of the ship-of-the-line. The British sailors fighting on the main deck cheered loudly as Brooks and his men boarded with howls and ear-splitting yells. They were exhilarated with their recent victory, blackened sweat streaked faces grinning and shouting as they fell remorselessly on their enemy.

For a moment there was confusion written on the faces of the French sailors, for they were now faced with additional numbers of British sailors as the Starlights swarmed aboard. The schooner's compliment of men was almost complete, the *Starlight* had only lost a few men, and the extra British sailors tearing into the battle would soon outweigh the French. And they knew it.

The *Phoebe* was devastated, with the spar deck in ruins. The mizzen was the only mast left standing, and the blue, white, and red tri-color was still flying . . . weakly fluttering in tatters.

In the ward room it was all over. The French surgeon sat with his head in his hands, overwhelmed and exhausted he could do no more for his men. He sat unarmed for he was technically listed as non-combatant personnel. If the French struck their colors, he would be taken prisoner, naturally. He expected to be treated with respect by the British though, and would be obligated to help with *their* wounded.

Henry and Joshua slipped away silently. The surgeon looked up at them for a brief moment, but said nothing. Henry pulled Joshua by his shirt sleeve towards the place where he had hidden the sword. His heart was in his mouth as they stumbled down the small passageway. He saw the door at last, and as he reached behind it his hand felt the cold metal. It was still in place, just as he had left it. Relief surged through him as he unhooked it from the hinge and revealed it to Joshua, who grinned with a ragged smile.

"Your sword, Mr. Henry . . . trust you," he chuckled. His face quickly turned to a frown. "You have a plan then?"

"No," Henry said regretfully. "I just felt a lot more secure knowing that I had the sword hidden. And now it is back in my possession. You never know . . . ." he trailed off as they made their way up the companionway ladder to the main deck, stepping over corpses as they went.

"You looks a mess, Mr. Henry!"

"You don't exactly look like Boston gentry yourself," Henry smiled back.

The two of them were covered in blood stains, and the clothes they wore were virtual rags. They were both filthy and stinking. Joshua stopped suddenly in his tracks, and stooping over one of the dead sailors, pulled out a pistol from the man's belt. "This will come in handy," he muttered quickly checking that it had been primed and had not yet been fired, then stuffed it into his own leather belt.

Henry and Joshua were not prepared for the sights and sounds that met them as they emerged from below decks. The carnage was sickening, and Henry felt as if he were an observer in a slaughter house. There were so many dead sailors of both nations, and their bodies had been carelessly tossed aside into the scuppers, as though they were merely a heap of rag dolls . . . discarded toys. Blood was running freely through the scuppers in a steady stream, and as it ran down the sides of the ship, its stained oak sides seemed red with shame.

The great ship-of-the-line seemed a lost cause as once again it listed dramatically to starboard, the deck canting at a steep angle.

The mainmast was broken almost at deck level, and lay in three massive pieces across the deck. The foremast had gone by the board long before, but was still trailing over the bow with all its shrouds and stays acting as a giant anchor. The mizzenmast with the spanker boom was still miraculously intact, and the driver, although hanging in tatters, was still moving the wounded ship along at a snail's pace, dragging the British ship with it.

Upturned guns lay strewn around everywhere as if they weighed nothing, and the limbs of the poor unfortunates that had manned them lay embracing them in a deathly grip.

Amongst all this wreckage was an unrecognizable group of men staggering and leaping over the broken timbers, locked in mortal combat. Screams and cries emerged from this moving mass of humanity as it staggered backwards and forwards. Looks of fear and hatred on faces unknown to Henry and Joshua, and on the facial expressions of the dead, blank stares of surprise, as though they were not expecting their lives to end so suddenly. And yet they had died so unnoticed Henry realized. Would he himself, and Joshua have a similar end?

Captain Weatherby had now joined the boarders. His stout but somewhat stiff body with his ruddy Yorkshire complexion, was now in the thick of the battle. His skilled swordsmanship finding its mark despite his portliness, as he thrust and parried while stamping his right foot forward with every lunge in a classic motion. In a matter of minutes he had put an end to two or three Frenchmen, who were showing signs of tiredness and fatigue.

Mr. Plumb, the old Master, had remained on board the *Dragonfly*, as per Weatherby's orders, to try to keep control of the *Dragonfly* as she continued to reel and grind against the ship-of-the-line, in the same manner a small dog would have its teeth stuck into the flanks of a Great Dane, and unwilling to release it's grip.

Meanwhile, Henry had drawn his sword and instinctively tightened his grip on the hilt in his right hand. Bent low as musket balls whined over his head and smacked into the bulwarks behind him, and with thick smoke still hanging in a soft gray canopy over the whole scene, made it difficult for him to discern what was going on. Occasional rays of sunlight would punch through the clouds and reflect on the swords and knives as they flashed in the awesome scene of battle that was raging around them. Henry pulled Joshua aside as a French marine made a vicious thrust with a deadly looking bayonet at them, then turned quickly to defend himself as another attacker came up from behind and struck him in the jaw with the butt of a musket.

There was confusion everywhere, as Henry quickly tried to analyze their dangerous situation. To the French sailors, he and Joshua would be seen as escaped prisoners and shoot them, or cut them down without a second thought. He heard cries and orders being shouted in English, and realized with mixed emotions running through him, that these were definitely British sailors fighting the French. Yet if he shouted to them in English, exposing his identity, he could be suspected of desertion and siding with the French. Yet if he said nothing, it would be assumed that he *was* French. To the English he was nothing more than a blood stained individual in rags with a sword in his hand.

Henry had not attempted to make his way back to his ship after his near drowning experience in Boston Bay. Besides the squadron was long gone by the time he had recovered. Yet the guilt had often plagued him. By revealing his true identity now it would only put Joshua in grave danger too. All things considered it made the British his enemy, at least for the moment. Joshua, as an American . . . he winced inwardly at the thought. He had to protect his friend no matter what the personal cost.

Yet, here they both were crouching against the bulwarks of the ship, he with a sword in his hand looking like a Madagascan pirate, and Joshua crouching next to him with his pistol ready. Fate made strange bedfellows, Henry thought.

"Stay down," Henry whispered forcefully, putting his hand firmly on Joshua's shoulder. He leaned over the larboard bulwarks in a quick movement, then ducked down again. It only took seconds for him to see a schooner jammed hard against the ship-of-the-line, forward of the main chains.

"There's a ship alongside!" he exclaimed excitedly.

"Another one?"

"A schooner, and flying the Ensign!"

Joshua looked puzzled.

"British! We're hemmed in. She's un-manned though, they must have boarded already!"

"You're not . . ."

"No, Joshua," Henry smiled ruefully, "I think that one's a bit too large for us to handle alone."

"Look, Mr. Henry," cried the big black man grabbing Henry by the arm. "Over there!"

Henry followed his pointing finger towards a tall figure in a deerskin shirt making short work of silencing a young English sailor. Henry gasped in astonishment, the shock of recognition made his mind ricochet.

"I'd know him anywhere," growled Joshua. "Captain Winters! Damn his eyes! What's he doing here?"

Of course . . . now it all made sense, Henry thought. That familiar voice shouting from behind the locked door near the ward room. The American drawl; the obvious barbarous nature, it all seemed to fall into place. Winters had been a prisoner of the French, and yet here he was now fighting the English. What could have turned the tables in his favor so easily?

Just as this revelation was rolling around in his mind, Henry saw Winters turn his head. He had spotted them both. Hatred flashed across his face as fierce as any red hot poker, and although he was knee deep in assailants he was making an obvious effort to fight his way to where they both crouched.

Winters sliced with his sword at all who stood in his way as he pushed and shoved through the fracas, and all the while he transfixed them with his eyes like a tiger preparing for the kill.

Henry leapt up, his body stiffened with a mixture of fear and anger, his hand gripping his sword tightly by the hilt as he squarely faced Winters.

"Never mind him, Mr. Henry," said Joshua shaking Henry roughly by the arm.

"I can't walk away from that man, my friend, and I'll certainly not turn my back on him a second time after he tried to run me through in cold blood on the *Lady Eleanor*. He's a dangerous coward, Joshua, and it's time someone did *something* to stop him!"

"Keep yer head down, Mr. Henry, lest you lose it before you gets a chance to settle the score," Joshua grunted as another burst of musket fire exploded around them.

The two men crept back along the gangway towards the quarterdeck, keeping their heads low for fear of them being blown off. Henry lost sight of Winters in the crowd of fighting men as they hurriedly stumbled up the steps to the quarterdeck. He was quick to observe out of the corner of his eye, another schooner lying a half mile off, and flying English colors. Close by it was a second schooner, slightly smaller, and badly mauled.

"Look, It's the *Lady Eleanor*, Joshua. My, she is in a sorry state, but I'd know her anywhere. All those months of fitting her out . . . I knew her inside and out! My, my, if Richard could see her now!"

Joshua's face wore an expression of shock. There had been times when he and Henry were alone in the little boat on the open sea, that he would have been pleased to clap eyes on the schooner again, minus of course Captain Winters. Her crew had been easily led astray by the deception of Winters and his maniacal ways. Now, she was sad and forlorn looking, as if disgraced. How many of his own countrymen had been killed? Bostonians like himself. Events were now happening too rapidly for his mind, and he felt burdened down with the weight of confusion.

Henry was also experiencing all the emotions of anger and wildness that men feel at the pitch of a battle. His every sense was heightened, and yet he and his friend seemed more like two extra stage hands in a play who were worthless and not needed, and had no impact whatsoever on the story that was unfolding.

In a split second, Henry was sharply aware of the English boarders on the starboard side of the quarterdeck. They surged forward towards Dupont, who was in the midst of a handful of French seamen that were fighting for their lives. There was only one other French officer standing with him amongst the mutilated bodies at their feet. One by one the French were being killed defending their Captain.

The Englishmen looked mostly in one piece. Henry saw a flash of dark blue as a midshipman's uniform with its white lapels and cuffs stood out amongst the seamen in their motley array of clothes.

It was easy to feel sorry for Dupont, it could not be easy for a Captain of a great line-of-battle ship to strike his colors to the enemy. It could not be much longer before the French were forced to submit.

Above the screams and cries of the mob striking mercilessly at each other, came a loud sound that seemed almost unearthly to Henry. A cry like the sound of a wounded animal that was enough to strike fear in any heart. Up the quarterdeck steps towards them ran Captain Winters, his face contorted with rage and his nostrils dilated as his breath came in short intermittent spurts. His sword was held high above his head as he lunged towards Henry, there was no doubting his intentions.

"You English bastard!" he wheezed. "I should have dealt with you a long time ago. Say your prayers, preacher! You've cheated me out of prize money, and I've lost my ship. You won't get away this time," he uttered bitterly.

"I believe *your* ship belongs to some good friends of mine," Henry said in a cool retaliatory voice, his face pale under the layer of sweat and dried blood. He quickly raised his sword to defend himself. He was not going to just stand there and let Winters cut him down without mercy.

"*My ship! My ship!*" shouted Winters in an almost childish manner. "What does Fitzroy know about war! He 'aint got no stomach for it, no more than his other Federalist Toadies."

"A fool has no honor or allegiance, Winters, and *you* are the fool!"

Winters was little more than eight feet away from him, and the air was filled with shouting and clashing of swords which rang in Henry's ears in a deafening manner, yet he kept his eyes glued on Winters. He waited for Winters to make the first move, strangely Henry didn't feel any fear. Perhaps deep down he had always known that it would come to this.

Just at that moment a French seaman slammed his whole body against Henry with brutal force, as his English attacker thrust a sword into his chest. The blood spurted over Henry like spots of red paint, and the force of the man's body weight made him stagger down onto one knee. As he pushed the dead sailor aside, he looked up to see Winters towering over him, with his face indescribably black with anger and leering. A glazed look of triumph was in his eyes as he held his sword high above his head ready to strike the death blow. A blow that would be the end for Henry.

It seemed as if time stood still for those few split seconds, and beyond Winters' dark silhouette, Henry noticed the clouds were strangely brilliant around the edges where the sun was struggling to emerge from behind them. It was more like a dream, his every sense was heightened. Although Henry's vision was greatly enhanced, strangely his hearing was nullified. It seemed quiet, as a deathly hush seemed to settle over the ship, yet reality told him the battle around him was loud . . . invasive . . . undeniable. Was this how death felt? Would this beautiful view of the sun framed by clouds be his last?

Henry heard a shot ring out somewhere close to him, the explosion seemed magnified a thousand times in his eardrums. Winters' sword was still in his hand as the man's frame closed the gap between them. Henry was helpless, he waited for the end, to feel the blackness of pain . . . then the sword in Winters' hand clattered to the deck. The American clutched at his chest with a strange look of surprise on his face. Henry watched as Winters glanced down in amazement at his own blood oozing through the deerskin shirt forming a large wet circle on his chest, and trickling slowly through the American's fingers. The man fell slowly to his knees with a groan, and before Henry could get to his feet, Winters doubled over and fell across Henry, pinning him to the deck. Henry watched the reclining light of life flick through his eyes for just a second . . . then he was gone.

As Henry looked up he saw Joshua standing against the bulwark, his right arm still held out straight, his smoking pistol telling the awful story. The big black man stood motionless as if frozen in time. Henry's friend showed no sign of emotion, his face was somewhat hard looking, and his lips set in a thin determined line. Henry thrust Winters' corpse aside and leapt to his feet.

Seeing Henry's look of surprise, Joshua cried, "I had to do it, Mr. Henry . . . I had to! I couldn't let him kill you!" Tears welled up in his eyes as the big man slowly let his arm fall lifelessly down by his side, his pistol still gripped with such force that his black knuckles looked almost white. Then he began to shake violently.

"It's all right, my friend," Henry said kindly, removing the pistol gently from his hand.

"God forgive me," sighed Joshua, shaking his head in bewilderment.

"You saved my life, *again*, Joshua, and I thank you for it. But there is no time to think about it now, what's done is done! Listen to me, we can't change it!"

"Strike! Strike! Strike!" the British sailors were yelling as they closed in tightly around Captain Dupont and his men. Dupont was wounded badly in the shoulder, but the look on his face spoke nothing of surrender. He would not strike to the British no matter what the cost.

Henry caught sight of a young British midshipman, with blonde hair sticking out from under his hat. The midshipman was locked in mortal combat with a French sailor. The boy couldn't have yet been fourteen years old, and despite his resiliency and remarkable swordsmanship for his age, he was no match for the heavy set Frenchman. The sailor took a swipe at the boy with both hands holding his cutlass. The boy ducked, and bobbed up again looking pale and harried. They both lunged and parried, again and again, with a vicious clanging of steel against steel.

Finally their swords became locked at the hilt, but the superior weight of the Frenchman was too much for the young English officer, and Henry could see the strength ebbing from the boy as he tried desperately to break free from his enemy. With sweat pouring down his face and his hat all cocked on one side, the midshipman took a step backwards, unable to keep his balance any longer, and as he did, he caught his foot on a ring bolt fastened to the deck, and fell flat on his back with a thud.

Winded and gasping for breath, the boy looked for his sword which lay out of his reach. He had no time to retrieve it . . . to defend himself. The Frenchman sneered as he raised his weapon to run him through. The midshipman yelled at the top of his lungs, and instinctively crossed his arms over his chest (as if human hands could stave off the deadly blade) in an un-conscious but futile effort.

Suddenly the French seaman's legs buckled under him and he fell to his knees. He had been stopped short with a knife protruding from his back.

Mr. Plumb's face grinned down at the boy. "Be thankful I chose to disobey orders, young Clark. Pick up your sword, lad, there's still a few more Frogs for us to finish off!"

"Th . . . Thank you, Mr. Plumb! Oh . . . Thank you, sir."

Clark picked up his sword with renewed courage, and quickly looked around him for another French sailor to tackle. All the time he was being pushed and jostled by the crowd of fighting men around him.

He caught sight of a couple of seamen close to the taffrail, noticing one was a big black man, while the other was white. So the French had some Black Jacks in their crew? They were both filthy. Don't the Frogs ever shave? The other Frog held a sword, but the black man looked unarmed.

In a split second, Christian made his choice; he would challenge the swordsman, who was half turned away from him, and looking in the other direction. He ran forward with all the agility of youth.

"On guard, sir!" he yelled weakly at the man, still breathless from his previous encounter. "Stand to! Defend yourself!"

Henry wore a look of surprise as he turned towards the youthful voice, his sword automatically raised in readiness to defend himself.

He looked steadily at the boy whose face was blackened with gunpowder and sweat, and dried blood daubed his uniform.

Man and boy stood staring at each other, weapons raised yet both rigid and frozen like statues. Suddenly a light of recognition filtered through Henry as he looked hard at the midshipman. Clark took a light thrust at him, and Henry easily stepped aside and opened his mouth to speak, but before he could utter a word, the English boy was knocked aside and flattened against the bulwarks by a violent bunch of desperate seamen, the last of Dupont's defenders.

"Christian!" Henry roared over their heads. "Hold on, lad, I can't believe you're here!" he shouted euphorically. "The *Dragonfly* . . . of course it all makes sense now!"

"Mr. Stapleton, upon my word it's good to see you again . . . we thought you were dead! Drowned! How did you . . . ? Never mind," the boy's face quickly broke into a smile. "I'm so glad you're alive, sir. Oh dear, I'm glad you are light on your feet . . . I might have killed you. What a sight for sore eyes you are."

"You too, Christian. You'll never know how much."

A shout broke out all around them, and Henry and Joshua looked up to see the tattered and torn French flag being hauled down, and the British ensign being raised in its place. All eyes followed it up the mizzen (the only mast left to raise it on) where it broke out in the strong wind, and streamed gallantly amidst the Dragonflys' cheers of, "Victory! Victory!" So the French had capitulated, thought Henry. It was finished. The official sign of surrender.

"Christian, this is my friend, Joshua Weller."

"Oh," Christian said with a puzzled look. "Pleased to make your acquaintance, Mr. Weller."

"Yours too, son," Joshua smiled down at the boy. Mr. Henry, is he . . . ?"

"Yes, he's an English officer, they start them young."

"They must do! Don't look old enough to catch a fish to me! You sure you 'ain't kiddin' me, Mr. Henry?"

Henry Laughed out loud.


The Dragonflys were going wild with exhilaration and frenzy. They had captured the French ship-of-the-line. She was now their prize!

Henry slapped Christian heartily on the back. Christian impulsively threw his arms around him like a son embracing a long lost father. It could have been his own son Benjamin. They were of almost equal age. Henry mentally slapped himself back to reality. This was now. This was what war was all about. Every crewmember aboard a fighting frigate longed for this moment. Prize money! Did the benefits outweigh the cost?

"Huzzah for the *Dragonfly*! Huzzah for the *Dragonfly*!"

"Huzzah for the *Starlight*, too," Captain Brooks's men rallied their voices in unisom, and the cry reverberated round the ship in a great energetic sweep.

With the battle over, and the bodies of the French dead unceremoniously cast over the side, the last of the French prisoners were being ushered by the red-coated marines down the forecastle hatch. It was now that the crew of the *Dragonfly* began to take on their personalities, as one by one the familiar faces registered into Henry's consciousness and immediately he began making his presence known to his old comrades. A homecoming of sorts? Suddenly he remembered Joshua . . . he turned his head . . . Joshua was with him . . . by his side. Henry had a feeling that he would always be *there*.

"It's all over then, Mr. Henry," Joshua said meaningfully.

"Or just beginning, my friend."

# CHAPTER ELEVEN

## A LONG SEA MILE

July turned into the heat of August, and after all the necessary repairs to the ships of the British squadron were complete, as well as the re-fit of the two prizes (which was a very arduous task to undertake while at sea), Weatherby was ready to return to Halifax. Dinner was being prepared in the Great Cabin of the *Dragonfly*.

Amongst all the hustle and bustle, Captain Weatherby's steward, Felkes, was interrupted by the arrival of all the ships' officers in their best uniforms, together with Henry Stapleton and Joshua Weller, who, although not suitably attired, had at least had the opportunity to wash their clothes.

This 'gathering of the ships' officers, was much to the annoyance of the crabby old Felkes, who although was a devoted servant of Captain Weatherby, tended to consider such occasions as the 'blight of inconvenience' to himself, and surely it would be the death of him.

In contrast, the Captain was in an uncommonly good mood, and justly so. His two prizes, the French ship-of-the-line, *Phoebe*, and the American schooner, the *Lady Eleanor*, were keeping their stations behind the British squadron in the capable hands of two prize crews. His mood was infectious, and high spirits were being displayed throughout all of the ships. No drunkenness, no seaman put on report, no swearing or bad behavior. Of course it had a lot to do with the prize money that each sailor was expecting to receive when they arrived in Halifax, the official home of the North American station of the British Navy.

After the deduction of the agent's commission, the prize money would be divided into eight parts. Old Vice-Admiral Sawyer would get his one part of course, being the flag officer of the station. The crews sniffed at that, seeing as the old boy, and his flag ship were not even present, for with Navy protocol the flag ship should be technically 'in sight of the battle' to have any rights to prize money. Weatherby would get three parts, naturally, then on, and on, down to the crew themselves, who got two parts, divided between them of course. Amounting to a few guineas for each man.

British sailors got a great deal of satisfaction in this method of dividing up the spoils, as their two parts combined amounted to infinitely more than someone like the tartar-faced Lieutenant Fox, who got a mere one part. It never seemed to bother them that the one part for lieutenants would probably only be divided by three or four, depending on how many lieutenants were on board each ship, and the sailors part had to be divided amongst many hundreds.

Still, despite all the talk and excitement, and the fact that all the ships were shorthanded because of the prizes, nobody cared about the extra duties, and everyone was willing to bear a hand.

In the Great Cabin the officers and midshipmen stood behind their chairs, the taller ones stooped over slightly because of the low deck beams overhead, waiting until their Captain was seated.

"Mr. Stapleton, why don't you sit here on my right," said Wetherby gesturing with his hand, "and Mr. Weller, you may sit next to him."

This must be the first time in British history that a black man had sat down to eat at a captain's table in the virtual sanctity of the Great Stern Cabin, Henry thought to himself. It brought a smile to his face.

"Now, Stapleton, although I've heard it already, you must tell us all about your adventures since you left our company on that infamous occasion in the Bay of Boston. We all thought we had seen the last of you, you know! A victim of Davey Jones," he laughed humorously. "Everybody at the table is privy to the fact, and I have already had the great pleasure of informing you when you first came on board the *Dragonfly*, after our defeating the French, that, for better or for worse, you are no longer a sailor in King George's Navy." Weatherby smiled with open satisfaction written all over his ruddy Yorkshire face.

"Your wife, Stapleton, must be a very determined woman if I may say so! For it seems that with the help of Lord Walpole, from you own home county, she did not allow their lordships at the Admiralty a wink of sleep until she had obtained your official release from the Service."

"God bless her," said Henry.

"The official letter arrived about a week after your unfortunate disappearance, together with your protection order. The Admiralty even offered to pay your passage home as a token of their . . . indiscretion you might say."

"How generous," said Henry smoothly.

"Is that all you have to say, Stapleton?"

"My apologies, sir. I must be overwhelmed with their generosity."

Joshua cast a quick glance at Henry. Watching him sit there in complete control of the situation, he marveled at his candor. Good for Mr. Henry, he thought. He's not intimidated by all these stuffed shirts and gold epaulettes. He's suffered enough under the hand of British injustice and political 'mistakes.' There was still a long sea mile to go before he would be able to sling his hammock in safety.

"Now, gentlemen," said Weatherby. "Let us eat!"

The guests at the table needed no second bidding, and attacked with their knives and forks, the uncommonly delicious looking roast beef, with all its trimmings, and including mint sauce, that Felkes had put up in small jars of vinegar over a year ago.

While they ate, Henry began his long discourse on the events that had occurred starting with the fire ship incident, and culminating in his eventually going overboard while defending the frigate *Restitution*. Every eye was upon him as he retold his near drowning experience. Every officer at the table showed particularly interest in his life ashore, and the American people who lived in the town of Boston. They politely stopped him at intervals to ask pertinent questions about how the American culture compared to life in England?

"Did you meet President Madison?" Lieutenant Fox asked facetiously.

"No, Mr. Fox," Henry replied, (he wasn't going to call him 'sir' now that he had a protection order in his pocket), Fox had no jurisdiction over him now. "But I did have the privilege of meeting former President John Adams, who happened to be visiting a very good acquaintance of mine, and was just leaving as I arrived. Adams is a very elderly gentleman now, but one who still has a keen sense of politics and religion. He lives on the outskirts of Boston, a farmer like myself. We had much in common!"

Fox sneered, but never bothered to comment.

"Ah, the two forbidden subjects of conversation, Mr. Stapleton," Weatherby commented in a candid manner. Politics and religion! Who can resist them?"

"Not I, sir!"

"Well, Henry, I give you joy of all your future conversations on whatever subject you wish to embark on. I know you will make a long passage of all of them!" Weatherby smiled, remembering vividly the long persuasive arguments that he and Stapleton had endured, right here in this same cabin on board the *Dragonfly* during that chilly month of May last year. How Henry had *insisted* that he be taken back to England, and how bumptious he had been in verbally declaring his 'rights' as a minister. On shore, and outside the limitations of the Royal Navy, Weatherby could have been good friends with such a man.

Henry happily answered all their questions as best he could. He was very careful, however, to avoid giving them any information about the French Count Thibadeaux, the fatherly friend he had met quite by chance in the Otis Coffee House on Long Wharf. He did not reveal that it was at the Count's own residence on State Street that he had met John Adams. He did not want to compromise the kindly old French aristocrat in any way, not while England was still at war with France. Anyhow, it was of no great consequence now. He was bound for England, and home.

The conversation at the table eventually resumed once more in a more formal manner, mostly discussing news of the war.

Captain Weatherby recounted how, Captain Lawrence, of the American thirty eight gun frigate, *Chesapeake*, had been killed when they had been engaged by the British thirty eight gun *Shannon*, while off the coast of Massachusetts.

"When did that happen?" Henry asked inquisitively. After all that he had gone through with Joshua by his side, who had saved his life in the way that he had twice over, and the friendship they had formed by their common sufferings, together with all that Richard and Eleanor had sacrificed for him to make his freedom possible in the first place, he found that he could not rejoice in Britain's victories like others around this table. Strangely, the welfare of America had become just as important to him as that of Britain.

"It was late spring this year, Stapleton," Weatherby continued in a very relaxed composure. "*Shannon*'s commander, was Philip Bowes Vere Broke. Came from a long standing naval family! His father before him too. From your part of the world, Stapleton! They have a great house in Norfolk ... people of title of course.

Broke had the *Shannon* for seven years, stickler for gunnery practice, and spoiling for a fight I'll wager. I am sure of it! Heard that he actually challenged Lawrence to come out with the *Chesapeake* in a single ship to ship duel."

"That was honorable," Henry replied.

"Yes! Mr. Stapleton, it was."

"Americans are high spirited you know, Captain Weatherby. They would never refuse a challenge. If Lawrence had achieved personal glory it would have been a tremendous boost to national morale."

Weatherby looked at Henry with his steel blue eyes trying to penetrate Henry's thoughts. That same awkwardness with the man again. The same way of 'turning tables' that Stapleton had.

Weatherby began again, "Lawrence had apparently only just taken command of the ship, no time to discipline his men. Barely knew his junior officers."

"Then he didn't have time to study their weaknesses either," Henry replied coolly.

"Hmm," Weatherby grunted.

"A hero is a hero, Captain Weatherby, whether in victory or defeat."

"You may say so, Stapleton, and of course you are right. You did not meet him personally while you were in Boston did you?"

"No, but I mixed with the gentry of New England, sir. I conversed with many, and shared their sentiments. Mr. Fitzroy was a very rich ship owner and entertained many noble guests during my time in Boston. War was the axis of every conversation you understand. James Lawrence was a national hero. He was second in command to Captain Decatur in a daring raid on Tripoli in order to burn the *Philadelphia*, so it wouldn't fall into the hands of the enemy. As commander of the *Hornet* he sunk the *Peacock* off the coast of Guiana. Before that he issued a challenge to one of Britain's brigs lying in a Brazilian harbor, then scorned them for not coming out to fight. Don't you see, he *had* to come out against Broke. He had to be true to his own conscience."

"Maybe," Weatherby concluded reluctantly. "Anyway, to get back to the story, and to give you the conclusion of what happened, Stapleton, if you will indulge me further," he remarked sardonically.

"Aye, aye, sir," Lieutenant Fox said banging his fist sharply on the table while throwing a withering look in Henry's direction.

"Thank you, Mr. Fox!" Weatherby said tersely. "The *Chesapeake* came out in the middle of the night against Broke. They were pretty equally matched, both ships carried fourteen long toms, larboard and starboard, and carronades on the spar deck. The *Shannon* was a hundred and fifty feet in length."

"The *Chesapeake* was one hundred and fifty one," said Henry dryly.

"Thank you for that information, Mr. Stapleton! As I was saying. The *Chesapeake* bore down on Broke in Massachusetts Bay. Broke assembled his men below the quarter deck. 'Remember your comrades from the *Guerriere*, the *Macedonian* and the *Java*. You have the blood of hundreds to revenge today,' he reminded them. The American's bow passed the *Shannon*'s stern, and the *Shannon*'s aftermost guns fired on them immediately, killing or wounding half the American gun crew. Broke said the American was making a knot of speed faster than the *Shannon*, then both ships were firing at point blank range. Horror on both ships, none of you need a description of how that would be after what we have all just experienced lately. Lawrence went down with a ball in his leg, but Broke seemed to be unscathed by the carnage. He jokingly said that his black silk hat scared the cannon balls away, yet one had flown right through his outspread legs!" The officers around Weatherby's table roared with laughter. Henry and Joshua couldn't help smiling to themselves at the mental image it conjectured.

"Three of the *Chesapeake*'s helmsman were shot down . . . wheel smashed, tiller ropes shot through, then, out of control, her stern started to drift towards the *Shannon*. Captain Lawrence must have given orders to rally some boarders from below. Two of his four lieutenants had been hit, a third carried out the order only to find when he returned on deck, that Lawrence had been hit again severely. He helped him below leaving the *Chesapeake* without a single officer on deck."

"Nobody to give orders," Henry replied shaking his head sadly. "When there is confusion the enemy has the upper hand unfortunately."

"Quite so, quite so, Stapleton. Anyway, Broke boarded the stricken vessel but received a saber cut that laid open his brain."

"Ah, his black silk hat became ineffective then," Henry said dryly.

"Stapleton, are you sure you know where your loyalty lies?"

Henry smiled at Weatherby, and then at Joshua, but said nothing in reply to this remark.

Weatherby continued, "He was delirious with loss of blood, but Lawrence's voice could be heard shouting, 'Don't give up the ship! Don't give up the ship!'"

"That's typical of the Americans," Henry stated. "It will be their battle cry for years to come you know, sir. The honorable John Wesley always said, 'They are fiercely loyal to their country, and would never give up their freedom.' Their ship, the *Chesapeake*, was to those sailors, *their* country."

"Blast me, Stapleton! But, they *did* give up their ship. In fact Lawrence gave orders for it to be burned when he realized it was all over."

"Or die in the attempt! I told you, sir. That is the way the average American thinks."

"I must say, Stapleton, you never cease to amaze me with your comments. I am sure the Admiralty will be very interested to hear of your exploits in America, as well as your analysis of the American character. But, to bring this account to a conclusion without any further interruptions, both Captains were given up for dead. Lawrence lingered for four more days, and died before they reached Halifax. The Admiralty insisted upon a burial with full honors. Broke confounded all the doctors, and made a total recovery!"

"Cheated the Grim Reaper, sir," commented Lieutenant Bradley kindly.

"Yes, indeed. And the end of the bloodiest engagement of the war so far. The battle lasted a mere fifteen minutes, and was over after the first broadside."

Henry saw a flicker of sadness come over Joshua's face, though he tried not to show it, as he ate heartily along with the others. This was the best food either of them had eaten in months, and Joshua was going to make the most of it.

Captain Weatherby tapped his fork against his glass. Felkes, who was standing behind the Captain, automatically assumed he wanted a refill, but the Captain waved him aside.

"Attention, gentlemen, if you please! It's time to get down to more serious business. I have a question for you, Mr. Stapleton. What, sir, are you intending with regards to Mr. Weller?" He coughed with slight embarrassment. "Of course you realize that technically speaking he is a prisoner of war, and as such, I have the authority to press him into our Service." He held up his hand as Henry was about to interrupt.

"But, as your . . . eh . . . servant, I could be persuaded to make an exception in this case. What do you say?"

"Captain Weatherby, with respect, Joshua is a free man, and a loyal friend!"

"Unquestionably so!" Weatherby raised his eyebrows slightly at Henry's response.

Henry continued, "I have no authority over him whatsoever, neither would I want to usurp any. He is, of course, quite welcome to accompany me to England if he so wishes. God knows he has saved my life several times over. I am deeply in his debt."

All eyes were fixed on Joshua, and there followed a short period of silence during which the only sounds that could be heard, were the gentle creaks and groans made by the *Dragonfly*'s timbers, along with the distant cries of those who were working on deck.

Captain Weatherby sat with his elbows on the table, lightly pressing his fingers together waiting for Joshua Weller's reply.

"Where Mr. Henry goes . . . I goes!" Joshua said simply. "I 'aint thinking of joining the British Navy, and that's for sure!"

The officers burst out laughing at this simple, but honest answer.

"That concludes the matter then," said Captain Weatherby. "Unless of course . . . ," he paused. "You would both like to be put on the ship's books as volunteers?"

Another chorus of laughter from those around the table, including Henry, who turned and slapped Joshua on the back. "Glad you're coming home with me, friend. I would have had it no other way." Joshua nodded. Henry could see the relief in his dark eyes.

"One more thing," said Franklyn Weatherby on a more serious note. "Mr. Stapleton, as you were not officially on the books at the time of our recent conquest, you are not lawfully subject to any prize money."

Henry shrugged.

"But I would like to offer you, as a token of appreciation for the part you played in our victory over the French, a little gift."

He turned, and reached out to a small side table which had a white cloth draped over it. Removing the cloth with a gesture of great flamboyancy, Weatherby revealed Henry's sword, embossed with its distinctive fleur-des-lis pattern, and superbly cleaned and polished by the ever faithful Felkes, who had undoubtedly restored it with as much fervor as the old steward could muster up. So much so, that it shone magnificently in the warm yellow glow of the candlelight that illuminated the Great Cabin.

"I am deeply touched, Captain Weatherby," said Henry as he leaned forward and took the sword from the Captain's hands.

"I give you joy of it, sir, and I'll warrant it will bring a pretty penny in London," concluded Weatherby heartily.

"Oh, I won't sell it sir! I know it may sound strange, but I think it will stay with me for a long, long, time. It certainly seems to have played an important role in my life."

Henry laid the sword carefully on the table in front of him amidst the host of dirty plates and empty wine glasses. He was momentarily overwhelmed by a certain amount of guilt, as he thought of Captain Dupont somewhere in the bowels of the ship under guard. The Dupont family sword.

Weatherby seemed to sense Henry's reluctance. "It is yours by right, Stapleton, it could go to no other."

Henry felt a little heartened by the thought that justice was finally done, what with the death of Captain Winters. Dupont must have some consolation in that fact, surely? Although personally it pained him to think that Winters' body was heaved over the side into the sea as callously as the body parts of the French. As a minister, Henry thought it the right of any man to have a decent Christian burial.

"And for you, Mr. Weller," Captain Weatherby said, as he again reached out, this time for a small dirty canvas bag. "I thought you might wish to keep this as a memento of your courage."

Joshua took the bag, and looked inside. Tears poured down his black cheeks as he withdrew the flag that lay within. It was easy to see what country's flag it was. The red and white stripes, the white stars still showing bright on the dark blue background, and even though it was badly stained and full of shot holes, it still smelled of smoke. Joshua felt a lump in his throat. To him it was most beautiful.

"Lordy, Mr. Henry, it's the flag from the *Lady Eleanor*. It's *my* flag."

"A fitting sentiment indeed," said Henry gently, while laying a hand on the big man's forearm.

"Captain Weatherby, there is a personal request that I feel compelled to ask of you."

"Pray continue, Stapleton," Weatherby replied with a puzzled look on his features.

"It's a word on behalf of Mr. Crook."

"Mr. Crook?"

"The *Lady Eleanor*'s Sailing Master."

"What of him?"

"Indirectly, he helped Joshua and I to escape when Winters tried to kill me."

"How so?"

"He cut the tiller ropes for us so as to give us a chance to get away in a small boat. He offered to do it! He was in favor of our cause, and I do believe he is a good man. Is there . . . any chance of leniency, sir?"

"Hmm . . . most unconventional under the circumstances. Of course it would not be my decision to make. Vice-Admiral Sawyer would be the one. But, yes, I will put a good word in for him. He will definitely become an American prisoner of war . . . in the prison at Halifax, but maybe we can arrange an exchange, eh?" he smiled.

"Thank you, Captain Weatherby, I am much obliged."

Weatherby nodded. "We'll carry on then! A toast, gentlemen, if you please," announced the Captain. "A toast to Mr. Stapleton, and Mr. Weller, and their safe return to England. I give you joy, sirs, you have both indeed shown your *true colors*.

And now gentlemen, the King," said Weatherby with sudden sobriety. Glasses were raised for the second toast.

Henry and Joshua raised their glasses in respect this time, although the wine stayed at the same level in their glasses. But no one noticed, and Henry gave Joshua a wink.

"The King," they all chorused. "God bless him."

"God Bless him indeed," Henry whispered to Joshua.

"Well gentleman," Weatherby said concluding the evening. "Duty calls! Be off with you all now."

There was a loud scraping of chairs as the men pushed themselves away from the table, a few of them a little worse for the drink. Others belched out their appreciation for the handsome dinner, as one by one they left the cabin and returned to their stations.

Christian lingered to shake Henry and Joshua by the hand. "Good luck, both of you," he said sincerely. "God speed you back to your wife and family, Henry."

"Christian," Henry said grabbing the boy by the arm. "Before you return to your duties, how is Freddie? I heard he lost his leg."

"Yes, sir! He is in good hands. We have one of the finest surgeons on the *Dragonfly*. If no infection sets in, I am sure he will recover. I am afraid it will be the end of his career most likely," he said sadly. "He will stay in Halifax for many weeks, there is no doubt about that fact."

"I shall visit with him as soon as I can, Christian. If not in Halifax then I will seek him out in England."

"Thank you, Henry. Freddie would like that immensely."

# Chapter Twelve

## A SAILOR'S WIND

For the next ten days on their journey back to Halifax, Henry and Joshua had plenty of time to talk. They were no longer officially crew members, although Henry had offered their services where they were needed. "No point in wasting a good fore-top man," he had informed Weatherby light-heartedly. The Captain had given them the same status as passengers on a King's ship, thus enabling them to stroll the decks at their leisure whenever they were not on watch.

These were sunny days, and the sea looked gloriously tranquil with its gently cresting waves with sparkling white tops. All five ships were under easy sail. The wind was warm in their faces and Henry felt for the first time in eighteen months that he could once again plan, with some amount of certainty, his own future.

Of course there was the matter of Joshua returning with him to England to carefully consider. That could pose problems while

England was still at war with America. He confidently relied on the fact that this devious notion of theirs, one of Joshua being his personal servant, would allay any fears. Country people in Norfolk seemed to have a habit of prying into other peoples' affairs, especially when it came to strangers appearing suddenly in their midst. He hated the thought of it looking like his own will was being forced upon Joshua, even though their personal relationship was quite the opposite. Joshua was as free as a bird, so to speak, and when he had put the question to Joshua about his decision to accompany him to England, his only reply was, "I think I'll try life in your country for a while, Mr. Henry, it will be an interesting experience."

Perhaps it would not be as complicated as Henry was imagining.

Weathering the Island of Nantucket on the larboard horizon, the frigate *Dragonfly* pushed her bluff bow lazily forwards on the next leg of Henry's journey back home. Captain Weatherby had mentioned that he would make enquiry upon their arrival back in Halifax, to find any British ship that may be returning to England in the near future, and that would carry them home: although he was careful to stress that it would not necessarily be right away, as most of His Majesty's ships stationed there would be on blockade duty somewhere off the eastern seaboard. They were still at war, he had reminded them.

Just the thought of going home though, was enough for Henry to take comfort. To see his beloved Elizabeth again; to hold her in his arms. He imagined Isabella and Flora, his two young daughters laughing and clamoring around him . . . and his son, Benjamin. His heart soared at the thought of him. Benjamin would have grown up during the time he had been at sea. Fourteen years old now, and . . . Henry realized with regret that he had just missed his own son's birthday, for the second time. How had he fared without his father for so long? He would have matured with all that responsibility on his young shoulders. Was he helping his mother enough?

Henry remembered Weatherby's words of how Elizabeth had been so diligent in not giving the Admiralty a moments respite in her endeavors to secure him a Protection Order. Would her beautiful face be showing signs of fatigue? All the anxiety . . . the sleepless nights? He hoped he could soon be with her and take away all her cares . . . relieve her from all the farm duties. Return to a normal life.

Funny how life at sea with a vast ocean around him seemed to evoke more time to think . . . to ponder, on his reunion with his family. No doubt other seamen had the same dream, but for them the reality was uncertain . . . maybe not at all. Perhaps they rehearsed the same homecoming in their minds after they had survived another battle? Until they heard the infamous 'beat to quarters' cry again. Then those thoughts had to be stripped from their minds as all sentiment had to be abandoned, as they prepared themselves to 'kill or be killed.'

Henry concluded, with a certain amount of sadness for his shipmates, that he was one of the very fortunate, and what stories he would have for his family. Every one of them would want to know every detail of his life since he had left Hawk Common House in the early spring of 1812.

Henry was very confident that they would quickly become attached to Joshua, just as he had himself. He was aware that when the villagers of Ludham met up with him, they would stare in astonishment. In Great Yarmouth, both a naval town and fishing port, it would not have been unusual, especially along the dockside. But in Ludham? Most of them had never clapped eyes on a black man before, and would probably conjure up images of natives from Africa . . . wild and hairy headhunters. Stories that had come home with the missionaries.

Yet how wrong they would be, Henry smiled broadly as he watched Joshua leaning against a shroud near the mainmast. The big man had more compassion in his heart for his fellow man than almost anyone he had ever met, high or low born. He had an inner strength that was intangible . . . like a rock that resisted the force of the sea.

The weather stayed remarkably pleasant as the ships sailed back into the big natural harbor of Halifax, with the *Dragonfly* leading the way and the prizes sailing between her and the schooners, which followed up as a rearguard.

Everything looked just as it did when Henry left it over a year ago. The sun was shining down on the roof of King's college nestled amongst the trees, and the brilliance of the various greens contrasted vividly with the colors of the wild flowers on the low hills surrounding the town. The smells of land wafted gently towards the ships. How different from shipboard odors they seemed. Even wood smoke and fresh fish were strangely inviting. It heralded in the beginning of a completely different way of life for Henry as he realized that it was well over a year since he had left Nova Scotia behind, and for most of that time he had been on the rolling deck of one ship or another.

The peacefulness and silence was broken as guns boomed out from the shore batteries, in the customary salute for a British squadron entering the harbor. Startled seagulls rose from the water shrieking out their loud protests at having been disturbed.

The smoke from the guns of the British naval station soon crept into the crew's nostrils, overriding the sweet pungency of the land.

*Dragonfly* returned the salute, with no shot loaded, and fired the appropriate amount of guns for the vice-admiral, who would, no doubt, be observing their arrival with great interest.

In the harbor the presence of the wind was almost non-existent. The sea was glassy and calm, with only a hint of a cats paw ruffling the surface. Already *Dragonfly* had clewed up her main and fore courses, and was sailing slowly and gracefully with only her topsails and jibs flying. Henry knew from experience that it would only be a matter of minutes before they too would disappear as if by magic, as the *Dragonfly* prepared to anchor.

"Let go the anchor!" came a cry from Mr. Philpot, the *Dragonfly*'s Bo'sun.

There was a smell of burning rope as the cable roared through the hawsehole, followed by a loud splash as the anchor hit the water and plummeted down until it reached the sea bed in the deep water of the harbor.

As the *Dragonfly* felt her anchor pulling and tugging on her bow, she slowly turned up into the wind and lay to it with ease. This mighty frigate which had experienced hundreds of battle stations and seen unlimited amounts of death and devastation was now as calm as a puppy on a leash. And now that the pressure of the wind was off of the topsails, they were neatly furled and her yards straightened. Her sister ships did likewise, and everything was stowed away in true Navy fashion.

Henry was surprised how few men-of-war were in the anchorage, other than the flagship *Africa*. Quite a different story from when he first set eyes on the harbor last year, when Freddie had first spotted the small ship-of-the-line and was so excited about his first glimpse of the British squadron. Today there was only one frigate, and that was being repaired and refitted. If there were so few ships, how would he get a passage back to England?

"Dreaming of home already?" said young Christian at his elbow.

"Absolutely, it's been a long time."

"It'll be shore leave for us as soon as the work is done around here," said Christian enthusiastically. "And for you too, no doubt. Not much chance of you deserting this time I'll wager, Mr. Stapleton," he laughed.

"I'll try not to, young Christian," said Henry. "And I'll remind you that I still cannot swim either!"

The midshipman was serious for a moment, then said, "Things may have turned out differently for you, Henry, if you could swim. Still, I think things worked out right in the end, eh?"

The next two weeks scudded by as Henry and Joshua patiently waited for a ship for their Atlantic crossing, but none was forthcoming. All through this waiting period the *Dragonfly*, and the rest of the squadron were busily taking on stores and supplies for their next voyage. The water hoys plied backwards and forwards with fresh water, while the men worked enthusiastically with happy and expectant faces at the prospect of spending time in a British port, and all the land based attractions that went with it.

Henry spent many pleasant evenings talking and playing cards with Mr. Plumb, the Master, and the Captain of the Royal Marines. He had great pleasure in teaching Joshua the popular game of Whist.

During this period of waiting, all the violence and sadness of the past months slowly took up residence in the deep catacombs of Henry's sub-conscious, and caused a lot of his past sufferings to ebb away like the tide. Things were about to change with only one last obstacle to overcome. A ship, and an Atlantic crossing.

He wrote a long letter to Elizabeth, then tore it up. It could not be mailed now: there were no post office packet ships at this time although Halifax was part of their regular route. Probably dodging American war ships. In fact no ship had yet entered the harbor bound for England, despite the beautiful weather and the favorable gentle south-west wind blowing. A perfect wind for England.

By the third week of August, Henry and Joshua were getting decisively irritable, especially as this morning the weather had done a complete turn around and they were awoken by loud rumbles of thunder and watched stabbing lightning streak across the sky with a vengeance. The wind had picked up dramatically and was blowing lustily from the north-west. The yards and halyards creaked and groaned under the strain, and a shrill whining could be heard as it sung through the rigging with a monotonous aggression.

As Henry came on deck he was awed by the angry looking sky which had a strange green color on the edges of the clouds, while the centers hung down in black sagging lumps that were shaped like a blacksmith's anvil. He looked up through the maze of freshly tarred rigging as the rain started. Large droplets fell suddenly, stinging his face sharply and forming wet blobs on the deck planking. The dry areas at his feet gradually began to fill in, and soon the rain was whipping across the deck in a horizontal spray as it streaked across. It reminded Henry of those vicious days in the English Channel, instead of the warmth and sunshine of North America.

The early morning light was slowly being eroded by a great blackness as the squall line advanced, and when it hit the *Dragonfly* broadsides on, it sent her rocking wildly from side to side. Held by her nose as she snubbed up with a jolt at her anchor, the waves foamed down her sides turbulently, and made her plunge violently as she crested the first large wave. Henry noticed that the motion was more uncomfortable and unnatural than any seaway he had encountered during his time at sea.

He stumbled down the companionway and shut the hatch with a bang. To be so close to his impending voyage home, and yet not being able to obtain the culmination of the event was maddening.

He burst into the small cabin that he shared with Joshua.

"Blast the weather," he snorted. "No ships will come into the harbor in these conditions, they'll be standing off for sure. And don't try to say anything that you think may appease me, because it won't!"

Joshua opened and shut his mouth silently, stunned by Henry's uncharacteristic behavior.

"I am sick to death of this way of life! Nothing is guaranteed. Nothing! And everything is dependent on the cursed weather. Will we ever get out of this place Joshua? Don't bother to answer!" Henry threw himself down on the bunk and laid down with his hands behind his head and his legs crossed.

"Does your wife allow you to put your soaking wet feet on your bed at home," Joshua smiled, staring at Henry's wet boots dribbling onto his bedding without him paying any regard whatsoever. "You'll have to re-learn old habits now you know!"

"You're in the right of it, of course, Joshua. It is something I would never have done in our bedroom, Elizabeth would have a fit. I'm afraid the Navy has taught me bad ways."

"Ah no! It's living amongst those Frenchies for so long that did us in," Joshua joked.

Henry didn't answer his friend. Elizabeth invaded his thoughts and feelings again. He could picture her in his mind . . . her face as he kissed her goodbye as he mounted his horse for the journey to Great Yarmouth. He never dreamt it would be their last kiss, and one that he would have to carry with him for all this time that they had been apart. But as he pondered on the memory of Elizabeth, it steadied Henry somewhat, and he lay for a long while in total silence.

"Joshua . . ." he turned suddenly to his friend, "I . . ." But seeing his friendly face, Henry paused briefly, then they both broke out in laughter, so loud that it almost drowned out the sounds of the storm erupting all around them. It couldn't last too long. Nothing mattered now.

Eight bells in the forenoon watch reminded them that it was time for dinner. They were eating most of their meals in the ward room with the lieutenants and midshipmen. Mr. Plumb ate there with them when he was not busy at the con. On this day, barely had Henry put a fork to his mouth, when an excited Christian Clark burst through the door.

"Henry you are in luck! A merchantman has just entered the harbor, and he is flying English colors. A small ship but sturdy looking enough. Maybe it will be *your* ship. Let's hope it is bound for old England eh? Soon be hearth and home for you, sir!"

Henry felt overcome with emotion at the news; his destiny was going to change at last, and he immediately resolved to enquire of Captain Weatherby about this ship.

"Thank you, Christian. That's the best news I've had in a long time," he replied sincerely.

"Hold your horses, Mr. Stapleton, let the fellow catch his breath. He only dropped his anchor five minutes ago! I know you are anxious to leave us, but we must exercise a certain amount of decorum in the matter. Who knows he may be outward bound for the West Indies, or sheltering from this blasted squall that just marched through. We shall see in due course. I shall send my coxswain over there this evening and make some enquiries."

"Thank you, sir, and I am sorry for my impulsiveness. My only excuse is my excitement at the prospect of going home."

"We all suffer from that disease," smiled Weatherby kindly. "Now run along my good fellow, and I will inform you of any pertinent news the moment it is to hand. Alright?"

"Thank you, sir, I am deeply grateful."

Henry sought out Joshua to inform him what Captain Weatherby had said. The two men sat on their bunks like young school boys cooking up a scheme to torment their schoolmaster.

Henry's excitement was evident to Joshua, but he was feeling a little more wary. He would be entering a new country as a servant. A country where few black people existed, and from what he had heard, England experienced cold and damp conditions in the winter, and summers where it rained incessantly. It would be an entirely new way of life. How long would he *want* to stay there. As a servant he may be cutting off his only freedom. And black men had few freedoms. Henry had told him that if it wasn't for the Gulf Stream, England's climate would be more like Iceland. He hoped he could adapt easily, for Mr. Henry's sake. His own race was not designed for cooler climates. It was the same with the native Americans, very few of them survived for very long in Europe. And Boston was bad enough. But *England* . . .

"What will we do for money when we initially arrive in your country, Mr. Henry?" Joshua said at last. Despite his misgivings he was a practical man. Prepared to work . . . it was all he knew. It was the only way to make an honest living for any man living under God's heaven. Perhaps he had been a fool to try privateering? Naw! I wouldn't have met Mr. Henry, he concluded quickly. He's a true friend.

"Frankly, Joshua, I don't know," Henry replied candidly. "I still have a few American coins, they will be worthless in England of course!"

"I still have my two pistols I could sell," Joshua added hopefully.

"And I still have my sword of course."

"No, not that . . . there's something about that French sword. I dunno what I'm sure, but there is! Anyway, Mr. Henry, it's rightfully yours, you earned it one way and another. The pistols I just took off some dead Frenchman, they mean nothing to me."

"They won't fetch much, Joshua, especially if they know we are penniless. Look at us, not a suit of clothes between us, just what we stand up in . . . Elizabeth has more elegant garments in her rag bag," he said shaking his head. "Anyway pawnbrokers are not the most congenial of men, you know. Nor honest come to that."

They looked at each other and couldn't help laughing again.

"What a couple of sorry souls we are, Mr. Henry, for sure!"

By seven that evening the storm had passed over, and the heat and humidity of the day was replaced by a cool breeze off the land. Green leaves from the nearby shore lay stuck to the deck, wet and plastered on the masts and spars; stripped from the trees near the water's edge where they had been carried out to sea with the violence of the winds. This change was refreshing to all of *Dragonfly*'s people, and the crew languished around quietly smoking their pipes, and generally relaxing as they watched the twilight creeping up on them from the eastern sky.

Henry looked down over the bulwarks to see Captain Weatherby's coxswain, Jenkins, in his blue jacket and white duck trousers, descending into the gig that was bobbing alongside the frigate. With the coxswain at the tiller, the men began to pull strongly towards the merchantman, which stood out in silhouette against the evening sky. She was English of course, they suspected as much, and Henry watched until he heard the coxswain hail the men who looked down over the side of the merchant ship at the arrival of gig bearing men from a British man-of-war.

"Captains Weatherby's compliments, sir. His Majesty's frigate *Dragonfly* 38, Jenkins, coxswain," he announced formally touching his hat to the commander.

"Captain Brown, of the *Day Star*, merchantman. Lately from Cuba. On the way home to Blighty. What can I do for you Jenkins," he asked warily.

"Short and sweet, That's what I always say. Captain Weatherby needs a favor!"

Captain Brown sniffed disdainfully, he had no regard for the Royal Navy. He had lost a lot of good seaman to the press gangs; plucked off his ship in front of his very eyes before he was even a few miles out of an English harbor, barely in the chops of the English Channel. These King's men left him critically shorthanded with the prospect of a long and dangerous voyage ahead of him, and with no possibility of picking up extra hands. What did they want of him this time he wondered.

"And what *favor* is that, may I ask?"

"We have two men aboard. One is a minister returning to England, (I can't explain too much about him.) The other is his servant. A black man. They are both strong! The Captain will pay for their passage, minimal of course, just enough to cover their keep. If you'll oblige Captain Weatherby, he promises not to press any of your men, though shorthanded we are, and that's a fact!"

Brown looked lost in thought for a moment as he rubbed his chin carefully. He really didn't have much choice in the matter. At least this way he gained two extra men, instead of losing half of his most experienced hands to a frigate captain. "I have the Captain's word on it then?" he said at last.

"On his honor, Captain! And you can count on it believe me, I've been wiv 'im for years now. Oh, and the two men, they are good seaman, they could 'elp you if you needs 'em."

"Never known a preacher to be a good seamen, Jenkins!"

"This one's . . . eh . . . *different*, Captain."

"Thank you, Jenkins. I accept the offer. Mind you they best not be trouble makers."

"Oh no, sir, they won't give you no trouble!"

"Tell them to be on board the day after tomorrow then. The *Day Star* leaves on the morning tide sharp . . . I'll not tarry here too long in case there's more of you buggers around," he snapped sarcastically.

"Pass the word for Mr. Stapleton," said Captain Weatherby to Felkes, upon the return of his coxswain, with the news from Captain Brown.

Henry and Joshua fairly raced to the Captain's cabin. "It seems you are to leave us very shortly, Mr. Stapleton," said Captain Weatherby with a broad grin on his face.

"God be praised!" Henry uttered. "What's the name of the ship, sir?"

"The *Day Star*, she is homeward bound from Cuba."

"Second Peter," replied Henry smoothly.

"Come again?" queried Weatherby. "Don't talk in riddles, man!"

"Second epistle of Peter, chapter one. From the Bible! It's a quotation, sir."

Weatherby looked puzzled. "I'm not much of a reader of the scriptures," he said defensively. "I am a devout Christian though, as my father was before me."

Henry decided to put the Captain out of his misery as he quoted from that particular verse. "*We have also a more sure word of prophecy; whereunto you do well that you take heed, as unto a light that shineth in a dark place, until the day dawns, and the Day Star arise in your hearts.*"

"That was verse nineteen," Henry smiled. "It refers to Jesus as the light of the world. One of my favorite verses. Makes one think of a lighthouse when a ship is in great danger, you can relate to that, sir, I am sure!"

"Quite so, quite so, although we need a great deal more of those worthy structures, but very appropriate for your circumstances I must admit," Weatherby said with a wry look on his face.

"Well, Henry it looks like you're on your way at last. I'm sorry to be losing you in a way. You'd have made a damned fine officer given time. You have what some men can never achieve. A single mindedness that will not give up when you know there's been an injustice done. Even if it means risking your life for what you believe in. There's real courage in that! I hope we shall meet again."

"I hope so too, sir."

"Well, it has been my pleasure to know you, and you too, Mr. Weller. All that remains is for me to wish you both God speed!"

"Thank you, sir, for all you have done," Henry said with genuine affection. "We will never be able to repay you. Especially for your generosity in paying for our passages." Henry held out his hand, and Weatherby shook it warmly and said, "Smooth sailing, my boy. Make sure you always keep the weather gauge," he smiled. "Whatever tack you take in life."

"I will, sir, you can count on it."


Henry and Joshua slipped through the entry port and climbed over the side of the *Dragonfly*, with a certain amount of sadness in their hearts. Henry felt awkward in a pair of Captain Weatherby's old breeches, although they were at least clean. Felkes had managed to drum up a white shirt and a blue jacket from somewhere for him. Mr. Philpot had given him an old cocked hat that had seen better days and was scarred with years of work and foul weather. To any observer Henry could have passed for a non-commissioned officer.

Joshua was a little harder to accommodate due to his size, but clothes were finally found for him amongst the seaman's slops, which took care of the last few coins that Henry had. Even slops didn't come free. The Purser made sure of that.

Henry kept his left hand on the hilt of his sword, to keep it from getting in his way as the two of them made their way down the side of the *Dragonfly* with ease, and leapt into the gig that rose up and down on the waves as it danced alongside the frigate.

"Shove off," Jenkins ordered from the stern sheets.

Henry sat upright, tightly gripping the sword by his side. He felt a certain amount of pride. For a fleeting moment he wondered if Elizabeth would recognize him with his sun tanned features, and wiry appearance. Ship's fare had robbed him of a few pounds, and when he had shaved this morning before they disembarked, he had noticed how his face was lined and drawn. His black hair, tied back neatly now for the first time in months, was gently ruffling in the breeze. He looked up at the bulwarks of the *Dragonfly* lined with smiling familiar faces, and a rippling cheer erupted. "Good Luck, Mr. Stapleton! Say hello to England for us," the men cried.

For a fleeting moment Henry noticed Christian waving frantically, and his youthful voice rang out above the rest, "Remember my uncle lives in Great Yarmouth, Henry. You never know . . ." the rest of his sentence was drowned out by the noise of the wind and the slapping of the waves around the boat.

The oarsmen dipped their oars, and the boat pulled strongly towards the *Day Star*, and Henry watched the frigate *Dragonfly* receding slowly in the morning mist. Was it truly the last time that he would clap eyes on that fighting frigate? It was dogged with memories.

Henry turned to Joshua who was staring hard, not at the frigate, but at the dim shoreline of his vast continent. His thoughts were miles away. In Boston perhaps? A single tear ran slowly down his black face, then he abruptly brushed it away with the back of his calloused hand.

"Weather's changing, Mr. Henry," he said at last.

"Yes, dear friend, we've finally got our wind."

# CHAPTER THIRTEEN

## WATCH FOR A STRANGER

"Try not to put those cakes on the edge of the table, Sarah, my dear. They may very well fall off, and that would be a great shame," said Elizabeth Stapleton.

The late September sunshine of 1813 shone weakly down on the little group of people preparing for their outdoor church service. The men had erected a small pavilion on the village green, in Ludham, where refreshments were to be served afterwards.

The tables Elizabeth was fussing over, were laden with food from the store cupboards of many of the womenfolk in the village. Pork pies, cakes, pickled onions, sausage rolls: the likes of which had not been seen since Delia Appleby's wedding, which event took place over a year ago, and was etched in the minds of today's culinary participants.

Elizabeth wanted the best . . . for God's service, and for her husband's memory. She had obtained the Protection Order, but it had been so long ago now. It was as Henry would have liked it, she consoled herself. A lump came up in her throat as she thought of Henry. Still missing . . . presumed dead. Yet somehow something deep inside of her could not, would not, accept that he *was* dead. There had been no proof. *Yes* he had gone overboard during a battle, or so the Admiralty had informed her, but there had been no body found. And this fact she desperately hung on to.

Elizabeth walked from the pavilion back out into the sun, which shone on her wheat colored hair and made it take on the appearance of fine bronze. She was as small in stature as Henry was tall, and they had made a handsome couple in St. John's church the day they were married. But today she wore a long simple yellow dress made of silk, which bore a tussy mussy of fresh flowers tied at her waist. Her daughter Flora, now six years old, had picked the bright blue Michaelmas daisies with their vibrant orange centers especially for her that very morning. The last flowers of the summer!

To any casual observer Elizabeth looked a picture of health, and calm in spirit. But a closer look would have revealed the tell-tale lines around her eyes, the result of many sleepless nights that followed long and hard days keeping everything running smoothly on the farm. Mr. Baldwin, her one and only hired worker, was aging, and found things harder and harder with each year that passed.

Elizabeth looked over with pride at Benjamin, her son, almost as tall as Henry now, and dressed in white breeches and a black coat with long tails. At fourteen he had matured quickly since his father had disappeared. He looked quite the parson, despite the fact that he had spent an hour scrubbing off the remnants of dirt from his duties of cleaning out the stables.

Benjamin spent a lot of time with Henry's big black horse, Viscount. He rode him often and hard, much to Elizabeth's consternation, and he would bring the horse back to Hawk Common House lathered in sweat from his gallops across the marshes. As his mother, Elizabeth understood, Benjamin had to deal with the loneliness and frustration in his own way.

So, today here he was taking his father's place, for he was to bring the sermon for them in the best way a fourteen year old boy could. Everyone was looking forward to his address. Young Benjamin (the locals affirmed) was a gifted preacher now in the absence of his father. He had had to take over the reins of responsibility, and spent many long hours studying his father's Bible. He had read other manuscripts too, which he had painstakingly plowed through in order to prepare himself for such an occasion as this. Inspirational books, such as Pilgrim's Progress, and Fox's Book of Martyrs. These particular two volumes he had studied fervently, until the candle in his room was burnt down to nothing, and finally guttered out.

Benjamin was particularly the old men's pride and joy, and he was, as they said in the county of Norfolk, 'A right good lad.' The same old men knew nothing, of course, about the wild rides that he took to try to forget all his responsibilities and come to terms with the loss of his father.

Isabella, the eldest daughter of the Stapletons, had blossomed into a very serious and deeply sensitive girl. Her knowledge of local people, and naturally charming social skills were quite beyond her years, and continually amazed her mother. Elizabeth was positive Henry would have been proud of each one of their three children for their own individual merits.

She looked up at the clock on top of the village church tower, it was five minutes to four. Almost time for the service to begin. Rows of benches had been set up in front of the pavilion, and Benjamin was to make his address facing the villagers. As yet there were only a few people sitting there. Mostly old folks that were struggling to stay awake as they enjoyed the sun and fresh air of a warm Sunday afternoon, while waiting patiently for the service to commence.

The other members of the Methodist group were busily making sure everything was in order. But despite this fact, the benches were still far short of being occupied.

Oh dear, Elizabeth thought, if only there had been more people turn out for the event. Would Benjamin be *too* disappointed?

Maybe they had left it too late in the summer to hold such an event? Maybe the weather was not quite warm enough for people to come out? Still, to have held it earlier would have been impossible. Almost everybody in the village had been busy with the harvest. No, there could have been no other time! What's done is done she thought to herself.

Elizabeth's small harpsichord had been carried up the half mile lane from Hawk Common House in a hand cart, pushed reluctantly by old Mr. Baldwin, who puffed and complained bitterly, as he set it up on the grass.

The woman who was now playing the instrument, Mrs. Willark, had been running her fingers over the keys with a look of annoyance on her face. The harpsichord was slightly out of tune, no doubt the consequences of it being moved out-of-doors into the fresh air. Mrs. Willark could be heard, tut-tutting and clicking her tongue in exasperation. She pulled out a small lace handkerchief and mopped her forehead and muttered, "This will never do. No! No! This will never do indeed! How can I be expected to play under these conditions?"

Elizabeth walked over to her side and gently said, "Are you almost ready, Mrs. Willark? It's almost four."

"As ready as I'll ever be," she snapped shrugging her shoulders in dismay.

"Just do your best," replied Elizabeth firmly.

At last everyone was seated, and moments before the service was to commence a carriage whirled onto the village green pulled by four white horses sweating and snorting as they were brought to a stop by the coachman. One of the immaculately dressed footmen leapt off, and opened the carriage door hurriedly, kicking down the small metal step, and Mrs. Braxtead emerged from her conveyance in a swirl of satin and feathers, followed by her five children. The young girls, with their satin bonnets all askew, squeaked and giggled while chattering incessantly, and the boys pushed and shoved at each other aggressively with scowling faces.

"Now, now, children! Hurry along and sit down, and stop being so unruly.

Good afternoon my dear Elizabeth," Mrs. Braxtead smiled as she smoothed down her dress and took a seat. "Sorry we are late! I fear I must blame it on the children, they never seem to follow instructions. It is so exasperating," she sighed flicking out her fan and sweeping it up and down frantically in front of her red cheeks.

"That's quite all right, Francesca, we are so glad you were able to come. It was good of you to make the long journey from Mundesley." She hasn't changed a bit, Elizabeth thought to herself, for it was only just over a year since the news that her husband, Arthur Braxstead, had been killed while serving on board the *Dragonfly*. The same nonchalant air that she had exuberated when Elizabeth had ridden over to deliver the sad news of Arthur's demise while serving in the Royal Navy. A service he had no intentions of making into a lifetime career, but merely to avoid the whole family ending up in the debtor's prison, for the same extravagance and elegant living that Francesca had always indulged in. And for which Arthur had needlessly laid down his life.

Elizabeth sat down calmly on the first row of seats as Mrs. Willark started playing the first few notes of one of Charles Wesley's hymns. 'Amazing love, how can it be; that thou, my God, should die for me . . .' one of Elizabeth's favorites. And as she closed her eyes and listened to the melody, she felt a soft movement at her feet. The family's border collie, George, had made his way into the village from the farm, and laid down beside her with his paws stretched out in front of him, and his head resting on the hem of her dress. She reached down to stroke him, and his course black hair brindled under her hand. Henry had loved this dog like his own child, they had been inseparable. She felt a tear start to roll down her cheek and wiped it away with the tip of her forefinger.

While the music continued to play, her mind began to grapple with all the grief and anxieties that had plagued her for the past year and a half. The disappointments that had occurred one after another seemed to culminate at this special occasion, as she pondered on the lack of people in attendance. The heartache that she felt must be affecting her mood more than she realized. She took a firm grip on her emotions. She must stay strong . . . composed in front of her children, and the members of the Methodist group.

Unexpectedly George began to growl, and stood to his feet. Elizabeth looked down at him and noticed that his eyes were fixed (as collies are apt to do when marking out a certain sheep in the flock) upon two strange men that had appeared as if out of nowhere. They stood some hundred yards away at the edge of the village green, with its line of oak trees pulsating with shades of yellow and gold on their dappled leaves as they rustled in the gentle September breeze and created a deep shade beneath the branches where sunlight couldn't penetrate.

The strangers stood staring openly at the little group of people who sat on the benches. They made no attempt to move, but held a statuesque position.

Elizabeth strained her eyes to look at them. It was difficult to see the men clearly, as she was staring directly into the bright sun that hovered above the trees and blended so well with the autumn colors. She held her hand over her eyes to shield them, and to obtain a good look at the strangers, but the deep shadows hid their features.

The two men were both tall and very sinister looking. Could one be black? Or was it the poor light. Hard to tell. The other man wore a black cocked hat which shaded the upper part of his features. Elizabeth noticed he wore a sword at his side that reflected the brilliant sun. A soldier perhaps? She noticed how easily the stranger's hand rested on the hilt, he was evidently accustomed to its use.

Elizabeth wondered if she should go and invite them to take a seat, it would boost the ranks of the congregation, but she was not sure, and felt a little nervous. Perhaps they were troublemakers . . . taken with drink maybe? That would truly be a disaster.

Elizabeth caught Benjamin's eye, he too, had noticed the strangers and looked somewhat restless.

Without warning the two men started to stride towards Elizabeth with great determination. George stood beside her, rigidly defensive.

A deep throaty growl rumbled from his throat, while the fur on the back of his neck stood up straight. Elizabeth instinctively put out her hand and grabbed his collar to restrain him. Suddenly the dog lurched forward, pulling free from her grip. She jumped to her feet calling his name, "George . . . George . . . come here!"

Ignoring her frantic cries, the dog raced towards the two strangers at top speed, barking loudly as if he was herding sheep through the farm gate. George covered the distance across the grass in seconds, sending clods of earth flying everywhere as his big claws bit into the turf. To any stranger he must have seemed ferocious.

The big dog crouched a few feet away from the men ready to attack, then suddenly he was wagging his tail furiously, and leaping up at the man wearing the sword. It was just as if he had known him all his life.

Elizabeth couldn't believe her eyes, but started walking slowly towards the men, completely oblivious that the hymn had finished playing, and she was the object of some strange looks from the rest of the congregation. As she walked closer, the men watched her carefully. Both were smiling broadly at her, and all the while George was jumping up with all four legs off the ground, and barking wildly around the two men in wild enthusiasm.

The black man knelt down and took George firmly by the collar, Elizabeth was afraid he might hurt the dog, but no man would go down on one knee to an animal except with kindness at heart she convinced herself.

Meanwhile his companion, the man in the cocked hat, strode quickly towards her. She should have been afraid, yet she felt strangely drawn towards this stranger like a magnet is attracted to iron. There was something familiar about this man . . . the way he walked.

All at once it was like the sun coming out from behind a cloud as the realization came, it was her beloved husband. How could she not have recognized him?

"Henry," she cried out, clutching one hand to her throat as she started to break into a run. Decorum left Elizabeth as she lifted up her silk skirt to her knees and let her feet take wings, despite the rugged turf of the village green that tugged at her heels. The wind tore off her bonnet and it lay abandoned on the grass behind her. There was not an ounce of propriety in Elizabeth as she flung herself at Henry, putting her arms around his neck as he picked her up and crushed her to himself. She felt so fragile in his arms as she looked into his deeply tanned face. Yet somehow Henry felt her inner strength pulsing through him. They were together . . . again.

"Darling, Elizabeth," he whispered staring into her blue eyes. "You don't know how I've longed for this moment . . . how many times I thought it would never come."

She tried to answer him, but words wouldn't come as the tears streamed down her face . . . tears of pure joy.

Henry kissed them away as he still held her tightly in an embrace that seemed to go on forever.

"They'll never take you away again," she sobbed into his neck.

Henry looked over his wife's shoulder to see startled faces watching them with fascination. He reluctantly lowered her to the ground.

"You made sure they can't, didn't you, beloved?" Henry whispered gently. And all the while he still looked deeply into her face as if every feature and familiar structure of her profile, was being re-carved into his memory. He smoothed the wisps of that wheat colored hair from her forehead.

"It is forever, isn't it Henry? The Protection Order, I mean? I couldn't bear to lose you again!"

"As far as I am concerned, dearest, it is forever!

Forgive me, my dear, but there is someone I would dearly like you to meet," Henry said turning to Joshua, who had politely given him a few private moments alone with his wife.

"This is Joshua Weller, my dearest. It is a long, long, story, but I owe my life to him, many times over. He has come to England to stay with us for a while."

"Welcome, dear sir. Welcome indeed," Elizabeth smiled and held out a small hand that Joshua shook most carefully.

"My pleasure, Ma'am," he replied shyly. "Mr. Henry, he never stopped talking about you, all those sea miles, and now I can see why."

Elizabeth nodded, "You are too kind, sir."

Hand in hand, Henry and Elizabeth walked slowly towards their children, who were currently racing wildly towards them. Here came Benjamin striding ahead of his sisters. He was almost a man now, and Henry couldn't help noticing how the lad looked broader across his shoulders. It was like looking back twenty years at himself in a mirror. He watched with pride until Benjamin was two feet away from him, then Benjamin slammed into his chest. Henry held him close. No words were exchanged. They didn't need any. Father and son were reunited.

"Mother has been looking after us," said Isabella shyly, and Flora shrieked with delight and said, "Benjamin has been looking after us too, Father! Except he won't clean out my rabbit's cage," she pouted.

"I should think not," replied Henry kindly. "Why a young lady of your age should be able to manage all the rabbits in the county! If not the whole of England," he said playfully.

"Father, don't be so silly," Flora said quite seriously, puckering her lips and nose, in an almost exact replica of a rabbit.

Joshua roared out laughing. "She'll break some young feller's heart one day, Mr. Henry! Let's hope he 'aint no naval man, eh?"

Henry felt a slight shudder pass over him. Was he really rid of it all? Was he as free as he thought he was?

"God forbid it should be so, Joshua, my friend." Their eyes met for a split second.

Henry, aware of the little crowd of people still gathered by the pavilion, turned to Benjamin and said, "Go back, son, pay my respects, and tell them I will call on them tomorrow. They'll understand."

"Yes, Father, I know they will."

Henry put his arm around his wife's shoulders, and said slowly and deliberately, "Let us all go home!"

# Author's Note

All the characters in **Shadow on the Water** are fictional, and bear no reference to anyone either living or dead. They do not play any decisive part in bending the course of history in any way. Although the story in this second novel in the Henry Stapleton series is interwoven with recorded historical events, and many naval heroes and prominent figures are mentioned, I have done my best to represent the lives and feelings of those who lived during those tempestuous times of war in 1812.

I hope you enjoyed sailing with Henry Stapleton by reading **True Colors**, and shared in his adventures. If you haven't . . . I urge you to get a copy and get up to date with this exciting nautical/naval fiction series.

Henry's drama continues in my third book, **To Stop a War**, to be published in the near future, so you will be thrilled to read about his urgent call to the British Admiralty in order to help orchestrate diplomatic relationships between the two nations. This third book is full of intrigue, mystery and betrayal. So cast off your mooring lines and set sail again.

You may order a copy of Shadow on the Water or True Colors
by contacting:

*www.daystarartstudios.com*

Or

*www.xlibris.com*

A limited edition full color art print 15" x 12" of the cover
painting of **Shadow on the Water**, signed and numbered by
internationally known marine artist Frank Roosa, is also available
for sale. You may order this picture as well as the cover art
print for **True Colors** by visiting us at our web site at, *www.
daystarartstudios.com* for these and other spectacular nautical art
prints and originals.